In The Blood

Lies the Dead Tell: Book 1

H.B. Lyne

ACKNOWLEDGEMENTS

My awesome Patrons; Andy, Isaac, Linzy, Richard,
Willow, Martin, Monica, Sonia, Emé, Faye, Laila, and Jay

My editor; Zoë Markham
My cover designer; Olivia Pro Design

My writing buddies who encouraged this work;
Angeline, Sacha, Ali and Imogen

My rock and formatting genius, Julia Scott
at Evenstar Books

ARE WE A PERFECT MATCH?

In The Blood is dark urban fantasy. In these pages you won't find sparkly vampires or teenage heroines with perfect hair.

This is NOT a romance. There are dark themes and scenes that may be of a distressing nature.

I write dark, gritty, emotionally compelling stories filled with flawed protagonists, anti-heroes and deliciously dark villains.

There will be plot twists that bring out your most colourful language and yes, I write in British English.
If any of these things bother you, turn back now.

If however, darkness is your poison, then read on and lose yourself in the shadows for a while.

For Kathleen

CHAPTER ONE

I NEVER REALLY KNEW MY PARENTS. I thought I did. Hell, with my gift, I thought I knew everything. I thought no one could keep secrets from me. But my parents had a whole life hidden from me, somehow.

When I learnt the truth, I honestly thought I would break. I questioned everything I thought I knew. I mean, if I could be so wrong about my own parents, how could I possibly trust anything else?

I'm getting there now. Slowly piecing it all together. I'm rewriting their lives, or the version I thought I knew.

I'm re-framing my entire life; what I am, my purpose, my place in all this madness. Everything I wanted before the big reveal seems so mundane now, so pointless. I was still a child, in comparison. Now I see it all. I see why I have this gift. I know what I'm supposed to do with it, finally, after years of questioning, doubting and denying it. Now I get it, at last.

My parents would be proud, I think. They would be honoured. Maybe this was what they wanted for me all along.

I'm beginning to understand why they kept it from me. I get that it's so much bigger than them and I get that they needed to protect me. I understand now. But damn, it's hard to accept. It's hard to sweep aside the hurt of being lied to all my life by the people who brought me into this world and who raised me to be honest and trusting.

It feels as though they didn't trust me with this.

But I know better, when I'm being rational.

They couldn't be bold; the risks they took were measured; they had a plan. They couldn't be open about it. That part was always meant for me. I'm the one who has to carry on their mission. I'm the one who has to lead, who has to be bold.

This is going to be legendary.

It scares the shit out of me, if I'm honest. But this is how it has to be.

It was one of those slate grey days. Those cold, November days that blend together because you're caught in that murky bit of the year when it's a bit too soon to get excited about Christmas, but you don't really have anything else to look forward to. The decorations were all up in the shops, but I'd walk past them with my Grinch-face on, determined to wait until a respectable time to get in the mood, like the 1st of December.

I'd just finished an essay and turned it in, but I can't remember now what the title was, or even the subject. It was my third and final year of university and I wasn't loving my course. A bit like the limbo of November, I was stuck between my core degree module and an elective that I was really looking forward to the following semester. But I had to get a pass in this crappy History of Art module first. I hate it. I'm no academic. I like the practical side, that's what I'd trekked all the way to Caerton for. My parents assured me that it was the best art course in the country.

Honestly, I didn't care much where I went, I just had to get away from home. Home was a ghost town. Oris was a reasonably big city, actually, full of people; but it was full of my personal ghosts. My mistakes. My regrets. I hated it and my parents got that. They didn't like the idea of me being far from home, but they understood why I had to go and they encouraged me to choose Caerton University.

They always supported me. Even when they found me on the bathroom floor, fourteen years old, in a pool of my own blood, both wrists open. I thought I was crazy. The voices in my head and the flashes of other people's lives; I thought I'd gone mad.

But my parents saved me. Literally, they saved my life, but after my physical wounds had healed, they let me know it was safe to tell them absolutely everything. So I did.

They were visibly relieved. My mum laughed. Not like a big belly laugh, but that sighing laughter people release when they've been holding on to too much tension. I think they expected me to come out with something worse than, "I can read minds".

But their relief didn't last long; they were worried and they got all guarded. But they supported me as best they could. They believed me. That was enough, really.

So when I was trudging back to my shared flat on that cold, November afternoon and I got a phone call from a number I didn't recognise, but with the local area code for home, something dropped out of the pit of my stomach.

It was the hospital. My parents had been found in their car in the bottom of the river. A tragic accident, they said. At first I was too shocked to even question it. There had been flooding reported in the news. That river was forever bursting its banks. Usually it was just property that was lost, but sometimes people, like my parents, were swept away.

I jumped on a train that afternoon. Just dropped everything and left. I must have called one of my professors on the way to let them know what had happened, but I barely recall doing so now. Everything was a blur of confusion and overwhelming sadness.

I got a message from one of the professors in a different faculty who I'd struck up a friendship with shortly after arriving in the city. She was cool and liked my artwork. Her message came through when I was halfway home. Just a simple, 'I'm so sorry for your loss, Eve. Let me know if you need anything.'

I couldn't even bring myself to reply. All I could do was stare out of the window at the rain and windswept countryside as it rushed by.

When I got to Oris station it was dark and the window was mostly black but dotted with lights. It was one of those grand, old stations with high, vaulted ceilings and a dozen platforms. I stood at the door as the train pulled in, the strap of my bag digging painfully into my shoulder. My fingers hovered over the button, ready to press it the moment it lit up.

I squeezed out between the doors even as they opened and ran along the busy platform, dodging the passengers waiting to board. I took the stairs two at a time. My calves were burning by the time I reached the top. I ran across the bridge as a train came rattling through beneath it.

My heart ached in my chest but I was desperate to get to Peter. I knew he was waiting for me on the far side of the barrier.

I gripped my ticket tightly in my gloved hand and hitched my bag up on my shoulder as I jogged down the steps on the other side of the bridge. There was a small line waiting to get out through the row of ticket barriers and I craned my neck as I waited, searching the crowd beyond for a sign of my tall best friend.

I couldn't see him and grew more and more frustrated as I made my way slowly to the front of the line. I shoved my ticket into the machine, silently praying that it didn't get stuck and flash up a red light, refusing to open the barrier for me. I got the green light and the little doors swung open to let me through.

I pressed through and strode forward, still searching for Peter.

'Eve!' his voice called over the hubbub of loved ones greeting one another. I spotted him moving forward out of the crowd towards me.

Tears began to stream down my face and I charged into his arms. I was wrapped up in a thick coat, scarf and gloves, but our cheeks touched briefly as he gripped me so tightly I couldn't quite breathe. There was a whisper in my ear and at first I thought it was Peter, but then I felt that whooshing feeling I always got with the visions and I knew he hadn't said a word.

'Does she know the truth?'

'The truth about what?' I almost blurted out. But the dizzy feeling stopped me. Peter put me down and took my bag. He knew not to try to hold my hand, or to touch me at all, really. The hug had been the expected gesture towards a grieving friend, he did what society said you should do to console someone. I'd invited it, which was rare, and he must have known that I needed it. I brushed the tears off my cheeks with a gloved hand and we set off walking.

We walked out through the vast foyer, which was bustling with people swarming around newspaper vendors and a large ticket office. Peter led me out to the car park in silence. My head was racing with questions, but I couldn't ask anything that would reveal I'd read his thoughts. I chewed on my lip and glanced sideways at him. Finally I settled on one safe question:

'When did you get a car?' I asked as we strode towards his little blue Honda.

'Last month.'

'You didn't tell me.'

'No. Well, we haven't been in touch as much lately, have we? And I wanted to surprise you at Christmas.'

'Oh.' The momentary relief ended. He was right. There had been some distance between us recently. I'd been busy with my life at university. I hadn't been the best friend. I tried to sweep aside my guilt. 'All that money you earned working in the chip shop but never spent. There I was taking you for a typical, tight, Yorkshire git. But you, clever clogs, you were saving for your own motor?'

'Yep. Impressed?' He smiled. He had the best smile.

'Well, I've already clocked up nearly thirty grand in student loans and I'll probably never finish my degree, so yeah. I think you made the smarter choice staying here and working.'

'Don't say that. You don't know what'll happen. You could go back after the funeral.' His smile had vanished.

My cheeks throbbed with the tears that were always just under the surface these days. 'Sorry,' Peter blurted. He opened the boot and dropped my heavy bag into it. I climbed into the passenger seat and took a deep breath, fighting the tears.

We drove to his house with the radio blasting out rock music and the windows down. The wind was like ice on my face, but it was exactly what I needed. Peter still lived with his parents about a five-minute walk from my parents' house. It was only a short drive from the train station, but 20-year-olds with their first car take any excuse to drive. Hey, my bag was pretty heavy.

We drove down the narrow street, cars packed in on either side with their wheels up on the pavement. There were potholes every few yards and Peter's car bumped up and down as he navigated slowly over them, the road too narrow to avoid them. About half way along the street, Peter pulled his car carefully up onto the kerb in a small space. I looked out of the window at the narrow terrace, its own windows bright with warm and welcoming lights.

The door was flung open before we'd reached it and Peter's mother was there, bathed in light, tears on her face and a handkerchief clutched in her hand.

'Eve!' she cried out and pulled me into a tight hug. I patted her gingerly on the back and she released me quickly. 'Come in and get warm.' She stood aside and ushered me into the narrow, terraced house.

The hall led straight to the back of the house, past a door on the right into the small living room and a passage that led upstairs. I stepped down a tall step and into the flagstoned kitchen. It was the homeliest place on earth.

Opposite the hall was a door into the back garden. Along the back wall was a wide window and under it a double sink. Over to the right was a dark green AGA that kept the room toasty warm all year round. It sat in a deep, stone fireplace and above it hung a dozen pots and pans. Right in the middle of the room was a large, pine table and six matching chairs. Along the wall beside the hall was a long settee, draped in a home-made patchwork quilt.

'I'll put your bag upstairs,' Peter said softly behind me, and he had disappeared up the narrow staircase before I'd even glanced over my shoulder.

'Thank you for having me, Mrs Wilkes.'

'Oh, it's my pleasure, sweetheart. I couldn't have you going back to that empty house. Not yet. You're welcome here as long as you need to be.'

I just nodded. I held back more tears and wished I was back in the car with the wind on my face again. Peter's mum bustled around me, taking my coat and handing me fresh hot chocolate with whipped cream and marshmallows. She ushered me into a chair at the table and before I knew it, the table was laid with a buffet of nibbles and she was insisting I eat. But I hadn't been able to eat all day. I picked out an almond from a dish of mixed nuts and put it to my lips to appease her worried, crinkled eyes, but I couldn't chew it, and discreetly knocked it to the floor and kicked it under the table.

The hot chocolate was nourishment enough and I sipped it slowly, welcoming the warmth and soothing creaminess of it.

Peter came back into the cosy kitchen, followed by his father. He was a greying, thin man with a fondness for baggy cardigans. He greeted me with a stiff smile but spared me any sentimental platitudes. I liked Kirk Wilkes very much. I'd spent more hours than I could count sitting listening to him playing the piano. It was the most soothing thing in the world when my gift emerged. I could drown out the voices and the unwanted images when he played.

There had always been a fondness between us and he had always insisted that I call him Kirk. I never really felt comfortable calling Peter's mum anything but Mrs Wilkes.

She was wittering on about the flood and all of the news items that had emerged over the last few days. I tried not to listen, afraid she would mention my parents.

That haunting whisper that had greeted me along with Peter came back and I strained to listen over the noise of the company in the kitchen. It was just a memory, nothing new, but I reached out for it, trying to grasp it in my mind. I needed to pull it closer and hear it again to understand.

Did I know the truth about what? What had my last

conversation with my parents been about? Probably something mundane like the cost of the machines in the laundrette. I couldn't remember. Why couldn't I remember? That should be something that stood out. It should be significant. I'd never hear my mother's voice again so I had to remember her last words to me. It was so important.

A hand pressed gently on my shoulder and Peter's dad was standing there, all blurred. I blinked and tears tumbled down my cheeks, accompanied by a sob.

Mrs Wilkes was silent for the first time since I'd arrived.

'I think I'll just go lie down for a bit.' My voice was barely more than a croak.

'Of course,' Kirk said softly. I got up and walked quickly to the stairs just off the hall before the kitchen step. Peter was right behind me and I let him follow, too broken to resist. My fingers brushed the walls, which pressed in tight on either side of the stairs. The narrow passage opened onto a wide landing and Peter brushed past me to get to the guest room door first. He opened it for me and I saw he had lit candles for me. There was even a small dish of chocolates on the night stand, probably courtesy of his mother. I forced a smile and went inside.

'Thanks, Peter,' I whispered.

'That's okay.'

'I really just want to be on my own.'

'Okay, sure.' He nodded solemnly and closed the door, leaving me in solitude. I sat on the end of the bed and stared at my bag, which was perched on a chair in front of the wardrobe. I don't know how long I sat there, staring, tears falling silently. At some point I heard the piano in the living room directly below me. It was a melancholy ballad, not a song I recognised, but I knew that Kirk was playing it for me.

CHAPTER TWO

THE NEXT DAY WAS A BLUR. I felt barely there, but Peter and his parents whirled around me, making things happen. Food appeared in front of me; I was moved from place to place. I was occasionally made to answer questions. I didn't mind, really. I couldn't function alone so I let my new, adopted family take care of everything. As long as I didn't have to make decisions I could manage not to cry.

That came to an abrupt halt at the funeral director's office late in the afternoon.

'We have this casket, very dignified. Simple, but classic.'

'Yeah. Okay. I don't think they'd mind.'

'And which church would you like us to—' He stopped, a concerned expression on his pale face. He was nice enough: calm, patient. He wore a black suit. He must wear that every single day, I thought. I could barely look at his face. I twisted my fingers around each other in my lap. He understood. He dealt with this every day.

'They weren't religious,' I croaked. 'No church.

Humanist, I guess. That would be nice.'

'I understand.'

Peter's mother put a hand over my fidgeting fingers, her other arm wrapped itself around my shoulders. I flinched but then my fingers fell still under her warm palm. I waited for a flash, but nothing came. I took a shaky breath.

After all of the decisions had been made, my face wet with silent tears, Mrs Wilkes walked me slowly out to the car, her arm still around my shoulders.

'You're too young to have to deal with all of this. I'm so sorry, my dear.'

'Thanks,' I mumbled as I climbed into the back of her hatchback. It was one of those bright, crisp days. The sky had been bright blue all day, but now it had turned pink with the sun low. Fluffy clouds rippled across the sky, disappearing into a haze at the horizon. We weren't far from the Minster. I remembered hanging around near there with Peter after school day every day. It seemed like a decade ago, but it had only been a few years.

The city buzzed with traffic and people, all going about their day with no regard for the weight in the pit of my stomach.

That night, Mrs Wilkes served up another meal and for the first time in two days, my stomach gave a low rumble at the sight and smell of it laid out on the kitchen table. I took a slice of baguette and covered it with butter.

Something easy and bland for me to break my unintentional fast. It was warm, fresh and soothing.

An hour later I was sick in the guest bathroom and sticky bread chunks came back up. I ate too soon.

I hid in the guest room and slept in my clothes. I felt as though the world would never be right again.

'We should go to the house today,' Mrs Wilkes was saying at breakfast the next day.

'I can't!' I blurted out, more animated than I'd been since I arrived. A rush of fear and panic swept through me and my cheeks burned scarlet.

'Maybe after tomorrow?' Peter suggested gently. 'After the funeral, Mum. Let her put them to rest first.'

'Okay, yes, that makes sense. I'm sorry, Eve. I don't want to push you.' But she was more brisk than she had been previously. She patted my shoulder and a stray thought made its way into my mind. She thought I needed a bit of a push to get me through this slump. She'd dealt with the death of a parent herself. While she was sympathetic, she believed there was a right way to go about this process and I was stuck in the early stages of grief, which is no good when estates need settling. This is why wealthy people have solicitors, I mused, to deal with the legal crap so the grieving don't have to.

I'd brought a pair of smart, black trousers with me from uni. I couldn't even remember why I owned them. But as I rummaged through my belongings in my bag I couldn't find anything to wear with them. I began pulling clothes out and tossing them to the floor, growing ever more frantic as I searched. Fresh tears stung my eyes.

'Stop crying!' I yelled at myself.

There was a gentle knock on the door and it opened. Peter stood there, gripping the edge of the door with a grim expression.

'Can I help?'

'I have nothing to wear tomorrow!' I shouted at him then slumped to the floor, surrounded by tops, jeans and underwear. I couldn't muster any embarrassment. He would just have to deal with seeing a couple of bras.

He walked over, his bare feet sticking slightly to the polished wooden floorboards until they made contact with the thick rug on which I sat. He sat down beside me and crossed his legs. His mouth did that wonky thing, like he was getting stuck into a puzzle.

'Do you want to go shopping? Or borrow something of my mum's? I might have a black shirt you could borrow.'

Peter was tall and skinny, his mum was not. I was built like a ballet dancer.

'Maybe your shirt?' I muttered, not wanting to look at him. I could work a man's shirt, probably. Part of me didn't care what I looked like. Another part felt like it was the most important decision of my life.

Peter patted my knee and got up to fetch the shirt. It was fine, it fit okay and when tucked into my trousers it was smart enough.

The next day I dressed and styled my hair, which I rarely bothered with. It was long and dark and had a tendency to curl whether I wanted it to or not. I pulled half of it up into a messy bun and let the rest hang loose over my shoulders. I put on a little make-up, but no mascara.

No one ate much for breakfast; it wasn't just me who didn't feel like eating. Conversation was sparse. Mrs Wilkes kept trying to smile and faltering. Mr Wilkes was wearing a suit. I'd never seen him in a suit before.

Peter leaned against the kitchen sink, a bowl of cereal in his hand, but the spoon sat in the bowl untouched. He was staring at the floor, just under the table, transfixed, a look of concentration etched onto his brow. He was wearing a dark grey suit with a navy shirt and tie. His mother fussed at him, brushing some lint from his shoulders.

'You should have a black one,' she muttered, disapprovingly.

'Yeah, for all the funerals I intend to have to attend. Mum, give over. I look smart, that's enough.'

'A black suit is versatile, isn't it, Kirk?'

Mr Wilkes let out a non-committal 'Hmm' and didn't lift his eyes from his paper.

'Well, I don't have one, so Mr and Mrs Rawling will have to turn in their graves.'

Mrs Wilkes' mouth popped open and she clamped a

hand to it before scurrying from the kitchen. I heard her crying as she hurried up the stairs.

Peter cast me an apologetic glance but to my surprise, I was smiling. A small chuckle even escaped my dry lips. He smiled back at me and we just hung there in that moment.

Kirk heaved a sigh, folded his paper and stood up, straightening his black tie, then cleared his throat and followed his wife upstairs.

'We need to go in five minutes, sweetheart,' he called.

Peter and I exchanged more furtive glances and half-smiles. He did look smart, he looked really good, actually. I'd never been attracted to Peter. He was firmly friend-zoned in our early teens. By the time we were sixteen I was confident he was gay and would eventually come out to me first, because I was his best friend. But he still hadn't taken that leap out of the closet.

Being intimate was difficult with my unusual gift. So I'd mostly steered clear of boys. With the exception of an awkward kiss with a boy called Billy in the last year of school. It felt like I was being attacked by a washing machine and was not an experience I was keen to repeat! Especially as I'd had a flash of a memory of him pleasuring himself to some awful porn. Yuck.

I'd had a boyfriend briefly while I was in Caerton. We had very awkward sex. I felt so vulnerable and hated it. It was rare for me to even be attracted to someone; the fear of getting a vision kept me from seeing people that way, for the most part.

But that morning, I did think Peter looked very handsome.

'Are you okay?' Peter's voice seemed to come from far away, pulling me back to the kitchen from my memories.

'Yeah. I actually am.' I looked up at him and smiled. I'd been thinking about something other than my loss, something real and human and painfully ordinary in a way. Aside from the intrusion of my gift, that is.

'You seem better today.'

'I think the waiting has been the worst bit,' I said, with a shrug. 'I have tissues.' I pulled the little packet out of my pocket and waved it. 'I'm ready.'

Peter smiled and dropped his untouched cereal bowl down on the counter.

'Come on. We'll go. My parents can follow.'

We left the house and walked quickly along the narrow pavement, between parked cars and houses. There were no gardens in front of the houses on Peter's street, the doors opened right onto the pavement. The dark stone felt too close, everything was too close to me these days and I walked quickly to get to a more open area. We walked single file to avoid bumping into any cars and I led the way to the end of the street and around the corner. It was only a five-minute walk to my house. My parents' house. We had grown up together, Peter and I, we'd played in the park at the bottom of his street. Our mothers were friends. Our fathers weren't exactly drinking buddies, but they talked and seemed close.

I had almost forgotten that Peter's family was grieving too.

We arrived at the house and stood on the pavement outside. I pulled my coat around me, bracing myself against the chilly morning air. Peter pulled me into his arms and tucked my head under his chin. 'Sorry, not sorry,' he said softly, his breath moving my hair.

I'd tensed at his touch, but I relaxed into the hug.

'You're just keeping me warm. That's fine. That's nice.' I smiled, even though I knew he couldn't see my face.

My head spun slowly, pulling me down into a vision and I tensed up again, fighting it. Peter was running along a dark, cobbled street. I could hear his feet pounding on the stone. I felt his heart hammering in his chest and fear coursing through his veins.

I gasped for breath and pulled out of his grasp. He let me go, he always let me go when I pulled away from him.

'What did you see?' His voice was soft and it took a moment for his words to register. I looked into his face, too stunned to reply. How did he know?

Footsteps hurried along the street behind him and his parents came into view. Mrs Wilkes' eyes were red and puffy and she clutched a handbag that swung wildly from side to side as she rushed towards us. Just behind them were two slow-moving, black hearses, followed by a sleek, black saloon.

'Just in time!' Mrs Wilkes huffed as she came to a halt next to Peter. Her husband sauntered more casually just behind her, his hands in his pockets. He gave me a small, apologetic smile.

The vehicles stopped alongside us and a sinking feeling settled into my body, pulling me back to the moment and what was really happening. Peter's startling question drifted out of my mind as I was led to the car and ushered into it. I couldn't look at the hearses and the two mahogany coffins inside them.

Peter slid in to sit next to me and grabbed hold of my hand, entwining our fingers. I looked into his face. The shock must have been written all over mine, but he didn't flinch, or pull away. He held my hand fast and stared resolutely straight ahead, avoiding my gaze.

'Sylvia and Jonathan were beloved members of their community.' The celebrant spoke clearly and solemnly about my parents. He told the story of their lives, pumped full of dignity and splintered with light humour. Those around me let out soft whimpers. Mrs Wilkes was quietly sobbing, a handkerchief pressed to her lips. Her husband kept a firm arm around her shoulders. I noticed his free hand clenched tight on his knee, the knuckles blazing white.

Peter had not let go of my hand and I hadn't pulled it out of his grasp. The image of him running through the dark kept resurfacing, but only the memory of the vision, it wasn't fresh. I kept expecting to get something else, as if he was transmitting. But my mind wasn't up for receiving the signal. Was my grief getting in the way?

Part of me wanted to be open to the vision. I needed to know if Peter was in real danger, and if so, from whom? I also didn't want to deal with the funeral. I didn't want to be there, I didn't want to hear about how my parents met or their thriving, five-star Italian restaurant. It wasn't all true anyway. So much of life was this polished presentation. The celebrant didn't mention the time they had nearly lost the business. In fairness, I wouldn't have known about that either if it hadn't been for my gift.

My parents were experts in keeping secrets, even from me. But on the day of the funeral I had no idea just how true that was, just how much they had kept from me.

With all of this distraction, I managed to get through the service without crying. But I was barely there. It took Peter standing and tugging me to my feet for me to realise that the service was over.

Mr and Mrs Wilkes went up to the coffins and pressed their hands to each in turn. I watched them, my eyes glazed. Was I expected to do that too? A surge of panic rose in my chest and I looked up into Peter's eyes.

'You don't have to do it,' he whispered, reading me expertly.

'I want to, but what if...' My voice trailed away. It was obvious now that he knew about my gift, but we had never spoken about it. People were waiting behind me to file out of the chapel. I walked forward and brushed my fingers across the top of my father's coffin, bracing myself. But nothing happened. I let out a slow, shaky breath and moved over to my mother's. Again, I just lightly brushed the tips of my fingers over where her head must be.

Like a jolt, an image shot into my mind and I stumbled back, right into Peter's arms. A second flash whipped through my mind and I felt so sick and dizzy that I was sure I was about to hit the floor. Someone nearby let out a little cry.

'Eve!' Mrs Wilkes called.

The two visions crashed through my senses simultaneously, fluctuating between one another and I felt as though I were drowning in them.

My parents were in their car, driving quickly through a rainstorm. The road was inches deep in water, and spray filled the air. Their headlights glared on the water, and the wipers swished frantically back and forth.

'I don't want to see this!' I screamed. I could feel Peter's arms around me, keeping me from collapsing completely.

But my parents didn't veer off the road, they didn't

plunge into the nearby river. There was a figure in the road ahead, facing their car, illuminated by their headlights. I couldn't tell if it was a man or a woman, the image was blurred and moving too fast.

Then Peter's past overtook my parents' deaths. He was hurrying home from work. It was night and the street was illuminated by dozens of lights from shops and bars; it was hot too and he was dressed in shorts. He passed a dark, narrow side street and a voice stopped him. Hands grabbed him and pulled him into the shadows. Fear swamped him and his head pounded as the man who had grabbed him shoved him against the wall and roughly searched him for his wallet and phone. He took a punch to the face and his nose broke with a sickening crunch. I was in his head, seeing it all through his eyes. Pain throbbed through his head. His limbs began to shake violently and something like a snarl erupted from his throat.

I looked down and saw his bare skin splitting. Instead of blood, thick, dark fur appeared in the cracks in the skin, gradually spreading to cover his arms. I tried to scream but no sound came out. His throat had morphed, no human sound could escape from it now. His broken nose was now a huge snout and his vicious teeth gnashed. The mugger let out a terrified scream. I could smell fresh urine. Peter's clawed hands reached for the man and wrapped themselves around his neck. As easily as a twig, Peter snapped it. He didn't stop there, his claws ripped the man's clothes and flesh, tearing him to shreds. A wave of sickness washed up over me as the blood poured out onto the dark stone.

Then Peter was running, human again, but terrified. It was what I had seen before, but now I knew what he was running from.

'Eve?' Mr Wilkes had hold of me and was gently pulling me along. I was outside the chapel, bathed in bright sunlight. 'Eve. Come on, I've got you. Come back to us.'

My eyes found Peter just beyond his father's face. There was a little crowd around him, concerned faces all fixed on me.

'Poor thing,' someone said. 'So hard, so unfortunate, just awful.' The voices chorused, mostly in my head. 'What's wrong with her? I've never seen anyone grieve like that. She's always been a bit odd.' I shook my head clear of those voices.

Peter stood still as people bustled past him. It was like he was standing in a rushing river, with water flowing swiftly past him on either side. Our eyes were locked together.

'What did you do?' I asked, the words never leaving my mouth.

'I changed.' His reply was firm, hard and certain. His lips never moved but I heard his words as clear as crystal in my mind.

CHAPTER THREE

WHEN I SETTLED BACK INTO MY SENSES, everything was quiet and still. The clear blue sky overhead was like a soothing blanket of colour and light. A soft, cold breeze cooled my cheeks and dried my tears. I breathed deeply and focused on the brightly coloured leaves on the ground. This was what was real – right here and now. The wooden bench beneath me was cool but dry.

'I'm in the graveyard next to the chapel,' I told myself in my head, looking around to orient myself. My parents were inside in their coffins, probably being moved to the crematorium, somewhere out of sight of the grieving family. People had laid vibrant flowers all along the path up to the chapel door. Almost everyone had gone now. The crowd of onlookers with their intrusive thoughts about my oddness were gone and my head was silent.

I looked around for Peter and found him standing near the funeral car, talking to the driver. He kept throwing furtive glances my way but our eyes didn't meet. An uncomfortable lump stuck in my throat and flashes of blood hitting cobblestones came back to me. I blinked them away and focused again on that azure sky.

Mrs Wilkes was talking to the Humanist celebrant, thanking him and shaking his hand.

'Will she be okay?' he asked, nodding in my direction.

'I'm sure she will. Such an awful thing to deal with at such a young age.' They both nodded solemnly.

Mr Wilkes was sitting next to me, I realised, his presence steady and calming. We sat in silence for what seemed like an hour.

'Shall we go?' I asked at last. My throat was hoarse and my words croaked out of my mouth like the crunch of dry leaves.

'If you like,' he replied, not looking at me.

I stood up slowly, unsure if my legs could take my weight, but they just about managed. We walked slowly to the car and the driver opened the doors for us. I crawled into the back and slid across to the far side, pressing myself against the door and staring out of the window at the empty cemetery. Peter's parents joined me in the back, but Peter sat up front next to the driver. I let out a little sigh of relief and released my tight grip on the door handle. I couldn't look at him without seeing the monster and the blood. I didn't want him near me.

I focused my thoughts instead on the first vision in the double-whammy. My parents. Who was that in the road? Had they swerved to avoid them? That wasn't what I saw.

The car was slowing down. My parents had glanced at each other and clasped hands. They were afraid, but resolved. I'd felt it.

Tears slid down my cheeks and I brushed them away. I'd seen what I was afraid to see, almost. But it hadn't been what I expected and now I had questions. Did Peter have the answers? What was he?

I glanced sideways at his father beside me. His face was unreadable. He held his wife's hand, gently stroking the back of it with his thumb. He had always been this calm and gentle man, but there was firmness there too. It was reassuring, and everything a girl wants from her father.

My own father had been different. He was strong and lean with broad shoulders that I knew could bear any weight. He could be aggressive at times and was always assertive. He never turned his temper on me or my mother, he was fiercely protective of us both. But he was rarely calm. He paced all the time and was always fidgeting. I always felt like he was restless, like he was a trapped animal.

My mother was the cook, and the one with the wits and patience to run a business. It was her second child, really, the restaurant, Cucino del Piero. My mother had named it after her father. He had taught her how to cook and although I never really knew him, I always got the impression that he had been proud of my mother's gift for cooking.

I had a hunch why my dad felt trapped. I'd stumbled upon the knowledge in the way I came by so much information that I neither wanted nor sought. I'd had a vision. When I was sixteen I found out that the restaurant was losing money. My parents were worried they would lose it. I remembered hearing them talking in hushed voices late at night and my father growing more short-tempered as they struggled to break even. I'd figured out what was happening without the aid of my gift. What I got from the vision was how they got out of the mess. They would never have dreamt of telling me what they had resorted to and I would never have known if it weren't for an ill-timed hug from my father.

The bank was about to repossess the property, but my parents were saved by their knight in shining armour.

The downside of running an Italian business in this city was that it got you on the radar of the Camorra. Britain isn't generally thought to have an Italian organised crime problem, but there are pockets. The Mafia wouldn't touch the city of Oris, but the Camorra settled in here at some point over a hundred years ago. Everyone knows, but no one talks about it.

The Camorra stepped in when the restaurant was about to close. They loaned my parents the money to keep it running. Every Friday morning after that, one of their foot soldiers came to collect the repayments. The Camorra effectively owned the business from that point on and my dad hated it.

Somehow, despite the stress that it placed on my parents, the business really started to soar. I guess they were strongly motivated to make it as successful as possible then.

Piero's had been closed since my parents had died but I was going to have to decide what to do with it. I doubted it could afford to stay closed much longer.

My thoughts drifted back to the vision. I saw the figure in the road again and recognition hit me like a truck. I reflexively reached out and grabbed Mr Wilkes by the hand.

'Oh!' I darted a glance at him and released his hand. Mrs Wilkes was looking at me quizzically. 'Sorry,' I mumbled, looking out of the window.

'That's okay,' Kirk said quietly. 'Everything all right?'

'I just realised something.' I knew who the figure in the road was. I had only ever seen him in a vision via my father, never in the flesh. It was Antonio Vitale. He and his sister, Lucia, were the joint heads of the Camorra in the city.

Now I knew what had really happened to my parents. Or I had a very good idea.

The Camorra killed them.

When we got back to the house after the funeral I retreated immediately to my room. Kirk was playing the piano downstairs, its melancholy melody floating up through the house to reach me.

Peter left it a respectable hour or so before approaching my door.

'Can we talk?'

'I suppose we have to.' I stood back to let Peter into the room. He walked in and flopped down into the chair by the wardrobe. He sank his head into his hands and I could see his shoulders shaking slightly.

I sat down on the end of the bed and crossed my legs, waiting for him to say something. When he finally looked up, his eyes were red and his cheeks were flushed.

'I'm not supposed to tell you,' he whispered. 'I'm not supposed to tell anyone. I want you to understand that.'

'I think I have an idea.' I arched an eyebrow and clasped my hands in my lap.

'Of course you do, sorry.' He leaned back in the chair and gazed at the ceiling. 'So, the summer after we finished school, something happened.'

'I saw.' I shifted my weight and averted my gaze to the rug. 'I saw you change into that thing and tear that man to pieces.'

'In fairness, he tried to mug me, and he broke my

nose.'

I raised an eyebrow and clucked my tongue. I didn't see how petty theft was deserving of what happened to him. 'I wouldn't have fought back if I were myself. I'd have let him take my stuff and I'd have taken a bit of a beating. Because that's how you don't die in a situation like that. Usually. But the adrenaline made me change. I had no idea what was happening, no one prepared me for it. It turns out I'm a shapeshifter.' He glanced my way with this boyish, apologetic expression on his face.

'Right.'

'I couldn't tell you. It's not allowed. We're supposed to conceal ourselves from humans.'

'Who says?'

'What?' he asked, blinking his big eyes at me.

'Who makes the rules? Who told you not to tell me?'

'I can't tell you that. It's not my secret to share. I'm telling you about me, but that's it. I'm sorry, but it's important.'

'Whatever.' I looked down into my lap as I twisted my nervous fingers around a tassel on the throw draped over the bed.

'It's for your safety, and other people's. The less you know, the better. I wanted to tell you right away. Keeping it a secret was the worst thing you can imagine.' I glanced back at him. He looked stricken at his own words and looked down.

'It's really not,' I snapped.

'No, I know. I'm sorry.'

We sat in silence for several uncomfortable minutes.

'You saw something else, didn't you?' he said at last. I nodded. A lump formed in my throat.

'My parents. They didn't have an accident. I don't know exactly what happened. It's possible they did really drown, but someone else was there. I think they were killed.'

Peter sat silently, watching me. His jaw was rigid and his lips set in a tight line. 'You're not surprised. Are you?' I asked.

'No. I'm sorry, but I'm not.'

'What do you know?'

'I suspect, that's all. I suspect that it was the Camorra,' he said.

I drew the inside of my left cheek between my teeth and nodded, fighting back tears.

'Why would they do this?'

'I don't know.' Peter heaved a sigh and something told me he was withholding something else. I didn't want to press it. I'd had enough revelations for one day.

'So, you can turn into a big, slobbering kill beast?' I asked with some attempt at levity. Something resembling a smile crept onto Peter's face.

'Yeah. It's called the Agrius. It's like half bear, half man. But I only did it that one time. I've been really careful not to let it happen again. It's horrible, being out of control like that. It was like all that made me sane and rational was gone and all that was left was this animal, this beast thing. It's dangerous to shift into that. I guess it used to be a survival thing for shifters, to be able to defend ourselves.'

'I don't understand.' A deep frown creased my brow. I was watching him intently, he had become more animated as he talked about it, more lively than he'd been all week. But I was confused. 'Is there more to being a shapeshifter than that beast thing?'

'Yep,' he said with a full-on grin. He jumped to his feet, moved into the middle of the floor, and his whole body shimmered, rearranging itself before my eyes. I slid back across the bed, my heart racing as I watched Peter disappear. In his place stood a tall and wiry fox. His fur was dark orange, with traces of grey around the nose and tail. He let out a gruff little bark and stepped closer to the bed. He jumped up onto it and flopped onto his side, like a family dog asking for a belly rub.

I laughed and inched closer. I couldn't quite believe my eyes. I reached out a tentative hand and stroked his side. His fur was coarse, like thick nylon. His eyes were black and shiny. He looked at me with such intensity it would have been unsettling, but I recognised my Peter in his eyes.

He shimmered again. Every inch of him vibrated, and bit by bit the fox was replaced with Peter, back in his suit, lying on his side on the bed beside me. He propped up his head on his hand and looked at me expectantly.

'That was different.' I smiled at him and he reached up, caressing my cheek with his thumb.

'I'm happy to see you smile.'

I cleared my throat and pulled away from him. His hand fell to the bed.

'Can you turn into anything else?'

'No,' he said, with a shake of his head. 'Just the fox and the Agrius.'

'And there are others like you? Here in the city?'

'I can't tell you that.' A sad sort of smile played on his lips.

'Were you bitten?'

'Like a werewolf?' He let out a bark of laughter and shook his head. 'No. It's just who I am, who I've always been. It just never happened until that night.'

'Is that how you knew about my... gift?' I'd never said it out loud before and the word stuck on my tongue, not quite wanting to come out.

'Sort of. I'd guessed, pieced it together from stuff over the years. I knew physical contact triggered it, that's why you hate being hugged and stuff. I'm guessing it's why you've never had a boyfriend, or a girlfriend, whatever.' He looked around awkwardly.

'Pretty much.' I avoided his gaze. I'd never told him about my boyfriend in Caerton, brief as that relationship was. Peter and I really had drifted apart. I guessed that was normal after school.

'I didn't go to uni because I needed to figure out what was going on with me. I freaked out after that night and didn't know what to do. I couldn't leave town; I thought I was dangerous. I didn't want to hurt – anyone.'

He'd nearly said "you", I was sure of it.

'You wanted to keep me at a distance, keep me safe?' I asked.

'Yes.'

'You'd hate Caerton. It rains all the time.' We both laughed. The irony not lost on either of us when we came from a city just as damp as the one I'd moved to.

'When I saw you that first Christmas, when you came home for the holidays, you'd sort of blossomed. That sounds cheesy, forget I said that.'

'Too late,' I said, giving him a gentle shove.

'You were different, you'd grown up. I couldn't tell you what had happened to me, but I knew that you saw things. Part of me wanted to grab you and hug you so you'd see. If you had a vision then I could be off the hook. You'd know without me telling you. But I stopped myself doing it. It was too fresh and too dangerous. I knew I had to keep you away. But this time, when you came home, it was too important to keep it from you any more. I asked if I could tell you and was told not to. But it's all got too big and too personal. You had to know. But I didn't mean for you to find out during the funeral. I'm really sorry.'

'It's okay.' I swallowed hard, tears threatening to spill yet again. 'I think my thing is a bit like yours.'

'What do you mean?' he said, staring at me with wide eyes.

'Just, you know, triggered by stress. Big, emotional stuff gets through easier. When I feel all vulnerable I pick up the visions much more easily. It's actually really annoying.'

Peter wouldn't meet my gaze. He was fiddling with a loose thread on the blanket.

'Right, yeah.'

'But you can control your thing?'

'Yeah. It took a bit of practice.'

'Do you think I could learn to control mine?'

'I guess so, yeah.' He looked up at me. I'd sprung onto my knees and was looking down at him with an eager grin. 'I can't teach you! I have no idea how your thing works or what it is.'

I slumped back down in a sulk.

'I guess. But this is a good thing. We both know each other's secret and we can talk about it and I'm not the only freak, hell, I'm not even the biggest freak!' I grinned at him and he grinned back. Gruesome murders notwithstanding, I knew that Peter and I would be okay. I had been terrified by what I saw, and yet I knew I didn't need to be afraid of him. Now that he'd explained so earnestly what had happened it all sort of made sense.

I wanted to know the rest, though. Who had told Peter to keep quiet? How many shapeshifters were there? Were they all around us humans? Was I even human?! Was my gift some sort of shifter-based power?

'Peter? Eve? Dinner!' Mrs Wilkes called up the stairs.

'Are you hungry?'

'Yeah, actually, I am.' I grinned at him and leapt from the bed, running to the door like I would have done when we were kids. He charged after me, laughing, and pushed past me in the hall. He bounded down the stairs three at a time and jumped the last five all together, landing with a huge thump in the narrow hall.

'Peter!' his mother shouted from the kitchen, and he glanced back up at me, still halfway down the tight staircase. He chuckled and winked at me.

'Sorry, Mum, I won't do it again.'

'You're not a little boy any more,' she scolded. 'That shook the whole house.' He tiptoed into the kitchen, mockingly. I sniggered under my breath as I followed him, my own light feet barely making a sound.

'Careful, Peter,' his father said softly, with a stern glare written on his face.

Peter dropped into a chair at the table and tucked into the food that had been laid out. I sat next to him and my stomach gave a loud growl.

'Sorry,' I said, clutching my belly. 'I guess my appetite

is back.'

'Quite all right, dear,' said Mrs Wilkes, passing me a plate of cold meats.

I loaded my plate high with food. Peter was already tucking into a chicken drumstick.

The four of us chatted about light, everyday things. The morning's event wasn't mentioned and it felt good to be somewhat normal for the first time in what felt like forever. As awful as things had been, it felt like a normal life might be possible again.

CHAPTER FOUR

IT WAS TIME. While I was busy grieving, the real world had kept on moving and now I had to face all the unpleasant, grown-up stuff. Monday seemed like as good a day as any to tackle it, a fresh week and all that. The funeral had been on Friday and messages had started piling up, mainly from the staff at the restaurant who wanted to know if they still had jobs to return to.

Kirk was an accountant and had been doing the books for my parents for as long as I could remember. He came with me to open up and sort everything out.

We arrived at Piero's before 9am. It was on a commercial street just south of the city centre and outside the ancient wall that surrounded the heart of the city. The street bustled with that morning rush hour energy. Cars swept along the road, sloshing the puddles up over the narrow pavement. People rushed along on foot, their heads down against the rain.

Kirk and I parked right outside the restaurant and I clutched the chunky bunch of keys in my hand as we dashed from the car to shelter under the red and white striped awning that ran across the front of the building.

A tinted window took up the entire width of the restaurant with a glass door in the centre. I unlocked it and stepped into the dark dining area. The chairs were stacked on top of the tables and the chequered floor looked dull in the gloom.

I looked around, memories flooding my mind. My whole childhood was wrapped up in this place. I saw my parents rushing through the busy dining area and myself sitting at an empty table doing my homework.

It was sad and empty without them.

I shook my head and set off between the tables to the back of the restaurant, Kirk close behind. We left the lights off and went straight into the office, which was next to the kitchen at the back of the building. I had my mother's address book with the names and contact details of the employees at hand and sat down in the office at her desk. Kirk pulled up a chair and sat opposite me, his kind eyes watching me intently.

'Would you hire a manager?' I asked him.

'Good question.'

'I'm 20. I don't know much about running a business.'

'No, I'm sure people would help if you asked, though.'

'Or I could sell it.' I sighed and leaned back in the chair. It was one of those spring-loaded office chairs that rocked back when you leaned back into it. My parents had worked hard to build up the business, they had sacrificed so much for it and ended up under the control of the Camorra for it. Selling it seemed like a very cold thing to do.

'You could, but I don't think that would honour your parents' memories very well.'

'No, I know.' I sighed again. 'I was just thinking that.'

Kirk had pulled out a ledger and was examining it. 'How does it look? How much damage have I done by leaving the place closed this long?' I asked.

'It's not great, but it can be recovered. Don't worry about that.'

A knock at the glass door at the front of the restaurant got both of our attention. I looked out through the open office door and saw a figure standing outside under the shelter of the awning. There was an ominous crack of thunder and the fine drizzle that had been falling when we arrived had turned to heavy rain.

The figure seemed to be a man in a suit and a long, black coat. His hands were in his pockets, his coat collar pulled up on either side of his face.

'Bit soon for debt collectors, isn't it?' I joked, but Kirk didn't laugh.

'I'll go,' he said solemnly. He stood up and strode out through the gloomy restaurant, between the tables with their chairs stacked on top of them.

He slid back the bolts at the top and bottom of the

door, retrieved a key from his pocket and unlocked the door, his gaze fixed on the stranger on the other side of the glass. I watched from the office, leaning back as far as my chair would allow.

The door opened and Kirk gestured for the man to enter. He was young, maybe only a few years older than me. He wore a dark grey suit, which I could tell was expensive, even in the low light.

'Mr Wilkes,' he said, his voice smooth like caramel. He had an Italian accent and a haircut that was probably as expensive as his suit. I took a deep breath and watched in silence. A horrible sense of apprehension had settled over the restaurant.

'Mr Esposito. I'm surprised to see you. How can I help?'

'I was hoping to catch Ms Rawling. Is she here with you?' He cast his gaze around the empty dining area. I had a split second to decide if I was concealing myself or making my presence known. I let the chair spring back to upright and rolled it on its castors quickly into the nook of the desk, hiding myself from view through the open door. It wasn't a silent manoeuvre and I cringed, knowing that there was a chance he'd heard the movement. I could just see the pair of them through the gap between the door hinges.

'It's still a bit soon,' Kirk said, his voice quiet but firm. 'Perhaps I can help.'

'I see.' The man's gaze lingered on the office door, but slowly returned to Kirk. 'Who will be taking over the day-to-day management of the restaurant?'

'It's too soon to say for certain,' Kirk replied, his hands buried deep in his cardigan pockets. 'I'm here now, though. Whatever it is you wish to discuss, you can do so with me. I'll be sure to pass on any relevant information.'

'How kind of you.' I'd never seen a smile so lacking in warmth. 'Mr Vitale would like to meet with Ms Rawling, or whoever is going to be running the business. The sooner the better. We want to ensure the smooth running of things. An interruption such as this is an inconvenience to all.'

'An inconvenience.' Kirk clucked his tongue and nodded. There was an edge of resentment in his voice. I realised that I was clenching my fists, my nails were digging into my palms. I released them quickly and shook my hands to take away the pins and needles that were starting. 'I'll pass along the message. Good day.' Kirk opened the door and held it wide, his intention clear.

The Italian gave a curt nod and left without a word.

Kirk locked the door and watched him leave. I scurried from the office in time to see the man getting into the back of a sleek, silver car. He had a driver, who closed the door for him before sliding into the driver's seat and setting off.

'Oh my god!' I gasped. 'He was Camorra, wasn't he?

My parents were up to their necks in this. Right?'

'I'm afraid so.'

'And he knew you!' I glowered at him and he avoided my gaze.

'Yes. Your parents aren't the only people I keep books for, Eve.' He walked away from me, back to the office, leaving me in stunned silence. I ran after him.

'You? You're in with them?'

'I don't think that's a fair assessment. They own me, like they own this place and half the people in this city.'

'But you... you help them launder money, right? That's what you meant?'

Kirk sat down in a chair and raised his eyes to the ceiling. He ran his hands through his greying hair.

'Yes. That is accurate. But, Eve, I don't have a choice. None of us do.'

I dropped back into my chair and stared at him. The kind and gentle man I'd known all my life was involved with organised crime. It was one thing for my parents to be indebted to the Camorra, I knew about that and hated it, but it was a peripheral thing that didn't change my life much. By the sounds of it, Kirk Wilkes did actual criminal work for them. That was bigger than I'd been prepared for.

'What do they have on you?'

'I'm sorry?'

'They must have some way of controlling you, right? You wouldn't work for them, break the law for them, if they didn't.'

'You are too clever for your own good. I'm not going to get into the details with you. You heard what he said, yes? You know who he was talking about? The man who wants to meet you is the head of the clan, Antonio Vitale.'

I swallowed a hard lump in my throat and nodded.

'I know who he is.' He was there the night my parents died. He was in the road. But no one could know that I knew that, least of all Antonio Vitale himself.

'They'll be back to set up the meeting. I don't see how you can say no to it. No one says no to them. I did my best to delay things, give you time, but they won't let you have long.'

'This is why I can't hire a manager, isn't it? I can't knowingly put someone else in their firing line.'

Kirk nodded, a grim look of regret on his face. 'If I sell the business, could I buy my way out of their debt? Would they accept that?'

'Maybe.' He wouldn't meet my gaze. I got the impression he meant "no" but couldn't bring himself to say it.

'Right.' I nodded and bounced slightly in the chair. I rolled up my sleeves, gathered up my hair and tied it quickly in a messy top bun. 'Let's get this place open for business, shall we?'

We spent the morning calling wait and kitchen staff. They were all glad to hear that we were reopening and even though I had started out saying we would open the next day, I was talked into opening that night. Mondays were usually quiet, I knew, but they were eager to get cracking.

'Excellent,' my mother's favourite chef, Giovanni said when I told him the news. 'I have three new recipes I'm itching to add to the menu.'

Kirk was wonderful. He made half the calls and he even called a contact he had at the local radio station to get an announcement out that afternoon. There wasn't time to get a cleaning crew in, but the wait staff arrived early and set about cleaning the place up ready for opening.

The kitchen staff cleaned out the kitchen, some stock had spoilt in the time that the place had been closed. The chef wrote a list and the two young pot washers went to the supermarket to buy fresh supplies. I'd have to get a delivery from our normal supplier later in the week. But Kirk showed me what I needed to know for that.

I wrote up the new menu items on the huge black board my mother used to write the specials on, and enjoyed the bustle and camaraderie that unfolded around me. I pushed aside the Camorra. That was a problem for another day. One I wanted to be able to face with a thriving business, not an empty shell.

The whole place felt alive once it was lit and set up for customers. It was warm and inviting, filled with amazing smells from the kitchen.

Our first patrons were Peter and his mum, who came

in for dinner to show me some support. I loved them for it. A little trickle of customers gathered pace as the evening went on.

'I'm so glad you're open,' I was told, more than once.

By 9 pm we were at capacity and the host, a woman called Tina, had to turn people away.

Tina had worked at Piero's since I was twelve. She was a petite woman in her forties with deep laughter lines and a kind face. She was always immaculately presented and no one knew the menu like she did.

Just as it was starting to quieten down and I was resting my feet in the office, trying not to feel too smug about the successful reopening, there was a knock on the office door and Tina opened it without waiting for a reply.

'You've been asked for.' She disappeared again. I groaned and slid my feet back into my shoes. There were still about half a dozen occupied tables, but the chatter had dropped to a low level. A waitress scurried past me on her way to the bar and her cheeks were flushed scarlet.

I looked in the direction that she had hurried from and felt my stomach lurch about a foot downward. A table in the window was newly occupied by two of the most beautiful people I had ever seen in my life.

The woman was tall, with long black hair that cascaded perfectly straight down to her waist. She had a regal nose, high cheekbones and flawless, Mediterranean-toned skin. Her eyes were dangerously dark. She was wearing a floor-length black dress with a slit up one side that went right up her thigh, and the highest heels I'd ever seen on a person in real life, as opposed to in a magazine.

Her companion I knew. It was Antonio Vitale himself. He was dressed in a light grey suit with a black shirt and tie. He too had long, black hair, which he wore tied back. He had the same nose as the woman, and chiselled jaw and cheekbones. He was stunning. The kind of man that you had to stop and stare at, whatever your sexuality.

Most of the customers, I would have guessed, had no idea who these people were, but they knew an Adonis when they saw one. That's why it had gone quiet.

I looked down at myself. I was wearing the same trousers I'd worn to my parents' funeral. I'd paired them with a short-sleeved, purple shirt and ballet flats. I didn't feel fit to be in their company, but I didn't have a choice.

I glanced around the restaurant and caught sight of Kirk behind the bar. He was emptying the register, but had stopped what he was doing to survey the scene. He looked my way and cast me a look of pity.

I had no time for that look. I'd had quite enough of that since I arrived home. I tightened my bun and strode over to Tina, who was standing at her post by the door. She was deathly pale. She knew exactly who she had seated. She pointed, wordlessly, in their direction. I nodded in thanks and walked slowly over to their table.

'Ah, Ms Rawling.' Antonio stood up and held out a

hand. He wasn't asking, he knew who I was. And he expected me to shake his hand. I plastered a smile onto my face and took his hand, bracing myself for a vision. Nothing happened. His hand was cool and his grip was firm. He shook my hand only briefly and then released it. His skin was totally smooth and his eyes were dark and deep.

My breath quavered slightly.

'How do you do? I don't believe I've had the pleasure?' We'd never met. He should have had no idea that I knew his face, or his name. He sat back down and draped a cloth napkin across his lap.

'Antonio Vitale. This is my sister, Lucia.'

'How do you do?' I cast a sideways glance at the woman. She really was breathtakingly beautiful, but cold and hard. She glanced at me with the expression you might cast at a mangy dog in your path.

'I really must congratulate you on such a successful reopening,' Antonio said, with a smile that didn't reach his eyes.

'Thank you,' I replied, still trying to smile with enough warmth for both of us. Lucia was a lost cause, I decided.

'I can't wait to sample the wine.'

'Yes, of course.' I plucked the wine menu from the table and opened it for him, passing it back to him. 'I'm afraid I can't recommend anything, I'm still very new to this.'

'That's quite all right.' He took the menu but didn't look at it. He was looking pointedly at me, taking in my messy hair, day-old make-up, creased shirt and the rest. But his face was inscrutable. 'I was very sorry to hear of your parents' passing. I wish I could have attended the service, but I had business.'

'Thank you,' I said stiffly, my smile slipping. He looked down at the menu at last and I relaxed a fraction. 'Did you know them well?'

'Oh not very, just, you know, through business.' He gestured around at the restaurant and I stiffened up again. This was my business now and I did not like him casually implying that it belonged to him. Something passed between us then, an understanding. He knew that I knew how he was connected to my parents and I knew that he had figured it out. 'We'll have half a bottle of the Lacryma Christi del Vesuvio Rosso.' He snapped the menu closed and handed it back to me.

'Of course.' I turned on my heel and marched to the bar.

'Are you all right?' Kirk whispered.

'Fine. I'm fine.' I gave the order to Marco, our bartender. He produced the bottle and two glasses on a tray and was about to take it over to the table, but he looked petrified. 'I'll take it.' I took the tray and swept back across the restaurant to the Vitales. I placed the glasses in front of them and began to pour the wine, as expertly as I knew how, which was not very. I knew that my hand was shaking slightly, but I was determined not to crack.

'I would like to meet with you privately,' Antonio said, so casually he might have been commenting on the weather.

'I see.' I put the bottle down and clutched the tray against my stomach. 'May I ask why?'

'We have business to discuss. I think you know this.' I didn't respond, I just waited for him to go on. 'You will come here, tomorrow at 8 pm.' He raised his hand, a white business card resting between his fingers. I took it and glanced at the address. It was somewhere I wasn't especially familiar with, the prestigious northern area of the city.

'Fine. I'll be there. Should I bring my solicitor?' I stared him down and to my surprise, he looked right back into my eyes and smiled.

'I don't believe that will be necessary.' He kept his gaze fixed on me as he took a sip of his wine. 'Very nice,' he said, finally looking away.

'It's not as good as the last vintage we shared,' Lucia said coolly. I glanced her way and noticed her smirk.

'No, it isn't.' Antonio nodded and smiled back at his sister.

I turned and stalked away without another word. What else was there to say? I set the tray down on the bar and strode into the office, closing the door with a little more force than was necessary. Kirk was right. You didn't say no to these people.

CHAPTER FIVE

IT RAINED ALL THE NEXT DAY and the air was thick with fog. There was an icy chill that had me layering up. Peter came with me to the restaurant to help open up.

'I could leave my job and work here,' he offered. I shook my head.

'No, stay away from this. It's too dangerous. If they find out what you are...' I stalled. It was too horrible to contemplate. He didn't argue and I felt like I wasn't the first person to say that to him when he gave me a withering look that screamed, "Heard it before".

I'd seen what he could do to a man, though, I couldn't pretend otherwise. Part of me wondered if Peter was exactly who was needed to stand up to Antonio Vitale. But no, that was selfish and foolish. Taking on the head of a dangerous Camorra clan was likely to mean suicide. Peter's strength wasn't exactly subtle, either. It was likely to get a whole host of innocent bystanders killed as well.

I was reasonably confident of surviving the meeting with Antonio Vitale. If he wanted me dead he'd just do it, he wouldn't meet me in public and invite me to his home, or office, or wherever I was going. He may own the police, but there were limits to what he could get away with. Weren't there?

'I should come with you,' Peter said as the time for me to leave grew closer.

'He told me to go alone.'

'No, he told you he wanted to see you privately, and not to bring a solicitor. I can at least drive you and wait outside for you. I don't see how he can object to that.'

'I suppose.' I didn't feel like I could say no to Peter any more than I could say no to Vitale.

I was wearing tight, dark jeans, a deep red sweater with a roll-neck and a navy blazer that I'd bought that morning. I needed some more smart clothes to wear at the restaurant. Even with the clothes I had left back in my room at university, I didn't have much that fit the bill. I opted for some wedge-heeled ankle boots that would keep my feet dry in the rain.

I wasn't sure whether it mattered what I wore. I didn't care, under normal circumstances, what people thought of my appearance. I didn't want to care now. I wanted to treat the Vitales the way I would treat anyone. But they weren't just anyone. I wanted to stand up to them, to reclaim my family's business and never have to deal with them again. But I was living in the real world and it was quite clear that it wasn't remotely that simple.

I was going to have to hear Antonio Vitale out. I didn't expect to have much choice in whether I accepted whatever his suggestion would be or not, but at least I would have the information.

Peter was wearing the same suit he'd worn to the funeral, his only smart clothes. I didn't suppose it would matter if he was staying in the car.

I left the restaurant in the fairly capable hands of Tina, and Peter drove me across the city to Herald Gate. It was a small area to the north of the city centre, close enough to the theatre, nice bars and restaurants but set away from the noise and bustle. The streets were wide and lined with large trees. Most of the buildings were white and Georgian, with grand columns and large windows.

'Wow,' I murmured, watching the beautiful buildings as we passed slowly. 'I hardly ever come up here. I'd forgotten how posh it is.'

'Yeah. Here reside the haves, as opposed to the have-nots, like us.'

We reached the address on the card Antonio had given me. I checked it three times. Set back from the road, beyond a deep pavement, there were tall, wrought iron gates between white stone pillars. A large, black "12" emblazoned on the stone told us this was the right place, but we couldn't see the house. High hedges ran in either direction away from the gates, concealing the property beyond.

'Wait here,' I said, my voice barely above a whisper.

'Not a chance,' Peter hissed. 'I want to be able to keep an eye on the house and be close enough to hear anything, like, you know, screams, or gunshots.'

'He's not going to shoot me, and if he did decide to kill me, it'd probably be swift and silent, no chance for me to scream.'

'That's not exactly reassuring,' he said, scowling. 'I won't budge on this, Eve. I'm driving you up to the door. Besides, it's chucking it down. You'll get soaked if you walk.' He had a fair point, so I settled back in my seat. Peter pulled the car off the road and up to the gates. They swung inward automatically and Peter proceeded through them.

The drive was made up of neat, clay brickwork and lined with tall pine trees. It swept in a curve to the left, then back to the right, where the trees gave way and the drive opened up into a wide paved circle in front of a huge mansion. A little fountain sat in the middle of the paved area. It burbled away, lit with several white spotlights.

The house was two storeys high but wide enough to fit at least five of the narrow terraced houses on Peter's street. Both floors were lined with tall windows and several of the downstairs windows were lit.

Peter let out a soft whistle and I gazed up at the house in awe. I looked around at the front of the property. There were no other cars parked, but the drive curved away to the left of the mansion and I could just make out a wide garage down a lit slope. It was three doors wide and there were two cars parked in front of it, one of which was the silver car I'd seen the day before.

'I'll be fine from here. You stay in the car and keep quiet.'

'Scream if you need me. I'll hear you.' Peter tapped his ear and gave me a grim smile.

The front door was up three wide steps and flanked by columns that reached all the way to the roof. I grabbed my umbrella and stepped out of the car.

I got to the large, black door and was looking for a bell or a knocker when it opened. A lean man in a dark suit stood there, peering down at me in the dark. The hall beyond flickered with candlelight.

'Ms Rawling?'

'Yes.'

'You're expected.' He held the door open wide for me and I stepped inside, fighting the urge to look back at the car. He closed the door and held a hand out for my umbrella. I folded it and passed it to him.

'Thank you,' I said, trying to smile. I don't think I succeeded. My palms were sweating and my clothes felt too tight.

'This way, please,' the man said, after stowing my umbrella in a nearby stand. He led me across the grand foyer, which was circular with a chequered floor. Directly opposite the door was the foot of a huge, sweeping staircase, lined with rich, red carpet. As my gaze followed it up, I caught sight of a figure leaning over the banister, watching me. She was draped in shadow, but a hunch told me it was Lucia Vitale.

The butler, I assumed, led me to the right of the stairs to a large, wooden door. He rapped hard on it and a voice inside softly called for us to enter. He opened the door and led me inside.

'Ms Rawling for you, signor.' His accent was distinctly English and the Italian title sounded slightly odd.

'Thank you,' Antonio Vitale said.

I looked around the large study. The walls were lined with books from floor to ceiling. The chequered floor from the foyer continued through into this room, but a large, dark rug took up a portion of the centre of the room and on it stood a magnificent wooden desk. Behind the desk stood Antonio, his fingers pressed into the wood. His long hair was loose and hung over his left shoulder. He was wearing a dark suit and tie, with gold cufflinks and tie pin. He was immaculate. So was the room. All those books and not a speck of dust.

The butler left and closed the door.

Antonio stood up straight and gestured to the chair in front of the desk. I walked to it, my wet shoes making a soft squeak on the polished floor with each step. The wooden chair was deep, with ornately carved arms and a thick, red cushion. I perched on the edge of it and looked up at him across the desk. He remained standing, though there was an opulent-looking chair just behind him.

'This is certainly private,' I said softly. I couldn't keep my nerves from my voice and it quavered slightly.

'My sister, Lucia, had misgivings about us meeting like this. She wanted to be here. But I felt it would help to put you at ease if she were not.'

I raised an eyebrow.

'You thought that I would be more at ease alone with you, in your house? A strange man that I just met? A man who is undoubtedly powerful and universally feared? The presence of another woman would certainly heighten the tension, yes.' Sarcasm dripped from my voice and I immediately regretted taking such a tone with him. His face was cold and hard. But after a moment he cracked into laughter and dropped down into his chair, brushing his hair back over his shoulder.

'Eve, you are quite something, aren't you?' He continued to laugh, but I remained tense. I wasn't going to let my guard down. It occurred to me that I could have come armed. Maybe I should have done. No one searched me. In fact, Antonio had no security that I could see. Somehow, that worried me even more. Men of power, it seemed to me in my humdrum life, were usually surrounded by protection. Senior politicians had secret service personnel with them at all times. CEOs had CCTV and metal detectors at their doors.

Antonio Vitale had a stony-faced butler and automatic gates. Was it confidence that no one would dare to make an attempt on his life? Or certainty that should anyone try, he could snap them in two himself before they could so much as wrinkle his suit?

Either way, I was not nearly as confident about my odds of getting out of this as I had been. I had never been more scared of this man than I was in that moment. I made a mental note to apologise to my parents' ghosts for ever judging them for making a deal with Antonio Vitale.

'What did you want to discuss?' I asked, my voice cracking in the middle. His laughter died out and he leaned across the table. The flickering candles that lit the room cast eerie, moving shadows across his face. He was smiling. The light glinted on his cufflinks and his eyes shone.

'Well now, to business. A simple matter, really. Your family owes an outstanding debt to me, as I'm sure you must know by now.'

'Is it the kind of debt that can be settled? Or is it the kind that always seems to grow?'

'Hmm.' He leaned back and looked at me with shrewd eyes. 'I haven't decided yet. I suppose it depends what you can offer me.'

'How much did my parents pay you?'

'Twenty per cent of their revenue.'

'I see.' I had no idea how much that was in practical terms, or how much the restaurant was making. I didn't know how much that stretched them. I had no idea if it was practical for me to match that. He seemed to see inside my mind as the thoughts wound their way through it. A small smile played on his full lips.

'Why don't you look at the books with your friend, Mr Wilkes?' His voice was almost musical, hypnotic. He seemed to be speaking with kindness, but I knew that couldn't really be the case.

'I will. I'd like to see if there is a way that we can bring this relationship to a close. Losing my parents like that, it's a difficult time and one I would like to be able to put behind me. I don't know if my future lies here or where I was living before. I didn't see myself taking over the family business.' I'd got up some steam and rambled on more than I'd meant to. I hadn't meant to tell him anything personal. What was wrong with me?

'I understand. But Eve, your parents left me with a gap in my income. They let me down.' He'd moved around the desk and was perched on the edge closest to me, leaning over me. When had he done that? 'You don't want to let me down, do you?'

'No, no of course not.' He was so close to me now. I was leaning forward too, my head felt foggy. He reached out a thin finger and brushed my hair away from my face, tucking it behind my ear. His skin was cold.

'Good.' His hand cupped my cheek and my eyes grew heavy. They flickered closed. 'You're young, and new to all of this,' he said, his voice soft and distant. 'You need the chance to catch your breath and figure things out.'

'Hmm,' I murmured in assent.

'I'm sure there is a way for you to get what you need and for me to get what I need.'

'Thank you,' I whispered. My mouth felt dry. My eyes opened and Antonio was helping me to my feet. He walked me slowly to the door.

'I will see you again soon, Eve. We'll come to an agreement then.'

'Yes. Okay.' The butler was seeing me out through the front door. The rain was cool and sharp on my skin. I seemed to snap out of the drunken fog that I'd found myself in and dashed over to the car. I leapt into the passenger seat and looked at Peter. He was staring at me expectantly.

'Well?' he asked when I failed to tell him immediately what had happened.

'I... I'm not sure.' I didn't have my umbrella. I looked up at the door, which was closed, and briefly entertained the idea of going back for it. But I reconsidered. I had a reason to come back another time for it. And I did so desperately want to find myself back here again soon, staring into those dark eyes.

CHAPTER SIX

'I DON'T LIKE THE IDEA OF YOU MEETING HIM AGAIN.'

'Well, it's not up to you.'

Peter looked stung. His face had gone pale. He turned and left the guest room, closing the door behind him.

I hadn't been able to tell him much about my meeting with Antonio Vitale. At first I didn't have a problem with that, but since getting back to Peter's house something had begun to feel distinctly wrong about the whole situation. I couldn't admit that to Peter, though.

My memory of the meeting was hazy at best. All I was really sure on was that he wanted to meet me again to finalise the terms of our agreement. Peter had not reacted well to this news.

I got changed into my pyjamas and curled up on the bed. I grabbed a book to read but didn't even open it. My mind was racing and churning over what had happened. I tried to focus on the bits that had unsettled me: Lucia watching me from the shadows; the lack of security; being alone with Antonio; his hypnotic eyes.

A soft smile crept over my face when I remembered the way he had looked at me. No one had ever gazed so deeply into my soul before. It was like he was lovingly leafing through a treasured book. I was the book. When he'd touched me I didn't get any visions. I didn't even flinch when he caressed my cheek. If it had been anyone else I would have done. But not him.

He was so beautiful. He looked like an airbrushed model in a magazine. He had that not-quite-real quality. He was no common gangster. He couldn't have amassed such wealth just from a few criminal dealings. Could he?

He had the air of old money about him. Italian aristocracy. The way he spoke, the way he commanded attention. He had lived an entire life of wealth and privilege. He didn't seem like a self-made man and yet there was great pride and self-assurance there too. I didn't know much about the Camorra, just that they came from Naples and had power and influence to rival the Mafia.

Maybe the Vitales were second- or third-generation Camorra clan leaders. Had they inherited their influence? Grown-up spoiled brats of harder-working criminals who now took their power for granted?

But I couldn't think about that now. I had to let my thoughts linger on those eyes a little longer. His face was relatively young, late twenties, maybe, but his eyes held the wisdom of many decades. He was surprisingly kind and gentle. I'd expected him to be cruel, but he'd given me more time and seemed open to negotiation.

I wanted to see him again. I wanted to feel his cool aura close to me, to feel his fingers gently touching me. I closed my eyes, my book forgotten on the bed beside me.

In my dreams I was with Antonio, running after him through the rain, and he was calling to me. I woke with a start in my brightly lit room in Peter's house. The house was still and silent, but I could hear rain pattering on the window. I stretched out and flicked off the lamp. My fingers brushed my phone and I tapped the screen to show me the time. It was 4 am.

I rolled over and stared at the window. I hadn't drawn the curtains and I could see the rain trickling down the glass in jagged trails. The sky was slightly orange from the street lights reflecting back off the thick clouds. It was still foggy, as it had been all day.

My eyes began to feel heavy and slowly sleep claimed me again.

When I woke up in the morning it was already getting light. I remembered my thoughts about Antonio's dark eyes and scolded myself for letting his good looks distract me from what a vile person he really was.

'He might have killed your parents,' I hissed at myself in the mirror as I brushed my teeth. 'What on earth were you thinking?'

I went down to breakfast and had to face Peter.

'Sorry,' I muttered at him as we passed each other in

the kitchen.

'What for?' He seemed genuinely surprised.

'For what I said last night. I wasn't quite in my right mind.'

'Oh, it's fine. All forgotten.'

'Today's the day, Eve, dear,' Mrs Wilkes said, bustling into the kitchen. 'Time to tackle the house.'

'Oh,' I said, staring at her. 'Yes, I suppose so.'

'I'll be there,' Peter said softly. I nodded, but no longer felt like eating my porridge.

The three of us walked around the corner to my parents' house after breakfast. Mrs Wilkes was chattering away, mainly to keep her own thoughts off the depressing task at hand, I thought. Peter and I trailed along behind her, not speaking.

When we arrived, Peter's mother used her key to unlock the door. She and my mother had had keys for each other's houses for as long as I could remember.

The house I had grown up in was in a slightly wider street than Peter's. The houses had little front gardens with walls and gates that set them back from the road. But they were still small, terraced houses. Our door was dark blue with a brass knocker in the middle. The garden was neatly paved, though the little wall had some loose cement between the bricks.

All of the houses were red brick and a bit newer than those in Peter's street. The walls were thinner, the ceilings lower, and they had much less character. There were no flagstone floors or wonky walls in my parents' house, no narrow passages.

We went into the carpeted hall and a musty smell greeted us. A little pile of post had mounted on the mat. Mrs Wilkes scooped it up and began straightening it out as she strode down the hall to the kitchen at the back of the house.

Peter led me after his mother. I glanced up the stairs as we passed them, and into the living room. Everything was dusty.

The kitchen was nothing like the Wilkes's. It was modern and bright. A bowl of fruit on the worktop had spoiled and Mrs Wilkes was already going about disposing of it. The smell was really unpleasant. Peter went straight to the window and opened it.

I just stood there, paralysed in the doorway. It didn't feel like my home. My home was full of life and family. This was a shell and it smelled of decay.

Peter looked at me and gave me a sad smile. He strode to the back door, unlocked it and went out into the garden. I followed him and as I reached the door I stopped, my breath caught in my throat. All of the flowers from the funeral had been brought here and laid out in the back garden. Rows and rows of wreaths, garlands, and bunches of carnations, roses and beautiful white lilies. Peter reached for a glass jar of lilies and brought them over to me.

'These will help with the smell.' We stepped back inside and he put them on the worktop where the fruit had been.

'That's perfect. Thank you.' I smiled and he draped an arm around my shoulders.

'Right,' Mrs Wilkes said, putting an apron on and rolling up her sleeves. 'I'll get this room sorted out. Eve, would you like to tackle the post or the dusting?'

I shrugged and let out a groan. Neither sounded appealing.

'Come on,' Peter said brightly. 'Let's tackle the post together.' He grabbed my hand and led me through to the living room, scooping up the pile of post from the counter where it had been dropped when we came in.

It was dull and tedious work. We opened everything quickly and made a stack of envelopes to recycle. Mostly the contents were bills and all the things I would have to make phone calls about; subscriptions to cancel, insurance to update. There were dozens of cards addressed to me with condolences from friends of my parents. Some of the names were familiar, but not all of them. I tried not to get stuck reading them all, or I would have been sitting there on the living room floor all day.

I cried several times and Peter, my rock, just squeezed my hand and encouraged me, silently, to keep going.

We could hear Mrs Wilkes pottering around in the kitchen. She cleaned out the fridge freezer, ran the dishwasher, which had been left with dirty dishes stacked inside for nearly two weeks. She cleaned every surface, took out the rubbish, and even cleaned the oven.

Peter helped me make the phone calls that needed to be made and when I cried down the phone at the insurance company because they wouldn't update the policy over the phone without me sending some document to them, Peter took the phone and gave them a piece of his mind.

It was one of the hardest days of my life, harder than the day of the funeral, in some ways.

Now it was real. Now it was the time for the real world to intrude upon my grief and I had to find a way to function. I'd been able to get the restaurant back up and running again because that part of it all was forward-facing. It was about what I was going to live on, people's jobs and moving forward. This work was about having to confront the past and dig into my parents' lives.

My mother had been the heart of the restaurant, of course, it was her passion and there were reminders of her all over the place, but it was warm and lively and full of positive vibes. Making copies of death certificates was none of those things.

When we were finished with the tedious post and

phone call tasks, Peter lay back against the sofa and stared at the ceiling. I paced the room, stretching out my cramped muscles.

'Is it too soon to think about their clothes and stuff?' he asked, not looking at me.

'Yeah. I can't. I don't want to part with anything. Later.'

He nodded and made to get up, but I caught his eye and started to speak, stopping him. But I didn't know what to say.

'Everything all right?' Peter's mother appeared in the doorway, drying her hands on the apron.

'Fine. Yeah. We're heading upstairs now to go through the stuff in the study.' Peter stood up, grabbed my hand and dragged me past his mother and up the stairs.

'What? Why are we doing this?' I hissed at him.

'So we can talk more privately.' He stomped up the stairs and I ran behind him.

My parents had a small home office at the back of the house. It was about as far removed from Antonio's study as possible. It was a tiny box room with a small desk and a single book case that was stacked with folders, papers, binders and books. The desk was littered with office supplies, stacks of post, more bills and documents.

Peter shut the door. I perched on the edge of the desk and folded my arms around myself. The office was like a freezer, and Peter's expression as he stared down at me wasn't exactly warm either. It occurred to me that people who crossed Antonio Vitale probably ended up in large freezers. I shuddered.

'Can't he just tell you over the phone what to expect? Or send one of his lackeys? Why does he want to see you again?'

'Look,' I whispered. 'I get it. It's creepy and weird and he might have killed my parents so this is a whole world of fucked up. And I came out of his house all weird and vague.'

'Yes, you did.' He shoved his hands into the pockets of his baggy jeans. 'Eve, it is so much worse than you know.'

'What's that supposed to mean?'

'Just that he is seriously dangerous. And don't underestimate Lucia. She's not just a pretty face.'

'No, I could tell. Peter, if you know something that I need to know, then now's the time to tell me. Are they shapeshifters too?'

'No,' he snapped, a little too forcefully. I cocked an eyebrow at him and he shook his head firmly. 'No, they aren't.'

'Okay. I believe you.' A lump bobbed in my throat. I did believe him, but I also knew that he was keeping something from me, something that was going to be important.

CHAPTER SEVEN

I FOUND MYSELF LOOKING OVER MY SHOULDER CONSTANTLY whenever we went anywhere for the next few days. I half expected to see Antonio peel out of a shadow and appear in my path at any moment.

We went back to the house repeatedly and I had to stop in at the restaurant every day. I was beginning to feel like I really didn't have a choice in what I did next. I couldn't go back to Caerton but I didn't really feel like I wanted to either. It felt like somebody else's life back there.

I sat down with Kirk and went over the accounts for Piero's. My parents had been skimming twenty per cent off the top for the Vitales and Kirk had helped them to hide it from the tax man. He showed me the paper trail, because there always was one, he said. But he was good. No one would find it, even if they were looking for it.

He had been doing the accounts for a dozen Vitale businesses for twenty years and had got very skilled at it.

'But they've never brought you into the inner circle?' I asked as we pored over the data.

'I'm not Italian, not part of the family,' he said with a smirk. I didn't think that was entirely the full answer.

'Peter thinks they're more dangerous than I realise. But I think I have a pretty good idea.'

'Oh?' He glanced up from the books and raised an eyebrow.

'I know what the Camorra are. I know what they want from me.'

'You went to his house, didn't you?'

'I did.'

'What did you think?'

'They didn't make all that money themselves from organised crime. Their wealth is old.'

'Yes it is.' He clucked his tongue and went back to work. But I was like a dog with a bone.

'Do you think my parents might have crossed them?'

'Why would you ask that?' He glanced up again, what looked like genuine surprise on his face.

'I think Antonio might have had a hand in their deaths.'

'Eve!' he hissed. 'You can't say things like that.'

'It's not really a leap.' He stood up and marched around the desk, turned me in my chair and gripped my shoulders.

'Eve, if it's true, and I agree that it's not hard to imagine, then voicing it could be very dangerous for you. These people go to great lengths to protect themselves.'

'It doesn't seem that way to me. There's no security at the house. Did you know that?'

'Did it occur to you that there was a great deal of it but that you couldn't see it?'

That caught me off guard and I pulled out of his grasp. A frown creased my brow and I stared up at him. Kirk's face softened and he got down into a squat in front of me, like a parent coming down to their child's level. 'You need to let this go. Please. I'm worried about you enough, without you getting more involved than you have to be. Agree to the twenty per cent, make the payments on time, and stay out of trouble.'

'How long for, though? I could be paying them for the rest of my life. My parents were trapped in this deal and they were never going to get free. It probably killed them.'

'No,' he said, heaving a sigh and looking down at the ground. 'Trying to get free probably killed them.'

My cheek trembled. He was right. But I was stubborn and didn't want to admit it. Kirk stood up and returned to his side of the desk. He seemed to think he had made his point sufficiently clearly.

The sky was shot with crimson as dusk settled over the city. I was about to head back to the house with Mr Wilkes, leaving the restaurant in the capable hands of the staff for the evening. Kirk was fastening the buckle on his leather satchel in which he had some important documents for the business. A familiar silver car pulled up at the kerb in front of the restaurant and an uncomfortable ache settled into the pit of my stomach.

I went out through the glass door, leaving Kirk inside fumbling with his bag. The driver got out and opened the back door. I peered inside and saw the man who had come to the restaurant that first day. He was sitting there, his arm draped across the top of the leather seats. He looked at me with a sneer.

The restaurant door opened behind me and Kirk stepped up to my side. He gently took me by the elbow and pulled me back a step.

The man slid out of the car, stood up and buttoned his jacket. His hair was slicked back and he wore gold rings on several fingers.

'Ms Rawling. We meet at last.' He held out a hand. 'Roberto Esposito.' I looked at his extended hand but didn't take it. I was wary of what sort of vision I might get from him. I didn't reply, there was no point. He already knew my name. After an awkward moment, he retracted his hand and cleared his throat. 'Mr Vitale requests the pleasure of your company this evening.'

'I'll come with you,' Kirk said softly beside me.

'I'm afraid my instructions were quite clear, Mr Wilkes,' Roberto said, icily. 'I am to bring Ms Rawling alone.'

I glanced at Kirk, he was shaking his head.

'I'll be fine. I was fine last time.'

'Don't assume anything,' Kirk said in what was barely a whisper. He was still holding my elbow. I gently tugged free of his grip and moved to climb into the back seat. Kirk tried to protest, but Roberto placed a firm hand on Kirk's chest, stopping him from getting any closer. 'Eve!' I looked over my shoulder at Kirk. His eyes were pleading. 'Be careful.'

'I will.' I got into the car and scooted all the way across to the far side. Roberto slid gracefully in beside me and the driver closed the door. I buckled up and kept my eyes fixed on the tinted window.

We drove quickly through the city. Lights were flickering on as we passed, the night coming to life as the sky slowly darkened. Roberto ogled me constantly and I kept my coat closed in my fist across my chest, constantly aware of his gaze on me.

When we pulled up in front of the Vitale mansion, the sky was a rich purple and dotted with stars. The driver opened my door first and I got out quickly, eager to get away from the creepy Roberto.

The driver led the way up the front steps, Roberto walked behind me and I felt his stare on my backside. As we approached the door it opened for us. The same butler from the other night stood there to admit us and I was led into the grand foyer. There was a round table in the middle on this occasion and on it was a huge display of white lilies. The smell was beautiful and they brightened up the candlelit space. A little tug pulled at my heart as I thought of the lilies at home.

People were bustling about, people in smart white shirts and some in aprons. I looked around with curiosity. I could hear the distinct sounds of a busy kitchen somewhere towards the back of the house and someone was playing piano in the room over to the left. It was some classical piece that I recognised but couldn't name. It was beautiful and haunting.

'There's a ball tonight,' Roberto said, watching me with shrewd eyes.

'Oh, I don't want to intrude.' I held up a hand and glanced back at the door.

'Your presence was requested. That's not an intrusion,' he said bluntly. I frowned.

'Am I... invited?'

Roberto laughed cruelly and strode away to the hall at the back of the grand staircase. I stood there feeling awkward for a moment, but the suited man who'd seen us in approached me holding out my umbrella.

'Apologies, Ms Rawling. I neglected to return this to you after your first visit.' I took it and shook my head to indicate that it wasn't a problem. I seemed temporarily lost for words.

The clacking of high heels on the foyer floor drew my attention towards the hall to the right, where Roberto had disappeared. Lucia Vitale walked briskly towards me. She was dressed in a bright red gown that skimmed the floor and plunged at the neck almost to her naval.

'You're back, are you?' Her voice echoed and several passing heads turned our way.

'I am,' I said, tilting my chin up.

'My brother is like an eager puppy with a new chew toy.' She didn't smile and passed by me, striding into the room on the left where the piano was playing. The music stopped; I could hear faint voices over the general noise of caterers, delivery people and other staff.

A moment later, Antonio appeared in the large doorway, framed by the polished oak. He was wearing an immaculate tuxedo, and a bow tie hung untied around his neck. His long, dark hair was tied back in a sexy man-bun. I tried not to stare.

He walked over to me and took my hand, drawing the back of it up to his lips. My cheeks grew warm.

'Was that you playing?' I asked, my voice a little shaky.

'It was.'

'Beautiful.'

'Thank you. Walk with me.' He marched for the stairs and I scurried along behind him, clutching my umbrella.

He is dangerous. He is dangerous, I chanted in my head as I followed him up the sweeping staircase. I didn't want to lose my head again. He took the stairs gracefully, his long legs easily taking them two at a time, while I practically had to run to keep up. I glanced down into the foyer, aware of how many people were passing through who might see me disappearing upstairs with Antonio.

I'd never cared a jot what people thought of me, my reputation was usually of no concern. But then, I'd never done anything to cause any negative reputation to arise. I realised as I dashed up those red-carpeted stairs that I cared more about that reputation than about any potential danger I was heading into. As I disappeared out of sight of the bustling foyer, I realised that it might be a good thing if a dozen impartial strangers saw me heading up those stairs if I never emerged again.

But then again, were they really impartial? Would they ever speak out against Antonio Vitale? I'd hardly be the first missing person associated with his name, and the police, I supposed, had never done anything much about the others.

I was being foolish. He wasn't going to harm me in his own house with all of these people right downstairs. He hadn't got where he was by being so careless.

Besides, he wouldn't be able to extort money out of me for many decades if I was dead in the next five minutes.

Antonio led me along a short corridor to the left. The red carpet continued and the walls were pristine white with charcoal-coloured doors on either side. Upstairs was deserted and the hubbub from downstairs barely reached us. He opened the door on the right and strode inside, not caring to glance my way. He just assumed I was following him. I stopped on the threshold. I saw what I had suspected. It was his bedroom.

It was a huge room with tall windows all along the opposite wall, the windows I'd admired at the front of the house on my first sighting of it. The windows were lined with blackout blinds and hung with heavy red drapes, which were currently tucked back. Between two of the windows, directly opposite the doorway where I stood, was a wide, low bed. It too, was dressed in fine red, and the carpet was thick with luxurious swirls of black and white.

Antonio had disappeared off to the left, but I stood frozen, unwilling to cross that threshold. He reappeared, holding a bottle of cologne, and stood in front of the bed looking at me with his head cocked to one side.

'I'm sorry, Mr Vitale, but I don't think it would be appropriate for me to go in there with you. Can't we discuss our business downstairs?' I'd found some courage from somewhere and for a moment felt rather pleased with myself.

He looked at me quizzically for a few seconds before flashing me a smile that showed too many teeth. He walked slowly towards me and I felt my resolve melting away. His eyes were locked onto mine and I couldn't look away. I took a step forward, then another, without realising what I was doing. I was dimly aware of him reaching past me and pushing the door closed. He was right in front of me, his chest almost touching mine. He smelled amazing. It was a coppery, musky smell.

His fingers brushed through my hair and a ripple of pleasure went through me. My eyes fluttered closed. A second later he was behind me, scooping my hair back and tucking it over my right shoulder. His smooth fingers ran up my arm, over my shoulder and up my neck. He clasped my chin and tilted my head over to the right, stretching my bare neck out. I groaned as he kissed my skin. His lips were warm, even though his fingers were cold.

The tiny, rational being that was still alive in my mind tapped me on the shoulder and cleared her throat. *It's not just money he wants from you.*

Antonio pressed his body against my back and snaked his hands around me to hold me firmly against him. I whimpered, powerless to resist the influence he had over me. His teeth grazed my skin. I gasped as he bit down, and that little rational voice clucked her tongue at me. *See, he's a damn vampire.* I wasn't listening, I didn't care. I melted into his embrace and let him feed.

My head was filled with fog and Ms Rational keeled over, passing out stone cold.

CHAPTER EIGHT

The fog slowly cleared and my eyes gradually opened, still bleary. I was leaning back against his hard chest, his arms still around me. I quickly did a mental body scan. I was fully dressed and although I felt limp and tired, nothing felt out of place or damaged.

'Eve?' His voice was close, soft and kind. 'Are you alright? You took a strange turn there, I was worried.'

I opened my eyes properly and focused on him. He was holding me upright, his face level with mine. Every part of my body felt heavy.

Antonio guided me to a nearby chair and eased me gently into it. I closed my eyes for a moment, a wave of nausea and unease rushing over me. When I opened my eyes again, Antonio was holding out a glass of orange juice and I took it from him, my hand shaking with the effort. I sipped and the juice felt cold and refreshing on my lips.

'Thank you.'

'Do you need a doctor?' he asked, his brow knitted in concern.

Ms Rational woke up and cocked a sceptical eyebrow.

'No, thank you,' I croaked again. I ran my mind over being in his arms. He had been totally still. I'd felt no breath on my shoulder, no heartbeat against me. He was so cold. It was true, then. He was a vampire. I had enough wit to realise that he thought I wouldn't remember. The way he was speaking suggested that he was trying to cover his tracks. So I stopped myself from feeling my neck. I had to play along.

'Are you feeling better?'

'Yes, thank you.' I was getting tired of saying that. 'We were going to discuss the financial arrangement.'

'We were.'

'I can match the twenty per cent that my parents paid.' My head was clearing quickly now and I felt more like myself. I was terrified, but I reassured myself with the knowledge that he had kept me alive. I had every reason to think that would continue to be the case.

'Very well.'

'But I would like a final payment date, please. I have no intention of remaining indebted forever.' I stood up from my seat on shaky feet and placed the glass on the nearby dressing table. He stood looking at me with a half-smile.

'If you let me take you to dinner then I will consider it. I feel I owe you a good meal.' His smile twitched but I held my face steady.

'Fine. One meal.'

'A date, Eve. A nice dress, food, drink, dessert.'

'In public.'

'If you wish.'

'With no obligation to return here with you. My body is not part of the deal.'

'If you wish.' I didn't even see him move, but he was standing right in front of me again and that intoxicating haze seeped back into my pores.

'Yes,' I said breathlessly, my head rocking back. Antonio took my hand and kissed the back of it softly. My heart raced wildly and I felt faint again.

He pulled away from me and I took a step back, breathing deeply to clear my head. What was he doing to me? Was it some sort of vampire mind trick?

'I'll see you to the car. Roberto will take you wherever you need to go.'

I must have pulled a face because he faltered and looked at me with his head on one side. 'Do you not like Roberto?'

'Not especially,' I said, not caring to check my tone.

'Very well. His driver will take you, if that's more comfortable for you.'

'You care about my comfort?' I asked, my voice laced with scepticism.

'Of course.' He looked a little affronted.

Antonio moved quickly to the door and opened it. I

made sure that my clothes were straight, my neck covered, still being careful not to pay attention to it too closely, and walked quickly out into the hall. He closed the door after us and led me back to the stairs, a little slower than he had led me up them. He took my arm to walk down them, attentive to my lingering weakness.

The party was getting started downstairs. The staff had largely disappeared, aside from a small handful of white-shirted people carrying trays of drinks and hors d'oeuvres. A few guests were milling in the foyer in their glittering gowns and smart suits. All eyes turned to us as we moved down the sweeping stairs. My cheeks were burning and tried not to catch anyone's eye.

Antonio stepped onto that chequered floor with me by his side with no hesitation or sense of impropriety. He was neither embarrassed by me nor concerned with the opinions of others. He flashed smiles at people and greeted his guests with warmth and charm, shaking hand after hand. I was fairly sure that one of the women he greeted was the Member of Parliament for Oris. He didn't introduce me to anyone, for which I was grateful. It was clear to me that I was not a guest in this situation, but he didn't rush me out of there either.

I became largely invisible as we manoeuvred slowly towards the large, oak doors. One pair of eyes were not diverted to the enthralling host, however, they were fixed on me in the tightest of scowls. Lucia stood in the doorway to what must be the ballroom, where Antonio had been playing piano when I arrived. She held a glass of red wine in one hand, scarlet lipstick staining the rim.

Lucia was surrounded by three men in immaculate suits. Two of them were fawning over her, trying to get her attention by chatting animatedly in hurried Italian. She was ignoring them. The third, a black man who was taller and wider than the others, stood still and silent as a pillar. His dark eyes followed me across the foyer, just like Lucia's.

I tugged my jacket collar up over my neck, clutched my umbrella tightly to my chest and averted my gaze until Antonio had led me safely to the door.

The circular driveway was lined with parked cars, with more arriving.

A moment later, the silver car was in front of me and the driver was holding the back door open.

'Take her where she wants to go. There's no need to tell Mr Esposito about this,' Antonio said firmly but quietly to the driver. I caught a glimpse of a crisp monetary note exchange hands and the driver pocketed it discreetly with a nod.

Antonio leaned into the car and smiled. 'It was a genuine pleasure. I hope you feel better after a meal and a good night's sleep.'

'Thank you.' I blushed again.

'I'll pick you up tomorrow at Piero's. I'll take you

somewhere else, don't worry.'

'Okay.'

He closed the door and I was whisked away. I turned in my seat to watch him out of the rear window. He stood to watch us drive away, even though a party of his guests were arriving and clamouring for his attention.

We turned down the drive and the trees obscured him from view. I turned back to face forward and wondered if it was all for appearances, all about extracting what he wanted from me. It was easier for him if I was besotted with him, but he could take it by force if he wanted. Or take blood from anyone that crossed his path for that matter. Why me?

My fingers darted quickly to my neck to check for punctures. The skin was completely smooth, if slightly tender. I would need to check in a mirror in a lit space for any sign of bruising, but it seemed from this initial examination that he hadn't left a mark. Was that part of the deal? The magic? Whatever it was.

It occurred to me that I should have been more alarmed at this discovery, yet I seemed to be taking it in my stride. The revelation that Peter was a shapeshifter had rocked my world view. I was still experiencing the shock waves and this was just another thing to add to the chaos. Somehow this just made everything make more sense, not less. Answers began to form as to why my parents were dead. Surely they had discovered Vitale's secret?

Threatened to expose it, maybe?

That made sense.

But what did that mean for me? Was he going to drink from me for a while then dispose of me once he was bored of me? What if I let on that his glamour trick didn't entirely work? Would he kill me as soon as I let slip that I knew what he was?

Just how much danger was I really in here? And did Peter know? Yes, somehow I was certain that he knew exactly what Antonio was. Lucia too, I suspected. She was too beautiful and too ugly at the same time to be human. The way she looked at me when we came back down stairs told me that I was in far more danger from her than from her brother.

CHAPTER NINE

I CLAMBERED OUT OF THE CAR at the restaurant and bid the driver a courteous farewell. I dashed inside and made a beeline for the staff restrooms out behind the kitchen. The fluorescent light flickered on automatically when I entered and I went straight to the mirror. My neck was pristine, not so much as a hickey.

For a second I doubted my memory. Had he really bitten me at all?

But I brushed away my doubts. He was definitely exerting a supernatural influence over me. The head fog that kept occurring was evidence enough on its own. One minute I was wary and sceptical around him, and the next I was swooning. I was caught between loathing and utter adoration.

My heart was racing as I stared at my neck in the mirror, running my fingers over and over the spot where he must have fed from me. There really was no trace. I'd held myself together for my own safety and now that I was alone and back in familiar surroundings, fear raced through my system.

I clutched the edge of the sink and gagged. My stomach heaved and I was spectacularly sick in the sink. It was mostly water, though tinged orange from the little juice I'd sipped. I'd barely eaten that day and I had no idea how much blood I'd lost. Another wave of nausea rippled up from my stomach and I dry-heaved, nothing left to come up.

'Everything okay?' A voice behind me dragged me back to the bathroom. Tina was standing in the doorway, clutching the edge of the door and looking at me with concern.

'I'll be okay in a minute. Thanks.' I held up a hand to wave her away and she took the hint. I ran the taps to wash away my vomit and cupped some water in my hand to wash my mouth out. I splashed my face and looked back at my reflection. I was pale. I had never really looked like my mother, who was half Italian. I'd inherited more of my father's northern-European genes. I had fairly pale skin and blue eyes, a real "English rose", they used to say. But the rose glow was absent from my cheeks and I looked drawn.

With a whimper of resignation, I left the restroom and headed into the kitchen. The chef, Giovanni, was in full swing, preparing several orders at once. I grabbed the elbow of a passing pot-boy, who looked at me in alarm.

'What's hot and ready?' He pointed at a simmering pot

of minestrone and I released his arm. I helped myself to a small bowlful and took it to the office to eat. I opened the door and found Peter leaning against my desk. 'What are you doing here?'

'I came to check on you. I wanted to make sure you were all right after going to his house.'

'I'm fine.' I pushed past him and sat down. I tucked into my soup with gusto, feeling like I hadn't eaten in days.

'Are you? Because I've never seen you eat like that before.'

'I need to recoup some energy.' I scowled at him and kept shovelling the soup into my mouth. It was warming and incredibly nourishing. I could practically feel the colour returning to my cheeks as I ate. Peter raised an eyebrow at me and crossed his arms over his chest.

'Been exerting a lot of it, have you?'

'That is none of your business!' I flinched at the harshness of my words, but he remained stoic.

'Eve,' he said, a note of caution in his voice.

'Peter,' I replied, dropping my spoon into the bowl and glowering up at him. 'Shut the door, would you?' He leaned over and pushed the door closed. Once it had securely clicked shut I stood up and slapped him hard across the face.

His palm went reflexively to where I'd struck him and his mouth hung open, but as his hand slipped down off his cheek I saw that I hadn't even left a red mark. But my palm stung so much I had to give it a shake.

'What was that for?' he hissed through clenched teeth. 'You could have set me off.'

'Sorry,' I said, blanching. 'I didn't think of that. But you knew. You knew what they were and you didn't tell me.'

'Ah.' He dropped his gaze to the floor. 'I wasn't allowed to say and I didn't want to put you in even more danger.'

'Well being alone with him without knowing what the real risks were did put me in danger.'

'Did he...?' Peter looked at me, stricken.

'Yes. He bit me.' I mouthed the words, suddenly afraid of the staff overhearing.

'I am so, so sorry,' he said softly. He grabbed hold of me and pulled me into a tight embrace.

'It's okay.' I patted his back and he released me.

'Did you get a vision or anything?' he asked in a whisper.

'Nothing. I don't think my gift works on him. But his doesn't entirely work on me either. He can make me compliant and I think he tried to make me forget what he'd done but it didn't work.'

'Interesting.'

'It gives me an advantage. I know exactly what he is, but he doesn't know that. But it also puts me in massive danger. I know his secret and if he figures that out...' I didn't need to finish that thought. We both knew what it might mean.

'You're seeing him again, aren't you?' Peter's voice was low and dark, full of pain.

'I have to. I have to play along or he'll know that I know. He has to think that he successfully hypnotised me, or whatever it is. Just for now. Just until I figure this out. But Peter, you know what this means about my parents? Right?'

'They knew.' He nodded, his arms wrapped tightly around himself. 'They always knew, Eve. Or for a long time, at least. But I reckon that when he found out they were resisting him... well, it can only have been days later that they died.'

'I see.' My soup threatened to lurch upwards, but I held it down. 'Is there anything else I need to know, Peter?'

He sighed and ran his fingers through his thick hair.

'I need to talk to someone first. Now that you know this I think we have to tell you the rest, but it's not up to me. It's about the safety of everyone involved.'

'I understand. I have to have dinner with him tomorrow.'

'Is that a euphemism?'

'Not on my part, but I think he has different nutritional requirements to me.' I cracked a smile, I couldn't help myself. Peter shook his head and the corner of his mouth twitched.

'Be really careful.'
'I will.'

I literally owned nothing that I thought would be acceptable for a date with Antonio Vitale. So the next day involved a trip into the city to shop for a dress. The sky was crystal clear and there was still frost on the ground when I set out. The city centre was quiet, as it was Sunday morning. Not all of the shops were open. Oris had that feeling of being paused sometimes; a time capsule of the old city in juxtaposition with the modern stores, and when it was almost empty like this it felt like a strange bubble, separate from the real world.

It took far longer than I'd have liked to find a dress because of the war raging inside me between the side that wanted him to take me – in all senses of the word – and the side that needed to keep cool and rational. I looked in a dozen different stores as they gradually opened over the course of the morning. I tried on so many dresses I was thoroughly bored by it all. Shopping was not my thing.

Finally I found a dress that seemed to make both voices in my head purr appreciatively. It was Chinese-inspired with a high collar, capped sleeves, and was a respectable length, with just a short slit up each side. It was black with a subtle dragon pattern to it that shone slightly in the light. I bought some black high heels and a clip for my hair that resembled chopsticks, just to finish off the look.

By the time I was heading home the city had come to life. It was bustling with shoppers and festive music blasted out from every open door I passed. Soon I was going to have to face the prospect of my first Christmas without my parents. I wished I'd got into the spirit early enough to at least exchange cards with my mum.

I got ready that evening at my parents' house, in my old bedroom. My posters were still on the walls, and my wardrobe was littered with the remains that I'd left behind when I went away to university. Everything was dusty, so I had to run the vacuum cleaner over the carpet and wipe the surfaces before I could do anything else.

I wasn't sure quite why, but I didn't want to get ready at Peter's house. Maybe it was because I didn't want to be questioned by either of his parents, especially his mother. But I think part of it was Peter himself. I couldn't stand the way he kept looking at me since our frank conversation in the office. His eyes were full of pity and something else that I couldn't place but made me feel uncomfortable.

I kept an eye on the sky outside, rather than the clock, knowing that it was more relevant. As the sky burst crimson, I set off for the restaurant, walking awkwardly in the high heels that I was so unused to.

'Should've worn flats,' I mumbled to myself as I walked briskly along the pavement. 'Just in case I need to make a run for it.' I shushed myself and took deep breaths.

When I got to Piero's it was bustling with activity. It seemed to be doing really well and I couldn't help but be pleased. I thought my mother would be proud. I did a quick check on things and reassured myself that everyone was coping. I made a mental note to offer Tina a small raise for the extra managerial work she'd been doing.

'You look really nice,' she told me. I blushed crimson.

'Thank you.' I dashed away before she could ask me if I had a date and with who. I suspected that she, and probably others, had an idea that I'd been dragged into something with the Vitales since their visit to the restaurant that first night. But I didn't want to confirm their suspicions and certainly didn't want anyone to know I was dating the most ruthless man in the city.

I saw the last hint of pale blue blink out over the horizon and stepped outside to wait. I walked down the street a little to where there was a space at the kerb and clutched my dark green coat around myself. It was about the same length as my dress and had a heavy hood, but was nice and dressy.

A few minutes later a stunning, black Maserati Ghibli with tinted windows pulled up at the kerb right in front of me. I braced myself as the driver's door opened, expecting to see a chauffeur. But Antonio himself stepped out. He was wearing a light grey suit with a metallic shine to it, and a burgundy shirt, undone at the top button and no tie. My breath caught in my throat. He was simply stunning.

'Hello,' he said, smiling as he approached me. 'Why are you waiting out here in the cold?'

I glanced towards Piero's and rocked slightly on my heels. 'Oh, I see.' He nodded. 'You want to make sure your staff continue to see you in a professional light.'

'Yes, something like that.' I didn't add anything about being associated with a known criminal that everyone was terrified of and certainly nothing about him being a blood-sucking fiend.

'Shall we?' He gestured to the car and I stepped carefully towards it. He opened the passenger door for me and I manoeuvred myself carefully into the seat, managing to keep my footing and not flash too much leg. The interior was as black at the exterior, and the seats were leather. It was comfortably warm and it occurred to me that that must be for my benefit, not his.

Antonio slipped into the driver's seat and cast a long look at me, taking in my outfit.

'You look beautiful.'

'Thank you.' I blushed scarlet again. 'You look very handsome.'

He smiled that small, hungry smile and looked me right in the eye. I tried to steel myself against his hypnotic gaze, but nothing happened; he didn't turn on the thing that made me go all weak in the knees. I realised as he started the engine that he hadn't needed to. I was right where he wanted me already. *Play the game, Eve*, I told myself.

We drove a short distance to a busier part of the city, where the night life was more lively. He parked in a small car park just off the tree-lined street and pointed towards a little French bistro tucked in between a brightly lit bar and a closed electronics shop.

'I hope you like French cuisine.'

'I do. Do you, um, know the owner of this place too?'

'No.' He smiled, taking my meaning precisely. 'But I have been here before.'

'With other women?'

'Sometimes.' A flash of jealousy coursed through me, taking me by surprise.

He got out of the car and strode around to my door, opening it for me before I had chance to open it myself. Part of me liked having doors opened for me everywhere I went these days, but Ms Rational scolded me for the thought. He held out a hand to help me out of the car and I gladly took it. I wasn't certain I could get myself to my feet on these high heels.

He kept hold of my hand, entwining our fingers, which also surprised me. We walked across the small car park to the bistro, I only wobbled slightly, and he again opened the door for me.

It was cosy and compact inside, with small tables draped in red and white chequered cloths, each lit with a candle. Most of the tables were occupied, but no one looked up as we entered. It seemed that Antonio's reputation didn't reach here. At least, not to the clientele.

A middle-aged waiter in a smart shirt greeted us with a smile.

'Welcome. Do you have a reservation?' There was no trace of a French accent. Any momentary illusion of being in Paris vanished.

'Vitale, table for two.'

The waiter's face twitched slightly, his smile faltering for the briefest of seconds.

'Of course,' he said, his voice not quite so bright. 'Please follow me.'

Antonio squeezed my hand and led the way after the waiter. We were seated in a corner at the very back of the bistro, out of sight of the window that took up the entire front wall of the dining area. I slipped my coat off and the waiter took it for me to hang on a nearby coat rack. Antonio held out my seat for me, which was a first. I wondered just how old he was. It seemed he was from a more chivalrous time. But I couldn't exactly ask without giving away the secret.

We were handed menus and the waiter rattled off the evening's specials. My head spun and I stared resolutely into my menu, hoping that I wasn't being rude. I didn't trust myself to look at Antonio. He ordered a bottle of wine and the waiter left us.

'Are you recovered from yesterday?' Antonio's voice was soft and casual. I chanced a glance and saw that he too was studying the menu.

'Yes, thank you. I'm not sure what came over me.' He looked up at me and made eye contact. I swallowed and tried to smile. Could he read my mind? Did he know already? He reached across the table and took my hand, caressing the back of it with his thumb.

'I'm glad you feel better.'

I told myself that his concern was sincere, but then I reminded myself what he was and that I couldn't trust anything, not even myself. I cleared my throat and eased my hand out of his grasp, taking up my menu again in both hands.

'Is there anything you recommend?' It suddenly felt like a foolish question.

'The chicken chasseur is very good. It will go with the wine.'

'Sounds great.' I smiled at him and he returned it.

The waiter brought us our wine and took our order. I had to admit, I was curious to see if Antonio would eat. He sipped his wine and looked intently at me. I felt hot under his gaze.

'I make you nervous.'

'Well, yes.' I let out a little laugh.

'I apologise.'

'Do you, though? Really? Don't you want people to feel

nervous around you?' I surprised myself at my boldness. He laughed a little. It was a beautiful sound, so natural.

'I suppose that's true. At least some of the time. I'd like to spend time with someone who was relaxed with me. It can be difficult, to do what I do.'

'What about your sister?' I took a large gulp of my wine and avoided eye contact.

'Family is family. It's different.' He took another sip as he shrugged.

'Your English is very good. How long have you lived here?'

'Many years.' Nice, vague answer, I thought.

'Do you go back to Italy often?'

'Rarely. Lucia and I, we have no family there now. Our home is here. Sometimes I have business back in Naples, but no more than once or twice every few years.'

'You're very young to be so successful.' I tried to keep my tone casual, but I wanted to tease something real out of him somehow.

'Am I?' He gave me a shrewd smile.

'I don't suppose you want to tell me your age.' I poked the nest and waited to see what would happen.

'How old do you think I am?'

I shook my head in exasperation.

'I'm really not sure. But you look youthful. How's that?'

'I'll take it.' He smirked and sipped his wine.

'Did your family have money?'

'You are asking a lot of questions.'

'I want to get to know the person I'm going into business with.'

'That is very wise.'

The waiter approached our table and I leaned back to make room for my food, only then realising that I'd been leaning across the table towards Antonio as I questioned him. The waiter looked anxious as he placed our plates in front of us and hurried away as quickly as was appropriate.

'That,' I said in a hushed voice, inclining my head towards the waiter's retreating back, 'is what I was talking about. He's afraid of you and you want it that way. It makes you feel powerful.'

'No, Eve, it happens because I am powerful. It's the side effect, not the intended consequence.' He picked up his fork and tucked into his fish. I watched him chew and swallow. With a slight feeling of surprise, I turned my attention to my own meal.

'So you like the power, but dislike the fear?'

'Something like that. You are still asking questions.'

'You said that was wise.'

'Hmm, so I did. But perhaps too much knowledge can be a bad thing?'

'Too much of anything can be a bad thing.'

'True. You are not typical for your youth.'

'In what way?'

'You're too sharp. Honed.'

'That's an odd thing to say. Is it a compliment?' I looked at him across our food and wine glasses. The candle flickering in the middle of our table cast the slightest shadow across his face.

'I'm not sure yet.'

We ate in silence for a few minutes, stealing glances at each other. The food was exquisite.

'Have you ever been to France?'

'Oui,' he replied, smiling broadly. 'Many times. I lived there for a while.'

'Oh, really?'

'In Paris, of course.'

'Do you speak French?'

'I speak six languages, including French.'

'Wow. But I guess that's not uncommon for other Europeans. It's just us English peasants who suck at learning languages.'

He let out a low, earthy chuckle. The low hubbub of the restaurant sounded miles away. There was a small bar near our table and I noticed the barman and the waiter exchanging whispers and glances in our direction. I tried not to let it bother me.

'Well, I would not have been so blunt,' Antonio said, his gaze fixed on my face.

'But you agree.' I grinned at him. 'I don't speak any other languages. But I wasn't very good at school.' I wasn't being entirely honest. My mother used to speak Italian to me as a child, before my grandfather died. But I hadn't used it much in years and was pretty rusty.

'Were you a bad girl?' He was looking at me with those eyes again. Those eyes that bore into me. My cheeks burned.

'What a question. No, that's not what I meant. I didn't do well academically.'

'I know what you meant.' His voice was gentle, the playfulness subdued. 'Why do you think that was?'

'I found it hard to concentrate.' I gave a shrug and looked intently at my food. I wasn't about to tell him why it was so hard for me to concentrate, or that the visions in my head had driven me to attempt to take my own life when I was fourteen, which meant I'd missed several weeks of school.

'I see.' He didn't probe and I was thankful for that. 'You'll want to save a little room for the croquembouche.'

'The what, sorry?'

'How do you say it? Profiteroles? They are a speciality here.'

'Oh, yes. Okay.' I smiled and put down my fork. I realised how at ease I'd become. He hadn't used his influence over me at all. I was certain of it. I felt clear-headed. 'Well, I think you'll be pleased to know that I feel much more relaxed with you.'

'I am very pleased.' He lifted his glass, tilted it towards

me in a little toast and took the last sip. He almost seemed human.

The waiter cleared our plates and Antonio ordered the croquembouche to share.

'Were you academic at school?' I asked, then took another sip of my wine.

'I didn't go to school,' he replied, looking at me and idly running his fingers around the rim of his empty glass. 'I was educated at home and then joined the family business when I was fourteen.'

'Oh, wow. That's young.'

'It was a different time,' he said with a shrug. 'But I have always loved to learn. You saw my library.'

'I did,' I said, nodding and blushing as I remembered that first meeting in his study surrounded by spotless bookshelves.

When the dessert was brought out of the kitchen I gave a little gasp. It was a stack several inches high, topped with a light sprinkling of cinnamon and dotted with bright strawberries. Antonio gently eased one of the little pastry balls onto a spoon and held it out for me. There was a little flutter of anticipation in my abdomen and leaned in to taste the treat. It was like I'd tumbled into a cheesy romantic movie and found that I liked it.

The pastry crunched slightly and the cream inside was thick and sweet. It was absolutely perfect.

'Wow. Definitely worth saving room for,' I said, after

I'd swallowed the profiterole.

'What did I tell you?'

'You were right.' We exchanged smiles and ate some more of the fabulous dessert. I couldn't manage more than a few as they were so filling. I picked at the strawberries a little too, as if the fruit made up for the cream and pastry of the profiteroles. I noticed that Antonio stopped at the same time as me, mirroring my appetite. I wondered if that was an Italian thing, or a generational thing, or a vampire thing. Why did it have to be so complicated?

Antonio paid the bill and tipped the waiter generously.

'To make up for making him nervous,' he whispered to me with a small smile. In that instant, although I didn't know it at the time, I fell a little bit in love with Antonio Vitale.

CHAPTER TEN

THE NIGHT AIR WAS CRISP and the black sky was dotted with crystal clear stars. Antonio took my hand and walked me to his car, taking long, slow steps in silence. The bar next to the bistro was buzzing with activity, but there were hardly any cars or people about on the street. I clutched my coat tight against the cold and my breath made little puffs in front of my face.

Antonio smiled warmly at me. I smiled back and was again surprised by him. His gentleness and charm were not what I'd expected from everything I'd heard about him. More than that, though, it was bliss to be able to hold someone's hand without a vision crashing into my thoughts.

When we got to the car he turned to face me and kept hold of my hand, stroking it gently.

'So, I had a nice time.' He seemed almost nervous and I couldn't help but smile.

'Me too.'

'You didn't expect to.'

'I didn't know what to expect.'

He stepped closer, pressing me against the car. My heart was racing with anticipation as his nose brushed mine. His body was firm and cool but mine was like jelly and was heating up, despite the cold night air.

He was so close, taking an agonising eternity to do what I knew was coming. When his lips met mine it was like an explosion inside me. Moments of yearning came crashing upon me at once. My eyes fluttered closed and I leaned into the kiss, welcoming it. His fingers released my hand and both of his hands went to my face, cupping it gently. He deepened the kiss, parting my lips and softly easing his tongue into my mouth.

The world was spinning too fast around us and my stomach fluttered uncontrollably. Butterflies. I'd never really experienced them. My hands gripped his waist through his suit jacket and I pulled his body flush against mine. I was pinned against the car and lost in a euphoric daze.

The kiss slowed and ever so gradually, Antonio brought it to a close. But he rested his forehead against mine. I was breathless, but he wasn't. I wanted him to be. I knew that if he could breathe, he would be panting as much as I was.

'I'd very much like to take you home. To my home, that is. If you would be agreeable.'

I captured his lips in another steamy kiss, totally

unsure of my answer. I longed to say yes, I was so very close to doing so. But Ms Rational was awake back there, her arms folded over her chest, tapping her foot and scowling at me. I broke the kiss and heaved a sigh.

'It's too complicated.'

'What do you mean?'

I pushed him back and stood up straight, bearing my own weight. My lips felt full and hot and things were stirring in my body that had rarely twitched before. I was tempted, so very tempted.

'Antonio...' I paused, a little surprised to hear his first name pass my lips. I'd never used it with him before. A slight glint in his eye suggested he'd liked the sound of his name on my breath. I glanced both ways along the street again, it was still quiet. We were alone. 'We have a business relationship and it's not an equal partnership. If you take more than money from me, I'm not sure what that means. I'm not sure what that makes me.'

'Can we not have a separate, personal relationship, outside of our financial arrangement?'

'I don't think we can. I don't think it's as simple as that even between regular people. But you aren't a regular person.' There was the slightest flicker of tension in his chiselled jaw. 'You're a criminal, I mean,' I added hastily in a hushed voice. 'You run a criminal organisation. Let's not mince words here.'

He looked at me shrewdly, his eyes narrowed slightly,

like he was appraising me. I took a step away from him, watching for his reaction. He let me move away without flinching, but there was yearning in his dark eyes. I took another step, heaviness filling my heart.

'Eve.' He stepped towards me and I backed away again.

'We've only just met. We hardly know each other. This is all happening far too quickly.'

'Okay.' He held up a hand to stop me and I stood still. I braced myself for him to turn on the glamour. If he was ever going to do it, now would be the time. If I was ready for it, maybe I could resist it. 'I'm not used to not getting what I want.' He smiled and shook his head. He was right in front of me in the blink of an eye and I gasped. He took my hand, raised it to his lips and kissed it softly. 'Let's say this: let's say we had a wonderful first date. I enjoyed our conversation, I am enjoying getting to know you. I would like to get to know you better and I will call you in a day or two. Shall we say that?'

'Okay,' I said, my voice barely above a whisper. 'That sounds very normal. Like the end of a regular first date.' I smiled.

He kissed me again on the lips, softly, with yearning.

'Very well. Good night, Eve. Take care getting home.'

'I will. Thank you for a lovely dinner.'

'You're welcome.' He released my hand and I backed away a few steps, careful not to topple on my heels. I turned and walked away, nice and slowly. I could feel his eyes on me. He hadn't tried to coerce me. Why not? He had the ability to make me do whatever he wanted but he hadn't even tried to use it. Could that possibly mean that he had genuine feelings for me and he wanted me to be willing?

I heard his car door open and close again a moment later. His engine purred to life and he drove away the other way down the street. I clutched my coat tight around my chest and only then realised that I had a tear on my cheek.

I was thoroughly confused and frustrated.

Movement in the tree between me and the road caught me by surprise and I let out a small yelp. I looked up and saw a large, tawny owl perched there, blinking as it gazed behind me down the street. It shuffled its feet on the branch and ruffled its feathers. I'd never seen an owl in the city before, just sitting there as if it were the most natural thing in the world. I walked on, casting a fascinated glance over my shoulder at it as I passed by.

I only managed to walk to the end of the row of shops when my feet gave up entirely. I leaned on a wall and pulled my phone from my clutch. I quickly ordered an Uber and a few minutes later my ride pulled up.

I was relieved to get into the back of the car and get off my feet. It was only a short drive back to Peter's house, but my mind raced over the evening several times in those brief minutes. The dark city flashed past the window and I stared without really seeing. I relived the amazing kiss, a smile playing on my lips.

We pulled up outside Peter's house and I came back to my senses.

'Thanks,' I said to the driver as I climbed out of the car, eager to get inside and have a hot drink with my feet tucked up under me. The wine had gone to my head a little, I knew that, but not so much that I had given in to the temptation of Antonio's offer.

His kiss had been incredible and I was certain that he must have significant prowess in bed. Was I a fool to turn that down? On balance, I thought not. Everything I'd let Ms Rational say to him was true. Never mind the fact that he was also a vampire and likely to suck my blood at any given opportunity. He could kill me accidentally if passion took over. Probably.

The house was still and quiet when I stepped inside. As soon as I was across the threshold I slipped out of my shoes, before I'd even closed the door. The hall was dark, but there was a light on upstairs and the light cascaded down. I closed and locked the door and tiptoed on aching feet to the kitchen. I flicked on the light and caught sight of Peter's dad sitting on the settee just below the switch. I startled and a hand darted to my chest.

'Kirk. You scared me. What are you doing sitting in the dark?'

'I'm sorry, I didn't mean to scare you. Sit with me, Eve,

please.'

'Okay.' I walked around him and sat down a few feet away, tucking my feet up under me and ensuring my skirt was straight across my knees. 'What's wrong?'

'Your parents were my closest friends.'

'Yes, I know.' I frowned, puzzled as to where this was going.

'I owe them a great deal and when I learned of their passing I swore to protect you. I'm finding that very hard to do.'

I said nothing, but I couldn't look directly at him either.

'You're taking a terrible risk. What you're doing with Antonio Vitale.'

'What do you think I'm doing with him?' I snapped, glaring at him. He wouldn't meet my gaze.

'I know you were at dinner with him tonight. I don't want to think about the details, frankly. You're like a daughter to me. But please believe me when I tell you that having any sort of physical relationship with him would be dangerous. You know this. You know exactly what I'm talking about.'

I blinked at him in surprise and my mouth hovered open, on the cusp of a question that I couldn't quite form. He knew the truth. And he knew that I knew. This tangled web of secrets was getting harder and harder to understand.

'Eve, you know what he is and so do I. He's not just a ruthless crime lord. He is a killer. A blood-sucking killing machine.' His last sentence was barely audible.

'How do you know that?'

'You're hardly his first victim. And I spoke to Peter today. He told me everything.'

'Everything?' My throat caught on a hard lump and I swallowed to clear it. Did Kirk know about his son?

'Everything I didn't already know. Eve, look.' He dropped his head into his hands, his elbows propped on his knees. 'I saw you tonight, with Vitale. I saw you and you saw me.'

'No I didn't. What are you talking about?'

'I followed you and I watched you outside, by the car.'

'Oh.' I blushed hard and looked resolutely at the flagstone floor. Kirk wasn't my father, but he was the closest thing to it now. I couldn't help but be embarrassed that he'd seen me locked in a passionate embrace with a man he clearly despised. But I really hadn't seen him. I frowned as I raced through my memories of the evening.

'I was the owl,' he whispered. His voice was muffled as he spoke into his lap, his head still cradled in his hands.

'I'm sorry?'

'I was the owl,' he said again, finally looking right at me.

'Oh!' I clamped a hand over my mouth and stared at him, eyes wide. 'You're like Peter,' I said, lowering my hand.

'I am, or he's like me. His mother knows nothing about it!' he added quickly, glancing in the direction of the stairs.

'How can she not know?' I was aghast. To spend a lifetime with someone and not know a thing like that.

'I have worked very hard to keep her safe. The fewer people that know, the better.'

'You instructed Peter not to tell me.'

'I did.'

'He didn't tell me, you know. I figured it out.'

'You had a vision of his first change at the funeral.'

'I—' I was caught off guard and simply gaped at him.

'I know about your gift. Your parents told me a long time ago. I thought there was a good chance some day of you finding out about me and then Peter. But I wanted to protect you for as long as possible.'

'Why did my parents tell you?'

'Because they knew about me.'

'But you just said—'

'I did.' He looked at me intently, daring me to ask the question. My head was spinning as it struggled against this realisation. I felt as though I was drowning.

'They were shifters too?'

He didn't respond. He didn't have to. I groaned and slumped sideways against the back of the settee. I was weak, dazed. It had been a big night. Kirk got up and fetched me a glass of water.

'Here,' he said, passing it to me. I took it and drank deeply. It was cold and numbed the tension in my throat. 'I hope you didn't drink too much wine tonight. You look well enough to suggest that he didn't feed from you.'

'No, to both.' I clutched the glass tightly in both hands and drank again.

'You know what he is, but you agreed to go out with him.'

'I had to. He doesn't realise that I know. I have to play along or he'll figure it out.'

'You could just make him believe that you're afraid of him because of his business practises.'

'No, I can't.' I sighed and put the glass down on the floor. 'He has some sort of glamour... thing. He can make people compliant and bend them to his will. It partially worked on me, but didn't make me forget. If I resist him he'll know his glamour doesn't completely work on me.'

'He used it tonight, I take it?'

'Um, yes. I think so.' I blushed and avoided his eyes. He definitely didn't need to know that my kissing him back like that was entirely of my own volition. I could let him believe I was missing a touch of free will.

'I see. Well, that makes it complicated.'

'It could be useful.'

'What are you thinking?'

'Well, maybe it would be useful to have someone close

to him. I could find out information.'

'No. Absolutely not. The moment he realises that you're doing it he'll snap your neck.' He marched across the kitchen and slammed a hand down on the edge of the sink.

'Okay, bad idea.' I was instantly worried we'd been making too much noise. Mrs Wilkes was sure to emerge from the hall any moment. 'I'll stay away from him. I'll find a way. I told him tonight that we needed to have a professional relationship. You saw me walk away, right? He invited me back to his place and I said no. I've set a boundary there and I think I can figure out a way to maintain it. I won't do anything reckless. I promise.' Inside I squirmed as I said it. I didn't think I could keep that promise, whether Antonio glamoured me or not.

'Okay,' Kirk said, nodding firmly. 'I'm glad you got home safely.'

'Thank you.'

He walked to the door, paused, glanced at me and looked as though he was about to say something else, but he shook his head and turned the corner to go up the stairs.

I sat in stunned silence for a few minutes, musing over the night's revelations. It was all too much and I cried silent tears. My parents were shapeshifters and I had never known. That maybe explained my gift. I hadn't changed, like Peter had, but I had this ability instead. I would have to ask Kirk more about that another time.

How had they kept something like that from me for all those years? How had I never had a vision of it? I would have to ask Kirk that, too.

Another troubling set of questions surfaced as I sat there. Did Antonio know about my parents? Had that contributed to their deaths? Was that why he was so interested in me? Because he thought I might be a shapeshifter too? Could he tell from drinking my blood that I wasn't? Or did my blood tell a different story?

I knew I wouldn't be able to stay away from him, despite my promise. These were questions that demanded answers and ultimately, it was only Antonio who could answer some of them.

CHAPTER ELEVEN

I DIDN'T SLEEP WELL. I kept waking with a start and finding myself feeling strange, like I was being watched.

After waking at 5.30 am and not being able to get straight back to sleep, I gave up and got out of bed. No one else was up yet and I padded softly downstairs to fix some coffee and crumpets for breakfast. It was still dark and I gazed out of the kitchen window into the garden. It was raining and there was a soft pattering on the window and the paved area outside.

Movement outside caught my attention and my eyes searched the shadows. My pulse quickened and I gripped the butter knife in my hand more tightly.

A fox crept into view and looked up at the lit window, its eyes wide. With a smile, I went to the back door and opened it.

'Is that you, Peter?' I whispered into the dark. There was a gruff little bark and Peter shimmered into view before me, stepping out of the shadows and into the pool of light from the open door.

'What are you doing up?' he asked, stepping in out of the rain and shaking himself all over, like a dog. I stepped back to avoid getting splashed, and giggled at him.

'I couldn't sleep. Have you been out all night?'

'No, just a couple of hours. We take turns.'

'You and your dad?' I asked, leaning back against the pine table and nursing my coffee in both hands. Peter blinked at me.

'He talked to you?'

'Yes.' He closed the door and I went back to buttering my crumpets.

'Is that why you had trouble sleeping?'

'Probably. Did you know about my parents too?' I glanced sideways at him and he shifted his feet awkwardly, not meeting my eyes.

'I'm sorry.' To his credit, he did look suitably abashed.

'It's okay. I get it.' It was true. 'Coffee?'

'Yes, please.' I poured him a cup from the steaming pot.

'What do you mean? You take turns?'

'Oh, patrolling. We keep an eye on the area, make sure there's no trouble.' He waved a hand vaguely towards the garden.

'What kind of trouble?'

'Suspicious activity.'

'Camorra sniffing around, you mean?' I asked, raising an eyebrow.

'Along those lines.'

I sipped my coffee and ate my breakfast at the counter. Peter busied himself making some for himself.

'I want to do some more sorting at the house today. You up for helping?' I asked after a while.

'Sure.'

'Now that I know, I need to look at things with fresh eyes. You know? Maybe there are important things that I overlooked before.'

'Yeah. Good idea. I'm going to go shower and get changed.' He leaned close and kissed my forehead. A vision flared into my mind and I staggered backwards with the force of it. I was inside Peter's head and he was a fox sprinting along a dark street. He darted from shadow to shadow along a cobbled street, past wheelie bins and yard gates. Light rain fell on the stones and landed on his wiry fur but I was barely aware of it. I had never felt myself move so fast. It was exhilarating. Then I was standing back in the kitchen, clinging onto the table with Peter looking at me with concern on his face. 'Sorry,' he said sheepishly. 'You okay?'

'Fine. That was... fun!' I grinned at him.

'What did you see?'

'You, as a fox, running.'

'Oh.' He grinned too. 'Yeah, it is fun.'

'Peter, why do you suppose I didn't change too?'

'I don't know. It's a bit random, I gather. I mean, it is

genetic, but like how you can have blue eyes even if neither parent does, as long as the gene is in there somewhere it can manifest. But having it on both sides doesn't guarantee it, either.'

'Okay.' I couldn't keep the disappointment out of my voice.

'You're perfect just as you are.' He took a swig of his coffee and put the cup down on the table. He rushed from the room before I could reply. I stared at the door long after he had disappeared through it, doubting his sincerity and wishing he hadn't said it.

Everything had changed. My whole world was upside down. Everything I thought I knew was wrong. My parents had a hidden life and were now dead. My best friend and his father were shapeshifters and had known about my parents. I had been the biggest freak I knew of, now I was the most normal. The gangster who extorted cash from my parents was attempting to seduce me and was actually a vampire. Worst of all, I wanted him to succeed in seducing me. I wanted to kiss him again and again. I wanted to feel that sensational euphoria again and I wanted to sink to the floor in his arms as he fed from me again.

How was I supposed to sort all of this out?

I washed up our coffee mugs and traipsed up the stairs. I could hear the shower running in the bathroom as I passed it and part of me wanted to barge in and challenge him on his parting comment. I hesitated outside the door, but shook it off and continued into the guest room, my room. I shut the door and leaned back against it, closing my eyes to keep from bursting into frustrated tears.

It was still raining when Peter and I set off for my house. We made it a brisk walk, with me under my umbrella and him making do with the hood of his coat.

'The rain doesn't really bother me any more,' he said, casually shaking it out of the front of his hair once we got inside. 'I get rained on most nights when I'm out in nothing but fur. I love it though! Being out in the dark, hunting and running through patches of moonlight.' He was grinning and I couldn't help but grin back. 'In fact, you may as well know now, we have these special names. They sort of come to us, choose us.'

'Oh.' I blinked at him in bemusement.

'Mine is Walker-in-Moonlight.'

'That's pretty.' I meant it, but I also felt a little left out.

'My dad is Moon Caller.'

'I'm seeing a trend.'

'Yeah.'

'What about my parents?'

'Mother-of-the-Forest and Red Wolf.' He looked at me with that sad smile that was all too familiar when people mentioned my parents.

'Oh. Nice.'

'Eve...' He stalled. There was nothing he could say.

I turned away and moved along the hall. I had to get on with something to take my mind off this mess.

My parents' house was less musty now than it had been when we first entered it, thanks to the cleaning we'd done already. But it was still cold and unlived in. I headed straight up the stairs to the office. It was little more than a box room and just as cluttered as the last time Peter and I had been in it. I didn't know what I was looking for. I just wanted some sign of their secret, some confirmation.

I began moving things around, flipping through stacks of papers and wading my way through the mess. Peter mirrored me and tried not to get in my way as I stomped about with mounting frustration.

'There has to be something,' I said, snapping under my breath at no one in particular.

'There may well not be. It's not like we have to identify ourselves on our tax forms.'

I brushed past him to get to the bookshelves and nudged the desk as I passed. It moved an inch and something dropped to the floor from behind it. I crouched down and saw a cardboard tube touching the floor at one end, the other still wedged up between the top of the desk and the wall. Frowning, I reached for it and tugged it free. I felt with my hand and found a small shelf hidden in the back of the desk.

'Peter!' I crawled right under the desk and felt all the way along the shelf, but there was nothing else there. It was only just big enough for the tube. I wriggled back out, the tube in my hand, and Peter helped me to my feet. I turned it over in my hands and saw that there were plastic caps on both ends. I popped one end off and peered inside.

'What is it?' Peter asked, his voice low and soft.

'I don't know.' There was a sheet of paper rolled up inside and I slid my hand in, grasped the edge of it and eased it out. Peter hurriedly cleared the desk, sweeping a pile of papers onto the floor in a dramatic flurry. I dropped the tube and rolled out the paper. It was thick and smooth and had been so tightly curled for so long, it didn't want to lay flat.

'Blueprints?' The paper was distinctively dark blue and covered in white lines. We grabbed objects to hold down the corners so we could see the whole thing.

'Weird.'

'It's this house.'

'Really?' Peter squinted and tilted his head from side to side. 'But they didn't build this. It's been here for decades, the whole street.'

I planted my finger in a small square.

'We're standing right here.'

Peter looked around the room and back at the plans. I ran my finger along the line that represented the exterior wall. 'That's their bedroom. That's mine.' I traced the lines of the house. 'And over here is the downstairs. That's the front door, the living room, the kitchen.' I ran my finger all over the blueprint and finally Peter nodded in agreement.

'I see it. What's that?' He pointed at a section in the bottom right corner of the sheet.

'The basement,' I replied.

'No,' he said, moving his finger to the left. 'That's the basement. Look, there are the stairs up to the kitchen.' I looked again and he was right. The basement was drawn up directly under the plan of the kitchen and the rest of the ground floor. But I hadn't recognised it immediately as the plans showed a large trapdoor right in the centre of the room. The area that I had first taken for the basement I knew had stairs in the corner and was about half the size of the actual basement. It clearly existed directly below the basement of my house.

'What the hell? Why would they build a second basement?' I grabbed the plans and bolted from the room without giving Peter the chance to answer. I was dimly aware of him running behind me. I sped down the stairs and into the kitchen. The basement was accessible through a door in the kitchen that was positioned under the stairs. I opened it on the closet, which was still filled with my parents' coats, shoes and boots.

There was a hatch in the floor, not hidden, with a brass ring in the middle that lay flat when not in use. I hooked my fingers into the ring and heaved up the trapdoor. A hook on the wall kept it in place.

A wooden staircase led down under the house. I flicked a switch next to the coats and a light blinked on at the bottom of the stairs. I'd hated these stairs as a child. I was always terrified I'd fall down them. If the hatch was open, I wouldn't even go into the closet for my coat.

I took a tentative step down and gripped the handrail tightly. It was thick with dust and I cringed as my palm made contact. The stairs had a heavy coating of dust on them too, and my footsteps were muffled by it. I went down slowly, my nerves on edge. Peter was right behind me.

The bulb hung from the ceiling with no shade over it. At the bottom of the stairs was a single room, exactly under the kitchen. The washer and drier stood side by side under where the kitchen sink was. There was a stack of shelves on the opposite wall, piled with boxes, my father's toolbox and some junk that had been there for as long as I could remember.

Peter grabbed a crowbar from the shelf and strode into the centre of the room.

'What are you doing?' I asked, panic lacing my quiet voice.

'Do you want to find out what they were hiding?' He looked at me, the crowbar poised in his hands. I nodded. He wedged the end of the tool between two floorboards and wrenched on the cold steel. There was a crack as the wood splintered. Peter yanked up the two loose boards and got to work on the next one. I grabbed a hammer and used the claw to help him rip up the middle of the floor.

Once we had pulled away half a dozen of the long, narrow boards, the air was filled with dust but I could see in the dim light that beneath the floor was a small gap and then another layer of wood.

I crouched down and wafted the drifting dust away. It was a trapdoor a lot like the one above us in the closet.

'Why did I never know about this?'

'They were protecting you.'

'People keep on saying that. Doesn't make it feel any more true.'

Peter bent down and grasped the metal loop in the trapdoor. He heaved and the door lifted open with a creak. The scattered floorboards shifted under the weight of the heavy door as Peter opened it up all the way and rested it carefully on the damaged floor.

Below us it was pitch black, the light from the single bulb in the basement unable to penetrate far into the hole.

'Why on earth is this here?' I whispered. My heart was pounding so hard in my chest I felt sure Peter must be able to hear it. 'Why would my parents have this built?'

'I don't know.' Peter glanced back at me. He tugged his phone out of his jeans pocket and turned on the torch on it. He shone it into the black space and I saw more stairs leading down.

'Peter, I don't like this.'

'It's okay. Take my hand.' I did as he said and we stepped forward together, very carefully. The ground was rough stone, covered in dust and tiny pebbles. The stone walls were only partially smoothed. It was cool but dry. The steps down were chiselled into the stone too. The passage was tight and we had to go in single file. I went behind Peter, clinging to his shoulders and peering over them into the torch-lit passage. He had to stoop slightly to avoid bumping his head on the rough ceiling.

The stairs didn't go down far, just a single storey. We emerged into a cave directly below my house and Peter shone the light all around it. There was a passage leading off into the black; the air didn't move down here. He shone the torch over the wall we'd just followed down into the cave and the light fell upon a dusty old switch. He flipped it and a fluorescent strip light blinked on, flickering slightly.

All around the cave were stacks of boxes. I peered inside the nearest one and saw canned goods. There were weapons too, axes, hammers and knives, all propped against the wall and coated in dust.

'What is this?' My voice cracked in the middle. I stared around at this alien place, right under my childhood home. Peter ran a finger over the nearest box and brushed the dust off it. I reached into the box and pulled out a can. I searched it for the expiry date and found it, stamped on the bottom. It was for two years ago.

'These have been here for years,' I said softly, turning the can over in my hands before dropping it back into the box.

Peter moved over to a stack of weapons and scooped up a machete. He blew the dust off it and swung it back and forth a few times.

'They were stockpiling for something.'

'And you don't know what?' My voice held a trace of accusation and I glared at him with wide eyes.

'No,' he said, looking at me in mild surprise. 'No idea. I haven't been a shifter for that long. I knew there was stuff I still had to learn. I wasn't brought in on anything involving this place. But my dad might have been. He might know what this is about.'

'I do.' Kirk's voice was soft but clear. I physically leapt into the air, nearly cracking my head on the low ceiling. He stepped into the light from the black passage at the back of the cave.

'Dad?'

'It's time you knew the whole truth.'

CHAPTER TWELVE

'WHERE DID YOU COME FROM? What's back there?' Peter was pale and shaking.

'One question at a time,' Kirk said, holding his hands up in front of him and easing himself towards Peter, who was still holding the machete. Kirk reached for it and eased it out of Peter's hand. Peter stepped back towards me and put his arm across my chest.

'What are you doing?' I asked.

'I don't know what's going on here. I don't like it.'

'He's your dad.'

'Is he?'

'Yes! Kirk, tell us what's going on, please?'

'It's a long story, Eve. You know that your father and I grew up together. What you don't know is that we each had a shifter parent and we both changed in our teens. We both became embroiled with the Camorra, one way or another, and both lost people to them. Your mother came on the scene later. But we were the only shifters we knew. After my mother was killed, I tried to fight them. But I had no training, no expertise, and I failed. I was no warrior. It wasn't in my nature, really. Your father, though. He was a full-moon shifter, a werewolf. He was stronger, faster and more fierce than I could ever be. He wanted to fight them. But alone, he was no match.

'Not long after you were born, we knew we had to resist them. We had to break the chain. Our parents had been fed on and controlled until it was our turn. The Camorra kept us weak and subservient. We wanted better for you two. We wanted the cycle broken.

'We couldn't fight them openly, but we could resist. We built this place at first just to stockpile provisions for an emergency. But it became more. It became the start of the resistance.

'This tunnel leads into catacombs that extend underneath the whole city. They're ancient. They were used by smugglers centuries ago. They were used by the vampires after that. But now they're ours.'

'Why didn't you tell me any of this?' Peter asked, hanging his head in disbelief.

'Because we had stopped years ago. We got scared. We boarded up the entrance and let it gather dust.' Kirk gestured up the stairs behind me. 'About six months ago your parents approached me and said they wanted to start it up again. I wish they had never suggested it. It got them killed.' He shook his head and rubbed the bridge of his nose. 'I don't have a choice now. You both need to know, you both need to be involved so that we can continue what Eve's parents and I started, so that their deaths weren't in vain.'

'I still don't really understand,' I said slowly. I looked around the cave and my gaze settled again on Kirk. 'How are you resisting? What is this place for?'

'This is a place to hide shifters that the Camorra don't know about. A safe place to hide and survive if necessary.'

'There are other shifters?' I asked, looking from Peter to Kirk with wide eyes.

'Yes,' Kirk replied. 'There have always been others. But not enough to overthrow the Camorra. We're bringing in help. Very gradually, over many years, we've been getting help into the city using these catacombs. We've been helping victims get out too, people who have been hurt too many times. We have allies. There are now nearly thirty shifters in the city.'

'What?' Peter spluttered. 'I thought there were just a handful.'

'There were, for a very long time. We were disorganised and only learned of each other by accident. But we knew that in order to overthrow the Camorra, we needed help.' Kirk looked tired but determined. I could see that it pained him to be telling us this. I felt confused and found my mind racing over my history, desperately trying to find confirmation of any of this hiding in my past.

'You can come through now.' Kirk tilted his head over

his shoulder, calling behind him into the shadows. A small, black cat emerged, brushing against his legs and purring. The cat shimmered and shifted, taking the shape of a petite woman with long, blond hair. A face I knew.

'Professor Melrose?' I gaped.

'Hello Eve.'

'You know her?' Peter asked, incredulous. 'From uni?'

'Yes. She teaches Physics. She wasn't one of my professors, but she liked my artwork.'

'I knew your parents, Eve. They were very brave. They sent you to me.'

'What?'

'They wanted you to be in Caerton. They encouraged you to choose that university, out of all the places you could have gone. They wanted you somewhere safe. You were safe there, with me.'

'And you're a cat?' I blinked at her, still in shock. She smiled. Her face was slightly lined and she had piercing blue eyes that shone right through the rimless glasses she wore.

'I can be. You may as well know my true name now. Most of the people who *really* know me call me Weaver-of-Sky's-Loom.'

I stood frozen, still half behind Peter, his arm across me. He didn't seem to want to move it and I was too stunned to object.

'What's so special about Caerton? Why there? It's the

other end of the country,' I muttered in disbelief.

'Numbers,' Kirk said. He lay down the machete and dug his hands into his cardigan pockets. 'Mainly numbers.'

'But also experience,' Professor Melrose said firmly. 'We went through a terrible war just over fifteen years ago and lost a lot of our kind.' There was something in her voice that hinted at a great personal loss, a crack in her otherwise smooth delivery. 'But we recovered, we rebuilt and reorganised. Here you have no structure. What few shifters there have been were not organised as they should be and it allowed these vampires to gain a foothold. Now that I'm here, I can help.'

'And what's the plan, exactly? Are you going to kill them?' A knot twisted in my insides.

'If we have to.' Kirk fixed his gaze on me and I squirmed.

'I'm sorry,' I said, shaking my head and finally knocking Peter's arm aside. I stepped towards the professor. 'I'm just having some trouble getting my head around all of this. How can this be happening? Everyone I thought I knew is turning out to be very different.'

'Because you are different, Eve.' Professor Melrose stepped towards me and put a hand on my shoulder. 'You have always been something not quite human and your whole world around you has shaped because of that. None of it is coincidence, it is all because of what you are.'

'And what am I?'

'Different,' Kirk said with a smile.

'You are shifter-blooded.' The professor's eyes were kind, but there was a hardness there too. 'Your parents were shapeshifters and you carry their blood. You may never have changed, but you have your gift because of their blood.'

'What do you know about my gift?' My voice was more harsh than I'd intended. It was all just so much to take on board and frustration was gripping me.

'More than you realise.' There was wisdom in her smile. 'You and I have something in common. You are very like your mother too, I see her in you.' She took me by both shoulders and looked right into my eyes. 'I want to give you a gift.'

My arms tensed under her firm grip and I wanted to pull away. But I was rooted to the spot and her eyes were so penetrating that I couldn't look away. I suddenly felt myself being pulled downward at great speed. My eyes rolled back in my head and the cave melted away.

I landed with a thump in the living room of the Wilkes's house. It was daylight, but the soft, pinkish light of a summer evening. Kirk and my parents were sitting together on one sofa. My parents were clutching each other's hands. Kirk was leaning heavily on the arm of the sofa. They all looked younger. I was pacing back and forth in front of them. I looked down at my hands and they were unfamiliar. Many rings adorned them and the fingers on my right hand were ink-stained. I was Weaver.

'Is it possible?' My mother's voice was soft and urgent. I looked at her. She was soft-skinned, kind and with disarming, dark eyes. Her hair was thick and dark, like mine, but she wore it short. She was slim but I remembered how strong she was. She never struggled with a jar or a heavy box. She always smelled faintly of spices.

'It's possible,' I said in Weaver's voice. 'It will be difficult and it will take time.'

I caught sight of my reflection in the mirror over the mantelpiece. I was a younger Weaver. My right eye was slightly discoloured and a shining red scar jutted down from the lower lid.

'We have time. We have to do it right, be careful.' Kirk was rubbing his temples as he spoke. 'But we don't have much time right now. Marianne will be back with the kids soon.'

'Your human wife?' Weaver said, looking at him with hard eyes. Kirk nodded. 'That never ends well, you know.'

'Only one of my parents was a shifter.'

'And did you lose them both?' Weaver's tone was almost cruel. Kirk looked down at the carpet. 'I'm sorry. But you have to be realistic about these things.' I was inside her head, her pain was my own. I saw the fleeting memory of her brother-in-arms on the end of a blade and of his human wife and child being sent away for their safety. It was still raw for her in this memory.

The scene rippled away and in its place there was a bonfire and fireworks. There was darkness beyond and I had no idea where I was. But I was still inside Weaver's head and I saw my parents laughing, singing, drinking. They were arm in arm and they kissed with the passion of youth. I wasn't even embarrassed, I saw their love and joy and all I could feel was that. Although it was tinged with loss and sadness, of course. I, as Weaver, watched their revelry. There were other shifters around the fire, I realised. A host of them, some in the monstrous form that I had seen in Peter's past. But they were celebrating and cavorting, not killing. I was in Caerton! This was when my parents went away without me when I was nine. I never knew where they'd gone. I stayed with Peter's family.

The scene rippled away again and I was sitting in a small cave, the walls were covered with writing and drawings. A large desk sat before me, covered in scrolls. Torches burned on the walls, flickering light filled the small space. I was leaning back in a chair and reading a letter. I recognised the handwriting, it was my mother's.

I'm sending her to you. She still struggles with the visions. I know you explained about this and about how she may never change, but still be afflicted with this. But I can't help her. That's not my gift, but it is yours. You understand it, you can teach her how to use it.

Believe me, I know how difficult that will be, how

limited you will be with what you can tell her. I have agonised over this for so many years. I had hoped she would change, so that we could stop keeping these secrets, but it seems she may not. That, surprisingly, comes as a relief to me, in the end. If she never changes she may escape Their clutches. If she is with you in Caerton, she most certainly will be free. I pray that Artemis keeps her far from harm, even if she isn't one of the "chosen".

You talk of this life as a gift, a privilege. I'm afraid I have never seen it as anything but a curse. We may always disagree on that point. An accident of birthplace makes such a difference, doesn't it? You know that better than most, I suppose.

Eve will arrive in a week. Please take good care of my special girl.

I was crying. I was back in the catacombs with Peter, Kirk and Weaver. She released me and passed me a white handkerchief. I took it and wiped my face.

'How did you do that?' My voice was hoarse.

'With practice. I share your gift, Eve, as you saw. Projecting images into another's mind can be learned. It was easier with you because you share the Sight. I transmitted and you are wired to receive, so the images flowed easily. But with time and patience, you may be able to learn to do the same to others. It can be useful.'

'I don't know if I want to. I don't know if I want anything to do with any of this. I only ever wanted a simple life.'

Peter put his arm around me and turned me to face him. He tilted my chin up to look into my eyes.

'If we defeat the Camorra, you still can.'

CHAPTER THIRTEEN

THAT NIGHT, having re-concealed the entrance to the catacombs as best we could by laying the floorboards back over the trapdoor, Peter, Kirk and I returned to their home. Weaver left us to hide somewhere safe. I didn't ask where.

Peter's mother fed us and talked enough for all of us. I wasn't sure whether she simply didn't notice how subdued we were, or if her chatter was her way of covering it up. I watched her bustle around the kitchen, making sure everyone's cup was full, keeping the food coming for as long as we were all there at the table. I found myself wondering again how she could possibly not know about her husband and son.

Maybe it was one of those things they talk about where a person believes what they want to believe, sees what they want see. Denial.

Everything that I'd learned since coming home needed time to percolate in my brain. I was in danger of overloading. I felt a strange detachment from the whole

Wilkes' family. It was far worse now than it had been when I first arrived and was simply grieving for my normal parents. That was a feeling that I understood, even though it was new and horrible. It was traditional grief.

Mrs Wilkes understood it too and treated me perfectly, even if it irritated me at the time. But now? What was this? I was grieving for a completely intangible loss. I had lost a perception. I'd seen the world a certain way all of my life and now I had to adjust to the way it really had been all along, even though I didn't see it.

I'd been in a room with my parents when they were younger. It had felt so real. I'd seen their fear and also their optimism. I'd seen them more free than I ever saw them in real life when I saw them at that bonfire. I had no memories of them being that happy, none of my own. Now I had Weaver's. It wasn't quite the same, but it would do for now.

I drifted away from the table having barely eaten, and made my way up to my room. I looked around at my things. I'd made myself quite at home over the two weeks that I'd been staying there. But it was time to go. I had my own house and knowing what was under the basement, I felt obliged to be there to protect it.

I started packing my things into my rucksack. I'd stay the night and leave in the morning, but I wanted to get the room tidied before I went to sleep. A gentle knock at the door stopped me. I sighed and turned to open it. Kirk stood there in the hall, his hands deep in his pockets, as usual.

'Can I talk to you?'

'Of course.' I stood aside and let him in. He cast his gaze around the room and took in my half-filled bag and open wardrobe.

'Are you leaving us?'

'I think I need to be at my house. I think someone should be there, you know, in case of anything untoward in the basement.'

'Okay. If that's what you want.' He closed the door and perched himself on the end of the bed. 'I know you've had a lot to take in.'

'You could say that.' I went back to packing. I needed to keep my hands busy.

'I am sorry that so much was kept from you for all these years.'

'I understand. I really do. I'm not angry or anything. Just, you know, processing.'

'Okay, that's good.'

'Was there something else?'

'About Weaver. What did she show you?'

'Memories of my parents. I saw the three of you downstairs here, talking to her about the plan. Then my parents in Caerton, and a letter my mother wrote.'

'Hm,' he said with a nod. 'Were they happy memories?'

'Partly. The bonfire was. What were they doing there?'

'They went to meet some of the other shifters and to start the process of bringing people here. I think they learned a lot. You know, when your father and I were young and newly changed, we used to joke about starting a pack and making changes here. He was idealistic then, we both were. But the Camorra changed that and for a good few years we were both a bit stuck in our lives. When you were born that all changed. You brought back that spark to your father, that desire to fight for a better world.'

I'd stopped folding clothes. I wasn't sure when. I looked at the man I'd known all my life. He still radiated peace and calm. I didn't associate him with fighting at all. But it made sense for my father. I could see him as a warrior.

'He didn't get the chance to fight,' I said, my voice soft and far away.

'He fought in his own way. He set things up for others to continue the fight. Your parents never meant for it to fall on you. They wanted you away from all of this.'

'In Caerton, with their friend.'

'At first, but they were confident you would find your own path.'

'Are there a lot of shifters there?'

'Yes.'

I raised an eyebrow when he didn't elaborate.

'Will I get to meet any of the others here?'

'Yes.' He smiled at me and I exhaled in exasperation at him. 'In time. We have to be so careful. Which brings me to what I really wanted to talk to you about.'

'Vitale.'

'Vitale. Both of them, really. But Antonio in particular.'

I dropped onto the bed beside him and dropped my head into my hands.

'I let him get into my head.'

'I know. Look, Eve, don't blame yourself for that. It's what he does. He's very skilled at that. He has this charisma that is almost impossible to resist. Trust me, I understand.'

'He's fed on you. Right?' I lifted my head and looked him in the eye.

'Not directly. He has taken my blood. His sister, Lucia, has fed on me. They've fed on all the shifters they know about. They seek us out and get us hooked into their business. I gather our blood is... special.'

'What? Like it tastes of strawberries or something?'

He let out a snort of laughter.

'Something like that. They've never specified. Don't want us armed with too much information.'

'Do you think my blood is like that?'

'Yes, I think it probably is. Maybe not to the same degree. But Antonio got his claws into you very quickly. I think he wanted to control you from the start.'

'And I let him.'

'I said not to blame yourself for that. But look, you said you have some control, right?' I nodded. 'So you can use it. You need to keep your guard up, not let him get back in there and use you. But you need to be really careful. We'll try to accelerate things now. That's why Weaver's here. We'll get you out of harm's way as soon as possible.'

'I need to help.' I looked at him with wide eyes, determination stirring in my chest. 'I need to continue what my parents started. Their deaths have to mean something.'

'That is certainly commendable, but they wanted you to be protected. I can't put you in harm's way. Shifters are strong, physically, very strong. You're a human girl. You are so breakable.'

'Don't patronise me. I'm more than capable of doing something to help. I might not be able to pick up a machete and wade into a brawl, but my gift can be useful and I can help. I want to.' I spoke firmly but made sure not to raise my voice. I could hear the soft murmuring of Peter and his mother talking in the kitchen below and knew that a word spoken just loud enough would carry to them.

Kirk nodded, a grim expression of resignation on his lined face.

'I thought you might say that. I can't stop you. I'm not your father, you're not a child.' He slapped his legs and stood up. 'Very well. I accept your help. When Vitale gets in touch, try not to be alone with him. Will you at least do that for me?'

'Sure.' I nodded and stood up beside him. He put a hand on my shoulder and gave it a squeeze.

'Okay, then we'll talk more tomorrow. I'll figure out a way to work you into the plan.'

'Thank you.'

He left the room and I went back to my packing. But after moving my things around aimlessly for a few minutes, I gave it up and flopped onto the bed.

My dreams that night were a confusing blur of my parents, various animals wandering in and out of rooms speaking to each other, and fires burning. Then there were Antonio's dark eyes alive with reflected flames.

I woke up the following morning feeling groggy and unrested. I rolled over and checked my phone. I had a message sitting there from an unknown number. I unlocked it and opened the message with a hint of apprehension. I had a hunch who it might be from.

I had never given Antonio my phone number, but had every confidence that he'd found a way to acquire it. I was right.

"Good morning, Eve. I trust this message finds you

well. I would like to see you again. There is a special performance of a film that I think you might enjoy tonight at 8 pm at the open air theatre in the museum gardens. Would you care to meet me there? Or I can collect you. Please reply and let me know your preference. I dearly hope to see you later. Antonio x"

The butterflies had started doing backflips in my stomach. But I appealed to them to settle down. I lay there staring at the message for what felt like an hour. I read it over and over again, telling myself that he was only after my blood. He only wanted to control me, extort money from me and potentially use me to find out more about what my parents had been doing. These were all far more plausible than him being genuinely interested in me romantically.

He was an ancient, wealthy, powerful and magnificent creature of the night. With a snap of his fingers he could bend any subject to his will. It was exactly what he had done with me. Even lying there knowing that, I felt myself falling for it again. He really was firmly lodged inside my head.

I tossed my phone aside without replying and got up. I went for a shower, all the while running over Antonio's message in my mind. I wouldn't be alone with him if we were in public. He couldn't very well drink my blood in the middle of a crowded place. He might answer my questions. This was probably the best way that I could help the cause.

I finished up and padded across the hall back towards my room, wrapped in a thick towel. Peter emerged on the stairs and looked flustered, his cheeks flared up bright red.

'Hi, er, sorry, I'll...' He pointed to his room, which was up the next flight of stairs, then back down the stairs he had just come up, not knowing where to look. I laughed and skipped quickly into the guest room and shut the door, sparing him from his indecision. I leaned against the door and continued to giggle. A quiet voice on the other side of the door stopped me.

'Actually, can we talk?'

I opened the door and looked at Peter. He fixed his gaze on the floor and shuffled his feet.

'Now?'

'Dad said you're leaving today.'

'Yeah. It's time.'

'Now? After yesterday?' He was whispering and still avoiding looking at me.

'Especially after yesterday,' I replied softly. 'Come in, will you?' I stood aside to let him in. He glanced awkwardly up and down the hall, then stepped inside and I closed the door. I made sure the towel was firmly in place and turned to face him. Peter had gone straight to the window and was sweeping the street. It was barely light out and rain pattered on the glass.

'Why?' he asked.

'Someone needs to be at my house, guarding the

entrance.'

'There was no sign that anyone else knew about it. It's been fine with the house empty for two weeks.'

'Yeah, but if we start using it that may well not remain the case. Besides, it's just time. Your parents have been great, really, but I can't live here forever. I'm a guest here, no matter how long I stay, and I really just want to be in my own home.'

'Okay, I get that.' Peter finally looked at me. I suddenly felt very vulnerable, standing there in just a towel, my hair dripping on the floor and my toiletry bag clutched in my hand. I hitched the towel a little higher up my chest and looked away from Peter. 'I'm sorry. I'll leave you to it. But let me help you take your stuff over.'

'Okay. After breakfast.' I smiled at him as he brushed past me and stepped out into the hall.

'Yeah.' He was avoiding looking at me again and he scurried up the stairs to his room. Why did boys have to be so awkward and confusing? Maybe that was what was so appealing about Antonio. He oozed confidence and grace. There was no awkwardness in him at all. Even knowing why, I was still in awe of him.

I picked up my phone and quickly tapped a reply.

"Thank you for the invitation. I would love to join you. I'll meet you there at 8. Eve x"

I didn't even care what the film was. But I absolutely wasn't going to let him bite me.

CHAPTER FOURTEEN

The rain eased off by mid-morning and the sun came out. Peter carried my bag to my house for me and didn't mention the awkward conversation or seeing me in just a towel.

'Has your dad said anything about meeting the others?' I asked as we entered the house. It was chilly and I went straight to the boiler to set the timer for the heating. Peter followed me and put my bag down at the foot of the stairs.

'Not yet. I have to work this afternoon but shall I come over tonight to do some more sorting or anything?'

'No, that's okay. I'm going to be out tonight.'

'At the restaurant?'

'Yeah, at the start of the night, anyway.' I turned to face him and took a deep breath. 'I'm seeing Antonio later.'

'Right.' He pressed his lips into the thinnest of lines and wouldn't meet my eyes. 'Are you sure that's a good idea?'

'No!' I blurted and gave his shoulder a shove. 'Of

course not. But I do think it's important. Last time I saw him he talked. Not very openly, but a little. He started to relax. I might be able to get information out of him. At the very least, I can keep tabs on him. We'll be in public the whole time and I will not fall for his mind tricks. I promise.'

'I'm not sure you actually have a say in that.' He gave me a grim, half-smile.

'Well, I can try. If we're going to take him down we're going to have to be clever about it and him trusting me is essential.'

'I suppose. I'm worried about you.'

'Don't you start on about my fragile human body. Your dad was bad enough.'

'I happen to like your body just as it is, not half drained of blood and covered in bite marks.'

'His bites don't leave marks.'

'Oh.' Peter looked stricken.

'I'm not going to let myself end up in a position where it can happen again and I am sick of making that promise to people. Will you please trust me?'

'Of course.' He'd gone red in the face. 'I have to get to work, so I'll go. Good luck tonight.' He swept away up the hall and I dashed after him. I didn't want him leaving in a temper.

'Peter.' He stopped at the door and turned to face me.

'I like that you care about my safety.'

'Okay. Good.'

'I will be careful. See you tomorrow?'

'Yeah. Tomorrow.' He grabbed me and hugged me. I let him. I was getting better at doing that.

He left and I locked the door. My room wasn't very homely these days. The walls were covered in old posters that no longer felt relevant. The bed was a single and I'd got used to the double in the guest room at Peter's house. I went to my parents' room and rolled up my sleeves. It was time to tackle the personal stuff.

Their room was twice the size of mine. It had a large window opposite the door that looked out on the front street. The double bed sat against the wall to the right from the door and the wall opposite was lined with fitted wardrobes. The wallpaper was fairly new and more floral than I would have chosen for myself, but it was pretty and it reminded me of my mother. I remembered her hanging it a few years previously and the way the house had smelled so strongly of the paste.

I got out their suitcases and packed as many of their nice clothes as would fit into them, then hauled them to the landing and stacked them up beneath the loft hatch. I would have to ask Peter to move them up there. The rest of the clothes went in bin liners, which I put by the front door to take to a charity shop. I emptied the bedside tables into a big cardboard box. It was mostly old nail files, tickets, pens and other random bits and bobs. The last book they were each reading, a necklace of my mother's and a scented candle were all things to keep.

I managed to get through it in a fairly business-like manner. It was only when I got to my mother's perfume and make-up that I got a little emotional. I sprayed her perfume on my wrist and took deep breaths. Memories flooded back to me and I wasn't entirely sure that it wasn't my gift firing up. But I didn't lose myself in it like I always had before.

I remembered last Christmas and my mother getting ready for our traditional trip to see the Nutcracker. She had looked so beautiful in a new dress. I went back to the suitcases, opened the one with my mother's things and found the dress.

It was long and flowing, dark green with tiny beads embellishing the neckline. I shook it out and returned it to the wardrobe. It would fit me perfectly.

Neither of my parents kept much of sentimental value and now I understood why. They hadn't wanted to have things lying around the house that might trigger a vision. It meant that their room was free of clutter and fairly quick to sort through.

With a heavy sigh, I decided to strip the bed. I'd buy some new bedding that was more to my taste, but for now, their best bedding would suffice. It was white with a teal runner and gold trim. It was pretty and simple.

By the time I was done clearing their room I didn't

have time to unpack my own things into the wardrobe, so I left my bag at the foot of the bed and went for another shower. I'd got quite sweaty and dusty sorting through all of their things and humping heavy suitcases around.

I didn't want to wear the same dress I'd worn to dinner, and thought that sitting on wet grass demanded more practical clothing. After blow-drying my hair and putting it up in a messy bun, I dressed in dark jeans, a long-sleeved black polo neck and red hoop earrings. My mother had some fairly new black boots with a low heel that fitted me perfectly, so I wore those and my green coat.

It was just getting dark as I gave myself a once-over in the mirror. Satisfied with my appearance, I set off for Piero's to check in there. I probably wasn't spending enough time there, I realised, but everything seemed to be under control.

It was quieter than when we first reopened, but still ticking along fine. The staff were coping, deliveries of ingredients and other things that we needed were set up and Kirk was keeping on top of the money. Thank goodness for Kirk, I thought.

At 7.45 pm I left the restaurant and walked across the city to the museum gardens. The Christmas decorations were up everywhere, with twinkling lights, bauble-covered trees in shop windows and festive music seemingly oozing from every pore of the city. I couldn't help but smile as I passed late-night shoppers, bustling bars and restaurants.

It wasn't quite December, but I allowed myself to feel a little Christmas spirit as I passed the pumpkin-spiced-smelling coffee shops and the huge tree in the square. The pine smell was still fresh and intoxicating.

I cut through one of the narrow, cobbled streets that led away from the hubbub and bright lights. The street twisted and turned, a remnant of the old city from hundreds of years ago. The buildings stood close on either side and leaned at crooked angles, the top floors jutting out another foot or so over the ground floor. It was one of my favourite parts of the city. Puddles stood between the cobblestones from the morning's rain, but it was dry enough now for the date that Antonio had planned.

At the end of the street was a broad, straight road that buzzed with passing traffic. On the opposite side stood two tall, stone pillars hung with wrought iron gates that were propped open. Beyond the gates were the vast gardens that wrapped around this corner of the city centre. The path from the road was well lit with old-fashioned street lamps and at this time of year, strings of coloured lights hung from lamp post to lamp post, casting their festive glow onto the glistening ground.

Standing beside one of the stone pillars, in a long black coat, was Antonio. He caught sight of me across the street and my stomach flipped over like a playful cat presenting its belly for a loving owner. 'Stop it,' I scolded myself under my breath. I smiled at Antonio, waited for a gap in the traffic and crossed the road to greet him.

Antonio took my hand and kissed the back of it. My cheeks blushed.

'I'm glad to see you. Shall we go in?'

'Sure.' He held my hand and led me through the gates. Under his other arm was a rolled-up picnic blanket.

The path was wide enough for a car and it swept in a curve to the left and down a gentle hill. Trees lined either side of the path and flower beds were interspersed along the way. We came to a fork in the path. The right led up to the museum, slightly up the hill and overlooking the gardens. It was a grand, Georgian building, but I'd never actually been inside. The left path continued down the hill towards the river, and we followed it. There were fewer lamp posts here and the dark shadows between pools of light seemed to stretch out further. But there was a steady trickle of people filing down the slope, so the tingle of apprehension I felt was kept to a minimum. I wanted to believe that Antonio wouldn't jump me in the shadows, but a little voice told me that nothing was out of the question.

We took a turn to the right at the bottom of the slope and emerged at the foot of a wide, grassy slope that led back up to the museum. The gardens here were beautiful. Deep flower beds housed roses, rhododendrons and, at this time of year, dozens of poinsettias. Little, warm yellow lights lined the flower beds, highlighting the bright red poinsettia leaves and casting long shadows.

At the foot of the slope was a huge projector screen and around fifty people sat in little clusters on the grass on blankets. Most of them had picnics, some sat on little folding chairs. There was a constant low babble of conversation and soft music was playing from the speakers on either side of the projector screen.

'You didn't tell me what film it was,' I said. Antonio was leading me up the slope, picking our way through the small crowd. He found a big enough spot and spread out the blanket on the damp grass.

'You'll see.' He knelt down and patted the space beside him. I sat down, fixing him with a playful scowl.

'I'm not actually that keen on surprises.'

'Really? I'll bear that in mind in future.'

He produced a small wooden box from his coat pocket, flipped the lid open and held it out to me. Inside were chocolate-dusted strawberries, much like the ones that had accompanied our profiteroles at dinner. I smiled and took one.

'Thank you, this is nice.' I watched him bite into his strawberry, still curious about his eating. 'You know, the people who care most about me aren't too happy about this.'

'About you eating strawberries?'

'No.' I concealed a smirk and raised an eyebrow at him.

'No, I'd imagine they are most concerned about you.

How do you feel about that?'

'They love me. They're worried I'll get hurt.'

'You didn't answer my question.'

'I suppose not. I think that I might get hurt too, but isn't that always a risk? We can't deny ourselves the things we want out of fear.'

'Very wise.' He shook his head and looked at the ground. 'You continue to surprise and impress me.'

'I do?'

'Yes.'

'Antonio?' He looked up into my eyes and for a moment I lost my breath and my train of thought. His eyes were shining in the twinkling lights at the edges of the slope and they seemed to dance right into my mind.

'Not many people call me that.'

'Sorry.'

'Not at all. I like it. I apologise, do continue.'

'I was going to ask if that's why you're interested in me. Because I surprise and impress you?'

'Yes.' He popped another strawberry into his mouth and smiled faintly as he chewed.

The screen down the slope flickered to life and there was a little ripple of excited murmuring from the gathered audience before they fell silent.

A simple black and white title screen displayed the word "Nosferatu" and an image of Max Schreck in the notorious role. I cast a sideways glance at Antonio and felt my brows knit together in puzzled wonder. He grinned at me and ate another strawberry. I was still holding my first. I looked back at the screen, smiling at his brazenness. I leaned back and finally ate the fruit.

I'd never actually seen the film before and even looking back now, I can't honestly say I've really seen it. All the way through I was distracted. I was so acutely aware of Antonio beside me, so achingly close. He watched the film with genuine glee on his face, which I glanced at often. The flickering of the screen highlighted his stunning cheekbones, and his dark eyes were entranced.

The irony of watching the original Dracula film with an actual vampire was certainly not lost on me and more than once I wondered what it must have been like to live through the invention of things as significant as film. I didn't really know how old Antonio was and I couldn't very well ask him.

Every now and then one of us would inch slightly closer to the other and I would feel a tingle shoot up my spine. I remembered the passionate kiss we'd shared at the end of our first date and I longed for a repeat performance.

But Ms Rational kept clearing her throat to remind me to keep my head. She stopped me from simply turning my head and capturing his lips with mine. Just.

As the final credits flashed up onto the screen, the people around us began to move, packing up their picnics and gathering their things. Antonio and I sat perfectly still, not speaking and barely looking at one another. The weight of everything unsaid seemed to lie over us like a heavy mist.

Gradually the park began to empty and we were left sitting in the dark. I had promised that I wouldn't be alone with him, but we were about to be completely alone and I was beginning to feel vulnerable. Yet I couldn't bring myself to move.

His cool fingers tucked a loose strand of hair behind my ear and a shiver ran through me.

'Did you enjoy the film?'

I nodded and closed my eyes, willing the butterflies to settle down. My head involuntarily tilted towards his light touch and I turned to face him. His lips brushed against mine, lightly at first, but quickly intensifying. Blood rushed to my face, my breath hot against his skin.

The sudden sweep of bright torchlight over us broke us apart. I put a hand up to shield my eyes. Antonio turned his head towards the source, his eyes dark and dangerous.

'Oh, apologies, Mr Vitale, sir. I didn't realise it was you.' I could just about make out the male security guard in his uniform on the other side of the beam of light. He scurried away without Antonio saying a word and we were left alone in the dark. Antonio moved to kiss me again but I pulled away, the mood broken and a twisting knot of fear taking root in my insides.

'I'd better be getting home.'

'Oh. Of course.' The disappointment was clear in his voice. I grasped his hand and kissed his palm.

'I have a promise to keep. But I wish things were different.' My voice was lower than normal, almost husky. The hint of those unspoken things heavy in my tone. He understood, at least in part. He stood up and helped me to my feet and we rolled up the blanket together.

We took a step towards the path but Antonio stopped and turned to face me. He pulled me tight against his chest and kissed me again, a kiss full of passion and enthusiasm. I leaned against him and welcomed the depth and intensity. His hand was pressed firmly against my back and I longed to feel it roam over my body, but he held it still, pressing me to him.

Reluctantly, I eased out of the kiss and his embrace. My lips felt raw and my blood pumped frantically through my veins.

He can probably hear your racing pulse. Ms Rational reminded me.

Shut up, I replied.

'Eve, I apologise. I haven't felt anything like this in quite some time.'

'How much time?' I pressed.

'Years. Decades, maybe,' he let slip.

'Oh.'

'You're intoxicating. I find I'm not quite myself around you.'

'Antonio.' I took his hand again and leaned close to him. 'I like who you are around me. It's the other guy that I'm scared of. The one that the security guard saw.'

'I see.' He nodded sadly and glanced at the ground.

'And you can't be this guy all the time. I know that. The other guy is what keeps the business going. Right?'

'Right.'

'So we take this slowly. Carefully.'

'Very carefully,' he agreed.

I pulled back, that knot of fear making itself known again. Our hands were still clasped, our fingers knitting together. There was a flicker of darkness across his face. He was thinking about the possibility of losing control with me and taking too much blood. He'd done it before. I was certain that had been his thought. As certain as I was that Weaver's memories of my parents had been real. My gift had just sparked into action with him.

CHAPTER FIFTEEN

'Okay.' We walked slowly up the grassy slope towards the floodlit museum, an uneasy silence hanging heavily between us. It felt surreal to step out of the darkness and onto the path under the twinkling coloured lights. The sounds of traffic and people began to reach my feeble, human ears as we approached the gates back out onto the main road.

The city was alive and oblivious to the turmoil I was experiencing.

I was certain that the lust I was feeling was mine and not the result of Antonio's hypnotic abilities. He hadn't tried to use it on me since that last time in his bedroom. He hadn't needed it. But even when I'd shown signs of resisting his charms he hadn't turned to it. I wasn't sure what that meant, but I wanted it to be a good thing.

People I'd known my entire life wanted to kill him and they expected me to want the same. But I was too deep in this romance, or whatever it was. I didn't want him dead. I couldn't see how to get out of this situation without losing something significant. I'd felt a lack of control ever since my parents had died. But now I was desperately fighting with myself to regain some sense of free will. I would have to make a choice and it was going to be painful.

Maybe it was possible to convince Kirk and the others that there was another way? Maybe I could convince Antonio to stop extorting my loved ones and feeding from the shifters? Maybe I had some influence over these things? I glanced at him as we walked slowly through the glistening city, and wanted to believe that I mattered to him.

'Does your sister know that we're seeing each other?' I asked, my voice wavering slightly.

'No,' he said with a small smile. 'It's not really any of her concern.'

'I don't think she likes me much.'

'She doesn't know you. She tends to be sceptical of the unknown.'

'Will she give herself the chance to get to know me? Would she, if she knew it was important to you?'

'Of course.' He looked at me with an expression of curiosity. I thought he probably believed it, but I doubted the validity of that belief. What little I had seen of Lucia Vitale so far did not endear her to me and I knew the feeling was mutual. She seemed like someone probably quite fixed in her beliefs. But maybe I should give her the benefit of the doubt. A smile crept onto my face and I tugged his arm closer to me.

'You didn't disagree that I'm important to you.'

'I thought I made my feelings quite clear in the park.' He didn't look at me.

'I suppose you did.'

'But I can't say that I'm clear on your feelings.' He did glance my way with that and my smile faltered.

'Neither am I,' I admitted. He seemed to accept that. We walked on in silence for a while, through the quieter cobbled streets and then onto the ones bustling with nightlife. My thoughts raced over the complexities of the situation that kept my feelings from being clear. There was so much I couldn't say to him. But there was one thing I could risk. 'It would be simpler if I didn't owe you money.'

'I see.' He nodded but didn't look at me. After a moment he stopped walking and turned to face me. 'Done.'

'I'm sorry?'

'No more payments. I'm sure next time I check my books I will see that your parents' debt has been paid in full.'

'Really?' I raised an eyebrow and rolled my tongue over my teeth. It couldn't be that simple.

'Really. In fact, I'm sure of it. If it makes things simpler.'

'It does.' *But what about everything else?* Ms Rational asked. How much was he willing to move for me?

'What about Mr Wilkes?'

'What about him?' Antonio frowned and cocked his head to one side.

'He's the closest thing I have to a father these days and he's not entirely happy with his employment.' Antonio's eyes narrowed slightly as he looked into mine. Had I made a terrible mistake dragging Kirk into this?

'I see. You know, I rely on him a great deal.'

'Do you?' I inched closer to him and looked imploringly into his eyes. 'I'm not sure he feels appreciated.'

'What would you have me do about that?' His lips were so close to mine. I didn't even care that we were in the middle of a busy street with people passing us and staring. I still had hold of his hand and I lifted it to rest on my hip. His other hand still clutched the picnic blanket. I put my hands around the back of his neck and pressed my body against his.

'Make sure he feels valued. Pay him well for the risks he takes for you.' Feeling emboldened and safe in the crowd, I took a leap. 'Make sure he's safe. Safe from blood loss.'

Antonio went rigid, his eyes blazed. My heart was threatening to burst out of my chest as we stood there, locked together. He looked like he wanted to rip my throat out, but I knew he wouldn't. I moved my head so that we were cheek to cheek and I whispered in his ear, 'You didn't expect me to say anything, but you're not surprised that I know.' Cogs were clicking into place and I pushed on, my voice low. 'You didn't choose that film tonight by accident. You drank from me in your bedroom that night and I didn't act the way you expected afterwards. You knew that I was at least a little resistant to your hypnotic gaze. That's why you haven't tried to use it again. You knew I would notice you doing it and you didn't want to spook me. I know, Antonio, and here I am, in your arms, kissing you.' I pressed my lips to his. He seemed to resist for a moment and I was terrified that I'd grossly misjudged. But he began to soften and reciprocate, kissing me back. His hand gripped my hip firmly and his kiss was hungry.

Someone wolf-whistled and someone else laughed. I heard a shout of 'Get a room!' but I didn't care. Neither did Antonio. His hand snaked up my back and grabbed hold of my hair. He tilted my head to one side and his mouth found its way to my neck, despite my polo neck. I gasped, certain that he was about to bite me right there, in front of everyone. But he stopped and set my head upright.

'What you just said was either very brave or very foolish.' His voice was low and dangerous.

'I know.' I was shaking all over. He roughly grabbed my hand and set off at a march. I scurried along in his wake, the crowds parting for us. The bars were closing soon, I realised, so the street was full of people moving on, either to nightclubs or home. I began to feel very frightened and part of me wanted to break away and make a run for it in the other direction. But part of me was glued to him.

The crowd began to thin as we approached the end of the street and turned away from the road that led to the train station and the route that would have taken me home. 'Antonio!' I called but he didn't respond. 'Where are we going?' The street we had turned onto was dark and quiet and he dragged me relentlessly on. I felt genuinely afraid for my life for the first time since he had walked into it.

A car swept past us, its lights passing by faster than I could think to attempt to signal the driver. Not that calling for help would do any good. People had the unfortunate tendency to not want to intervene when someone was in trouble.

As suddenly as we'd set off, Antonio came to a halt. He tossed the rolled-up blanket to the wet ground and slammed me against a cold, metal shutter over a shop window, his hand around my throat. It was almost pitch black but I could see his dark eyes fixed on me. I could hardly breathe and he was holding me up so high I had to stand on my toes. I held up my hands in surrender and tried desperately to get the word "please" to pass my lips.

His mouth crashed against mine and he was kissing me again with intense fervour. He released his grip on my neck and his hands held my shoulders firmly against the shutter. I couldn't help kissing him back but I'd been reminded, vividly, of how dangerous he was.

He hurriedly unbuttoned my coat and his cold hands tugged my top up so that he could press them firmly against my skin. They moved up my sides and he grasped my back. My own hands fumbled to find a way through his layers to his skin and eventually got there. I gripped his back, pressing my fingers hard into him. He was so firm, his muscles strong, and he held me in place as if I were nothing.

Antonio's mouth moved to my jaw and down to my neck, pushing the neck of my top aside as his lips searched for the right spot. His teeth brushed my skin and I squeezed him tighter, bracing myself. *This is how I die*, Ms Rational said, her voice grim and unwavering. There was a pinch as his newly protruding fangs pierced my skin. I tried to cry out but my voice caught in my throat and stuck there. There was only a moment of pain and then sweet surrender. My whole body went limp in his arms. His hand supported my head as he drank. I could hear him gulping and even though I should have been revolted, I found myself aroused. I felt his arousal through my jeans too and in that moment I desperately wanted him in every way possible. I whimpered and sank into the feeling of utter euphoria.

I had broken my promise but I didn't care. I would do it again and again to feel like this.

He pulled back but kept a firm hold of me. I blinked and tried to take my own weight, but couldn't. I was gasping for breath. His teeth almost shone in the dark and I saw my blood on them. He had two neat fangs showing that weren't there before and I watched in awe as they slowly receded back into his gums.

'Fine. Done. You get your wish.' His voice was husky and trembled slightly. 'You get everything you asked for.'

I had no idea what he was talking about and blinked at him, still half in la-la land.

'What?'

'Everything. As long as it means that I can do that again.'

'I... I can't think straight right now.'

'I'm sorry.' He kissed me softly and stroked my hair, which had tumbled down out of its bun. 'You asked for your debt to be clear and for Kirk to be safe and fairly paid. They were complications that got in the way of your feelings for me. I want them out of the way. I want your feelings for me to be crystal clear.'

'Okay.' I was beginning to understand. I tried again to stand on my own, with a little more success.

'I take it this was another complication,' he said softly, gesturing my neck and his teeth. I nodded, feeling almost numb. 'Well now it's out in the open between us. I know, you know. The elephant in the room has been addressed.'

'How can I trust that you won't kill me?'

'I don't know. That's what trust is though, yes?' His accent had deepened, like he was lost in somebody he used to be. I nodded again. 'I'll get you home. We'll talk tomorrow.'

All I could do was nod. I felt far away, like I wasn't quite in my own body. Surely all of this was happening to somebody else? I was dimly aware of him making a call and then lifting me into his arms and carrying me back to the main road. He set me down against a wall and a moment later his black car pulled up at the kerb. A driver got out and held the back door open for us. Antonio helped me into the back seat and gave the driver my address. *He did know it,* Ms Rational said, her voice heavy with sleep.

CHAPTER SIXTEEN

I FELT MYSELF PRESSED AGAINST HIS SIDE, his arm around my shoulders. The lights of the city flashed past the tinted rear window of the car. My head was a blur and time seemed to slow. I was faintly aware of being in danger, but the blissed-out feeling still coursing through my veins kept me from minding. *He'd stopped feeding*, Ms Rational said sleepily. I was alone in a dark side road with him, he could have drained me and dumped my body with no one seeing. If he was ever going to do it, it would have been then, right after exposing his secret like that. We weren't in his home, or mine, where a dead body would be a serious problem. But he didn't kill me. He drank and he stopped and he told me I could have everything I wanted.

I had no doubt that he was a ruthless killer. But I also now had no doubt that he had genuine feelings for me.

I'd wanted things to be simple, but they'd only grown more complicated. If he'd wanted to kill me then going along with the shifters would have been easy. But now I was firmly wedged in the middle of a war.

One big question still stood in the way of my feelings for Antonio and I was far too frightened to ask it. For all my boldness in the street, I now felt like a vulnerable and foolish girl.

The car gently pulled to a halt outside my house. Antonio slid out and smoothly eased me onto the pavement. I was coming fully to my senses now and managed to stand with only a slight wobble. Antonio held me tight and helped me to the door. He fished my keys from my pocket and unlocked the door for me. With one hand he opened the door, with the other he pressed my keys into my palm.

'You're home.'

'Thank you. Would you like to—' He pressed a finger to my lips to silence me.

'Before you ask, you should know that I can't enter your home without an invitation.' His finger slipped from my lips and caressed my cheek.

'Oh.'

'It's only fair that you have all the information. Once you invite me in I can enter any time I wish. I could slip into your bedroom while you sleep and drain you dry before you can scream.'

He was so close to me, his voice barely audible. My breathing quickened as I imagined him sliding up my bed while I slept.

'I see.' My voice sounded far away.

'So don't invite me in now. Sleep on it. See how you feel tomorrow. If you decide never to extend that invitation but wish to continue on this path with me I would understand. If you need a safe place to retreat to, I understand. This thing with me, it puts you in danger. I want you to truly appreciate that.'

'I think I do.'

'Good.' He kissed my forehead and stepped away from my door. 'Buonanotte, mia cara.'

I watched him get into the car and drive away before going inside and closing the door. I leaned heavily against it and closed my eyes. It had been a long and exhausting evening. Tomorrow would be complicated. But for now I just needed to sleep.

I eased off my mother's boots and dragged my heavy legs up the stairs. I fell asleep on top of the covers, fully dressed. I don't remember dreaming that night but I woke up the next morning feeling groggy and weak.

I went to the bathroom, peeling off my clothes as I went. I looked at my reflection in the bathroom mirror. Ugly purple bruises had developed on my neck where he had gripped my throat.

I cringed as I examined it. My muscles felt tender. The memory of him pinning me against the shutter came back to me and something unpleasant squirmed inside me. He could have killed me. The fear was paralysing. I hated how helpless I had been and remembered why I was doing all of this. But I didn't want anyone to see the bruises. I felt ashamed of what had happened and couldn't let Peter or anyone else worry even more about me.

After I had showered, washed my make-up off and shaken off the lingering fog, my mind was clear enough to recognise that I was desperately hungry. I suddenly wished that I were at Peter's house, where Mrs Wilkes was sure to be serving a substantial breakfast. After establishing that all I had in my kitchen was a loaf of bread and some sausages in the freezer, I pulled on my coat and boots, wrapped a thick scarf around my bruised neck and set off for Peter's house.

I felt faint and the walk was a challenge. But the icy breeze kept me alert enough to make it around the corner. I knocked on the door and opened it without waiting for an answer.

'Hello?' I called as I moved down the hall. The house was quiet, but I could smell bacon.

'Eve?' Mrs Wilkes called. 'Is that you, dear?'

'Yes. I hope you don't mind.'

I stepped into the kitchen and found her sitting alone at the table with a coffee and a stack of bacon and eggs.

'Not at all, dear. Come on in.' Her eyes were red and puffy and I instantly felt as though I were intruding. 'You look pale. Are you all right?' She stood up and bustled about, fetching me orange juice, coffee and bacon.

'I'm okay, thanks. Just ready for breakfast. I haven't

had a chance to get food in at home yet.'

'Of course, of course. Here.' She served me some eggs and went to put bread in the toaster.

'Are you all right?' I asked, not quite looking at her.

'Oh yes. I'm sure everything is fine.'

'What do you mean? What's happened?' I couldn't eat the eggs. My heart was pounding.

'Peter didn't come home last night. Kirk says young men sometimes stay out and that I shouldn't worry. But of course I do.'

'Of course. I'm sure your husband is right, though.' I ate a mouthful of eggs, desperate for nourishment, despite the gnawing worry. 'Maybe he met someone and is busy getting to know them.' I tried to smile reassuringly and hoped that she would take my thinly veiled reference to her son's sex life as it was intended.

'Oh, Eve. I think we both know he only has eyes for one girl.' She smiled indulgently at me but I merely blinked at her. Girl? Peter? Didn't she know? She sat back down and picked at her own breakfast. 'But thank you,' she said. 'Maybe you're right.'

'Where's Mr Wilkes?'

'He had to go to a client early this morning. Some sort of tax issue.' She waved a hand dismissively. I nodded solemnly and continued to eat. The food was doing the trick and I was starting to feel more present and satiated. The hot coffee was the best part, warming my insides and giving me a slight buzz. 'I gather things are going well at the restaurant.'

'Hmm.' I hurriedly swallowed a mouthful of bacon and nodded. 'Yeah. Thanks to Mr Wilkes really. He's been fantastic. And the staff, they're troopers.'

'Don't sell yourself short. I'm sure you've kept everyone going.' She smiled again.

'Thank you.' I looked down at my food, doubting that was the case. 'Did you know that my parents wanted me to go to university in Caerton because they had friends there?'

'Yes, I remember something about that. They knew someone who moved there, I think, and went to stay once. You stayed here for a few days.'

'Yes, I remember. I was nine.'

'That's right.' She nodded wistfully. 'I think they got on well with the people they met on that trip because they stayed in touch.'

'Did any of them come here to visit?'

'From time to time, yes. I know that when you and Peter were considering your university options, your parents talked about you going there and it was their strong preference.'

'They knew a professor at the university.'

'That's right, yes. I met her once or twice. Interesting woman.' She emphasised the word "interesting" in a way that suggested it wasn't exactly what she meant. I stifled a laugh. 'Why are you asking, dear?'

'Just curious really. I feel a bit like I never really got to know my parents very well. I think that relationship changes when you become an adult. I missed out on it.'

'True.' She gave me that sad smile that I was so accustomed to these days. 'But you knew the most important thing; that they loved you very much and wanted you to be happy.'

'Thank you.' A tear filled my eye and I brushed it away, looking resolutely at my coffee cup.

'Hello?' Kirk's voice called from the hall and the front door clicked shut. I hadn't heard him come in. Mrs Wilkes jumped up and dashed down the hall to greet him. 'Any word?'

'No, not yet. Eve's here. She hasn't seen him.' The two of them entered the kitchen and Kirk and I exchanged meaningful glances.

'Would you mind taking this upstairs, sweetheart?' Mr Wilkes held up his briefcase. His wife took it and disappeared up the stairs. He sat down wearily next to me. 'His phone wouldn't work if it was on his person when he shifted form.' His voice was very low.

'Right. So he could just be gallivanting about as a fox somewhere then?'

'Yes. You're safe and well, then?'

'Yes. Listen, I need to talk to you properly.'

'Likewise. Can you meet Weaver and me this afternoon?'

'In the catacombs?'

'Yes. It's the safest place.'

'Okay.'

Mrs Wilkes' footsteps were jogging down the stairs and we both fell silent and inched away from each other. I picked up my glass of orange juice and drank it all in one go. The sugar was much needed. I stood up, my chair scraping noisily across the flagstone floor.

'Are you going already?' Mrs Wilkes asked, her face a little panicky.

'I'm afraid so. I need to get some shopping in and then go to Piero's.'

'I'll see you out.' Kirk stood up and held a hand out to indicate for me to go ahead of him. We walked quickly to the front door.

'Will Antonio be asleep? Does he sleep in a coffin all day?' I whispered hurriedly.

'He can't go out, but I don't think he sleeps. I don't really know. Why?'

'I'll ask him about Peter.'

'Careful.' He grasped my arm and glared at me. 'Antonio?' He raised an eyebrow.

'Vitale.' I tugged my arm free and opened the door. 'So I'll see you at the restaurant this afternoon to go over the books?' I raised my voice louder than was strictly necessary so that Mrs Wilkes would hear.

'That's right.' He glowered at me, more angry than I'd

ever seen him. I swept out through the door and marched down the street. The bright light was dazzling after the dull light of the Wilkes's kitchen. I was flustered and irritated. I wanted to tell Kirk that he didn't need to be afraid any more. But bitterness tainted the news that I'd made a good deal with Antonio. He would see, once he knew the full story, that I'd saved his family.

As I walked, I held my phone in a trembling hand and called Antonio's number. It rang for a full thirty seconds, which felt like an age. I was nearly at my door and sure that it was about to go to voicemail when the ringing stopped and a slightly groggy voice greeted me.

'Eve?' It was him. I let out a shaking breath.

'Morning. I'm sorry to trouble you, it's just that my friend is missing and I wanted to check—' What on earth was I going to say? Did you eat him?

'I understand,' he said softly, his voice a little weary. 'I know of no reason why anyone you know would be missing. I promise.'

'Okay. Thank you. I'm so sorry that I had to ask.'

'Not at all. You're checking all bases. I'm sorry to have put you in that position in the first place.'

'Thank you. I'm sorry if I interrupted anything or if you need to sleep, or something.' I felt my cheeks burning as if he was staring me down, even though he was just on the phone.

'I need very little sleep, don't worry.' I could hear a

smile in his voice.

'Oh, okay. Good. Well, I'll see you soon.'

'Are you all right?' His question stopped me from ending the call. I leaned heavily against my front door and rubbed my eyes with my free hand.

'A little tired. I've had breakfast. I'll be okay once I know where Peter is.'

'I see. Make sure you drink plenty of water. You'll be fine, I promise.'

'Thank you.'

'I hope you find your friend. If there is anything I can do to help please just ask.'

'Thank you,' I said again, a little surprised and touched. 'When will I see you again?'

'Hmm, I'm not sure.' I could hear that smile again and knew he was teasing me. 'I have business to attend to this evening. If you feel up to a late night I could see you later. Midnight?'

'I could probably manage that.' I found myself smiling broadly and drew my lower lip up between my teeth.

'Excellent. I'll call you once my business is concluded. Is that all right?'

'Sure.'

'Take care of yourself, Eve. See you tonight.'

'I will. Bye.'

I ended the call and lingered there on my doorstep, staring at my phone without really seeing it. With a heavy sigh, I unlocked the door and went inside. I made my way to the kitchen and was about to pour a glass of water when a clattering sound in the basement stopped me in my tracks.

I went to the hatch in the closet, it was closed. I quietly opened it and peered into the shadows below. It was pitch black but there was definitely movement. A shape moved into the shaft of light from the open hatch.

'Eve?' Peter's voice croaked.

'Oh thank God!' I hooked the hatch against the wall, flicked on the light and bolted down the wooden stairs. I flung my arms around him and he held me tight. 'Your mother is worried out of her mind.' I pulled back and whacked him on the arm. He flinched.

'I'll go home in a bit.'

'Are you all right? Are you hurt?' I looked him over and saw that he was struggling to put any weight on his right foot and he clutched at his side.

'I got into a bit of a fight. I'm fine. I heal fast.' He staggered sideways and sat awkwardly on the edge of a crate.

'Who were you fighting with?'

'Not a who. A what.'

'A vampire?' I asked, my throat tight and teeth clenched.

'Something else.'

'What else is there?' I blurted the words, not caring to

keep my volume down, and he winced slightly.

'Other stuff. I can't really explain. It's complicated.'

'Try.' I crossed my arms over my chest and stared down at him.

Behind him the trapdoor to the cave stood open, the floorboards askew from where he had pushed his way through and made that noise.

'There's another dimension, sort of.' He stalled and frowned, still clutching his side. I tapped my foot impatiently. 'Sorry. I'm trying to use words you'll understand.'

'Hey!'

'Sorry, it's just different, we have this whole other language.'

'Oh.' I looked sheepishly at the floor and shuffled my feet.

'It's a place called Hepethia. Normally only shifters can go there, but sometimes there are doorways that humans can go through. Anyway, there are other things there, demons, basically.'

'Demons?' I glared at him and then glanced at the trapdoor. 'Can they get through?'

'It depends on the demon. Don't worry, nothing followed me. There's nothing here.'

'Demons, though?' I felt as though the wind had been knocked out of me and I let out a slightly hysterical laugh.

'It's a lot to take in.'

'Yeah. It really is. I'm glad you're okay.'

'Right back at you.' He glanced towards my neck, which was still wrapped in my scarf.

'Oh I'm fine. Worried about you, but otherwise peachy.'

'Did you have a good date?' There was a sourness on his tongue and he didn't look at me directly.

'It was productive, actually.'

'Oh?'

'I'll tell you later. We're meeting down there this afternoon.' I nodded my head towards the trapdoor. 'I'll tell everyone together.'

'Okay, that sounds... interesting.'

'Don't worry. It's good news. Very good news.'

CHAPTER SEVENTEEN

"Just wanted to let you know that my friend turned up. He's fine. Just had a big night out. Boys. Thanks for understanding why I rang. See you later x"

I stared at the text and read it six times before hitting the send button.

I gave Peter some toast and coffee and by the time he had eaten he was no longer limping or clutching his side.

'Apologise to your mother for worrying her,' I warned him as I saw him out of the door.

'I will. See you later.' He hugged me again and set off for home.

Antonio hadn't replied to my message and I tried not to let it bother me. It was best to keep busy, I decided. I ran my errands and ate a good lunch. I was just washing up when my phone bleeped with an incoming message.

"I'm pleased your friend is ok. See you tonight x" It wasn't much, but I couldn't help grinning when I read Antonio's words.

Just before 3 pm, there was a knock at my front door.

I went to it and Peter and his dad were standing there.

'Hi, come in.' I stood aside and they passed me to head back to the kitchen.

'Weaver will meet us down there,' Kirk said over his shoulder. I closed the door and locked it. It would be getting dark in just over an hour. Even though Antonio had explained about not being able to enter my home, I didn't want to chance any intruder gaining entry while we were tucked away under the house. Although given what I was learning about the world, I supposed that a simple lock wouldn't keep much out.

I had left the hatch open and closed the kitchen blinds, but Kirk and Peter waited for me in the kitchen. Kirk fixed me with narrowed eyes, his arms crossed over his chest.

'So, I was called out to the Vitale house this morning.'

'Oh?' I asked, unsure where to look.

'Vitale told me that I was getting a pay rise and that my donations would no longer be required.'

'Donations?' Peter asked, frowning. A moment later he caught up and smacked his own forehead lightly.

'I take it I have you to thank for this?' Kirk said, looking pointedly at me.

'Well, yes,' I replied.

'He just did what you asked?' Peter asked, disbelief written on his face. 'No strings attached?'

'He has feelings for me,' I said, not looking at either of

them. I couldn't tell them about the strings. I kept my hands resolutely away from the polo neck of my shirt. 'That gives me some influence, it seems.'

Kirk let out a gruff "hm" and shook his head. He wasn't as pleased as I'd wanted him to be. I'd expected some sign of gratitude, but he just seemed annoyed with me.

I cleared my throat and moved over to the closet. 'Shall we head down there then?' I set off down the stairs into the basement without looking back but I heard them following me. 'It's a little unsettling, you know? Knowing that people can get into my basement down here.'

'I bet. Sorry about surprising you this morning.' Peter sounded suitably contrite and I wondered what he had told his mother. He passed me at the foot of the stairs and lifted the trapdoor as easily as if it weighed nothing. I hadn't bothered to cover it with the floorboards that morning. It was too much effort if we were going to be using the door regularly. I would have to figure out another way to conceal it.

The three of us filed inside and Kirk closed the door behind us.

The strip light in the cave below lit the way down the narrow steps. I was relying on Peter to lead the way, feeling carefully with my feet for each step.

We stepped down into the cave. It felt like such an odd thing to have under my house. I was still somewhat puzzled by it all. Weaver was sitting on one of the crates, one leg crossed over the other. Her fingers glistened with rings and her hair hung loose over her shoulders. She looked up at us over her glasses.

'Everyone all right?' she asked, her wise eyes narrowed slightly as she looked over each of our faces.

'Fine.' I slapped on a bright smile. Peter and Kirk made non-committal noises from their throats.

'I see.' Weaver got to her feet. 'Let's go, shall we?' She set off along the dark passage away from my house. Peter followed close behind and I grabbed hold of his hand to help guide me. I could hardly see a thing, but I guessed their eyes were sharper. I lit the torch on my phone to help me pick my way along the passage.

The shadows danced up the curved walls and I remembered what Peter had said about demons. I found myself glancing nervously over my shoulder every few steps but all I saw behind me was Kirk, half in shadow and looking determined.

'Where are we going?' I whispered after a while.

'Deeper in,' Weaver said softly from the front of our bizarre caravan.

Soon after, the passage widened and Peter no longer had to walk with a slight stoop. We had been heading steadily downhill, shallow enough that I didn't notice right away, but now the path levelled out and I realised how far down we'd come. The air was tight and cool. The passage was absolutely dry and the ground slightly dusty. The walls were smooth and the ground fairly level. It had the feel of a place designed for easy passage, rather than a natural formation.

Every now and then I caught sight of the white torchlight glinting on tiny fragments of precious stones in the walls, crystals of every hue peeked through the rock. We came to a short set of steps down, neatly formed brick steps that contrasted with the bare rock. At the foot of the steps a vast cavern opened up. It was too big for the torchlight to reach the walls or ceiling, and as our feet made contact with the ground the sound echoed all around us. I shone my light overhead to see an archway of large, sandstone bricks set into the rock above the passage entrance.

Shadows across the cavern moved and I flinched, clinging tightly to Peter's arm and shining my torch into the black. Weaver lifted her hand over her head, her fingers were splayed out. With a flick of her wrist, a small flame erupted in her palm and she waved her arm in a great arc over her head. The fire danced out of her hand and burst out in a dozen small balls of flame. They sped away from her and landed in torches set into the walls around the cavern.

Light blazed all around us and I gasped as the whole place came to life. The source of the movement became clear. Around a dozen animals stood there in silence.

Badgers, cats, foxes, owls and wolves made up the odd menagerie.

One by one, they shimmered and shifted form until a group of ordinary-looking humans faced us. Well, almost ordinary. I couldn't help but notice some oddities about some of them. One woman was dressed in shorts and a vest and her skin was completely covered in tattoos. She had at least half a dozen piercings on her face. One man, who had been a wolf to one side of the group, was nearly seven feet tall and had a huge axe strapped to his back.

I was still clinging to Peter and I looked up into his face. He was looking back down at me with a broad grin.

'What do you think?'

'I'm kind of speechless.'

'I thought you might be.'

'Do you know them all?' I was whispering and my voice was covered by Weaver and Kirk's animated greeting of each of the shifters.

'No, only a few.'

'Who's the human?' the man with the axe said in a booming voice that echoed off the walls. He shook Kirk's hand but his eyes were fixed on me. My skin broke out in goosebumps.

'This is Eve,' Kirk replied. 'Daughter of Mother-of-the-Forest and Red Wolf.' It felt strange hearing my parents referred to by their shifter names, names I had only heard for the first time so recently.

'Or Mum and Dad, to me,' I mumbled. Peter let out a throaty chuckle and tugged his arm free in order to throw it around my shoulders. He dragged me forwards into the loose circle that had formed. People were talking in hushed voices, shaking hands and slapping one another on the back. I had never felt so out of place in my life.

'Thank you all for coming,' Kirk said, his voice carrying and bringing the others to silence. 'You all know Weaver-of-Sky's-Loom, our friend from the south.' There was a murmur of recognition. 'And Eve is here as my special guest. She may be unchanged, but her blood is shifter-kind. Her parents began this initiative and their deaths have brought Eve into the fold. She had a right to know who her parents really were, why they died, and to have a role in avenging them, if she wishes.' I stared at him with wide eyes. He was a fine orator, a trait I had never witnessed in him before. But his talk of vengeance startled me. Heads nodded all around the circle and the man with the axe folded his thick arms across his chest and fixed me with an intense but not unkind stare.

'When are we making a move on the Camorra?' one of the women called. She had a rough voice and short, spiky hair.

'All in good time,' Kirk replied.

'They've killed two of us. It might not be long before they move to take out more.'

'Yes, but if we move too soon we could all be killed in

the attempt,' Kirk said, a little weariness seeping into his voice. I got the feeling they had gone over this many times.

'But when will we be ready? What else needs to happen?' the woman with the tattoos asked.

'You've all heard me say it before, but you really need to be ready to take on the guarding of the veil.' Weaver's voice was almost musical. I turned to face her, as did every other eye in the cavern. I had no idea what she meant, but I longed to hear more. 'Each of you needs to be ready for that. You've been paying the Camorra to do it for you for over a hundred years. You can't take them out without structures in place to pick up the job.'

There were murmurs around the circle, some nodded, others were shaking their heads.

'We've decided how to divide up the city. We've started to assemble into packs. I know we still have a few disagreements to iron out, but we're nearly there.' Kirk looked around the circle as he spoke and I wondered where the rest of them were and why each of these shifters was here when others were not. Were these the leaders of the packs? 'We also have an ace up our sleeves. An advantage that we can hopefully utilise.' Kirk glanced sideways at me and gave me an encouraging smile. He expected me to speak. I shook my head and leaned closer to Peter. He squeezed my shoulders and ducked his head to whisper in my ear.

'It's okay. Speak, or not, it's your call.'

'Eve here is a Seer,' Kirk said and every head swivelled to look at me. 'We've never had one resident here before. Weaver's visions have proved useful, but as she is rarely here and only occasionally sees things pertinent to our situation, it may be beneficial to have Eve in the fold. Further to that, she is partially immune to the Vitales' powers.'

Loud cries of surprise rippled around the circle. I felt terribly awkward and withered under the gaze of the strange shifters.

'What was your good news?' Peter asked me, just loud enough to be heard by those closest to us. They fell quiet and the others gradually turned their attention to us. I cleared my throat and a strange guttural noise leaked out but no words.

'Ah, yeah, well, I wasn't expecting to share it with a room full of shifters, so...'

'It's okay.' Peter squeezed me again.

'You didn't seem too pleased when I told you in my kitchen,' I said under my breath.

'Right, well, it's a lot to take in,' Peter replied, his grip on my shoulders loosening.

'You're telling me.' I shook my head. Everyone was still looking at me. The man with the axe had his arms crossed over his chest and was glaring at me, his jaw twitching. I cleared my throat. 'I— I have the favour of Antonio Vitale.' Someone across the circle snorted. I swallowed hard and went on. 'He likes me. He took an interest in me after my parents died and I went along with it. Not out of choice, I think you all know how it is.' Most of them nodded, some shifted their feet and looked at the ground. They knew exactly what I meant. 'I figured out what he was when his glamour didn't quite work on me. I've been able to spend some time with him completely in my right mind.'

'Have you got any information from him?' the tattooed woman called.

'Not exactly, but he— he seems to be open to giving me things.'

'What things?' Axe Man asked.

'Things I ask for. Favours.' I could feel my face burning and my palms were sweating. Why was this so hard? I was afraid to give the whole truth and was picking my words.

'It's true,' Kirk said. Silence fell again. 'Vitale told me this morning that no one would be feeding on my blood any more. He said that he values the work I do for him and he wanted me to know that I was appreciated and safe.' He gave a shrug and glanced warily at me. 'Eve made that happen,' Kirk finished.

'How?' demanded Axe Man.

'We had quite a frank discussion and he agreed to what I asked,' I replied.

Gasps and incredulous looks shot around the circle.

'A frank discussion?' Kirk raised his eyes to the ceiling.

'He knew that I knew,' I said. 'He's not stupid. So I took control of the situation and told him that I knew what he was and used his infatuation with me to my advantage.'

'And what does he get in exchange for my safety?' Kirk looked as though he knew the answer. Peter had gone completely rigid beside me. His arm was no longer around my shoulders. I looked from father to son, a sinking feeling in my stomach. They weren't as pleased as they should have been and I felt like I had massively trampled all over their plans.

'A relationship with me.' I held my chin high and fought back the tears that were tingling the corners of my eyes.

'Eve...' Kirk shook his head and let his chin drop to his chest.

'That was very brave,' Weaver said softly. She was suddenly by my side and she slipped her arms around me and pulled me into a hug. 'I think your parents would be proud.'

'No, they'd be terrified.' Kirk's voice was stony.

Weaver released me and squared up to him.

'Yes, they would. But they would be proud as well. Eve stood up for her friends and family, she has taken on a huge risk in order to protect those she loves. I think she is becoming exactly the young woman they wanted her to be.'

'Thank you,' I croaked, my throat suddenly tight.

'We don't have much time before sunset.' Weaver looked around at everyone. 'Keep your counsel about what you've heard here today. We don't know yet what it may mean. We proceed with the plan, so organise your packs, patrol your territories discreetly and keep any arrangements you currently have with the Camorra until we give the word. We can't let their human allies know what's happening. So keep up appearances. I know how that makes you all feel, but it's so important if we're going to succeed.'

The circle broke up into lively chatter and people kept sneaking glances at me, but I saw them all. I hugged my arms around myself and felt a shiver go through me. Peter moved away from me, shaking his head, and went to talk to a couple of shifters on the other side of the cavern.

I watched him go, feeling confused and abandoned. Weaver turned back to me and looked at me with sympathy. 'May we talk?' she asked. I nodded and she led me away towards the arch that we had entered under. 'Has he fed from you?'

'Yes.' My voice trembled.

'Has he got into your head?'

'Yes.'

'Have you had trouble distinguishing your decisions from his will?'

'Early on, yes. But not now.'

'I see. Have you considered that he has more of a hold

on you than you realise? What feels like free will could really be him controlling you.'

I blanched and felt a wave of nausea come over me. I couldn't answer her. 'It's okay. Every shifter in the city has been in the thrall of one or other of the Vitales. They all understand. Your parents were made to submit to regular blood donations and they did so willingly, or so they thought, for many years. Kirk too. He didn't want you to fall into the same trap, he loves you like a daughter and he wanted to spare you all of this.'

'I know.' I looked across at Peter. He was listening to the others talking, but he seemed a million miles away. Was he as worried about me as his father?

'I think he's hurt,' Weaver said softly. I looked at her, frowning. 'He may see it as a betrayal, you being with Vitale.'

'That's nonsense.'

'It's just a theory.' Weaver patted my shoulder. I nodded solemnly and turned my thoughts away from Peter. It was too confusing to try and get my head around.

'You didn't approach me in Caerton because of my art, and you never mentioned knowing my parents.'

'No. Well, no, your art is spectacular, actually. I draw, not like you, but it's something I do. So I did like your art, I never lied about that. But your parents and I thought it would be best if you didn't know of our connection immediately.'

'How did you ever meet in the first place?'

'Your mother and I had a common ancestor, several generations back, before the war here. Two brothers went their separate ways and one of them ended up in Caerton. My family was descended from him. Artemis sent me a vision of an ancient conflict and it prompted me to examine my family tree. I set out to trace the missing line that we had no record of and I found your mother. It was a hard time for me, I had recently lost people in a terrible war, including my own sister. I felt that all family was precious and reached out to your mother. We wrote to each other at first and then arranged to meet. She told me about shifter life here and I didn't entirely like what I heard. So I agreed to help put it right.'

'Why has it taken so long?'

'Because there were only half a dozen shifters here then and they didn't all know each other. Nothing could be done with such small numbers. But if I had marched into the city with an army it would have been slaughter and humans would have been caught in the middle. It had to be done carefully. My own community was still weakened after the war we had endured, so we couldn't leave Caerton in large numbers either. But we were organised; we were good at tracing potential shifters who might change and sorting them into packs as soon as they changed, so our population was growing swiftly. We began syphoning willing volunteers to move here. Too many at once would have got the attention of the vampires. So it was just one or two a year at first. Your parents wanted to stop about five years ago. So we did. I was never really sure why. Then six months ago they said we had to pick it up again. Just before your parents died we decided the numbers were favourable here at last.'

'Do you think that's why they were killed? Do the Camorra suspect?'

'I think that is entirely likely.'

'Do you think I'm right to try to stay close to Antonio?'

'I can't say. I know that you have good intentions, and it may be possible to find out what he knows, if you're careful.'

'I'll try. I'm seeing him again tonight. I want to make my parents proud. I don't want their deaths to have been in vain. What they started here...' I gestured around, '...I want to finish it. I want everyone to be free.'

Weaver nodded and patted my shoulder again.

'I'm glad to hear it.'

'Profess— sorry, Weaver, when you gave me those memories, I felt your loss and something about a child. Who was that?'

'Amy.' Weaver smiled. 'That was Amy.'

'Was she yours?'

'No. She was the daughter of my Alpha. You should know, under normal circumstances, it is quite common for shifters to send their children away for their protection.

Usually much younger than you were.'

'I see. Alpha? What is that?'

'The shifter in charge of a pack. Kirk will be the Alpha of his pack when they settle it all. He's the eldest and most experienced.'

'Are you the Alpha of your pack?'

'No,' she said with a wry smile. 'Alphas don't tend to leave their packs alone. They shouldn't even leave their city. My Alpha can spare me for a few days at a time.'

'Whatever happened to Amy?' I asked, curiosity burning and a strange connection to this girl forming.

'She's doing just fine.' Weaver smiled warmly. 'Come, let's straighten things out with that boy of yours.'

'He's not my boy.' Weaver raised an eyebrow and swooped away, her long skirt billowing out behind her. I gave a little shake of my head at her odd remark and followed her. I felt a little better about things and more certain than I had been about what side I needed to be on in this insane battle.

CHAPTER EIGHTEEN

SOME OF THE SHIFTERS HAD DRIFTED AWAY down various tunnels that led out of the cavern. Kirk was talking to Axe Man and Tattoo Woman, as I had taken to calling them in my head. Peter was with an older woman with a shock of wispy, grey hair. She had a crossbow strapped to her back and looked wild and fierce. Weaver led me towards Peter, smiling at me over her shoulder.

There was a sudden rumble and the ground shook beneath my feet. Dust sprinkled from the ceiling and every head in the place whipped from side to side to locate the source. Weaver struck out her arm to halt me but I had already stopped and was sheltering my eyes from the falling dust.

Another rumble shook the cave and an ear-splitting roar echoed all around us. A scream caught in my throat and I stood paralysed in terror. The shifters scrambled frantically into a cluster around Weaver and me. Those with weapons drew them. There was Axe Man, the woman with the crossbow, and various other swords and hammers. I looked around, quickly counting nine remaining shifters.

A third rumble that felt nearer echoed all around the cavern. From one of the wider passages leading away from the place came a slight billow of dust and tiny, loose stones. I watched, wide-eyed, as a dark hand with huge claws appeared out of the shadows and wrapped itself around the edge of the passage, gripping the stone and pulling itself through the opening. There was a loud scraping sound like nails down a blackboard and I clamped my hands over my ears.

The thing dragged itself out of the passage like something emerging from an egg, uncurling itself for the first time. It was midnight black and covered in hard plates like armour, underneath which ran rivulets of bright lava. The whole thing smoked and hissed and its enormous feet landed with thuds that shook the floor.

'Demon?' I asked in a petrified squeak.

'Demon,' Weaver said. How was she so calm? 'Okay guys, we've got this.'

'We've never faced anything this big before.' Peter's voice shook.

'Size is irrelevant,' Weaver said. Several shifters around me whimpered with doubt. 'Kirk, talk to it.'

'Talk to it?' His head whipped around to glare at her.

'Talk to it. That should always be the first course of action. It's in the wrong realm, it might be frightened and trying to get home. Crystal, get ready.'

I looked from face to face to identify who Weaver was talking to. It was the tattooed woman. She looked stony-faced and gave a firm nod. She pulled a small pack from her back and began rummaging through it. Kirk stepped out of the cluster slightly and held up his hands.

The demon looked down at us all; its huge red eyes shone and sparks flew out of them. It roared and hot air blasted down from its maw, blowing my hair and stinging my eyes.

'Blazing Furnace,' Crystal hissed, pushing past me to get to Kirk. 'That's its name.' She stood beside Kirk with a fist closed tightly around something.

'Blazing Furnace,' Kirk said, his voice booming out with authority. The demon tilted its head and peered down at the tiny figure that had spoken. 'We mean you no harm, but we will defend ourselves. State your reason for being here.' The demon took a step towards us and roared again.

'Okay, I don't think it's capable of reason,' Kirk said, stepping back. Crystal opened her palm and a blinding white light erupted from it. I squinted through the dazzling light and saw the demon flinch.

'I want you to run for the passage we entered through,' Weaver hissed in my ear. 'On my signal.' I nodded and got ready to bolt.

One by one, the shifters around me began to shudder. Their bodies were growing larger, hair erupting from under their skin, their faces became the muzzles of bears. Weaver moved between them and flicked her hands out ahead of her, small flames bursting to life in her palms. 'Eve! Run!' I hesitated just long enough to see her shift into a beast in a second flat, far faster than the others.

I sprinted out from the circle of terrifying beasts and into the arched passage. I skidded to a halt and crouched in the shadows, clinging to the rock as I watched the eruption of utter chaos.

Crystal hadn't shifted, she was standing there with her hand raised over her head and that bright light glowing like a flare in her hand. The demon was shielding its eyes from the light and staggering sideways.

I couldn't make out one shifter from another, except Weaver, whose palms were still on fire. She threw a fireball at the demon and struck it on the shoulder. It hissed and smoke billowed out from the plate that she'd hit. I wanted to know which of these creatures was Peter, but they all looked much the same to me.

They piled forward to attack the demon. Roars, snarls and growls rent the air and fur physically flew in all directions as their savagery was let loose. Weaver continued to hurl fireballs at the demon and Crystal held still though I could see her arm shaking.

The demon thrashed out with its talons and ripped through flesh. Splatters of blood whipped out from torn limbs, leaving streaks across the cavern floor.

I crouched there, silent and shaking, tears flowing down my face.

One of the shifters was thrown back from the fight by a sweep of the demon's arm. It skidded across the floor towards me and lay still, its eyes open and fixed on me. I covered my hand with my mouth to stifle a scream.

'Don't be Peter, please, don't be Peter. Or Kirk. Please,' I whimpered quietly to myself and whatever deity might be watching over these events. I couldn't watch any more. I turned away, pressing my back against the cool stone and closing my eyes. I could still hear the fight. The roars, howls, thuds of the demon's feet stomping the ground, the hiss of smoke, the ripping, tearing sounds. The air was thick with the smell of smoke and hot from the fire. I could taste ash as I gasped for breath.

There was a loud clatter and something that might have been a cheer from the snouts of shifters. I chanced a glance and saw that someone had wrenched off the chest plate of the demon's armour. But the cheers were short-lived as lava oozed free from the demon, spilling onto the ground with a violent hiss, scorching everything it touched. Shifters yowled and leapt away, their fur and skin burning.

Crystal was wavering, she staggered away from the fight and I saw her arm begin to drop, the light flickered and threatened to go out. Without even thinking, I ran to her and held her up.

'Can I take it? Will it work for me?'

She shrugged, apparently unable to talk. She was trembling all over and she gave way, slumping against me. I reached for her hand and saw a small piece of clear quartz tucked into her fist. I uncurled her fingers and took hold of it. She clasped my other hand and nodded. I thrust my hand upwards and felt a rush of cool air as if I were standing on a strong air vent. My hair billowed around me and the quartz burst to life in my hand.

The demon again backed away from the shifters, blinded by the light. It stumbled into the passage it had crawled out of and got wedged there.

Lava was creeping across the floor towards myself and Crystal. I tugged on her arm and we stepped backwards, though she was barely on her feet. I began to understand why. My arm was shaking and my body was growing weaker. Whatever power was fuelling the crystal was draining energy from my body. We stumbled together towards the edge of the cavern and watched as the shifters tore into the prone demon. It roared in pain but all it could do was thrash in place.

'It's weak enough now. We have to send it across the veil,' Crystal whimpered.

'I don't know what that means,' I said, looking at her in horror.

She peeled the crystal from my hand and thrust it up into the air again, but the crystal flickered feebly. 'Weaver!' I screamed, searching the fray for her. Her fireballs had gone out and she looked just like every other beast in the fight. 'Weaver!'

A figure peeled itself out of the fight and bounded over to us on four strong legs. She shifted form mid-bound and landed gracefully on two human feet right in front of us.

'Good job, both of you. Let me take that now.' She prised the quartz from Crystal's hand and threw it up into the air. With a flick of her wrist she sent a fireball up to meet it in mid-air. The two collided and there was a crack of thunder. A flare blazed out from the crystal, filling the cavern with blinding light. There was another snap and the demon shimmered and vanished, along with all of its spilt lava, though the ground remained scorched and partially melted in places. The quartz dropped to floor, glowing dimly in the torchlight.

The shifters slowly regained their human forms and I searched their faces for Peter and Kirk. With a shaking sigh of relief, I saw them both, their arms around each other. Kirk was limping and Peter supported him. They were both bleeding.

The body on the floor remained unmoving and someone went to it.

'He's alive,' Weaver said, without needing to go closer. 'He would have reverted to his human form by now if not. See to his wounds and he may yet survive.'

'You could try for a little more sympathy,' Axe Man snapped at Weaver.

'That was sloppy. It's a miracle no one died. None of you are ready. You need to learn how to fight as a unit. If not all of you together, then at least in your packs. Get out of here now and go and get ready. When you face the vampires they won't spit lava but they will have sharper minds.'

She turned and swooped away up one of the passages. The rest of us looked at each other, shock written on every face.

'Yeah, but, demon,' Peter said, a grin spreading over his face.

'That was actually seriously cool,' Axe Man said and he broke into a gruff laugh. Others laughed in relief and everyone began to relax.

'Will you be all right?' I asked Crystal as we helped each other to our feet and brushed dust off ourselves.

'Yeah. Thanks for your help. Look, I didn't know your parents. I only changed a couple of months ago. But I reckon they would be damn proud of you today. What you're doing with the vampire is really brave and what you did here today, well, I reckon you saved lives. So, be proud of yourself.'

'Thanks,' I said, blushing and looking at the floor. 'How did you know the name of that demon?'

'I'm a crescent moon. It's my gift from Artemis.' She spoke as if it were obvious. I smiled and nodded as if I understood. My questions about moons and Artemis would have to wait.

A few of the shifters were moving the unconscious beast, sharing the weight to take him away. Kirk and Peter made their way over to me.

'What you did was commendable,' Kirk said, not quite looking me in the eye.

'Yeah. You could have been badly hurt, or worse.' Peter was still helping his father stand, but he looked a bit sheepish and boyish. 'I'm glad you're okay.'

'Thanks. I couldn't do much.' My eyes ached. My skin felt awful; dirty and sweaty and that uncomfortable feeling of dried tears on my face. 'I really want to go home and get cleaned up.'

'Of course. We'll walk you back.' Kirk heaved himself away from Peter and gave his lame leg a shake. Peter threw him an expression of concern and Kirk waved a dismissive hand. 'I'll be all right, just need to walk it off.'

We bid farewell to the other shifters and everyone went on their way. Kirk led the way up the passage we had entered along, with me in the middle and Peter at the back. Kirk's limp did gradually wear off as we walked, healing as swiftly as I'd seen Peter heal before.

I tried not to think about what I'd witnessed in the cavern, but flashes of it intruded as we walked in silence away from the scene.

'Will that demon be able to come back?' I asked tentatively.

'I don't know,' Kirk said soberly. 'It depends how it got here. Demons are from another realm. They can usually only get into Hepethia or the human world if summoned, or if extraordinary events pull them here.'

'Do you think someone could have summoned it here, then?' I asked, unable to hide the alarm from my voice.

'Yes, I do. One of the ways the vampires have controlled us all these years is by guarding the veil between worlds for us. They know all about the veil and demons. It's normally a shifter responsibility. It's our reason for being on Earth. But after the great war, there were too few of us to do it. The Camorra arrived and offered to do it for us, if we paid them. Of course we agreed, we had no choice. Over the years, even as our population began to recover, we forgot how to do it, or even that we had to. We didn't form packs any more, we weren't organised and we didn't fulfil our responsibilities. That's what Weaver is helping us to get on top of.'

'She was pretty angry back there,' Peter piped up from behind me.

'She was right to be. Most of us have rarely shifted into the Agrius before, let alone fought a mighty demon like that. We didn't have a clue what we were doing. We have a lot to learn.'

'Why haven't you been preparing? You've been sneaking shifters into the city for years. Shouldn't you have been training to fight too?'

'Some of us have. Not everyone was here today. We were down a number of capable warriors. But what we've been lacking is teamwork.' Kirk's voice had softened as we walked up the narrow passage, he sounded tired but less stern than he had been. I hoped that his attitude towards me was softening too.

When we reached my basement, we concealed the entrance to the catacombs and headed upstairs to the kitchen. It was dark and Kirk turned on lights and went about making us all coffee. Every part of me ached. The clock on the wall showed 6 pm. As if on cue, my stomach rumbled.

'I get like that after a fight too,' Peter said, a chuckle chasing his words. We both laughed and Kirk joined in with a gruff little laugh of his own.

'I'm sure Marianne would be happy to feed us all,' Kirk offered, while pouring steaming water from the kettle into three coffee cups.

'I don't want to impose,' I replied. 'You've fed me so much since I got back.'

'It's not an imposition, Eve. You're family.'

I smiled and Peter pulled me into a one-armed hug. A vision coursed through my mind, causing every muscle to go rigid.

I saw Peter shifting form and leaping into battle. Kirk too and the others. But it wasn't a memory. This was something else. There was a demon twice the size of the one we had just vanquished. It had slick, black tentacles that thrashed at the shifters attacking it. Among them was Antonio. I recognised his long hair, but everything else about him was frighteningly alien, with claws and vicious fangs protruding from his top gum. Lucia was there too, no beauty left in her features. The two sides clashed in a brutal and bloody battle. The demon's roars filled the air and shifters were dropping left and right.

I shook out of it and found myself in Peter's arms, with Kirk standing right in front of me looking worried.

'What did you see?' he asked.

'The end,' I said, shaking and trying to stand. 'The end of everything.'

CHAPTER NINETEEN

I was supplied with strong coffee and a biscuit. The three of us sat at the kitchen table in silence after I recounted my vision.

'So, they can definitely summon demons, then?' Peter said at last.

'Looks that way,' Kirk replied. His hands were wrapped around a steaming mug and he stared intently into it.

'It's not certain though, is it? Aren't these visions supposed to be warnings? That's what Weaver says.' Peter was looking from me to his father with the bright-eyed enthusiasm of a puppy. I shrugged. I had no idea how my gift worked. I had generally only picked up memories and present thoughts before. Seeing the future was new territory.

Kirk said nothing. We slowly drank our coffee and once Kirk had finished his cup he stood up, his chair scraping across the kitchen floor.

'Let's go eat. I'm sure this will be dealt with in due

course.'

Peter and I exchanged nervous glances.

'I have to shower. I'll meet you there in a bit. Let your mum know to expect company, okay?' I said. Peter nodded and followed his father to the door. I locked it after them and went upstairs, stripping off my clothes on my way to the bathroom.

I started running the shower in a haze, still shaken from the battle and the vision. When I stepped inside the narrow cubicle it was like entering a soothing cocoon. The water was hot and the glass quickly steamed up. The water flowed over my hair and skin, soothing every ache and washing away the grime. Looking down I saw the dirt swirling at my feet before disappearing down the drain. It was strangely symbolic, I thought.

Once I had shampooed and conditioned my hair, and washed away all of the dirt, I stepped onto the cool bathroom floor and grabbed a thick towel from a stack in the airing cupboard.

I checked my neck in the mirror. It was already turning yellow, the bruises were healing quickly. I dried and dressed quickly, constantly fighting the images that flashed through my mind. I felt better for the shower, but the unwanted thoughts kept returning.

I was due to meet Antonio late that night but nerves twisted in my stomach and I wasn't sure I wanted to see him. Weaver's words hung like a heavy chain around my neck. He had successfully hypnotised me at his house twice. I had feared that there was a lingering effect on my judgement but had convinced myself that my free will was driving my actions since then. But Weaver made a convincing point and I couldn't dismiss it.

I had a part to play in this madness and I was determined to do whatever I could to help. I kept one eye on the photograph of my parents on the dresser as I applied a little make-up and blow-dried my hair before I walked briskly around the corner to the Wilkes's house.

I opened the door and was greeted with warmth and wonderful smells.

'Hello?' I called as I entered. There was chatter coming from the kitchen and I followed it. The three of them were laying the table, engaged in easy, breezy conversation. I didn't know how Peter and Kirk switched it all off like that. I was a little in awe. They had both changed their clothes, I noticed. All signs of blood and dirt were gone. I wondered briefly how they had got in and changed without giving anything away to Mrs Wilkes.

'Eve, come on in.' Mrs Wilkes ushered me across the threshold and thrust a basket of rolls into my hands. I smiled as warmly as I could manage and put the basket on the table next to the butter dish.

It was an odd dinner. I felt so out of sorts, yet the others seemed perfectly normal and happy. I wondered how tiring it was for them to lead such a double life. Was it worth it? I could understand what Weaver had told me about shifter families. My parents had hidden their true identities from me my entire life. To keep something so fundamental from the people closest to you was a terrible burden, I imagined. I was sure I couldn't do it.

What did that mean for my future? Would I ever have a normal marriage and children? Changed or not, I had shifter blood. There was always a chance my children would turn at some point. If I had a non-shifter partner, would I have to conceal the truth about our children from him?

I watched this apparently happy family and knew that a family with secrets could function well enough, but I wasn't convinced it was healthy.

My quietness wasn't remarked upon, thankfully. I ate consciously, not wanting to eat too much or too fast in case anything disagreed with my slightly turbulent stomach. But I was deeply in need of nourishment. Thankfully, Mrs Wilkes's cooking was exemplary and the meal she laid on was healthy and plentiful.

Peter ate like there was no tomorrow, shovelling food into his mouth with little thought for table manners. He made me smile more than once with his infectious enthusiasm.

But my mind was partially elsewhere, ever mindful of the time and waiting for that call. I helped to wash the dishes once we had all finished eating and kept glancing at the clock. 7.50... 7.55... 8 o'clock.

'You're waiting for him to call, aren't you?' Peter asked me in a hushed voice as we stood at the sink, him washing, me drying.

'Afraid so.' I cast him a sideways glance.

'I won't stop worrying about you being with him, you know?'

'I know. I appreciate you caring, Peter.'

'No problem. Don't get yourself killed.'

'I'll try not to.' I smiled up at him and he returned it with a dimpled smile of his own.

Once the dishes were done, I needed to do something. I couldn't sit around waiting.

'Thanks for dinner,' I said to Peter's mother.

'Any time, dear. Take care.' She gave me a gentle pat on the arm.

'I'm going, Peter, stuff to do.' He nodded gravely and saw me to the door. He helped me into my coat and at the last moment, pulled me into a tight hug. I patted his back, dreading another vision, but nothing happened. He released me and looked into my wide eyes.

'Be really careful.'

'I will. I'll call you tomorrow.'

He opened the door for me and I stepped out into the cold night. I didn't head in the direction of home. I turned the other way and set off towards the city centre. It was a bit of a walk to Antonio's house, but I didn't mind. The fresh air was bracing after my time in the catacombs, and the city thrumming around me made me feel connected to things in a way that had been lacking.

I'd lost track of the days somewhere along the way, but the city buzzed with evening energy. It was still early, really, and at this time of year the shops stayed open late for Christmas shoppers. Music spilled out through open doors, nearly all of it festive, and my apprehension eased away. There was too much childhood nostalgia in the season for me to remain solemn and dwelling on the scary events in my life.

I passed through the shopping area of the city centre and into the northern area where one of the city's two theatres stood beside an art gallery and across from a museum dedicated to the ancient wall that still encompassed much of the city centre. I passed under one of the wall's many old gateways and out onto a quieter road that led out to Herald Gate, the residential area where Antonio lived.

Cars swept past me and I kept glancing toward their dark windows, always wondering if the occupant was anyone that I should worry about. I ducked off the main road and onto a quieter side street that turned behind the nearest row of terraced houses. At the end of the street, the terrace gave way to larger, detached houses. The back streets were deserted and not well lit. My nerves were jangling as I got closer and closer to his house. I didn't know if the gates would open for me, or what I would find by arriving unannounced, but I knew I couldn't wait to be summoned. If I was going to turn the situation to my advantage, then I couldn't wait for the censored version of his life that he was willing to share with me. I would have to try to catch him unawares in order to see anything that he didn't want me to see.

I thought about the information I wanted to get from him. I needed to know if he knew that Peter was a shifter and if he knew anything about what was being plotted against him. I had no idea how I would get that kind of detail from him. But I had to try. I couldn't let the shifters be slaughtered like I'd seen in my vision. Then there was my parents and how they died. He was there. I had to know what role he played.

I took deep breaths, clearing my head. I reached the end of Antonio's road and approached his grand mansion with my head held as high as I could muster. As I approached, the gates swung open and a black car I didn't recognise crawled out between them. I paused, a strange sense of glee mixed with apprehension swelling in my chest. The car pulled slowly across the pavement and swung out into the road, turning right and away from me. The gates started closing and I jogged to them and darted through the gap before it closed completely.

I walked quickly up the drive, which was completely dark, the trees on either side blocking any light from either the road or the house. I tugged my phone out of my pocket and used the torch on it to light my way. Sneaking onto the grounds probably wasn't my smartest move, but I was fuelled by the certainty that I was doing something important.

As I walked carefully up that paved drive in the dark, my hands and face freezing, doubt began to set in. What was I going to do? Peer in through the windows? Getting caught might mean my death. I had to be smart about this.

I drew a deep breath and picked up the pace, walking decisively up the centre of the drive and straight up to the floodlit house. I turned off the torch but kept my phone in my hand and set it to the camera. I stepped up to the front door and rang the bell.

The now-familiar butler opened the door with a curious expression on his normally stoic face.

'Ms Rawling? I don't believe we're expecting you until later.'

'I know, I'm sorry to arrive unannounced. I need to see Mr Vitale. Is he here?'

'He's in a meeting. But I'm sure he wouldn't want you to wait out in the cold.' He opened the door wide and stood aside. I smiled in gratitude and stepped into the foyer. He closed the door and something felt rather final about it. 'May I take your coat?'

I unbuttoned it and passed it to him. He disappeared briefly into a closet just next to Antonio's study. My eyes lingered on the polished, oak doors, which were firmly closed. I could hear movement in the room beyond and the house felt alive with activity that was tucked out of sight. It was warm and voices carried to me from different directions.

The butler reappeared and gestured for me to follow him. He led me past the study and down a corridor to the right of the grand staircase. We passed another closed door on the right, then a door on the left that had a round window set into it, rather like the kitchen at Piero's. I glanced through it and saw a chrome kitchen beyond. The next door on the right burst open and Roberto Esposito stepped into the wide hallway. He was shrugging his suit jacket onto his beefy shoulders. I caught a glimpse of blood on his white shirt, and bloody cuts on his knuckles. In his other hand was a black holdall that looked full and heavy. He sneered at me as we passed each other. I ignored him and peered into the room he'd left. As the door swung slowly closed, I saw a man being hoisted from the floor by a third man in a dark suit. The prone man had blood hanging in a grotesque string from his mouth and bruises all over his swollen face. I silently snapped a picture on my phone just before the door closed.

I shoved my shock deep inside and picked up my pace to keep up with the butler. This was Antonio's normal business, Ms Rational pointed out. I couldn't dispute that.

We reached the end of the corridor and entered a

beautiful parlour at the very back of the house. There was a huge orangery stretching out into the rear grounds, although I couldn't see anything of them in the dark. One wall was lined with bookshelves and the other walls were hung with modern art. Two deep, burgundy couches faced each other in the centre of the room and a vintage drinks cabinet sat against the wall.

'Can I fetch you a brandy? You look as though you could use something warming.'

'Yes, please.' I smiled graciously and he went to fix me a drink, returning quickly.

'Please take a seat, Ms Rawling. I will let Mr Vitale know that you're here.'

'Thank you.' I took the drink and moved over to the sofas, choosing the one facing the door. The butler left, but not through the same door. I noticed another door to my left and watched him knock and go through it. He closed it behind him, but not all the way shut. I edged over towards it and heard Antonio speaking quickly in Italian. It took me a second to tune in and recall the sound of the language that my mother had used more when I was a child and my grandparents were still around.

'Lo apprezzo, Commissario. Cerchi di stare tranquillo, ormai abbiamo le elezioni in pugno. Non ci sarà nessun problema. Ci incontreremo la prossima settimana per discutere i dettagli e metterci l'anima in pace. Che gliene sembra?'

It was evidently a phone call, as I didn't hear a reply, but Antonio went on to bid farewell and end the call. He'd been talking to the Commissioner about meeting to set his mind at rest about an election, if my memory was serving me correctly. I swallowed a lump of nerves in my throat.

'Ms Rawling is in the parlour, signor.'

'I see.' Antonio sounded agitated. 'Where is my sister?'

'I believe she is entertaining guests in her room.'

'Good. Let's hope that it stays that way. Grazie.'

I skipped silently back to the sofa and dropped down onto it. I knocked back the brandy and put the empty glass down on the table. The alcohol was indeed warming and it soothed my aching insides. I lay my head back against the back of the sofa and allowed my eyes to close for a moment. The butler didn't return, but after a minute or so I heard the door swing open and my eyes sprung wide to see Antonio standing in the open doorway, leaning with ease against the frame, his arms crossed over his chest. He was wearing a suit and his hair was loose down his back. He smiled softly as I sat up straight and looked him over.

'You're early.' He was wearing a slight smirk and his tone was gentle. I smiled.

'I couldn't wait to see you.'

'I see.' He moved towards me, as gracefully as a big cat. 'I told you I had work tonight.'

'I know. I'm sorry to intrude.'

'Does anyone know that you're here?'

'Of course,' I lied. 'Why? That almost sounds like a threat.'

'That is not my intention. But you must understand that I cannot necessarily guarantee your safety if you come here when I'm not expecting you. People come and go and not everyone here is as friendly as me.' He was still smiling as he perched on the edge of the sofa opposite me.

'I know. I saw Esposito.' I wrinkled my nose.

'Did you? He's the least of my concerns, frankly. Come.' He stood up and held out a hand. I took it and he pulled me to my feet. He kept hold of my hand and led me from the parlour. Rather than going back the way I had come, he led me into the room he had entered from. It looked like a boardroom with a huge, black table dominating the room, surrounded by high-backed chairs. At the far end of the table was a stack of papers and a black phone with blinking red lights on it.

Antonio led me through the boardroom and through another door to the right into a dimly lit corridor with no doors or windows. It was quiet back here, away from the front of the house. The corridor must have run parallel to the one the butler had led me along, with the rooms I had passed in between. Internal rooms with no windows. Perfect for vampire dealings, I thought.

We turned left at the end and headed up a narrow spiral staircase, which came out at the end of the corridor where his bedroom was. The upstairs was silent and dark.

Some light shone at the other end of the landing where it opened up to the lit grand foyer, but it was otherwise dark and I clung to Antonio's hand as he led me quickly to his room.

He opened the door and ushered me inside, without turning a light on. The blackout blinds weren't drawn and faint moonlight entered through the huge windows, casting pale patches on the carpet. He closed the door softly behind him and stood leaning against it, gazing at me with hungry eyes.

'Don't you still have business to conduct?' I asked, my hands on my hips in defiance.

'I do. Which is why you need to stay in here, quiet, and keep the door locked. It opens from inside, you are not a prisoner, but you must stay here. For your safety.'

'Okay.' I gulped awkwardly, suddenly acutely aware of how serious he was. He had stopped smiling. I nodded earnestly. 'I'll be quiet as a mouse,' I said in a whisper.

'Quieter. We can hear mice.' The corner of his mouth twitched. I nodded silently. He really was trying to protect me.

'I'll be back as soon as I can.' He strode over to me, crossing the room in a flash, and planted a passionate kiss on my lips. It was all too brief, however. He pulled away, leaving me breathless. 'Lock the door behind me.'

'I will,' I whispered. I followed him to the door and did as he said, my heart pounding hard and my head spinning.

CHAPTER TWENTY

I LOOKED AROUND THE ROOM, my eyes wide and straining a little in the dark. I went to the bedside table first and quickly looked through the drawer. There were a few bookmarks, some nail scissors, a couple of old, slightly creased tickets, a paper clip and absolutely nothing incriminating. I slid the drawer shut quietly and turned to the bed. I ran my hands over the edges of the mattress and pulled up the corner. It was heavy, and it was too dark to see much underneath it, but there didn't seem to be anything hidden under it. I checked all four corners, working quickly and as quietly as possible.

I blew a strand of hair out of my face and looked around. There was a vanity station under a large mirror. The surface was completely clear, but it had drawers. I dashed over to it and tried the top one. It was locked. The second one down opened, but like the bedside table, was practically empty. There were two different colognes, a box with cufflinks in, and a few sundries.

I turned to the door on the opposite wall, which I was

pretty sure led to his bathroom. I went to it and listened carefully at the crack. It was silent and no light crept under the door. I tried it and it opened. It led into a large walk-through wardrobe. On either side were rails hung with dozens of suits. I stepped inside and ran my fingers gently over the soft fabric. I peeked at some of the labels and saw a pattern of famous Italian designers that even fashion-phobic me had heard of.

There was a shallow drawer containing rows of watches and more cufflinks and tie pins. Another shelf held more cologne and still nothing I could use. The door at the other end of the closet almost certainly led to a bathroom. But I stopped and took a deep breath. He was careful. I knew that. He wasn't going to have a dossier marked "Evil Plans" lying around, certainly not in a room that he had locked me in alone. But maybe I could learn something about the man from what I could see.

He didn't keep clutter, or sentimental items, aside from the tickets. I went back to the bedside table and looked at them more closely. They were both theatre tickets. One was for Swan Lake, a performance at the theatre I'd passed on my way here. It was dated from about two months previously. The other was from a theatre in Caerton from the previous year. I turned it over and examined both sides in slightly stunned disbelief. What had he been doing in Caerton? The ticket had been to a play I'd never heard of. Had it been one of a pair? Or had he gone alone? Not that I should care. I ran my fingers over the ticket and heaved a sigh. I carefully put both pieces of card back where I'd found them and looked around the room again.

I'd carefully put everything back as I found it and sank now onto the end of the bed to wait for him.

Alone with my thoughts, I ran over what I'd seen when I arrived. I shuddered at the memory of the man who'd been beaten and wondered what had been in the bag. Money or drugs, probably. I pulled out my phone and looked at the photo I'd snapped. It was slightly out of focus, but I could make out the man, face down and being hoisted up. The man holding him was familiar. I'd seen him when Antonio led me out through the start of his party. He had stood with Lucia, watching me. He was tall and broad, with skin like black coffee and dark eyes.

The Camorra's main business was extortion and good old money laundering, but I was sure they must have their fingers in many pies. I wouldn't be surprised to learn that drugs were involved somewhere in the chain. I was vaguely aware of the grip the organisation had in Naples, but had to admit that I didn't know nearly as much as I ought to, given my situation.

The big thing I knew that most people didn't, was that this particular clan was headed by vampires. I sat bolt upright and strained to listen to distant noises in the vast mansion. From Antonio's extreme caution, it occurred to me that Lucia might not be the only other vampire in the house. I'd never really considered before that more of the Camorra might be likewise afflicted with the condition.

I looked at the picture again. The big man that I'd recognised was hoisting that bleeding man up with one hand and showing no strain. He had to be a vampire.

I'd seen Esposito in daylight and he wasn't slick enough to be one of the undead. But I knew there must be others that I'd seen and plenty I hadn't. I was sure that Antonio was in charge, though. But he had said he couldn't guarantee my safety, not even in his own home. As powerful as he was, as much authority as he had, there were creatures here that might do whatever they wanted and he couldn't necessarily stop them. He might have just been thinking of his sister, but something told me that wasn't true.

Lucia was supposedly in her room, but I didn't know where in the house that was. She could be right across the hall. I grimaced and folded myself up, wrapping my arms around my knees. I'd been so bold coming here and now fear coursed through my veins.

I typed a hurried text message to Peter letting him know where I was, just in case I didn't make it out. My hand shook as I tapped away and I just about jumped out of my skin when I heard a key in the lock. I hit send and quickly concealed my phone, my eyes not leaving the door.

'It's me,' Antonio's voice whispered on the other side

of the door and I relaxed a touch. I jumped up and ran to the door just as he opened it. He slipped inside and I flung my arms around his neck. 'Are you all right?' The door clicked shut and he locked it again before wrapping his arms around me. I was trembling and just about managed to nod against his chest. He took hold of my shoulders and gently eased me away from him so he could look into my eyes. 'Eve?'

'I didn't like being here on my own.' My voice was so quiet I didn't think mortal ears could hear it. But he didn't seem to have any trouble. He scooped me up and carried me to the bed, laying me softly upon it and lying down beside me. He stroked my hair off my face and gently kissed my forehead.

'I'm sorry if my words caused you alarm.'

I shook my head, even though that was exactly what had happened. He nodded slowly, gave a half-smile and then glanced around the room. 'Did you find what you were looking for?' he asked, his smile widening. I stared up at him and blinked hard, unsure how to answer. 'It's okay. I expected you to look around.'

'How did you know?' Again I whispered desperately faintly.

'Little differences. Don't worry, by the way, we're quite alone now.'

'Alone?'

'More or less. Frederick is downstairs and I think I

have a cleaner somewhere.' I guessed that Frederick was the butler. It was nice to have a name to go with the face. Antonio was grinning at his own joke and I mustered a smile.

'No Lucia?'

'She's gone out.' He dipped his head and kissed my cheek.

'Oh.' He kissed my jaw and ran a finger down my shoulder and arm.

'Does anyone else live here?'

'Hmm...' His lips were busy on my ear and jaw. He paused. 'People come and go. But there is no one else here at present.' His lips went back to my jaw and his fingers tugged the neck of my sweater aside so his lips could wander down to my neck. He stopped abruptly and his gaze flickered between my neck and my eyes.

'What?' I asked, searching his face.

'The bruises. I did that.' He looked at me with wide, concerned eyes.

'You did.'

'Eve, I am so sorry. I should never have been so rough with you. I deeply regret it.'

'I shocked you. You reacted. I'm okay.' The half lie stung as I said it.

'It will never happen again, I swear to you. I don't want to hurt you.'

I nodded meekly, hoping he was both honest and truly

able to make good on his promise. A flicker of his thoughts wormed their way into my mind. I swallowed hard and felt the colour drain from my face. He was thinking about a girl, sixty years ago. The girl he had loved with all of his cold, dead heart. She'd died in his arms. An unfortunate loss of control. I didn't like what I was starting to see when I let my guard down with him. I wanted to go back to the blank canvass, the way normal people had to stumble blindly, not knowing what those around them were thinking.

A question burned its way into my thoughts, one I couldn't ignore. I was afraid to voice it, but equally afraid to let it fester in my mind, unanswered.

'How many people have you killed from over-feeding?'

'Eve, why would you ask me that?'

'You're the one who wants me to know how dangerous you are.'

'You're right,' he said. 'But I don't think you really want to know the answer.'

'No, probably not. But I think I need to know just how big a risk I'm taking here.'

He shook his head sadly.

'I have lost control with a young woman in my bed precisely once in my two-hundred-year lifetime. It was a long time ago and I regret it nearly every day. I loved her.'

'Oh.' I knew this much, although he had just informed me of his age, which was new. 'Have you ever loved anyone else?'

'Once or twice. I had a wife when I changed. She died of old age many years after I stopped ageing with her.'

'I'm sorry.'

'It was several lifetimes ago, Eve. I have made peace with it. I've had other lovers, many. I've killed some of them on purpose.' I blanched and felt myself tense up. 'I have lived a long and cruel life.' There was little emotion in his voice. He said it as casually as one might mention liking cats over dogs. 'I've killed enemies. I've drained tasty specimens for sport. But I wouldn't still be here if I wasn't careful and somewhat wise. I do not kill people I care about, or people with attentive families and friends.' He looked right into my frightened eyes and I saw a hint of sadness in his. 'Would you like me to try to help you forget this conversation?'

'No.' I shook my head and a tear ran down my face and into my hair.

'I told you you did not want to know this.'

'You did. But it's good that I know.'

'You think I'm a monster. That brave girl in the street telling me that she knew but was still in my arms is shrinking away from me as I speak.'

'You are a monster.' I reached up and caressed his cheek. 'I am scared. But I still want to be here.'

He leaned down and kissed me tenderly. He didn't feel so cold, his lips were warm and moist and his body warmed as it pressed against me. I welcomed the weight of him on top of me and wrapped my legs around him. Ms Rational wasn't just silently observing, or even passed out. By the time Antonio had removed my clothes she had completely left the building.

CHAPTER TWENTY-ONE

MY EYES FLICKERED OPEN SOME HOURS LATER. For a second I was confused and didn't recognise where I was. The room was filled with the dull grey light of pre-dawn. My skin was goose-bumped in the cool early morning air and I was momentarily surprised to find myself naked and under thin, silk sheets. I was alone in the bed. I raised myself up on my elbows and looked around. My body ached and I remembered the paces it had been put through in the night. A smile crept onto my lips and heat flushed into my cheeks.

The closet door stood open and I heard the door beyond it open. Antonio was framed in light from the bathroom behind him, a toothbrush sticking out of his mouth. He leaned on the door frame, naked, and resumed brushing his teeth as he gazed at me. I rolled onto my side to face him and smirked at the sight of him.

'You brush your teeth?'

'Of course,' he said thickly, through the minty foam. He turned and disappeared into the bathroom for a moment and returned without the brush or foam in his mouth. He flicked off the light and strolled towards me. His skin was pale and smooth, his body utterly perfect. I grinned as he stooped to lay a soft, fresh kiss on my lips. His mouth was cool and I could taste the mint.

I rolled onto my back and gazed up at him, lost in erotic memories mingled with future desires. As if reading my mind, he grinned back. 'Later.' He turned and went to the furthest window, wincing as he drew close to it. The cool light on his skin seemed brighter than it ought to and there was a faint trace of a hiss as it touched him. It reminded me starkly of what he was and my smile faltered. He reached up and pulled down the blackout blind, then drew the heavy, crimson drapes across the window. He repeated this with each of the four windows in the room, gradually shutting out the dawn sun and plunging the room into utter darkness. I lay there watching him, questions bubbling to the surface of my mind. He clicked on a small lamp on his bedside table and crawled into the bed beside me.

'Does it burn?' I ran my fingers over his chest and stomach. The skin was faintly pink, where before it had been like pure, pale caramel.

'It does.' His voice was soft, but emotionless. I leaned down and kissed the pinkest part on the top of his chest. 'The hotter the sun the more dangerous it is. This feeble English winter dawn is nothing.' He smiled faintly and I tried to smile in return, but it was hard to joke about something that might kill him.

'Is that why you came here? Is it worse in Italy?'

'Hmm, partly. It was more about the opportunity for my family and clan. But the weather certainly encouraged us to stay.' He lay back and put his hands behind his head.

'How did this happen to you?'

'I was turned. "Abbraccia la notte," they used to call it. I was a mortal man before.'

'You said you had a wife?'

'I did. My family was all Camorra, they were there at the start of the organisation. A match was arranged for me with a daughter of a rival clan elder in order to broker a peace. But we were lucky enough to fall in love. When my father passed away I was to take over. One of my uncles took me aside one night and told me the truth about my family. That in each generation two were given special gifts, while the rest would be tasked with continuing the family line. He told me that I had been chosen to "embrace the night." He made me a vampire. My sister too.'

'Oh.' A dull ache rose in my chest as he spoke. He was calm and there was a sadness to his voice, but it seemed so distant he may as well have been recounting the plot of a film he'd seen.

'I sent my wife away for her protection, I was afraid of what might happen if she stayed. I could no longer give her children, or the life I had promised her, so I released her from any obligation to me. I checked in on her from time to time, from a distance. I saw her grow old and die peacefully surrounded by family. She had a good life.'

'What about you? Have you had a good life?'

'It depends what you mean by good.' He looked at me and smiled that sweet, seductive smile. 'I've travelled, I've made a fortune, I have power and influence. I'm a success, I suppose. I've loved passionately. I've lost much. Yes, I suppose you would call that a good life.'

'Are you happy?'

'I am very happy with you naked in my bed, yes.' He grinned, rolled over and pushed me onto my back. 'You ask too many questions.' He kissed me, halting any reply from leaving my lips. His hands pinned my wrists to the bed as he inched my legs apart with his knees. I gladly wrapped my legs around his hips and whimpered into his mouth, welcoming his intentions.

A sharp rap on the door broke the mood in an instant. Antonio's eyes went dangerously dark and his head whipped around to look at the door. He looked back at me, released me and pressed a finger to my lips. He was gone from on top of me before I could blink and was striding to the door, while tying a floor-length, silk gown around himself. I pulled the sheet up to my nose and kept my head low.

'Tony, answer the door.' Lucia's voice was crisp. My heart was pounding and my pulse racing.

Antonio opened the door and placed himself firmly in the narrow gap, blocking her view into the room. I could smell her perfume and feel the resentment oozing off her, even without seeing her face.

'What do you want? I have company.'

'I know! I heard you going at it, repeatedly. Disgusting. Who have you got in there? You don't normally let them stay all night. Fuck, feed and discard.'

Something unpleasant crawled around my insides.

'No, Lucia, that's your attitude. I thought you were out last night.'

'I was. I was with Dante and some pretty little thing we picked up at a bar. But I came home hours ago, which you would have known if you weren't so engrossed. Who *is* she?' I could sense her trying to crane her neck to see around Antonio, and wriggled down in the bed, making sure I was hidden. I hated hearing her talk to him like that. My skin crawled.

'What did you do with her?' Antonio asked with heavy resignation.

'Who?'

'The girl from the bar.'

'I'm not telling you the details of my sex life, Brother.'

'No, I mean when you were done. Do I have another mess to clean up?'

'No,' she said breezily. 'Dante dealt with it. You know how good he is about that sort of thing.' Antonio leaned heavily against the door.

'Will you please stop leaving a trail of corpses everywhere we go? It affects me too, you know?'

'Ugh, you are so boring these days. Remember when we used to swan around Paris every night? Drinking, dining, fucking whoever we pleased? Was it a duchess you bedded that time?'

'I have advised you countless times, Lucia, that it is far more sustainable to catch and release your prey. My companion will walk out of here alive and well later and will gladly donate again in a few days.'

'Yes and your way is dull and not what we were made for.'

'Was there a point to you darkening my door this morning?' His voice was dark and threatening. I was desperate for him to lock the door and return to my side. I felt so vulnerable lying there alone and naked.

'Yes. I'm still upset with you about our conversation yesterday. If you hadn't taken my favourite vintage off the menu I wouldn't have to discard as many humans.' Lucia didn't sound upset, she sounded like she was toying with him in a sulk.

'I explained about that,' Antonio said, heavy resignation in his voice once more. 'I need him kept whole.'

'He was fine being fed on for years. Why now?'

'Because he is important to the business. You know, that thing that keeps you supplied in designer dresses and shoes?'

'I was taking good care of him, wasn't I?'

'Yes, but I can't afford any mistakes. Besides, there are still some bags of his in the freezer downstairs.'

'Ugh. I hate you,' Lucia said in a mock whine.

'No, you don't.'

'I suppose not. Who kept you so occupied all night, anyway? Is it someone special?'

'That is none of your business.' He closed the door and locked it with a firm click. He stood there, one hand on the door, his head hanging low for endless seconds while Lucia huffed indignantly on the other side. I heard her footsteps stomp away down the carpeted hall and finally Antonio returned to me. He sat on the edge of the bed, not looking at me.

'She didn't seem to care if I heard all of that,' I finally said, not daring to raise my voice above a whisper.

'No,' he replied. 'She'll assume that I will make you forget everything.'

'Will you?'

'Not if you don't want me to. I don't even know if I can. You are oddly resistant.' He looked at me, his head on one side, regarding me quizzically.

'Am I someone special?'

'Yes. Very. Not just to me personally, I think.' He crawled across the bed towards me, still looking at me with narrowed eyes. 'How can you resist my glamour? Do you have any other interesting mental abilities?'

'I have no idea!' I scoffed, looking away. 'I don't even really understand what you mean.'

'You are a terrible liar, Eve.' He was giving me that sexy half-smile. I edged away from him, laughing nervously. 'What is it about your mind?'

'I honestly don't have a clue. Can't you read it?'

'No,' he said, his eyes narrowing further, still stalking slowly towards me. 'But that isn't within my usual skill set, anyway. Is it within yours? What are you, Eve Rawling?' He made to pounce on me and I leapt from the bed, darting into the closet. He was right on my tail and I squealed with delight when he caught hold of me and hoisted me up in his strong arms. I was giggling, but my heart had never beat so fast. He carried me into the bathroom, slammed the door shut with a kick of his foot and deposited me on the cold, marble basin rim.

His mouth crashed against mine in a deep kiss and he made love to me for the fourth time. Still with so much unsaid between us, and yet so much revealed.

CHAPTER TWENTY-TWO

'I MUST FEED YOU. You've been here for hours and had nothing except that brandy. I'm pretty sure it's lunch time.'

'I'm fine, honestly. It's not like you've been feeding on me. Not this time.' I tried to act coy, but I don't think I got it quite right because rather than smiling or kissing me, Antonio looked embarrassed and turned away. 'You wanted to.' I put a hand on his chest as we lay in bed facing one another. 'I saw it in your eyes, especially the first time.'

'Yes. The two go hand in hand so often. I did have the urge to bite you. But it hasn't been long enough since I last had your blood. You need time to recover.'

'Like with blood donation,' I said, trying to be helpful. 'They only let you donate every couple of months or so because your body has to replenish the blood.'

'Exactly.' We both tried to smile. I was exhausted. I didn't want to admit it, but I'd hardly slept and even though he hadn't fed on me, I'd exerted a lot of energy to keep up with his other appetite.

'But I do need to go home.'

'Of course.'

'Can I use your shower?'

'Yes. There are plenty of towels in the bathroom.' I kissed him softly and scooted away from him. I scooped up my clothes from the floor around the bed and carried them to the bathroom. The light was still on from our last visit, when he had taken me vigorously on the sink. I blushed at the thought.

The shower was huge, taking up the length of one entire wall, and easily three feet wide. The tiles were terracotta and dashed with something lighter that glinted like gemstones in the warm lighting. There were three large shower heads and a range of controls. I blinked as I looked at them, trying to work out how to turn anything on.

There was a sudden, loud buzz that echoed around the tiled room and I jumped sideways. My jeans were pooled on the floor by the sink and my phone continued to vibrate in the pocket, rattling against the floor. I scooped up my jeans and fumbled for the phone, desperate to shut it off. I tugged it free and saw Peter's name on the display. I glanced at the closed door and, knowing that Antonio would certainly hear every word with his supernatural hearing, I reluctantly answered.

'Hi Peter. I can't really talk right now.'

'Right. Just wanted to make sure you were okay.'

'I'm fine, great, actually.'

'Are you still at his house?'

'Mm-mm.' I nodded in the affirmative, looking anxiously at the door.

'Can you speak freely?'

'Ish. I'm just getting ready to leave, actually. I'll be at Piero's in a little while. Will you be there?'

'I can be. Are you sure you're all right?'

'Yes, I promise. I'll see you later.'

'Okay. I can come and pick you up.'

'No, there's no need. I'll just meet you there.'

'Fine.' He didn't sound at all happy, but he let it go. I put my phone down carefully by the sink and cringed at the thought of what I would need to tell him and the others. I returned to the shower, tried a dial and hot water burst from one of the shower heads. I stepped inside the huge cubicle and felt the water pound against my skin. I closed my eyes and relished the refreshing feeling.

I finished showering quickly, got dried and dressed and returned to the bedroom, towelling my hair dry. Antonio was wearing black, silk pyjama bottoms and sat in a chair by the vanity, reading a newspaper. There was a little silver tray next to him with orange juice and a small stack of pastries. He put down his paper and smiled warmly at me.

'I hope you don't mind, but I must insist that you eat something before you go. I had Frederick bring these up.' He gestured to the tray. I grinned and perched on the edge of the dresser to eat a cinnamon swirl.

'Thank you.'

'When you're ready, I'll have a driver take you home, or to the restaurant. Wherever you want to go.'

'That would be nice. Thank you.' My smile faltered slightly. There was a little edge to his words that reminded me of my hushed conversation over the phone. 'Peter was worried about me. So he called.' I decided to just address it and give him a window to acknowledge that he'd overheard. He nodded, avoiding my gaze.

'Of course. I hope he was reassured.'

'I think so.'

'Eve,' he said, glancing quickly at me and then looking away. He paused on the brink of saying something. I ate and waited. 'It is important that I know if my security is compromised.'

'Right.' I blinked and found that the pastry had seemed to harden in my mouth as I chewed. I swallowed, painfully, and reached for the juice. I expected him to elaborate, but I feared I didn't need him to.

'What does your friend know about me?'

'Um...' I took a drink to delay answering. He knew I was a bad liar and I had to lie my way through this. 'He's afraid of you, like most people who know your name. He hates that I'm involved with you.'

'Is he your... are you... have you been...' He seemed flustered as he fished for the right words. I tried not to laugh.

'He's not my boyfriend. He's like a brother to me. We've never been intimate.' I answered each of his half-asked questions and grinned when I saw him blush. 'How do you even blush? Or have sex, for that matter? Isn't your body basically dead?' I cringed. I'd had sex, repeatedly, with a dead man. My stomach lurched uncomfortably.

'Good to know, and I really don't know. It defies modern science. My body is dead in that it does not age, it is immune to infection and disease, I cannot father children. Nor do I breathe unless I exert the effort to do so. But blood does circulate around my body and I can manipulate where it goes, to some extent. Like choosing to harden the right part of me over and over again.' He stood and moved over to me. He pressed against me and looked into my eyes. It was my turn to blush.

'Yeah, I noticed that.'

'Yes, you did.' He kissed me and I leaned into it, happy to not have to answer any more questions about Peter. Antonio pulled slowly, reluctantly back from me. 'So, I don't have to worry about what he knows?'

'No, I don't think so.'

'What about his not liking you being in my bed? Would he act on that? Seek to prevent it happening again?'

'I don't think so, but as you said to your sister, it's really not any of his business.'

'Would you tell him that?'

'Yes, of course.' I was only half lying.

'Very well. I won't worry about him.' He turned to move away from me but I caught hold of his arm.

'Antonio.' I paused as his gaze landed on my hand gripping his arm and then turned to meet my own. 'Erm, that conversation could have gone differently. If I hadn't been able to reassure you about Peter, what would you have done?'

'I don't think you want to know.' He eased his arm out of my grasp and stalked away to the bathroom. I heard the shower turn on and sat there in uncomfortable solitude. I tried to take another bite of my cinnamon swirl, but had lost my appetite. What was I doing? Whose side was I even on in all of this? Every time I thought I had clarity, something changed and I lost it again.

No, I was on my parents' side. I was doing this for them. I had to be close to Antonio and this was the only way to achieve that. I also happened to enjoy being with him. It made it easier to get the answers I needed. But when the time came, I would stand with the shifters and make sure that my parents didn't die for nothing.

At some point, I realised, Antonio and I would have to acknowledge to each other the existence of the shifters. I didn't know how long I would be able to keep my ability secret from him when it was obvious he already suspected.

I was so lost in my thoughts, I was caught by surprise when Antonio emerged, fully dressed, with his hair tied neatly back.

'Are you ready to go?' he asked.

'Sure.' I slid off the dressing table and looked around for my boots. I spotted one sticking out from under the bed and crossed to fetch it. But Antonio was quicker. He had scooped it from the floor and located my other before I'd taken my second step. 'Thanks.' I took them and bent to put them on.

'Give me a moment.' His voice was low and firm, a distinctly more business-like tone than he'd taken with me since I arrived. I couldn't help feeling a little disappointed. As I was fastening the laces, he went to the door and opened it. He looked out into the hall and tilted his head from side to side. Apparently satisfied, he opened the door wide and indicated for me to follow him out into the hall. I scurried across the room and stepped out into the dark, quiet corridor. The window at the far end was covered just like his bedroom windows. But the end that led to the grand foyer was bathed in sunlight from the huge window over the front doors.

'Are we alone?' I whispered.

'Not quite,' he replied softly. He took my hand and led me quickly to the back stairs that we had come up the previous night. There were no windows this way, I realised. He led me down the stairs and along the dark and empty corridor, towards the sunlit foyer. He stopped in the shadows, a far-off look in his dark eyes. I leaned against him and kissed him softly. His hands clasped my face and he kissed me back with yearning.

We pulled apart and I stepped away from him, into the sunlight. A throat cleared behind me and I spun to see Frederick standing there in his neat suit with my coat over his arm.

'I had a really good time.' I gave Antonio a smile and he returned it.

'Good. Me too. I'm afraid I've neglected some business that I must attend to tonight. I'll see you tomorrow.'

'Okay. Call me?'

'I will. Frederick will see you to the car.'

'Okay.' I nodded and turned to go. The butler held up my coat and helped me into it. 'Thank you,' I said softly, unused to being waited on.

'Quite alright, miss,' he replied, kindness in his voice. He opened the front door for me and I glanced over my shoulder to see Antonio watching me leave from the safety of the shadows.

The sun was so bright in comparison to the dark mansion that I had to blink several times as my eyes adjusted. Antonio's Maserati was idling at the bottom of the steps, his driver standing waiting for me. He opened the door as I approached. I turned to Frederick, who'd followed me down the steps.

'Thank you,' I said again, feeling distinctly awkward with all of this servitude around me.

'Not at all. Good day, Ms Rawling. I hope to see you again soon.'

'Yes. Likewise.' I got into the car and the driver closed the door.

'Where to, miss?' he asked after sliding into the driver's seat.

'Piero's. No, actually, I'd better go home first.'

'Very good.'

'You remember the address?' It'd been this driver who'd taken me home the night Antonio had bitten me in the street. I blushed at the memory. The driver's face was impassive in the rear-view mirror.

'Of course.'

The city looked all wrong in the bright, November sunlight. I had quickly become accustomed to the dark, the night, the twinkling lights and deep shadows. I found my thoughts drifting to what the process might be for changing someone into a vampire. I knew how it worked in the movies. But was that true to life? What had Antonio gone through? Had he ever changed anyone else? I loved the Italian phrase for it, it was so romantic. *Embrace the night.* I found myself smiling serenely as I gazed unseeing at the sunlit streets, shops and people.

I thanked the driver as he helped me out of the car, and watched him drive away before going into my house. I went inside, shut the door and leaned heavily against it, suddenly aching with exhaustion.

'Well?' snapped an impatient voice from down the hall.

CHAPTER TWENTY-THREE

I STARTLED AND MY HAND LEAPT TO MY CHEST. My eyes fixed on Peter, standing in the kitchen doorway with his arms over his chest.

'You can't keep sneaking into my house, Peter,' I shouted at him and stomped down the hall towards him. I pushed past him and went straight to the kettle. I needed coffee and lots of it.

'Sorry, but we can't talk freely at the restaurant, you know that. I had to meet you here. You were ages.'

'I had to shower and eat first. I got here as soon as I could.'

'You were with him all night.'

'Yes and I'm not going to go into the details of that.' I bustled about, fetching mugs and busying myself to avoid looking at him.

'Fine. I don't want to know, anyway. I just want to know what you found out.'

I pulled out my phone and went into the photos app. The picture I'd surreptitiously snapped was there. I passed him the phone.

'I saw a bit of what goes on there. But just glimpses. I heard him on the phone to someone high up in the police, I think. He was speaking Italian.'

'The commissioner is Italian.'

'Well, that's probably who it was. He said something about the election. But isn't it still a couple of years until the next one?'

'The next General Election, yes,' Peter said, passing me my phone. 'The police commissioner election is in May.'

'Okay, so it was probably about that. I think he's rigging it.'

'Right.' Peter rubbed the bridge of his nose. 'Anything about us?'

'Not a jot. It's a hard subject to broach. I can't very well come out and say "so, about all my shapeshifter mates that you keep feeding off and extorting, did you know they're plotting to overthrow you?"'

Peter flinched at my sharp tone and I cast him a furtive, apologetic look as I poured our coffees.

'Obviously,' he said, more calmly than I expected. He put my phone down on the table and wedged his hands into his jeans pockets.

'But you came up.'

'Oh?'

'He asked if you know what he is. I said no. I said that

you were as afraid of him as anyone, but for no supernatural reason.'

'You don't need to protect me.'

'Of course I do!' My voice was higher than I meant it to be. 'That's what all of this is about. This massive risk I'm taking by literally getting into bed with that monster is all to protect you and your family!' I slammed a hand on the counter, surprising myself with my anger. Peter stared at me with wide, fearful eyes.

'Eve,' he started, his voice full of pity. He moved over to me and planted his hands on the kitchen counter.

'Don't. Don't say anything. Look, this is what I can do to help. This is my choice and I don't mean to put it on you. You never told me to do any of this; you tried to stop me. I'm very tired and it's confusing. Honestly. The whole thing is really confusing. I don't know if I'm coming or going half the time.'

'Why is it confusing?'

'Because he's a killer.'

'And?'

'And I like him. I like the way I feel when I'm with him. It's not his glamour, it's real.'

'Yeah, that does sound confusing.' Peter stood frozen, his fingers gripping the edge of the counter so tight his knuckles had turned white. 'You don't have to help us. We can do this without you. But do me a favour and don't get in the way.' He stormed towards the door.

'Peter!'

He stopped and looked over his shoulder at me.

'What?'

I was seething and had no words to offer him. I grabbed the nearest coffee cup and hurled it towards him. He easily dodged and the cup smashed when it hit the wall. Black coffee trickled down the powder blue wallpaper. We both stared at it in stunned surprise.

'Sorry,' I said breathlessly.

'I'll help you clean it up.' He walked back into the kitchen and picked up a cloth. I stood there, numb and alarmed, while he wiped the coffee off the wall. I found my feet and went over to pick up the broken pieces of porcelain.

'Thanks,' I mumbled, taking the wet cloth from him. 'I just said that it was confusing. Not that I wanted out. I have to do this, for my parents.'

'Okay.'

I dumped the broken mug in the bin and the cloth in the sink. I leaned heavily against the sink and closed my eyes. Peter walked up behind me and put a hand on my shoulder.

'I'm just worried about you.'

'It's not just that, though, is it?' I asked, turning to face him. 'You don't seem worried. It's more like jealousy.'

'No!' He recoiled. 'I don't like you being with him because he could kill you.'

'So could you.'

'What?'

'You could turn into that beast and rip my throat out. Don't pretend like you're just a meek human guy. There's a monster inside you too.'

'Is that what you think?' He looked devastated.

'Well, yeah. But my point is that I know you wouldn't do that. I trust you.'

'Good.' He looked flustered and still shocked by my words.

'I need to figure out how to find out what he knows. I could try bringing up my parents, but if he suspects that I know he was involved in their deaths he might just kill me on the spot.' Peter flinched. 'I don't think he will, though. He has strong feelings for me. I don't think he'd kill me unless I gave him no other choice.'

'I hate this.'

'Me too.'

'How can you have feelings for the man who killed your parents?' His jaw was clenched.

'I don't know. I wish I understood it. You don't know what it's like to not be able to touch someone without being afraid that you're going to see something horrible. I've shied away from intimacy since I was twelve years old. I don't even remember the last time I hugged or kissed my parents. Imagine your parents dying with you having not hugged them in nearly a decade. Then this man comes into my life who is not only gorgeous and mysterious, but who doesn't trigger my visions. He can hold me in his arms, kiss me, even make love to me and my head stays in the present. I don't know his thoughts, I don't see flashes of him killing people.'

Peter turned away and covered his face with his hands.

'I'm so sorry. I didn't really think of any of that and I never wanted you to see my first change. I didn't know what you'd see when I held you that day. I just wanted you to know my secret.'

'I know. And I don't blame you at all. It is what it is. But the relief I get when I'm with Antonio, it's priceless. And what if he didn't kill my parents? We don't really know, do we? There's no proof. It's all just guesswork.'

'True.'

I couldn't confess that my gift had triggered with Antonio and that I had seen death in his past at his own hands. That wasn't my secret to share and it weakened my argument. I knew that.

'How are the others after Weaver's cutting remarks?'

'Fine. Well, you know, processing it. These guys are all really just learning how to be shifters, even the ones who've been around for a while, like my dad. Weaver basically came in and told them all they've been doing it all wrong. That's not an easy pill to swallow.'

'I bet.' I poured fresh coffee for both of us and handed

a mug to Peter. I took small sips, feeling the heat run down my throat. The caffeine was just what I needed. I could feel the familiar buzz as I drank.

'On which note, I need to go,' Peter said, chugging back a few big gulps of coffee. 'There's some training thing I have to go to.'

'Okay. Watch out for demons.'

'I will. You too.' He gave me a meaningful look and I brushed him away. He went straight down into the basement, rather than to the front door. I followed him halfway down the stairs and watched him slip away through the trapdoor. It was a wonder that it'd remained hidden from me for so long. There was no way my parents came and went through it the way Peter did.

I shut the hatch and went back to my empty kitchen. The afternoon had brought wispy clouds across the blue sky and the shadows had grown long in the back garden. It would be getting dark soon. I glanced at the coffee stain on my wall and sighed. I'd never liked the blue walls in the kitchen, so maybe it was time for a new coat of paint anyway. I made another coffee and took it upstairs with me to drink while I got changed and ready for work. If I had to go a night without Antonio, I'd spend it at the restaurant and keep busy.

By the time I set off for Piero's, it was dark and every step of the walk there I was on edge, hoping that his car would pull up beside me, and praying not to run into

Lucia. The city wasn't that big, after all. I shuddered at the thought of her killing that woman the night before, and god knows how many people before that. A new victim every night for two centuries? I tried not to think about Antonio doing that.

He didn't want to feed on me too often. But if he had to feed every night then who else was he feeding from? A spark of jealousy ignited inside me. I didn't want him seducing other women and taking them home with him. But I also didn't want him feeding callously on the shifters. He'd mentioned a freezer and Kirk's blood being bagged up in there when he was placating his sister. I cringed at the thought of rows of blood bags stacked up somewhere in that house. But that was better than Antonio going out and finding fresh victims.

It was an impossible situation and I wondered for about the hundredth time how I had gotten into it.

CHAPTER TWENTY-FOUR

THAT WAS THE LONGEST NIGHT OF MY LIFE. Piero's was fairly busy and one of the wait staff was off sick, so I was helping Tina, waiting tables and helping behind the bar. I worked hard on my feet all evening, rushing between the kitchens and tables. It was a job I'd done for two years in my teens, so I knew what I was doing, but it wasn't exactly work I enjoyed. It involved far too much contact with other people for my liking. But it was exactly what I needed to keep my mind off Antonio.

When things finally started to die down around 10 o'clock, I slunk into the office, slipped off my shoes and drank a litre of water straight down without stopping. I hid myself away in there until closing and decided to stay late to order stock and make plans. Now that the business was free from debt to the Camorra I could contemplate bringing in a manager to keep the place running for me. I could do it, but I didn't love it and I was so distracted with my complicated life that I wasn't doing the job justice.

Tina was the last of the staff to leave and I made my

way around locking all of the doors behind her. There was a service door at the back of the building, just off the kitchen and another back door that the staff used. I came to the front door last, which Tina had bolted at closing time, but I locked up with my keys as well.

The street outside was quiet and still. There were no cars parked on the road, no lights on in neighbouring buildings and no one out walking at this time of night. I stood and looked out at the road, bathed in orange street light, breathing deeply in the stillness.

Piero's was eerie when it was closed. It didn't feel real, or certainly not alive, like it did when it was lit and filled with people. I didn't like being alone there.

I brewed a pot of strong coffee and got comfortable in the office. I left the door open so that I could see out into the dining area. Every little noise out on the street got my attention and kept me from my work.

With how jumpy I was, it took hours to get everything done. It had taken a constant flow of coffee to keep me going all evening and I had caffeine-induced jitters once I was alone in the quiet.

Finally, at 2 am, I was ready to leave. I gathered my things and headed home. It wasn't a long walk, but every step was agony after being on my feet so much. The streets were still almost deserted, but each car that swept past had me on edge. Damn that coffee.

I was desperate for my bed and partially regretted how

little sleep I'd had at Antonio's. I smiled to myself as I walked home, remembering the excellent reasons for my lack of sleep.

At last I made it to my front door. Peter was sitting on the step waiting for me. I groaned and stood at the gate, staring at him.

'Sorry,' he muttered. 'We need to talk.'

'Peter, no. It can wait until morning. As in, daylight. As in, after I sleep for about fifteen hours.'

'It can't.'

'You think it can't, but it can, I promise you.'

I strode up to him and heaved him up by his arm. I unlocked my door and went inside. I made to close the door between us, but he thrust out a hand and planted it on the wooden door, holding it half-open.

'Eve, seriously.'

'Fine.' I swept away from the door and dumped my bag and coat at the foot of the stairs. I stomped up to the landing and was dimly aware of him following me, having shut and locked the door. I peeled off my clothes on my way along the landing, not caring about Peter trudging along in my wake. 'What is it? Quick,' I snapped at him over my shoulder. I was down to my underwear when I kicked my bedroom door half-closed. Peter, to his credit, stopped outside and I saw him lean against the door frame and cast his gaze to the navy blue carpet.

'Weaver had us do this ritual to officially form our

pack.'

'Right.' I was fishing pyjamas out of a drawer and had only a passing interest in this news. My bed was calling to me.

'Me, Dad, Crystal and Strikes Twice.'

'Who?'

'The big guy with the axe.'

'Oh. Yeah.' I changed into my pyjamas and brushed my hair, only half-listening.

'Your house falls on our territory, so we have to patrol past it. With your nocturnal habits you need to be aware, in case you see us.'

'Peter.' I swung the door open and looked him in the eye. 'This really could have waited.'

'All the packs have formed, Eve. Aside from having an actual plan, we're all set.'

'Right. Good. Is that all?' I was livid. I needed to crash and he was delaying me for no good reason.

'I suppose.'

'Why couldn't this wait until tomorrow, Peter?' I brushed past him and went into the bathroom to brush my teeth.

'I thought you'd want to know.'

'You're not planning to surprise him at dawn with flaming torches and stakes, are you?'

'No,' he said, looking down and blushing. I clucked my tongue and set about brushing. 'I'm sorry. I guess I was scared that you were with him.'

'I was working,' I said thickly through toothpaste foam, not looking at him.

'I know. But I thought you might go to him afterwards. Every time you see him you're in danger and you risk losing sight of what we're doing here.'

I spat, rinsed and cleaned my brush, breathing deeply before responding.

'You're making excuses. Why? What's really going on here?'

'Nothing. I'm sorry I bothered you.' He stomped away down the stairs and had slammed the door shut before I could force my sluggish body to react. I stared after him and heaved a sigh.

'What is wrong with him?' I muttered as I trudged down the stairs, locked the door and dragged myself back up to my room. I collapsed onto my bed feeling more muddled than ever but too tired to dwell on it. I fell into a deep sleep and didn't even dream.

The sun was bathing my room when I woke. My eyes were thick with crusted sleep and I spent a while slowly rubbing them clean, listening to the birds outside and the occasional car trundling down the street. I still felt groggy, but about a thousand times better than when I'd hit the pillow. I finally opened my eyes properly and reached for my phone. It was 12 pm. I sat up quickly and shook my head clear. It was rare for me to sleep more than about six hours. But I had really needed to catch up.

When I got down to the kitchen, having showered and dressed, I noticed a note on the table. I looked around, but nothing seemed out of place. I picked up the scrap of paper and recognised the neat, narrow slanted writing of Professor Melrose.

Didn't want to wake you. Can you meet me in the usual place when you get this, please?

I folded the note and stuffed it in my pocket. I made myself some chicken, rice and vegetables and took my time eating, defiantly taking as long as possible. It was gone 1.30 before I descended the stairs into the basement and opened the trapdoor. I stepped into the dark and narrow passage and turned on the torch on my phone before closing the trapdoor. I hated this passage and resented having to go down it on my own. What if there were demons?

I made my way slowly down the steps and into the store room. The strip light was blinking slightly. Weaver sat cross-legged on top of a crate with a heavy book on one knee and a notebook on the other, a pen in her hand. She looked up at me with a small smile.

'Hi,' I said, not smiling back.

'You must have been tired.'

'I was.' I perched on the edge of the crate opposite her. 'Where are you staying?'

'With one of the other shifters, Crystal, the one you helped. She has an entrance to the catacombs too, so I can get around the city without going onto the streets. It's best if I'm not seen.'

'Why? Would someone recognise you?'

'Maybe,' she replied, cocking her head to one side. 'But if the wrong thing caught my scent then we could lose the element of surprise.'

'Right, yeah. That sense of smell thing.'

'You're angry.'

'Frustrated. I don't want this to be my life.' The strip light flickered and I looked around nervously. If it gave up and went out we would be in the pitch black. Everything in the cave was coated in dust.

'You wanted a normal human life.'

'Yeah. Didn't you?'

'No, I was raised knowing what I was, knowing I might change. I never expected a human life. Eve,' she said seriously, putting her pen and books to one side. 'When I was about your age I had a pack mate who felt like you did, at least in part. She was constantly torn in two between her humanity and her shifter blood. It nearly destroyed her.'

'What happened to her?'

'She lost everything from her human life. She lost

herself for a while, too. Don't let that be your story. I know that you crave normality, but you are not normal, you never have been. You need to make peace with that as soon as you can so that you can hold on to what's important and let go of what isn't.'

'How do I decide what's important?'

'I can't tell you that.' She gave me a sad sort of smile. 'But I've found that blood family can be a bit of a mixed bag. The people who believe in you and who have your back are your true family. That kind of loyalty is valuable.'

'You were related to my mother, right?'

'Yes, that's right. Our ancestors were what's known as Furies. In Caerton they were shifter royalty. It's not certain here, much of the history has been lost. There was a great war and most of the shifters died. The Furies were so few that their ideology was lost, they blended with the other shifters. Your mother never knew her heritage or the dangerous ideas that the Furies used to espouse.'

'What ideas?'

'That shifters are superior to humans and should treat humanity like cattle.'

'Ugh. But you aren't a Fury? You don't believe that?'

'No,' she said with a smile. 'I was saved from that fate. But there were disadvantages to the shifters here losing sight of all of that. Furies would never find themselves enslaved to vampires.'

'No, I suppose not.' I shifted my weight and looked

away.

'It would be simpler if you had changed. You would understand about being part of a pack and wouldn't be stuck on the fringe.'

'Yeah, thanks.' I raised an eyebrow and crossed my arms over my chest defensively.

'I apologise. I don't mean to offend you.'

'Sure. Your friend, the one who lost herself, did she come to terms with what she was?'

'In her way, yes. She was different, too. You'd like her, I think.'

'Was? Is she...?' I couldn't say the word, I was afraid of saying the wrong thing.

'That's a whole other story,' Weaver smiled. 'I asked you here to talk about the future. Walker told me about what you learned from visiting Vitale.'

'Walker?'

'Peter, sorry. He is Walker-in-Moonlight to me.'

'Oh, yes. It's hard to remember all these names, especially when I've known people all my life by different ones.'

'Of course. Peter said that you heard something about rigging an election?'

'Yeah. And other apparently human criminal stuff. I didn't really get any closer to uncovering what he knows about all of this.' I gestured at the cave around us. 'But I can keep trying. I know you need a plan of attack, and knowing how much of an advantage you have is important for that. I don't want anyone to die.'

'No one?' She raised an eyebrow and leaned towards me slightly.

'No one who doesn't have to.'

'You have your head straight about Vitale, don't you?'

'Yes, of course. He probably killed my parents, he enslaved my family's people. He's the head of a dangerous organised crime syndicate and has done terrible things. He's a monster.'

She fixed me with a shrewd look and simply nodded. I felt as though she saw right through me. But she didn't challenge my words.

'Right then. I'm going to train the others. Want to watch?'

'Sure.'

Weaver picked up her things, summoned a flame into her palm and held her flaming hand ahead as she led the way down the other passage out of the cave. 'How do you do that?' I asked in wonder.

'It's a gift from Artemis.'

'People keep saying stuff like that. But I don't really understand. I've heard of Artemis, she's a Greek goddess, right?'

'That's right. Shifters believe that we have been chosen by her to protect humanity from the demons and other creatures that threaten it. She chooses our form for us depending on which moon phase we change under for the first time, and she grants us each one or two special powers to help us fulfil our role.'

'Oh, wow.' I followed close behind her, watching my step while also trying to listen carefully to what she said.

'We can also create talismans, objects with special powers, by making deals with fae and constructs and sometimes demons.'

'Aren't demons dangerous?'

'Yes, but to different degrees. Sometimes we can make deals with them but you have to be careful, they can twist your words.'

'Right. What are the other things?'

'Fae are like spirits of nature, they come from another realm, Alfheim. Constructs are from Nidavellir and are beings of machinery and things man-made.'

Her words were immediately scrambled by my brain but I held my tongue. Weaver chuckled and stepped out into the vast cavern at the heart of the catacombs. There were over a dozen shifters assembled and engaged in some very serious-looking practice combat in pairs and threes. I drew a breath and held it as I looked around.

Three shifters I didn't recognise were taking on a hulking heap of bricks and mortar with thick, metal poles jutting out from its joints. The sound of grinding stone echoed, as did its rumbling grunts as it lunged helplessly from one shifter to another.

I raised a finger towards it and leaned close to Weaver's ear.

'Construct?'

'Yep.' She grinned at me.

On the other side of the cavern were Crystal and Strikes Twice, engaging a swirling sandstorm. They'd backed it into a corner between two tall rocks but seemed to be at a loss for what to do with it.

'Fae?' I asked, pointing towards it.

'That's right. It's rare that we have to fight them, but sometimes they pose a threat and don't respond to reason, so it's worth practising.'

'Are they here willingly?'

'Yes, they agreed to help. Crystal!' Weaver bellowed as she strode towards the clueless shifters in the corner. 'You're the rite mistress. Time to send it back.'

Crystal nodded and started throwing something I couldn't make out at it from a small pouch. The sandstorm collapsed to the ground and vanished. Weaver patted her on the back.

All around the cavern were other small practice fights with demons and constructs, things that took my breath away. Shadowy figures with tentacles, shining metal men, something that was oozing dark liquid that might have been tar.

Kirk and Peter weren't there, I noticed. I followed Weaver over to where Crystal was still being congratulated, though I didn't really understand why.

'Hi, Eve,' Crystal said, smiling and leaning in to give me a hug. I flinched and pulled out of it as quickly as possible. Crystal looked a little confused and offended.

'Sorry,' I said quietly enough that only she could hear me. 'I'm not much of a hugger. Physical contact like that triggers my visions and they can be pretty horrible.'

'Oh, I'm sorry. I didn't realise. Noted for future reference.'

'Thanks. What was that thing you did?'

'Oh!' Crystal showed me the pouch she was carrying. Inside was lots of fine, brightly coloured grit. 'Ground Hepthian crystals.'

'I don't really know what that means.' I gave her a sheepish look and she chuckled.

'That's okay. I didn't at first. Weaver showed me how to collect crystals from Hepethia, which is sort of like our home realm. I grind them up and can use them to send things across the veil, like that sandstorm fae.'

'Oh, that's kind of cool.' I grinned at her and she smiled back. 'Is that where you get your name? Crystal?'

'Yes.' She grinned at me. 'I have a special affinity with them.' She was as scantily clad as the first time I'd seen her. Her arms and every other bit of visible skin seemed to be covered in intricate tattoos and I noticed that many of them were of crystal formations. She looked a few years older than me and I remembered her saying that she'd only changed two months previously.

'Do shifters change at all different ages?' I asked.

'Mm-hmm,' she replied, busying herself with putting away the pouch of ground crystals. 'But I was a relatively late bloomer. Normally it happens in the teen years. It's usually triggered by violence or a really stressful experience.'

I nodded. I wondered if it might still happen for me. Although my life recently hadn't lacked for stress and life-threatening situations. If a change hadn't been triggered by any of that then I thought it unlikely to ever happen.

I couldn't quite decide if I was relieved or disappointed.

CHAPTER TWENTY-FIVE

WHEN I EMERGED FROM THE DARKNESS OF THE CATACOMBS it was late afternoon. The shadows were stretching out in the fiery orange glow of the approaching sunset. My phone started going crazy with notifications once I was back in range of a signal. I unlocked it with a frown. I'd had two missed calls from Antonio and one from an unknown number. I had a string of text messages asking me to call him back as well as three alerting me to voice messages. My heart began to race as I considered why he might be so desperate to get hold of me.

I was about to call him when my doorbell rang and a knock accompanied it before it even finished chiming. I went to the door and put the chain on before opening it a crack.

Antonio's driver stood there looking concerned.

'Ms Rawling,' he greeted me with a courteous nod. 'Apologies for the intrusion. Mr Vitale was most anxious to contact you and was unable to do so. I've been sent to collect you and take you to his house.'

'Oh. I'm fine, I was sleeping all day.'

'Of course. My apologies again. Please, would you accompany me?'

'Okay, just a minute.' I closed the door and returned my attention to my phone. I dialled into my voicemail and listened to the messages.

'Eve, I hope you are rested. I would like to see you tonight. Will you call me back, please?' Antonio sounded calm enough in his first message. The second was an hour and a half later.

'Eve. Are you all right? Please return my call.' He sounded a little anxious.

The third message was from the unknown number whose call I had missed just a few minutes before returning from the basement.

'Ms Rawling, this is Mr Vitale's driver. I'm outside your house to collect you. Are you all right? I'll try the door again shortly.'

The text messages filled in the picture a little.

"Eve, I'm worried about you. If you're coming to see me tonight, I would prefer you to travel in daylight."

I got the distinct impression that I'd need to speak to him to fully understand why he was so anxious. A little red flag popped up in my mind as I considered this slightly stalker-ish behaviour.

I jogged up the stairs and quickly packed a small bag to take with me. If I was going to be there all night I wanted a change of clothes and my toothbrush.

I ran back down the stairs and flung open the door. The driver was waiting for me by the car, so I gave him a quick smile before turning to lock my door. By the time I reached the car, he'd opened the door for me and I climbed inside.

It was dusk, the sky had turned to misty pink and orange. We drove a little more quickly across the busy city than I was strictly comfortable with. I had the distinct impression that his orders were explicit: get me there before dark.

I was beginning to feel quite uneasy about the situation and didn't feel at all safe going to the house in such a rush or with such an ominous cloud hanging over me.

I was still gripping my phone and I called Antonio, hoping for some reassurance, I supposed, or to reassure him at least. He answered on the first ring.

'Eve.' He would have sounded breathless, if he breathed.

'Hi. I'm on my way. What's going on?'

'I'll explain when you get here. Where were you?'

'Sleeping. I needed to catch up.'

'Of course, yes, of course. I'm sorry.'

'No, I'm sorry to have worried you. Is that why you're rushing me over there? Because you were worried?'

'Partly. I will explain. I need you to hurry, it's almost

sunset.'

'We'll be there in about two minutes the way he's driving. Shall I tell him to slow down?'

'He is following my instructions.'

'And if we crash and die you'll make that known, will you?'

'You won't crash. You'll be fine. I'll see you soon.' He was uncharacteristically short with me and ended the call abruptly. I felt a little stung, even with all of this urgency and uncertainty, I still wanted my smooth Antonio.

We were pulling up in front of the house a few minutes later. The sky was blazing orange in the last burst of daylight. The sun's rays were warm on my skin and took a moment to bask in the safety of the sunlight in front of the house. But the door was swung wide by Frederick and I felt the driver's presence ushering me towards it.

Frederick was impeccably calm and yet even more efficient than usual in taking my coat and seeing me in through the brightly lit foyer. He led me up the grand staircase and straight to Antonio's room. When we were still several feet away, the door flew open and Antonio darted out and scooped me into his arms.

'Quickly,' he whispered as he ushered me into his room. Frederick turned smoothly and swept away down the corridor without a word. The blinds were drawn and the room was dark and it took a few seconds for my eyes to adjust. Antonio locked the door and pulled me into his arms again, kissing my forehead.

'What's going on?' I whispered, impatiently. 'You have your servants rushing me about. They're totally cool and collected on the surface but I can tell they're going nuts on the inside. I don't know if they're genuinely afraid for my safety, or just worried about their own necks if they let you down.'

'Both,' he said, still holding me firmly against his chest. 'You're okay.'

'Of course I'm okay. Why wouldn't I be?' I prised myself free of his tight grip and fixed him with my most severe glare. 'Tell me.'

'Lucia. She's... she's not happy.'

'And you think she wants to hurt me?'

'She doesn't know about you yet. She suspects, she knows something, but she wants to hurt someone, yes.'

'Wouldn't I have been safer in my own home, the one she hasn't been invited into?'

'Not if she found a way to drive you out of your home.'

'Why would she hurt me, anyway? Ruthless killer, I get that, but does she make a habit of killing your girlfriends?'

'No, she doesn't.' He shook his head and let out a low snort of laughter, his hands buried in his crisply pressed trouser pockets.

'Am I a special case?'

'Maybe.' He looked at me with deep, dark eyes.

'Did you really just want to get me here for something else?' I smiled seductively at him and moved towards him. His eyes flickered down my body and he licked his lips.

'That wasn't my intention. But seeing as you're here.' He grabbed my hands and pulled me against him again, this time capturing my lips in a hot kiss. One hand pressed against my back, the other held the back of my head. Blood rushed to my lips and my head began to feel lighter. I broke the kiss and gasped for breath. He was looking into my eyes with hunger and I blushed.

Antonio lifted me up and walked me to the bed, where he lay me down and crawled on top of me, his intentions perfectly clear. He kissed me again with that intense passion and I began fumbling with the buttons of his shirt.

A rap at the door abruptly halted things and Antonio tore from me, leaving me panting on the bed alone. He was at the door even as Lucia tried the handle. The door was locked and didn't budge. He pressed himself against it and called through it.

'What do you want, Lucia?'

'Before you get going— is it the same one as the other night?' There was eager excitement in her voice. She didn't wait for a reply. 'I'm meeting the others. Do you want us to bring you a snack? Or are you all set for dinner?'

'I'm good, thank you.'

'I will find out who has got you all giddy, you know? I need to talk to you later about that situation.'

'Later, yes. Have fun.'

'You too, brother dearest,' her voice sing-songed as she moved away from the door. Antonio turned to face me, though he tipped his head back against the door and closed his eyes.

'She sounded happy enough.' I raised an eyebrow at him.

'Because the sun has set and she can go out to eat.'

'You're afraid of her.' I propped myself up on my elbows and looked at him through narrowed eyes.

'She is dangerous. Not to me, directly, but she is not in her right mind and hasn't been for a long time. She's reckless and I can't control her like I used to.'

'Big brother isn't as influential as when you were both younger?'

'Exactly. She does her own thing, she has done for a century, more. But she used to listen to me. She doesn't any more.'

'Maybe she doesn't trust you.'

'Why would you say that?'

'Well, does anyone really trust you?'

'I suppose not. Fear and trust are not the same thing.'

'They're kind of opposites,' I said with a wry smile. 'When people trust that you'll kill them if they step out of line, that's not the same as trusting that you won't.'

'Very true.' He looked at me with those big eyes filled with wonder. 'You are one of a kind.'

'Aren't we all?'

'I've lived long enough, Eve, to know that people are mostly the same. But every now and then, someone surprises you.' He gave me that smile that made my heart flutter, and stalked back to the bed. He pounced and I squealed. He did his best to keep me as breathless as possible for several thrilling hours.

'Who were the others Lucia mentioned?' I asked as we lay staring into each other's eyes later that night.

'Celino, Dante and Laguardia.'

'Are they vampires?'

'Yes.'

'Did you make them?'

'Yes. Well, Lucia made Dante. Why are you asking me this?' He'd tensed up slightly and his eyes narrowed a little.

'Because I think my safety might depend upon knowing. Are there any other vampires?'

'Not here, no.'

'In Naples?' I asked, running my fingers gently over his chest.

'Yes.'

'Lots of them?'

'No, just a few, as far as I know.'

'You've been here a long time, haven't you?'

'Yes.' His chest heaved as if he were sighing, and he rolled onto his back, resting his hands behind his head. 'I came here in 1863.'

'Why?'

'To make my family proud.'

'Human family? Or vampire?'

'Yes.' He turned his head and smiled softly at me. I looked at him, this perfect man, his skin almost iridescent in the moonlight streaming in through the windows. The blackout blinds had been rolled up at some point between my orgasms. 'Why am I telling you all of this?'

'I have special powers that make you susceptible to my questioning.' I wiggled my eyebrows at him and grinned.

'That's usually my forte. But not with you, somehow.'

'Does Lucia have her own human servants too?'

'Yes. That's what worries me. You aren't necessarily safe in the day if she decides to play with you.'

'What does that mean?'

'If she decides that I'm too attached to you, or not paying her enough attention, or worries about what you know, she might take matters into her own hands. Very few people know what we are, for good reason.'

'Frederick knows.'

'Yes, and a small handful of others closest to us. Lovers don't tend to know.'

'They probably clue in when they get bitten.'

'Yes, but then they forget.' He raised his eyebrows and poked me hard in the shoulder. I swayed slightly but returned to my position on my side, gazing at him. 'Why didn't you?'

'No idea,' I lied with a shrug. 'How did you get here? Back in 1863? It must have been very dangerous to make a long journey in those days.'

'Yes,' he replied with a grudging nod, allowing me to deflect his question. 'We had to travel by road at night across Europe and as passengers on a pirate ship across the North Sea from the Netherlands.'

'How did you keep safe from the sun before blackout blinds?'

'Carefully.' He chuckled. 'Did you know that Oris has a network of catacombs running underneath it?'

'I heard something about that, yes,' I replied vaguely.

'They go right out to the coast. Smugglers used them. That's how we got to the city. When we were on the road, sometimes we buried ourselves.'

'Oh god. And clawed your way out after dark?'

'That's right. But that never suited Lucia much. We found safe places, manipulated people into protecting us, built houses with hidden rooms with no windows. It wasn't always easy, but we're still here.'

'Is it just sunlight that can hurt you? Or were there other dangers?'

'The stories are mostly true. A wooden stake to the heart is— Eve.' He shook his head and looked away from me. 'What am I doing?'

'Trusting me?' I leaned over and kissed his cheek.

'I'm a fool.'

'Why?' I asked, genuinely surprised by his tone.

'This pillow talk could kill me.'

'Yes, it could. Me too. How does it feel?'

'Vulnerable.'

I let out a laugh and shook my own head.

'Now you know how I feel.'

He rolled back to face me and pulled me up against him.

'Stop it,' he growled, his nose almost touching mine.

'Stop what?'

'Stop making me fall in love with you.' He kissed me. It took me a moment to shake off the surprise and give in to his kiss, but when I did it felt even more intense. My head swam in dizzying spirals and every inch of contact between our bodies felt like a spark of electricity. I lost myself in the smell of him and the heat of our bodies as we made love yet again.

'Bite me,' I urged as he moved in me, tilting my head to give him access to my neck.

'No,' he snarled between passionate kisses. 'Too much, too soon. Next time.'

I cried out as he brought me to my climax and before I came down I knew that I loved him too, but to say it out loud was too big of a risk to myself and to him.

CHAPTER TWENTY-SIX

'I NEED TO GO HOME,' I said with a whimper. 'I need to actually sleep and I have to be at the restaurant tomorrow.' I'd come prepared to stay overnight, but knew I would lose another night's sleep if I did.

'You're safer here with me,' he replied, placing soft kisses on my collarbone.

'You can't shield me forever, and besides, you might be worrying about nothing.'

'Maybe. But I can't count on being able to get you out of here without being seen.'

'We have to take that chance. This thing is intoxicating, Antonio.' He groaned as I said his name and I shoved him away from me, trying to extricate myself from our tangled limbs and the bedsheets. 'We could stay in here forever, but what would happen to my family's restaurant, or your criminal empire? We have lives to live.'

'Speak for yourself,' he said with a huff, falling hopelessly onto his back.

'You may be missing some key signs of life, like a

heartbeat, but you are living. However that's possible, you're here when you should be long dead. You didn't live this long by getting lost in passionate love affairs. You need to put your cool head back on for a bit.'

'Why is it that every time we speak it is you, with your paltry twenty years, who speaks with such wisdom?'

'Maybe I have an old soul?' I grinned and climbed out of the bed. I padded across the thick carpet to the bathroom, running my fingers over his suits as I passed through the wardrobe. I was just at the bathroom door when the wardrobe door behind me slammed shut and I was plunged into pitch black. I heard the main bedroom door open and Lucia's voice cut through the pounding in my chest.

'I'm bored. Ugh, why are you naked?'

'Lucia, get out.' Antonio's voice was unmistakably irritated but he affected a tone of boredom.

I suddenly felt extremely vulnerable, standing there in the dark, with not a stitch on. My skin erupted with goosebumps as I stared at the thin line of dim light around the edge of the door. I tiptoed to the bathroom and lifted a white towelling robe off the hook on the back of the door. I slipped into it and instantly felt warmer, though the tiled floor was still cool against my bare feet. I crept back to the wardrobe door and listened.

'I've hardly seen you lately. Dante decided to go off and you know I can't abide being with the others on my own. Why aren't you downstairs, anyway?'

'I was busy.'

'Still? Is she still here?'

'No, you just missed her. What a shame. I can't wait for you two to meet.' His voice dripped with sarcasm.

'Not funny, Tony,' Lucia whined in a mock baby voice. 'If she's important to you then I should meet her.'

'Hmm. Two things: she's not important to me, and if she was you would be desperately jealous and not likely to play nicely.' I cringed a little, but I knew he was protecting me.

'If she's not important then why are you spending so much time with her and keeping her hidden?'

'Because she tastes delectable and I don't want to share.'

'Fine, be that way. Come out with us later. We're going to some after, after-hours thing at a club that Celino heard about.'

'After, after-hours?' I could almost hear his eyebrow arching.

'It's going to be fun. There will be all sorts of flavours there. There might even be some of your favourites. I heard it's under new management, one of the beasts we own.'

My stomach clenched. Whether she meant humans or shifters, referring to them like that was sickening.

'What?' Antonio snapped. I hadn't expected that

reaction. I listened more closely.

'That's what I heard.'

'Why didn't I hear that? They shouldn't be starting new businesses without my say-so.' I heard movement and the jingle of his belt buckle. He was throwing clothes on. 'Get out and find Dante.'

'If he's still with his quarry he won't be easy to track down.' Lucia sounded pleased.

'You have your ways. Get him here as soon as possible. Try to make sure he doesn't leave a corpse for me to dispose of this time.'

'I'll do my best, Brother. I like seeing you back to your old self.'

I heard her heels on the carpet and the door slam. I stood in the shadows, aching all over, and felt a tear on my cheek. The door opened slowly and Antonio stood there in jeans, his face dark and serious.

'I'm sorry you had to hear that.'

'No, it's okay, it's the reality.' I brushed past him and looked around the room for my clothes but they were nowhere to be seen. Antonio ducked down and fished them out from under the bed, along with my bag. I was crying in earnest now. The illusion felt as though it had been shattered.

'It's me protecting you the only way I know how.'

'I got that.' I sniffed and nodded as I hurriedly yanked my jeans up. 'But the last bit... "beasts you own"?'

'Eve.' He caught hold of my arms, stopping me from pulling my top on. I looked into his eyes, they were glistening. 'That's the way she thinks of people and that was me protecting you too. Lucia expected that reaction from me and I had to deliver it. It got her out of here so that you can get home safely.'

'What's she expecting you to do next?'

'Discipline the person who has tried to extend their reach. I will, but they'll be fine. I promise.'

'You can't go soft on my account.' I was trembling. I tugged free of his grip and finished getting dressed.

'You don't want me to be the Camorra clan leader that got me here, Eve. You wouldn't be able to look me in the eye.'

'No, maybe not. But I'm not going to ask you to change for me.'

'Why not?'

'Sorry?'

'Why won't you ask me to change?'

I wiped my cheeks and avoided looking at him. I had no idea what to say. All I could think about was the shifter who was about to face trouble and the terrible lies that still existed between us. How much love would it take to undo those lies and uncover the secrets?

'Would it make a difference if I did ask?'

'Maybe.' I looked into his eyes. I wanted to believe him. I wanted my life to be simple. It had never been more complicated. 'Ask me.'

'Change for me. Don't kill anyone. Don't extort anyone. Stop making everyone around you afraid of you.' It was a huge thing to ask and something twisted around in my gut as he stared at me, unblinking, for an agonisingly long few seconds.

'What would I do instead?'

I blinked up at him, caught off guard.

'I don't know. Start an honest business?'

'If only it were so simple. How about, for now, I promise to not kill anyone? That's the big one? Right?'

'I suppose.' I looked away. 'I have to go.'

'Wait a moment.' He grabbed a shirt, flung it on and slipped his feet into a pair of shoes. He swooped to the door, opened it a crack and listened intently. 'Okay.' He ushered me forward and put his hand on my back to guide me towards the grand staircase. 'There are people downstairs,' he said softly as we reached the top of the stairs. 'No one I'm concerned about, but let's get you out of here quietly. Okay?'

'Okay.' I was still shaking and my cheeks were cool from the tears drying on my skin. Antonio wrapped his arm firmly around me and I leaned on him as he led me down to the foyer. Frederick appeared from the study, where I could hear voices talking animatedly, and moved swiftly to the closet in the corner of the hall, returning a moment later with my coat.

'Is miss all right?' he asked, glancing from me to Antonio and back again.

'I'm fine,' I lied.

'Would you have Nicolas bring the car around, please?' Antonio said softly.

'Of course.' Frederick disappeared into the study and Antonio led me to the door. He opened it and took me out into the cold night. The sky was clear and the moon cast its silver glow on the paved drive. The trees in front of the house swayed gently.

'I don't want to be a secret that you smuggle in and out of your house,' I said, turning to look into Antonio's face.

'I understand.'

'Either something changes so that we can be together openly, or this has to end.'

'I see. You understand how that puts me in a difficult position?'

'Yes, and I'm sorry. But there are all sorts of reasons why this whole situation is madness. The reality outside of your bedroom is bitter.'

'It is.' He nodded sadly.

The car pulled up beside us and the driver got out to open the back door for me.

'Call me when you work it out.'

'I will. Make sure she gets inside safely,' he added to the driver as I got into the car. Nicolas nodded and closed my door. I watched Antonio through the tinted glass, my heart aching.

CHAPTER TWENTY-SEVEN

WHEN I GOT HOME IT WAS THE MIDDLE OF THE NIGHT, but I couldn't put off the call that I had to make. I found Peter's number in my phone and hit the call button. He answered after just a couple of rings.

'Everything okay?' he asked, an edge of panic in his voice.

'With me, yes. But I wanted to warn you, the Camorra are moving on someone who has apparently taken over running some club without permission from them. I'm sure it's one of your friends.'

'Shit. Now?'

'Now. I heard Lucia telling Antonio about it.'

'I'll ask Dad who it is. You didn't get a name?'

'No. Sorry. Peter, he promised that whoever it was wouldn't be harmed.'

'Really?'

'Yes, but he can't control his sister. She's crazy, and dangerous.'

'I know. Thanks for the warning. I'll take care of it. Are

you sure you're all right? Where are you?'

'I'm home. I'm okay. Just tired. I'm going straight to bed now. I just had to call you first.'

'Are you safe?'

'I hope so. It's a relative term these days.' I let out a humourless laugh. Peter remained silent. 'I'll see you tomorrow.'

'Yeah. Thanks again.'

'No problem. Bye.' I hung up the phone and trudged up the stairs to my empty bed.

Peter called me the next day.

'He kept his word,' he said, his voice cracking.

'I'm glad no one was hurt.'

'Me too.'

'Don't tell me what happened,' I said. 'I don't want to know.'

'Are you sure?'

'Yes.'

He respected my request and I didn't hear any more details about the shifter who had been in trouble or what the consequences were. The less I knew about how Antonio did business the better. I couldn't face it while I was stuck in this limbo.

The next few days were agonising. I stumbled from

one mundane task to the next, my head stuck in a fog of confused love, infatuation and resentment. This was not the life I'd asked for or expected, even with my gift, I'd still had my sights on something resembling normality.

But I hated moping and tried to keep busy, even though I constantly had one eye on my phone, waiting to hear from Antonio, hoping to hear him tell me he'd handed the business to someone else and was giving up his life of organised crime for me.

But life wasn't a fairy tale and Antonio wasn't a prince.

It was a painful three days of nothing. I was on edge the entire time, waiting for something to happen.

December had arrived and the staff at Piero's insisted on putting up a tree in the window. I watched from the office door as Tina and two of the kitchen staff decorated it while singing loudly to Christmas music blasting from the sound system.

I interviewed a few people for the manager role at Piero's, while doing the job myself somewhat competently, despite everything going on in my personal life. It was ludicrous; someone my age, as inexperienced as I was, interviewing people twenty years older. I kept wondering why I was bothering to hire someone. If my romance with Antonio was over I'd need something to keep me occupied.

But then I'd think of Caerton and my life there. Part of me yearned to return to university, though it was looking more and more like I'd have to restart my final year if I did go back. I wasn't sure I could make up the time that I'd missed.

Peter and Kirk came and went a few times, flitting in and out of the restaurant and my home between their human and shifter responsibilities. I was always on the outside looking in, it seemed. I didn't feel like I was a part of any one thing in my life. I didn't really fit anywhere. I had felt like that my whole life and it felt insurmountable now that I knew just how complex the world really was. I didn't quite fit with the shifters, or humanity, and I certainly didn't feel at home with the vampires.

I hadn't felt at ease in Caerton, although I had a group of friends there, I was always a bit different from them. But nor did I feel right running Piero's in my home town. I wondered if I would ever find my place. I fought against the idea that it was only to be found in Antonio's bed, but that truly was the only place I'd felt comfort and joy.

I missed him with an ache in my chest that made me feel as though I were living in slow motion. As those days dragged on I wanted nothing more than to have him tell me he would do whatever it took in order to be with me.

At the same time, I had to hear snippets of news from the shifters about their plan to retake control of the city. I knew that they planned to kill Antonio and Lucia and I felt utterly powerless to change that. I still didn't know what I was going to do if it came to a choice. I was completely torn in two between people that I thought of as family and the love of my life. Every time I felt like I'd made a choice my mind would change. Constant nausea from indecision plagued me.

'What do you mean, you and Vitale are taking a break?' Kirk asked me on Monday afternoon after the interviews.

'I asked something huge of him and I'm waiting for him to give me his decision,' I said wearily. 'I don't want to see him until he decides. It's too confusing. This is way too personal to discuss with you,' I hissed at him over the desk in the restaurant office.

'You've given us valuable information, I appreciate that. But ultimately I just want you to be safe. You know I never wanted you to get close to him. I'm glad that you're putting some distance between you.'

'But?' I raised an eyebrow and tapped the end of my pen on the pad of paper on my desk.

'We may need your help to enact the plan. We may need you to get in touch with him.'

'When?' I asked with a sigh.

'When we're ready, which should be any day now. We can't talk about it here.' His eyes flickered to the door.

'No, we can't. Are you going to let me in on the plan?'

'Yes. What did you ask of him?'

'Something I hope will mean he doesn't have to die.'

'Eve,' he said, looking at me with pity in his wrinkled eyes.

'I support you, Kirk, I do. I want you all to be free. That's what I'm trying to achieve. Aren't you?'

'Of course.'

'If that can be accomplished without any bloodshed, then isn't that the ideal result?'

'Yes, I suppose it is.' There was reluctant acceptance in his weary face and voice.

'I never took you for the vengeful type.' I picked up my things and stalked from the office without waiting for a reply.

I didn't hear from either of the Wilkes men for a whole day. When I did it was just a text message from Peter.

"Meet me under the house in an hour."

With a nagging sense of apprehension deep in my bones, I made my way into the catacombs.

I could hear the shifters before the white torchlight touched the edge of the tunnel down under the city. It sounded like the roar of a waterfall flowing over a high cliff. My hand was slippery with sweat on my phone and I swapped hands to wipe my palm on my jacket.

The passage opened up and I stepped into the vast cavern. I flicked off the torch, my mouth hanging open as I saw them all assembled there. There were flaming torches burning in brackets on the walls and two bonfires roaring at opposite sides of the cavern, filling the whole place with warm, flickering light. Between the fires were what looked like around thirty shifters, many in their beast form. My breath caught in my throat.

They were jostling, laughing, roaring; some were fighting and being cheered on by onlookers. The noise was like nothing I'd ever encountered.

From out of the crowd, two familiar faces emerged: Peter and Weaver made their way to me. Peter was grinning, but Weaver looked serious and determined.

'You came!' Peter caught me in a one-armed hug, which he quickly released me from.

'Is this normal?' I asked, glancing warily over their shoulders towards the throng.

'Oh yes,' Weaver said, smiling slightly. 'You should see the gatherings in Caerton.'

'Maybe I will one day.' I was a little afraid of what I was seeing, but infinitely more curious.

'Maybe.' Weaver patted me briefly on the shoulder and the three of us set off walking across the cavern towards the fire to the right. I gazed at all of the shifters, arranged in clusters of five or six. Some groups merged and then separated again, like leaves blowing together and then drifting apart. There was a lot of laughter and camaraderie between them, but it was so physical and their bestial forms so alarming that it didn't look entirely friendly to my eyes.

I spotted Kirk towards the head of the crowd, standing with Crystal and Strikes Twice, deep in serious conversation. We steered towards them, weaving carefully between other groups. Peter kept himself between me and any jostling, shielding me from getting accidentally hurt. When we reached the others Kirk abruptly stopped what he was saying and greeted me with an awkward smile.

Crystal grinned and gave me a little wave, which I returned with a smile of my own.

'Hey,' I said in greeting. 'Is this everyone?'

'It is. Every last shifter in the city,' Kirk said, nodding, his fists deep in his cardigan pockets. He still looked so dad-like here among the big and brutal.

'Woah.' I looked around again and felt the closeness of the Agrius beasts beside us. I stepped away, closer to the fire at Kirk's back. 'Why are they here? Why am I here?'

'We need to discuss the plans and your insight may prove crucial,' Weaver explained.

'How are you going to hold a discussion with so many shifters?' I couldn't see how they could even be called to order, never mind engage in any sort of reasonable discussion when they all kept shoving and punching each other.

Weaver winked and raised a hand. The fire behind me roared and the flames leapt higher, licking the high ceiling of the cavern. I darted away from the heat and flung myself against Peter, who caught me skilfully and swung me around to the outer edge of the crowd and away from the fire at the same time. When he placed me back on my feet, smiling down at me, the crowd had settled to near silence and all faces were turned towards the immense blaze.

'Form a circle, please,' Weaver called, her voice echoing off the stone walls. The crowd parted and jostled quickly into a large circle. I found myself between Weaver and Peter. Kirk, Crystal and Strikes Twice lined up on Peter's other side. 'Thank you all for coming,' Weaver called out once everyone was in position. The fire died down behind us, back to the modest blaze it had been when I entered the cavern, its roar no longer loud enough to drown out Weaver's voice. 'You've come so far since I arrived. From being packless and disorganised, to what I see today. I'm impressed. Thank you all for hosting me and for taking my advice so readily. It makes what we need to do much more achievable. For too long you've been under the thumb of those who mean to keep you subservient, and you've neglected your duties to Artemis. But you're ready to resume your role as guardians of the veil between worlds. I'm so proud of you all.'

There was a ripple of muttering around the circle as the shifters took Weaver's praise on board. A number of eyes were flickering in my direction and I felt as though a spotlight were shining on me as I stood there beside Weaver, the lone human amid this army of powerful shapeshifters. Not all of them had seen me before and even those that had didn't really know me or what I was doing there. I could feel them growing beyond curious and into suspicious. Fingers pointed my way and not-so-quiet whispers carried across the circle.

'For those who aren't already acquainted,' Weaver said, her voice commanding silence from the assembly. 'This is Eve Rawling, daughter of Mother-of-the-Forest and Red Wolf. She is here in their place and is as entitled to be here as any of you.' Her voice was firm and I noticed a number of scowls disappear from faces around me, those doubters suitably chastised.

'We need to hear the plans you've been considering in your packs. The problem we face is city-wide and requires us all to cooperate,' Kirk said, his voice carrying clearly. 'We need to agree on a course of action.'

The circle erupted with shouts and eager suggestions. I cringed against the wall of noise that hit me. I heard little distinctly in the chaos, but it was clear from the angry tone and violent gestures around the circle that no one had considered sitting down with the vampires to talk it out.

'One at a time!' Weaver's voice roared out over the uproar, again settling the others to grudging silence.

'Dane?' Kirk said, gesturing across the circle to a tall, broad man with a long beard. The smaller, leaner man beside him clapped him on the shoulder and his face shone with pride. Dane nodded and stroked his beard slowly, apparently soaking up the silence and rapt attention he now had.

'The Yorviks have been talking about going up to the house in the daytime and shattering all of the windows.' Shouts of agreement and bursts of laughter shot around the circle. I tensed and felt my fists clench at my sides. Peter put a hand on my shoulder and squeezed it.

'That won't work,' he called. There were more shouts, not everyone heard Peter, but some did and were attempting to argue the case. 'I get it!' he shouted loudly and the shifters quietened to listen. 'I get why you would suggest it. But it won't work. It's not targeted enough. Too much could go wrong.'

Again there was an eruption of noise. My palms were sweating and my heart thudded angrily in my chest. I looked up at Peter, thankful to him for speaking out, but frustrated that they didn't get it. I wanted to explain, but didn't feel as though they would listen.

'Have you got a better idea?' a woman shouted in challenge from Weaver's other side.

'Yes, as it happens,' Peter replied. 'We know they're planning to rig the election next May. We have a plan to disrupt their political business and take out a big branch of the influence they hold over the city.'

'Rubbish!' jeered the woman who'd challenged Peter. Other shouts and frustrated gestures followed.

'We need to act now!' someone called.

'It's not enough!' called someone else.

'Kill 'em all!' Their voices became the roar of a rabble and my breath quickened as I began to fear for my own safety if a fight broke out.

Weaver caught hold of my hand and I looked into her shrewd eyes.

'You had something to say?' Her voice was low, just for me. I shook my head. 'It's okay. They need to hear from you.'

I whimpered and felt my back crumple. I turned away from the circle and begged her with wide eyes not to put the spotlight on me. She squeezed my hand again and waved her other hand at the fire, again stirring it into an inferno. The rabble died down gradually and all eyes turned our way once more.

'Eve has comments.' She released my hand and turned me to face the crowd. I gave her one last withering look, desperate to get out of this. 'It's okay,' she whispered.

I looked at Dane, the big guy, and nodded, swallowing a hard lump in my throat.

'There are people in there.' My voice was feeble and seemed to flop to the floor just in front of me. I knew it hadn't carried and cleared my throat before trying again, louder and clearer. 'Your plan, I get why you would suggest it. It's better than some sort of full-on assault which would likely see massive casualties. Sneak attack during the day when they're vulnerable to sunlight is a good idea, in principle.' I hated defending the idea, but I had to win favour if I wanted them to listen to me. Dane was watching me with narrow eyes, stroking his beard again. 'But there are people in the house, living humans. They could get hurt.'

'Too bad!' someone shouted with callousness in her voice.

'Yeah. Conspirators deserve whatever they get.'

'Yeah!' Shouts rang out. I swallowed hard again and felt a tightness in my chest.

'They don't all know the truth!' I shouted above the mounting din. A hush fell. 'They're glamoured, or manipulated. The Camorra have what they have through careful compartmentalising. No one knows everything. Not one of us here and no one in that house besides the Vitales themselves, and even there there's a rift!' I regretted it the moment I had said it. Questions began flying at me from all directions and I looked from one eager face to another. Weaver clasped my hand again and held her other hand up to command quiet. It came and I was gently urged on. I looked up at Peter, who was looking down at me with an expression of curiosity. 'Antonio and Lucia don't see eye to eye on some things.'

'How do you know that?' Dane called.

'Eve is our eyes on the inside,' Weaver said, saving me from having to answer. 'That's all you need to know.'

'I see and hear things,' I said in an attempt to elaborate. 'The point is, I don't want anyone innocent to get caught in the crossfire. Yes, you could smash every window in the house and let sunlight flood in. But it wouldn't instantly kill every vampire in there, even assuming they were all in there at once. They would wake if sleeping and find shelter to recover from any burns they had. They would send their human protectors out to gun you down.'

'Bullets aren't much of an issue for us, love!' one man shouted and others laughed.

'They might be if they're silver!' Peter shouted back, more angrily than I would have expected. It wiped the sneers and grins off their faces though.

'Why would they have silver bullets?' someone asked.

'Because they know they work against us,' Peter replied in a sarcastic tone. 'They aren't stupid. They know what we are and have been controlling us for a century. We can't expect to overthrow them overnight, or in one day. We need to be clever.'

'That's what my parents were working for most of my life,' I added, my voice echoing in the stunned silence. 'They wanted you to do this right so that no one gets hurt.'

'What would you suggest?' Kirk asked, leaning out of the circle to look into my face. He was calm and smiling softly. I felt his pride radiating towards me.

'I don't know,' I said, taken aback. 'Coordinate everything. You need to take down the Camorra clan in its entirety or someone else will just take the place of the

Vitales at the head of it. You need to remove their political sway and take over the veil work that Weaver mentioned. Then, maybe, you can think about a physical assault on the vampires. But even that has to be coordinated and targeted so that you don't hurt anyone else.' I thought of myself being in Antonio's bed during such an attack, or some other ignorant human in Lucia's bed. I thought of Frederick and the cleaner that Antonio had joked about somewhere in the house going about their business.

My cheeks were burning and my back was soaked in sweat from being too close to the fire. I wanted to bolt out of there now that I'd said what needed saying. They didn't look like they were about to storm the mansion now, so I felt I'd done my job.

Peter was looking at me with mingled sadness and pride and I dodged eye contact, fearing tears coming to my eyes.

'Thank you, Eve,' Weaver said softly. She turned back to the crowd and raised her voice. 'There was a time when my city faced a great threat that required the packs to unite. It was a struggle. The plans that were put in place took months to enact and come to conclusion. Eve's family has been working on this for years. It requires precision. Sadly, with their passing, much of what had been put in place was lost. You had a massive setback, but I believe you can do this.'

The shifters rumbled in agreement and the circle

began to break up into smaller discussions.

'I have to get out of here,' I whispered to Peter.

'Of course. Want me to come with you?'

'Yeah, okay.' I let him walk me out of the cavern and away from the heat and noise. The tunnel back to my basement was cool and quiet, just what I needed. 'How do you know about the silver?' I asked him.

'The other day when we found Night Thorn, the shifter you warned us about, Lucia had got to her first and tortured her with silver.'

'Oh god. Peter, I'm sorry.'

'She's okay. Antonio got her to stop. He let Night Thorn go with a warning. She healed.'

'Do you believe he wasn't in control of Lucia?'

'Night Thorn does.'

'Right.'

'Okay, we're here,' Peter said as he saw me into the safety of my basement and stood awkwardly in the entrance to the hidden passage. 'Do you want me to come up?'

'I need to sleep. I'm so tired.'

'Sure. Here, take this.' He pressed a coin into my hand. It was old, big and gold but tarnished and the markings on it impossible to read.

'What is it?'

'It's a talisman. If you need me just squeeze it and whisper my name. I'll hear you wherever I am. There's no phone signal down there, or on the other side of the veil, and I can't answer the phone if I'm not human anyway.' He smiled his boyish smile, complete with dimples.

'Thanks.' I put it in my pocket and turned toward the stairs.

'I'll let you know what happens down there,' he called. I turned and nodded.

'See you later.' I watched him pull the trapdoor closed, disappearing back into the catacombs.

I dragged my aching body upstairs. It was dark already and I closed all of the curtains, checking the street outside for signs of vampires, but there were none.

A cool shower was calling, so I peeled off my dirty, sweaty clothes and stepped into the shower. I washed off the strain of the day and by the time I was clean I felt relaxed enough that I thought sleep might be possible. I pulled on a nightdress and climbed into my bed. I was asleep in moments, but my dreams were filled with fire, smoke and the sounds of ripping flesh.

CHAPTER TWENTY-EIGHT

THE KNOCKING CREPT ITS WAY INTO MY DREAM AT FIRST. A strange banging that seemed out of place in the burning corridors of my old school. As my conscious mind began to become more aware, the doorbell ripped through the dream and tore me from sleep. I sat up in bed; the room was near dark. The bell rang again, followed by more knocking.

I leapt from the bed, shoved my feet into my slippers and threw on a robe as I hurtled along the landing and onto the stairs. I bolted down them and into the dark hall.

'Eve?' a male voice called on the other side of the door. 'Eve? I hear you.' It was Antonio. I unlocked the door and threw it open.

The sky was tinted pink and an eerie glow hung over the street. Antonio was leaning heavily against the door frame and his skin was hissing and smoking. He clutched his jacket across his chest and I could see dark blood seeping through the fabric and onto his hands.

'What's wrong? Are you hurt? Is that your blood?'

'Always the questions. Much. Yes. Yes. Please, I need your help.' He glanced over his shoulder at the lightening sky.

I stood suspended on the cusp of something important. I had seconds to decide whether to invite him into my home or not. If I didn't he would burn to death right there on my step. That would be hard to explain to the neighbours. I glanced anxiously up and down the empty street.

'Okay, come in.' I stood aside and he stumbled forwards into the hall. I slammed the door, shutting out the worst of the sun. The little window over the door still allowed some of the dawn light to enter, casting a patch of light onto the wall. 'Come to the back of the house.' I moved past him and led the way down the hall to the kitchen at the back. The blinds were drawn and the back of the house faced west so it would be a while before much sunlight penetrated them.

Antonio sat down heavily in one of the dining chairs and gingerly eased off his blood-soaked suit jacket. It was ruined, no dry cleaner could get that much blood out. I watched him cautiously, pulling my robe tight across my own chest against the morning chill.

His shirt was ripped right open and was even more soaked in blood. I couldn't just watch. I moved over to him and helped him peel the wet sleeves off his arms. There was a gaping slash from his left shoulder to his right hip.

'Oh my god! How did this happen?' I grabbed the shredded shirt and bundled it up, then pressed it to the middle of his chest where the wound seemed deepest.

'A demon.' His voice was hoarse and wavered as he blurted the words.

'What kind of demon?'

'The angry kind. That won't help.' He brushed away the shirt even as I tried to apply pressure. 'My blood won't clot.'

'Oh.'

'I need to feed.' He wouldn't meet my gaze and his voice was desperate.

'Oh,' I said again, stepping back. 'Did this happen nearby? Or did you go out of your way to get here?'

'Neither.' He coughed hard, reflexively raising his hand to his mouth, and blood spattered against his clenched fist.

'Oh god. Don't bleed out all over my kitchen!'

He looked up at me with narrowed eyes that screamed a sarcastic apology right at me.

'I need shifter blood to heal,' he said with a groan in his voice. 'It's the only way with a wound like this. Shifter blood, the like of which flows in your veins.'

We hung there, suspended in a moment of brutal honesty.

'I'm not a—'

'I know. But your parents were. You share their blood.

Please, Eve. Please help me.'

I stared at him, my thoughts racing. He was at my mercy. He couldn't go outside without frying. He would bleed to death right there if I let him. He had no choice. Wasn't this what the shifters had been working towards? It was within my power to end this generational feud without anyone else getting hurt. No one except the man I loved. The dead man. The man who was likely responsible for my parents' deaths.

I took another step back and my back bumped against the sink. If I saved him, if I let him drink my blood, in this state was he more likely to lose control and take too much? I could die in his arms right here in my home. I looked down at my hands. They were coated in his blood. There were splatters of it on the sleeves of my dressing gown. My hands were shaking.

'How do you know my blood will help?' I asked, not looking at him.

'I've tasted it already. I know that taste. I'd know it anywhere.'

'Because you fed on my parents.' I looked at him then. He looked back at me, pain in his eyes.

'Yes,' he said, dropping his head.

'Did you kill them?' I was shaking. He looked up, still hunched over and clutching his gaping chest, his eyes dark but wide.

'I did not. I swear to you. I tried to save them. I grieve

for them.' He was telling the truth. I could see it in his eyes. 'I won't feed on you by force, Eve. My fate is in your hands. I am not accustomed to begging for my life, but I ask you to please, trust me. Save me.'

Tears were flowing down my face. I nodded numbly and stepped towards him.

'I have more questions.'

'I wouldn't expect anything else.' He tried to smile but he was too weak. I could see his skin growing paler by the minute as his blood continued to flow out of his chest.

'Later, then, when you feel better.' I stepped up close to him. The metallic smell of the blood was dizzying. I pulled him to his feet. Then I stretched my head to one side, exposing the skin of my neck. Antonio wrapped his arms around me and with one last searching look into my eyes, he closed his eyes and sank his fangs into my vein. I gasped and my fingers dug into his bare back.

I could feel my life flowing into him; I could hear him gulping down my blood. My vision blurred and my eyes flickered closed.

I was standing on a dark road. Rain thundered on the black tarmac and I was soaked to the skin. My long, black hair clung to my face and neck. Trees lined the roadside and the rain dripped in great, heavy drops from their last autumnal leaves and mostly bare branches. The sides of the road were a foot deep in fallen leaves that now lay in muddy clumps.

The headlights were growing bigger and I could hear the tyres swooshing through the standing water on the road. I saw their faces faintly illuminated by the lights on the dashboard. Sylvia and Jonathan Rawling slowed to a halt right in front of me and I ran to the passenger door. Jonathan jumped out and grasped my hand. I pulled him into a brotherly embrace and we patted each other on the back.

'Stay in the car, Sylvia,' I called in my deep voice and thick Italian accent. She stayed behind the wheel, the wipers still swiping swiftly back and forth. 'Jonathan, are you going to Caerton tonight?'

'Yes,' Jonathan replied, breathless and flinching slightly against the pounding rain. 'We have to go to Eve.'

'Good. Stay there until I can fix this.'

'But what about—'

'I'll take care of everything, but you must get out of the city. It's not safe any more.'

'What about you?'

'I'll be all right. I'm a survivor.' The corners of my mouth tugged up into a smile.

'Does she know about you?' Jonathan asked, his face creased with concern.

'No, and I intend it to stay that way. Now get out of here before she traces your whereabouts and figures out where you're going.'

Jonathan nodded and climbed back into the car. I

leaned down and peered across him to Sylvia. 'Look after your girl, cousin.'

'I will. Thank you for everything you've done for us, Tony. Let us know when we can come home.'

'I will.' I closed the door and waved them on their way. They drove quickly, but not too fast for the conditions. Then I went back to my own dark car and climbed into the back seat. 'Follow them, carefully,' I said to my driver. I turned on the heated seat to dry myself and watched carefully out through the windscreen as we drove, with no lights, after the fleeing Rawlings.

We had gone no more than a mile and a half when it happened. I could see far beyond the capabilities of normal human sight. I saw their car brake hard and lift up and spin through the air, the lights twirling in a dizzying spiral. I saw Lucia's face, laughing maniacally, in the flashing of spinning headlights. The car landed upside down with a crunch. 'Stop,' I said quietly and my driver did as instructed. We sat there watching from a hundred yards away, my car dark and quiet. Lucia approached the car and dragged Jonathan out through the smashed windscreen. She crouched beside him and tucked into his neck.

There was nothing I could do without revealing the truth. The Rawlings were dead either way. 'Let's go home,' I ordered, my voice low and dark.

'Si, signor.'

With a rush of light and breath, I was yanked from the

vision and back into the present. I was sitting on the kitchen table, my night dress hanging off my shoulder, my robe undone, with Antonio wedged between my thighs, still drinking hungrily from my neck. His hands gripped the backs of my shoulders and he was murmuring with pleasure. Slowly, reluctantly, he pulled back and retracted his fangs. His chin was stained with my blood and I felt a little of it trickling down my neck. He dipped back to lick the drop and I remembered thinking, "Waste not want not", something my granny used to say, before everything was plunged into darkness again.

It felt as though I was slowly sinking into cool water. It was peaceful; the dappled light above me shifted and swirled. It was pretty. I felt like I could go now. I knew the truth and that was enough. Even though sadness hung over me, I didn't feel heavy any more and part of me looked forward to seeing my mum and dad again.

'Eve!' The shout echoed dully under the water. It was enough to wrench me from the serenity I felt, but I continued to sink slowly down. 'What have you done?!' The voice was louder. Peter's voice.

'No...' I managed to croak. I was being pulled up, back to consciousness. Antonio pulled away from me and I rushed up faster into the light. I reached out for him but grasped only cool air. 'No!'

'Eve? Are you all right?' Peter was scooping me into his arms. I could feel his heart pounding in his chest, his body warm against mine. I grew warmer and finally opened my eyes.

'My mother... she was a Vitale?'

'Yes. Distantly, but yes.' Antonio's voice was closer now.

'What? What are you talking about? What have you done to her?' Peter lay me down on the table and tore away from me. He lunged at Antonio, who was covered in blood, but no longer bleeding profusely. My blood had already begun to heal him. Peter grabbed Antonio by the throat and rammed him against the sink unit.

'No! Please!' I could hardly raise my voice loud enough to be heard over the snarls that both men were issuing. I tried to move towards them but barely shifted a few inches across the table.

'My, my,' Antonio managed to rasp, his throat held tight in Peter's hand. 'What big teeth you have.' He was smiling viciously.

'All the better to eat you with,' Peter snapped in reply.

'So, you take after Daddy. Maybe we should take this outside?'

'Suits me just fine. It's daylight,' Peter said through gritted teeth.

Antonio chuckled and raised a hand. One nail

extended, growing into a neatly pointed claw. He traced an arch through the air. From his nail came a glittering, gold line like a sparkler being swept through the air, leaving a trail of sparks behind it.

I watched, unable to lift myself up as a doorway opened and Antonio pulled Peter roughly through it. With an enormous effort, I pushed myself up and dived off the table, straight through the doorway after them. I fell with a thump onto a hard floor. It was dark, but for a cool, crescent moon shining in a star-studded sky. The door hung there in the air, sparkling gold at the edges and I could see my kitchen beyond it. Yet all around the door was dark night sky and I lay on what looked like a floor of smooth crystal.

Snarling, snapping sounds came from just behind me and I turned to see Peter in his Agrius form and Antonio with his teeth and claws bared, circling each other like wolves about to fight.

'Stop,' I whimpered, crawling towards them. 'Stop it at once, both of you.' They didn't seem to hear me, they just kept walking in those slow circles, their eyes fixed on each other. I raised a hand, my other supporting my weight and trembling with the strain of it. I drew upon every ounce of will in me. They had to stop. I couldn't let them kill each other. My outstretched hand held firm, even though my supporting arm felt as though it would give way at any second. 'Stop,' I said through gritted teeth.

I pushed out with my thoughts and swept my arm out wide. Peter went flying backwards and tumbled to the floor, rolling away across the crystal ground. Antonio stopped pacing and his head snapped towards me, his eyes wide. He ran to me and I collapsed in his arms.

'Did you do that?' he whispered. I nodded. 'You had a vision, didn't you? You saw the truth?'

'Yes.' My throat was so dry my voice scratched it and I was sent into a violent coughing fit. Antonio sat me up and held me, stroking my back. When I stopped coughing I looked up to see Peter walking cautiously towards me.

'Eve?' His voice trembled.

'You weren't listening,' I croaked. 'I told you to stop.'

'So you made me?' He crouched down in front of me and started to smile. But his eyes flickered towards Antonio and the smile faltered.

'She saved my life,' Antonio said softly, stroking my hair. 'She willingly saved my life.'

'I did, Peter, I did it willingly. Please don't hurt him. He's on our side.'

The two of them exchanged bitter glances. I didn't think their opinions of each other were likely to change much, but it seemed that for now, at least, there was a truce. 'Is this Hepethia?' I asked, looking around. The pale moonlight glittered on the ground and somewhere in the distance I heard something like a bark followed by a howl that trembled on the still air. If we'd been in the human world, I would have thought they were dogs, but here in Hepethia, the realm of shifters and god-only knew what else, I thought it unlikely to be anything so mundane.

'It is,' Antonio said.

'You have no right to be here,' Peter spat.

'I have every right. Because for over a hundred years I've been doing your job. I've been single-handedly guarding the veil.'

My whole body was shaking and my eyes were fluttering closed.

'We can hash this out later. We need to get Eve home.' Antonio scooped me up and I wrapped my arms around his neck. He walked me back to the golden arch and stepped through it, back into my kitchen, Peter right behind us.

'Whose blood is that all over her?' Peter asked.

'Mine,' Antonio replied. He glanced at Peter and stood looking around my kitchen. I could barely keep my eyes open but I saw the door shimmer away, the sparks framing it disappeared and my kitchen was back to normal. 'Where's her bedroom?'

'Follow me,' Peter said, his voice low and dark. Antonio carried me after Peter into the hall and up the stairs, taking care to make sure my head didn't bump against the wall. He carried me as though I weighed nothing at all and my foggy mind wondered just how strong he was.

Peter led Antonio along the hall to my room, formerly my parents' room, at the front of the house. My body made contact with the soft bed; the duvet was still ruffled from when I'd leapt from it to answer the door. Antonio tucked me in and I slipped into sleep. His hand was on my face.

'I'm getting you some help. You're going to be all right.'

'Hmm,' I murmured. My lips were so dry. 'Questions.'

'Later. I promise. Rest now.' He kissed my forehead and I drifted into a heavy sleep.

CHAPTER TWENTY-NINE

RED LIGHT FILTERED THROUGH MY EYELIDS as consciousness returned. My limbs ached and my throat felt like rusted metal. I became aware of a strange feeling in my left arm, a little like when you wake up with a hand that's gone numb from being lain on for too long. I flexed my fingers and peeled my eyes open.

Sunlight filled the room, the pale curtains across the window weren't intended to block out light. My eyes settled on the crook of my left elbow and saw a needle taped there. My gaze followed the tube that was attached to it up my arm, to a metal stand beside my bed with an IV bag full of clear fluid hanging from the top of it.

'Hey, you're awake.' Peter's soft voice came from the corner by the window. I turned my head and saw him sitting in the white armchair between the window and the wardrobe. He stood up and approached my bed, sitting gingerly on the end of it.

'Antonio?' I looked around.

'He's just outside. He can't come in here right now.'

Peter indicated the patch of bright light right across my bed. His face was pale and his voice was strained. I realised I'd upset him by immediately asking about Antonio. I reached out for him and he moved up the bed to take my cool fingers. He was so warm. I grasped his hand and clung to it. 'He got a doctor here to set up the IV. He did everything he could to make sure you were all right.'

'Eve?' Antonio's voice was dull on the other side of the door, but unmistakable. Peter released my hand, stood and went to the door. He opened it and Antonio was standing there, his hands on the door frame either side of the door, just out of the reach of the sunlight. He was dressed in faded blue jeans and a creased, faded Grateful Dead t-shirt with partially peeled print on the front. I let out a hoarse giggle.

'Are they my dad's old clothes?' I asked and my throat burned. I winced and clutched my neck.

'Here,' Peter said softly, at my side again in an instant and holding a small glass of water. He helped me to sit up and take a drink. My eyes flickered back to Antonio, who hung there in the doorway looking frustrated and mutinous.

'Thanks,' I rasped between sips of the cool and soothing water. 'Have you two already talked about what happened?'

'Not really,' Peter said, flashing Antonio a wary glance.

I nodded and passed the empty glass back to Peter. He

took it and placed it on the bedside table. I glanced down at myself and saw that I was in a different nightdress, one not coated in Antonio's blood. I looked up at Peter and then at Antonio, wondering who changed me.

'He did,' Antonio replied to my unasked question, his voice venomous. 'I could only put you into bed before the sun rose too high.' He banged the side of his curled fist against the door frame and it cracked. He looked at the splintered wood in surprise. 'I'm sorry.'

'It's okay, it's only wood. I'm glad you're okay. Are you all healed?'

'I am. Thank you.' He dipped his head. 'How do you feel?'

'Rough, but a bit better than before. Thank you for getting a doctor. Someone you trust, I take it?'

'Absolutely. Rest and plenty of fluids, she said. You lost about two pints, I think.' He rubbed a hand across his forehead and wouldn't meet my gaze.

Peter stiffened on the bed beside me and I put a hand on his knee to steady him. I felt his anger oozing out from his very pores. He didn't relax at my touch so I poked him hard with my index finger and his face snapped towards me, his eyes wide.

'What was that for?'

'You didn't have to change me. You dirty perv.'

'You were covered in blood. I didn't think you'd want it getting on the bed, or that you'd particularly like sleeping in it.' He had the good sense to blush and avoid my eyes. 'I'd really like to know how you came to be in that state.' He looked pointedly at Antonio.

'I was in Hepethia, attempting to deal with some unpleasant business, which is none of yours.' Antonio glowered at Peter. 'There was a demon, some sort of pain aspect. It had tendrils with razorblades on them. When it attacked me I was badly injured.' He touched his chest gingerly and paused. He seemed to be recalling the pain. 'When I crossed back into this world it was dawn and I was too far from home to get to safety there. I came here and Eve let me inside.'

'You invited him in?' Peter asked, looking sideways at me.

'I did. I didn't do it lightly, Peter. He was bleeding and barely standing. He would've caught fire on my doorstep too, which I thought might be hard to explain to the neighbours as they emerged to go to work.'

'Fair point.' Peter nodded solemnly.

'He had a huge gash across his chest. There was so much blood.' I gagged, remembering the smell.

'I can heal swiftly,' Antonio said meekly from the doorway. 'But some wounds bleed too quickly. My blood doesn't clot like yours.'

'Like the living, you mean,' Peter shot at him, spitefully.

'Indeed. Shifter blood accelerates the healing process.

This is something my kind established centuries ago. Eve's blood is strong enough to do the same. A theory I put to the test. I regret having to do so.' He hung his head and leaned against the door frame, his arms crossed over his chest.

'You won't be able to feed on her again for months, you realise,' Peter said, standing and taking a step towards Antonio.

'I know.' Antonio looked up and fixed Peter with an angry scowl.

'You could have killed her. You were more concerned with your own immortal neck than her life.'

'That's not true. You don't understand—' Antonio took a frustrated step into the room but stopped at the edge of the shadow from the hall, snarling like a cornered animal. Peter smirked with satisfaction.

'Peter,' I said softly, pulling his attention back to me. He turned and looked down at me, his face softening. He dropped back down onto the bed and pulled me into his arms. The IV tugged at my arm and I winced.

'Sorry,' Peter said, setting me right and checking the connection of the equipment.

'It's fine. Antonio, explain, please.'

'I was thinking only of your safety,' he said, looking at me sadly. 'I have to live in order to protect you. There is no way I would have lost control and killed you in error this morning. I was too consumed with being able to protect you.'

'That sounds like a contradiction,' Peter said, grumpily puffing his chest out.

'Right now I am the best chance you have of getting what you want, Dog Boy. My sister killed Eve's parents and she will kill Eve too if she figures out what Eve knows or how close she is to all of you.' Antonio spat the words angrily, his accent thickening as he spoke. I caught a muttered Italian insult as he turned away and began to pace in the hallway.

'I had a vision,' I said, drawing Peter's attention back to me. 'I saw it happen. I saw Antonio meet them on the road out of town. He embraced my father like a brother and called my mother "cousin". They were friends, allies. He was urging them to leave the city and come to me in Caerton, for their safety. But Lucia intercepted them just up the road and she—' I stalled, remembering what I'd seen. My voice caught in my throat and a tear came to my eye.

'She killed them? Are you sure?' Peter asked, glancing towards the door. Antonio was standing there, his hands in his hair.

'I'm sure. She flipped their car. She tossed it through the air like a toy.' Peter's gaze flickered dangerously in Antonio's direction again and I knew what he was thinking; he was worrying that the vampires might be a match for shifter strength after all.

'She drained them and threw them and their car into the flooding river next to the road,' Antonio said, his voice a low whisper. 'There was nothing I could do. If I had shown myself she would have known that I was working with them and all would have been lost.'

'What do you mean, you were working with them? They were trying to bring you down.' Peter's jaw was tight, his hands balled into fists in his lap.

Antonio shook his head and let out a mirthless laugh.

'No. They were, originally, but for the last six months we were fighting the same battle.'

'What battle is that?' Peter asked, disbelief in his voice and on his face.

'To have your people resume their role and to stop my sister killing any more shifters.'

'Right. Why didn't my father know anything about this?'

'Because my sister favours him. If he knew the truth and she used her glamour on him, she could find out everything.'

'Favours him? Do I want to know what that means?'

'She likes his blood best,' Antonio said, tilting his head to one side. 'She doesn't sleep with him, as far as I know.'

'Ugh. Right, well, that's good. Oh god, my mother!'

I grabbed Peter's hand and pulled it close to my chest, holding it tight with both hands.

'Your mum's safe. Your dad's faithful. He can't help

the feeding thing, but that's why we're doing all this. Right?' I squeezed his hand and he looked at me.

'Right,' he murmured, staring down at the rug between the bed and the doorway.

'You knew I had visions.' I looked up at Antonio. He nodded.

'I did. Well, I guessed. But when it happened while I was... it was clear that your mind was somewhere else.'

'What about seducing Eve. What was that about?' Peter was scowling again. 'If you were working with her parents, why go there?' My cheeks glowed crimson.

'I told Lucia that I would establish what Eve knew. I had to make a show of business as usual too. I didn't expect to develop feelings for you.' He looked pointedly at me, rather than Peter. 'The plan was to meet with you once or twice, glamour you to find out what you knew, tell Lucia you knew nothing and then never see you again. I meant to keep you at a distance in order to keep you safe from her. But I got selfish. I fell in love and I put those desires before your safety, for which I apologise unreservedly.'

Peter was on his feet and charging at Antonio before I could react. He grabbed Antonio by the throat and slammed him against the wall opposite my bedroom door. I pulled myself from the bed, grabbed the metal stand that I was attached to and dragged it across the carpet with me.

Antonio let Peter manhandle him. He hung limply in Peter's grip, his face impassive. I lumbered out of the bedroom and put a hand on Peter's shoulder. He flinched and glanced my way for a split second.

'You fucked up,' Peter snarled in Antonio's face; spit flecked from his lips. 'You got too close and now Eve is in even more danger from Lucia. Now tell me again about needing to stay alive to protect her.'

'Peter,' I said, tugging fruitlessly at his shoulder. 'Yes, you're right. I'm in more danger now that Antonio is so close to me. But if he dies now, there'll be no one who can even vaguely control Lucia. She'll be let loose on this city, not just on me.'

Peter's grip on Antonio loosened slightly and his shoulders relaxed a fraction. I ducked under his arm and put myself between the two men, my back pressed against Antonio. Peter faltered and released Antonio with a growl. He turned away and stomped along the landing to the stairs. He stood there, one foot hanging over the top step, staring back at us. Antonio's arms had snaked around my body and his temple rested against the side of my head. Peter's face twisted into a bitter expression and he bolted down the stairs and out through the front door.

I turned to face Antonio and placed my hands on either side of his face. 'I love you.'

He blinked at me, taken aback.

'I love you too.' He dipped his face and kissed my lips softly. When he broke away he stroked my hair and smiled. 'I will do whatever it takes to make you safe.'

'What if that means killing your sister?'

'If it comes to it, if it must be done, then I will do it. It should be me. Family can forgive much, family should do so. But when someone is out of control and has to be stopped, then that too should fall to family to resolve.'

'Okay. I hope there's another way.'

'So do I.'

CHAPTER THIRTY

ANTONIO HELD ME RIGHT THERE IN THE SHADOWS until the sun had tracked its course far enough west to no longer be streaming in through my bedroom window. He helped me to the bed and sat me down on it.

'I'll get blackout blinds,' I said. He looked over my shoulder at the window, still a glowing crimson square behind the curtains. Antonio stayed on the door-side of the bed, away from the last rays of light that filtered through. He knelt down beside me and took my hand.

'If you wish.'

'I want you to be safe in my home.'

'Eve.' He smiled and shook his head. 'You are too kind.'

'It's not kindness. I want to be able to have my wicked way with you all day long.' I grinned at him and he burst out laughing. It was a rich and full laugh, quite unlike anything I'd heard from him before. He kissed my hand and stroked my arm.

'Best wait until you've recovered a bit more.' He

gestured up at the IV hanging above me and I grudgingly wriggled my way under the blanket. 'It'll be dark soon. I'll have to go straight home and get changed. I have things I need to attend to.'

'Sure.' I nodded. I didn't want to be left alone though and he must have detected the reluctance in my voice because he leaned close and laid a soft kiss on my lips.

'Ask Peter back.' There was tenderness in his voice and only a trace of apprehension.

'Are you suggesting I have another big, strong man here in my bedroom without you?' I asked, teasing him. He smiled, showing his teeth.

'I'm not remotely threatened by him. Besides, he can genuinely protect you. Not that it will be necessary.'

'I hope you're right.' I cast a nervous glance towards the darkening window. 'Will you call me later? Don't disappear again.'

'I will, and I won't. I'm sorry if it felt as though I had abandoned you. I had to see to a few things before I could give you what you asked for.'

'And are you giving me what I asked?'

'I am. No more killing, or extorting. I'm getting out of the business.'

'You'd do all of that for me?' I gazed at him.

'Of course. I can't explain everything now, some things are already in motion that cannot be reversed. I have to see those through and I can't tell you about them. But what I was working towards with your parents was intended to make the shifters in the city safe and get the Camorra out of it. These things take time. The business is like a hydra, you cut off one head and another grows in its place. It's not enough for me to walk away, if I even could. It's not enough to kill Lucia either. Someone else would just take her place.'

'When do you think it'll be done?'

'I can't say. But I assure you, it's all I want now. I will make it happen.'

I tried to smile, but a part of me felt as though he was spinning a tale. Wasn't all of this the sort of thing bad men told the dupes in their thrall? The promise of change with no real evidence of it? 'I have to call Nicolas and get him to meet me here the moment the sun sets. Will you be all right for a moment?'

'Sure.' He gave me a small smile and left the room, closing the door behind him. I looked at the window again. It had fallen to shadow and the light had turned from crimson to dull blue. My phone lay on the night stand and I grabbed it, intending to call Peter. Something stopped me and I found myself staring at the dark screen. I remembered the talisman he gave me and looked around the room for yesterday's clothes. They were piled on the floor next to the chair that Peter had been sitting in when I woke up.

I swung my feet to the floor, grabbed my IV stand and

hobbled gingerly over to my clothes. I scooped up my jeans and felt in the pockets until I found the coin. I tugged it free and gave it a squeeze. 'Peter,' I whispered, my breath fogging on the tarnished gold.

The coin felt suddenly warm and I looked it over, but nothing about it had changed as far as I could see. I moved slowly back to the bed and just as I reached it the door swung open and Antonio stood there looking grey. 'What's wrong?'

'One of my contacts has been killed. I need to go and sort this out.'

'Of course. I'm sorry.' I felt suddenly strange, standing there in a long cotton night shirt with a cartoon pig on it, clutching a metal pole on wheels in one hand and an old gold coin in the other.

'Why aren't you resting?' Antonio asked, suddenly all bossy and business-like. He hurried to my side and helped me back into bed.

'I am, I'm fine, don't fuss,' I rambled in protest.

The front door opened and quickly slammed. Peter's familiar footsteps bounded up the stairs two at a time and he appeared in the doorway looking flustered and windswept.

'Are you all right? There's a car outside.'

'That'll be for me,' Antonio replied, settling me back into bed. 'I have to leave. Look after her. She needs rest and something to eat.'

'Of course,' Peter said, not looking at him.

Antonio bent and kissed me with unnecessary sensuality, his tongue flicking between my lips. When he pulled back he cast an unpleasant smirk Peter's way and I rolled my eyes in Peter's direction by way of an apology.

'I'll call you later,' Antonio said softly to me.

'Yeah, great.' I waved him away and he strode across the room. Peter filled the doorway and the two of them faced off, each refusing to move aside. 'Oh, get over yourselves,' I called out. Peter turned sideways and held out a hand, indicating for Antonio to pass. The vampire snorted derisively and slid past him without a word. His footsteps were quiet on the stairs and I had to strain to hear the door open and close again, in contrast to Peter's noisy entrance.

'Are you okay?' Peter asked, moving to my bed and perching on the end of it.

'Fine. I just didn't want to be alone. Were you doing anything important?'

'Everything's important these days,' he said, snorting gruffly. 'But you're my top priority.'

'You'll make me blush.'

Peter made sure I was comfortable then disappeared downstairs, returning a few minutes later with a sandwich and glass of juice for me.

The food was hard to chew, my throat was still so dry, but it tasted good and eased my trembling considerably.

After I'd eaten, I cast my eye over the IV. 'I really want this out so I can go shower.'

'It's re-hydrating you,' Peter said, frowning.

'Yeah, I know. But I'm gross.' My skin was still crusted with dried blood where it'd soaked through my nightshirt.

'Okay,' he said, scepticism in his tone. He peeled back the tape holding the needle in place so gently I didn't even wince. He smiled nervously and slowly removed the needle. It tugged as it came clear of my skin but I managed not to let the discomfort show.

'That's better,' I said, flexing my arm and wriggling my fingers. I made to stand up and found I had more strength in my legs after eating.

'Don't lock the door,' Peter instructed as I crossed the hall with my fluffy towel draped over my arm. 'In case you fall or something and need help.'

I nodded and did as he said, but I felt steady enough.

The water was so hot it made my skin tingle. It was physically and emotionally cleansing, washing away the blood, sweat and dirt. When I closed my eyes I saw moments from the memory that I'd seen when Antonio fed on me. I began shaking and crying silent tears as I saw my parents' deaths. It was so brutal. They'd been on their way to me. If they'd got away just a bit sooner they'd be here now, or more likely we'd be together in Caerton. Would I know what they were? Would I ever have met Antonio?

I would have traded the truth to have my parents

back, maybe the love too. The love was intoxicating but it was complicated as hell.

But this was my life now. As painful as it was, I had to accept it. Lucia killed my parents and Antonio had been working with them. He was the good guy in all of this madness, or relatively so.

I needed him to call me. I needed to hear his voice, even though we'd only parted an hour previously. I needed to know that he was okay, that Lucia wasn't onto us all. Her behaviour since I arrived in town suggested that she believed she had dealt with the insurrection when she killed my parents. She wasn't acting like someone who was worried about her grip on power.

But what would she think if she knew about me and Antonio?

This was coming to a head, I knew; secrets would have to come out soon and I would have to face Lucia. I wasn't going to let everyone else fight my battles for me, even if everyone I knew was a supernatural being with strength and powers.

I finished my shower and dried off. I could hear Peter standing just outside the door, the floorboards creaking with each shift of his weight. I hated him hovering over me, but felt it would be pointless to resist. He wanted to make sure I was safe and it wasn't hurting me to let him get on with that.

I wrapped my towel around myself and stepped out

into the cool hall. Peter gave me an awkward smile.

'Better?' he asked.

'Much. Thanks. I'm going to get dressed. You don't need to protect me while I do that.' I smirked at him as I brushed past and moved into my room. I closed the door, leaving him where he stood. 'Have you told the others yet?' I called through the door as I slowly dressed in jeans and a clean shirt.

'About your vision?'

'Yes!'

'I told Dad. He was going to relay it to some of the others.'

'It changes things,' I said.

'Yes, it does.'

I pulled my sweater down over my top and flung open my bedroom door.

'He's on our side.'

'Yes.' He looked at me, not quite meeting my eye.

'What?' I narrowed my eyes at him. I knew that look. It was one of mild disbelief and scepticism.

'What if you saw what he wanted you to see?'

'I don't think people can direct my visions, Peter. They've always been honest.' I grabbed my phone from by the bed and looked at the blank screen. Why hadn't he called yet?

'Okay, but I just think a healthy dose of caution is a good idea here.'

'Why? Why are you so intent on keeping him the bad guy? He's on our side, he has been for ages.'

'Then why has he still been drinking shifter blood? What was he actually planning with your parents? We don't know, Eve. My dad knew nothing about it. Why? He was your dad's best friend.'

'Antonio explained that. Lucia could have found out.'

'So he says. You're taking a lot on faith here.'

'Because I have to, because my whole world fell apart and nothing is what I thought it was. Nothing!' My voice had risen and my palms grew greasy. I checked my phone again. Peter reached out and snatched it out of my hand. 'Hey!' I shouted, reaching to grab it back.

He flung it across the room, where it fell with a thud on the thick carpet. I turned to fetch it, but Peter grabbed my wrist and pulled me back.

'Stop it!' he shouted in my face. 'Stop checking your phone. He isn't going to call. He's off doing vampirey things somewhere.'

'What is your problem?' I tugged my arm free and glowered up at him. 'You've been acting weird ever since I got back, and especially since I started seeing him. Why do you have such a big issue with this?'

'You are such an idiot sometimes!' he shouted. He turned and stepped out onto the landing, running his hands through his shaggy hair.

'That's rich. Seriously, stop acting like an

overprotective big brother. If being with him is a mistake then it's mine to make.'

'Is that what you think of me?' he asked, wheeling around and staring at me with wide eyes. 'That I'm like your big brother?'

'Well, yeah.' I blinked at him, the anger ebbing away.

'Eve!' he snarled and paced away from me towards the stairs, then turned and strode back, glowering down at me. 'I'm in love with you. I have been since we were thirteen. I don't like you being with him because I want you to be with me!'

CHAPTER THIRTY-ONE

'WHAT?' I BLURTED, almost laughing, but catching myself at the look on his face. 'Are you serious?'

He grabbed my shoulders and pressed his lips to mine, kissing me forcefully. I was too stunned to react. His lips pressed hard against mine and my body refused to either reciprocate or push him away. My head spun and tipped down into darkness. It wasn't a vision, but I felt his feelings as keenly as my own. He was deeply, passionately in love with me. He had fantasies about us, he'd dreamed of this moment, of telling me the truth and finally kissing me. The dream had been nothing like this. He'd never meant to do it in anger.

I pulled away from him, my lips feeling tender and my face flushed with heat.

'I'm sorry,' he said, looking away. 'I shouldn't have done that. You saw something, didn't you?'

All I could do was nod. I gently touched my shaking fingertips to my lips. My head was still reeling from the strength of his feelings and I felt like a fool for never seeing it. My memory raced over all of the times he'd come to my aid, stood by me or otherwise been there for me. I remembered his mother's comment about him only having eyes for one girl—it was me. She knew. She saw as clear as day how her son felt about me, when I'd assumed that his lack of interest in other girls had been because of his sexuality.

'I didn't know. I'm sorry. I should have known how you felt.' My voice sounded hoarse and as if it was on the other side of thick glass. I was still light-headed and began to sway.

Peter caught hold of me, lifted me easily into his strong arms and carried me to my bed.

'I should have said something before now. I'm sorry. Are you okay?'

'I'll be all right in a minute. It's the blood loss.' I could feel the heat in my cheeks. I didn't want him to think that I was swooning over him. This made everything even more messy than it already was. Peter was like a brother to me. I loved him dearly, and his parents. They'd been amazing since I'd returned from Caerton. But I was in love with Antonio and that wasn't about to change.

How could I eat with Peter and his parents like a member of the family now that I knew how he felt? I couldn't lead him on but nor could I treat him like a brother or friend when I knew he felt so differently. I felt as though I was losing my family all over again. My chest ached and my cheeks trembled with the threat of tears.

'Peter,' I rasped, reaching out for him. He took my hand and crouched beside the bed; finally he met my eyes. 'You're my best friend. I want it to stay that way.'

'I know.' He kissed my knuckles and released my hand. 'I'll let you rest for a bit. When you feel up to it, we should go to my house. We need to talk to my dad.'

'Sure.'

'I'll be downstairs if you need anything. Okay?'

'Yeah. Thanks.' I gave him a weak smile. He backed out of the room and closed the door, leaving me alone in the lamplight with my mangled thoughts.

I woke before I even realised I was falling asleep. I sat up immediately and the room spun. I reached for the glass of water on my nightstand and drank deeply. It calmed my shaking hand and steadied my spinning head.

I reached for my phone but it wasn't on the nightstand. I remembered Peter throwing it across the room and looked over to where it had landed. It seemed like a mile away. There was a sinking sensation as I recalled what'd happened with Peter. I swung my feet to the floor and tried to stand up. My legs shook but I managed to take my own weight and take a few steps towards the phone. I stooped to retrieve it and checked the screen. It was gone midnight and I had a single text message. It was from Antonio, asking how I was feeling.

I quickly typed a reply explaining that I'd been asleep but that I was okay. "How's it going there?" I asked.

My legs felt so heavy as I took a few steps towards the door. I stopped and breathed deeply, my head had started to spin again. I closed my eyes and when I opened them everything was still. I walked forwards and grasped the door handle.

My phone buzzed in my hand and I held it up to see a reply from Antonio. I opened the message, which read, "I'm glad you've had some more rest and feel better. I've been busy, hardly a moment to spare. Not seen Lucia. Next time she shows up I'm going to have her followed. Be careful."

I gave his message a thumbs up, then opened the door. The landing was dark and it took a moment for my eyes to adjust. I was about to take a step when I saw Peter slumped on the floor next to my bedroom door, his head resting against the wall, his eyes closed. He didn't look comfortable. I squatted beside him and shook his shoulder gently. He startled awake and stared at me with bleary eyes.

'I'm awake. You all right?'

'I'm okay. We should go to your house, speak to your dad.'

'All right.' He clambered to his feet and rubbed his

eyes. 'I'll be glad when all of this is over and I can get a good night's sleep.'

'You used to sleep for ten hours straight.'

'I really did. That seems a lifetime ago. Do you need any help on the stairs?'

'Maybe.' I put a hand on his shoulder and let him lead me to the top of the stairs. I'd slept in my clothes and felt uncomfortable, but I couldn't be bothered to change them. I didn't even care if I had bed hair. I just wanted to get to Peter's house.

Peter went ahead of me down the stairs; he walked slowly and put a hand out to make sure I couldn't fall past him. I was shaky and weak, but not so bad that there was a chance of falling. I appreciated the gesture, though.

We made it down the stairs and he helped me put my boots on, then my coat. He stepped out into the cold night in just a t-shirt.

'Aren't you cold?' I asked, my teeth chattering against the freezing night air.

'No. I have a high tolerance for the cold these days.' He grinned at me and held out a hand. I locked the front door and took it. Mercifully, no vision struck. I wasn't sure I could remain standing if my head tipped into a vision right now.

We walked so slowly it must have been agonising for Peter, but he didn't complain and he didn't rush me. Each step was heavy and carried the risk of me collapsing. It occurred to me that I should have stayed in bed, but it felt as though we were right on the brink of something and I didn't want it to happen while I slept.

We got to Peter's house and I could see the hall light shining through the small, frosted glass panels in the top of the door. He went to open the door and paused with his hand on the handle; his face had gone white.

'What is it?' I asked in a whisper.

He gave a single shake of his head and opened the door slowly, careful not to make a sound. I hung back as he stepped inside. I could barely see past him down the narrow hall to the dark kitchen.

'I'm disappointed.' A cold, hard voice carried down the hall. Lucia's voice. 'I thought this would motivate you, Kirk, darling.'

Peter stood frozen just inside the doorway for a moment. Then he bounded full pelt towards the kitchen. There was a crash and a small scream. I hurried after him, my blood pounding in my ears and my vision blurring as I exerted the effort to keep pace.

He burst into the kitchen and I reached the door a split second later. I caught hold of the frame on either side of the door and stopped, suspended in horror as I took in the scene.

Kirk was in the firm grasp of Dante and one of the other men I'd seen with Lucia at the party. Lucia had Mrs Wilkes in her arms and a plate lay smashed on the stone floor. Peter's mother's face was deathly white and suspended in an expression of shock, her mouth hanging silently open. There was a red line across her throat and it was expanding. I blinked, not trusting my eyesight as my head spun and my ears rang horribly.

Blood was beginning to pour down Mrs Wilkes's neck and chest.

Lucia looked up at Peter and me, a cruel smile spreading across her face. 'Oh look,' she sing-songed. 'The whole gang's here.' She let go of Mrs Wilkes, who crumpled to the floor. I watched in horrified silence as her blood spread across the flagstones and pooled in the groove between two of them.

I was dimly aware of Peter and Kirk erupting into their Agrius forms, Kirk shaking off his vampiric captors. There was a cacophony of sickening sounds; chomping, snarling, ripping.

When I finally managed to tear my eyes away from the pale and frightened face of Mrs Wilkes, I saw the table on its side, with Kirk pinned against it by the two male vampires. Lucia was grinning maniacally as Peter desperately tried to claw at her while she held him easily in a headlock.

Her dark eyes settled on me and her smile faltered. She grabbed Peter's head and yanked it sideways with a stomach-turning crunch. I tried to scream but no sound came out. Lucia tossed Peter to the floor next to his mother.

'You don't look well, Eve, my dear. You look positively drained.' She sneered the last word even as I sank to the floor, half sitting on the step, half leaning into the kitchen. Tears streaked down my face and every muscle screamed for relief. 'Has my dear brother been getting carried away with you?'

I couldn't answer, even if I wanted to. My gaze drifted sideways to Kirk, who was still restrained and seemed to have given up fighting it. His big, sad eyes stared towards the floor and his form slowly morphed back into his human one.

Lucia stepped over the two bodies on the floor, her feet in pristine, black shoes with a ten-centimetre heel. She crouched in front of me, pinched my chin between her carefully manicured thumb and forefinger and tilted my face up to look at hers.

'I don't think I need to bother finishing you off. It looks as though you'll be departing shortly anyway. Maybe then I'll get my brother back. Quite the distraction, you've been. He'll remember himself once you're gone.'

She stood up and with a single jerk of her head, her faithful servants released Kirk, stood and followed her, each of them stepping over me and swooping down the hall and out of the front door.

CHAPTER THIRTY-TWO

'KIRK,' I CROAKED. I slipped down off the step and crawled across the floor. The cold, hard flagstones were painful against my palms and knees. He sat slumped, staring at his wife's blood, which was inching its way closer and closer to his outstretched feet. 'We need help, Kirk.'

He still didn't move.

A groan rumbled from my left and I tilted my head towards Peter. My heart throbbed painfully in my chest. My pulse raced and I staggered sideways away from his body. Panic coursed through my veins. His arm moved, followed by his back arching. There was a crunch as he turned his head, popping the bones back into place. Fresh tears burst from my eyes and I let out a loud whimper. Confusion and fear raced through me.

Peter pushed himself up to sitting and rubbed his thick neck with one hand.

'You're alive!' I gasped, crawling slowly towards him.

'It takes more than that to put down one of us,' Peter replied, his voice hoarse.

I reached him and leapt into his arms. He wrapped them around me and cradled my head.

'I couldn't do anything,' Kirk said, his voice barely a whimper. 'I couldn't stop her.'

'I know, Dad. I know.' Peter's jaw was clenched as he spoke and he gripped me a little tighter. 'What did she want?'

'She wanted to know if her brother had betrayed her. She thought I would tell her if she threatened Marianne. I couldn't... I couldn't save her. I tried. I couldn't betray the pack and I couldn't save both. I...' His words failed him and he dropped his head into his hands. Vocal sobs filled the kitchen and his hunched shoulders shook.

'What do we do?' I asked, looking up into Peter's face. 'Do we call the police? Or do you want to handle this privately?'

'We have to call the police,' Kirk replied. His voice was dull and toneless. His eyes still fixed, unseeing, on his wife's blood. 'But it's pointless to tell them who did it.'

'Maybe,' I said, my voice a hoarse whisper. 'Maybe not. Antonio made me a promise and I trust him to deliver.'

'Even if the police don't get paid off any more, they won't act against the Vitales. We deal with justice ourselves.' Peter's jaw was still clenched even as he spoke and he held me just a little too tightly. He slowly released me and slid out from under me, placing me carefully on the floor next to his mother's body. 'Don't touch anything. We found her like this.' He got to his feet and pulled his phone from the back pocket of his jeans.

I couldn't look at the body, I didn't want to look at Kirk either. He was still sitting there, stunned and sobbing softly. Peter left the room with his phone pressed to his ear. 'Yes, police and ambulance I think. But I think it's too late.' He stood in the hall looking towards the door as he spoke to the operator and all I could do was look at him as my own blood pounded dully in my ears. I could hear him relaying the scene and answering their questions, but he sounded far away and indistinct.

My own phone started buzzing in my pocket and I fumbled awkwardly to retrieve it. Antonio's name showed on the display and with shaking hands, I answered.

'Are you all right?' he asked before I could speak.

'No. Mrs Wilkes is dead.'

'Porco Dio!'

'The police are coming,' I said softly, ignoring Antonio's colourful language. My eyes were fixed on Peter as he re-entered the kitchen. His narrowed eyes were on me.

'Has Lucia left you there?'

'Yes. She thinks Peter's dead too, but he's fine.'

'And Mr Wilkes?'

'In shock, but physically intact.'

'I am so sorry. I should have acted sooner. I should

have known something like this was going to happen.'

'It's done. It's not your fault.' I rubbed my face wearily.

'Eve,' Peter said, crouching in front of me. I looked at him and held the phone away from my face. 'We need to get you out of here before the police get here. You look like death and they'll be interested to know why.'

'I heard that.' Antonio's voice came quietly from my phone. 'I'm on my way.'

'Not here!' Peter snapped. 'You are not welcome at my house!'

'Peter. He's trying to help.'

'I know, but he's still not welcome. I'll take you home. You can collect her there!' he called into my phone.

'Fine. I'll see you in a few minutes, Eve.' I pressed the phone against my ear again and fresh tears began to fall.

'I love you.'

'I love you too. I'll be right there.'

I hung up the phone and clutched it as Peter lifted me to my feet.

He wouldn't meet my eyes and I realised how awkward he must feel hearing my declaration when he'd only hours ago made the same one to me. I clung tightly to him, not even caring if a vision struck or not.

'Dad, I'm taking Eve home. Dad?' Kirk looked up at us, his eyes red and unfocused. 'Call Weaver. Get ready in case the police get here before I get home. Okay?'

'Okay. Call Weaver. Police.' Kirk still just sat there,

tears on his cheeks.

'I'll be right back.' Peter helped me limp to the back door, carefully avoiding the pool of blood. He opened it then looked back over his shoulder at his father. 'Dad? How did they get in?'

'Hmm?' Kirk looked up at his son, his brow furrowed.

'How did they get into the house?'

'She invited them in.'

'Why would she do that?'

'I was upstairs. She answered the door. I couldn't stop her. She didn't know.' Kirk's face crumpled and he broke into renewed sobs.

'Stay with him,' I said, pushing myself away from Peter and grabbing hold of the open door. 'He needs you. Stay. I can get home.'

'No you can't. You can barely stand.' Peter looked from me to his dad, his mother's body in a heap on the floor between him and his father. 'She could still be out there.'

'You can't leave him in this state, Peter. Stay.' I stepped outside and closed the door.

It was ice cold and the clear sky was studded with stars. A siren was growing closer in the otherwise silent night. I pushed myself away from the door and stumbled quickly up the garden path to the back gate. Peter didn't follow me. I figured he must have heard the siren too and taken my advice.

I unlatched the iron gate and slipped through it,

closing it again as quietly as I could. The back street was almost pitch black. A few twinkling Christmas lights inside people's windows provided a little light, but I didn't really need it. I knew this street like the back of my hand. I walked slowly along the narrow pavement, careful not to slip down the step onto the cobblestone street. I could hear the river rushing by on the far side of the trees that lined the opposite side of the street. The trees swayed in the wind and their bare branches creaked.

My fingers brushed the top of the stone wall of the gardens on my right to keep me on track and steady. My head was pounding and nausea swept over me. I could still smell Mrs Wilkes's blood. I paused for a moment, gripping the wall as I swayed dangerously. I took a deep breath. All I could really smell was wet grass.

When I set off walking again, a security light in the back garden of the house I was passing came on, flooding the garden and street beyond in bright, white light. I squinted and kept walking, gathering as much speed as I could manage.

I was beginning to seriously doubt my ability to get myself home. Every step was a huge effort and I grew more and more dizzy. For just a moment, I regretted letting Antonio feed from me. I hated feeling this weak, especially with what had just happened.

I stumbled on in the dark. The crack of a twig under the trees sent me staggering into the wall, my pulse reached a new high rate and a creeping sensation of being watched made its way up my spine. The end of the street was so close. The warm, orange glow of the street lights was almost within reach. I fixed my eyes on that glow and continued walking steadily towards it.

The sound of my own breathing was all I could hear now. The babble of the river was too soft for my foggy brain to focus on it. The little puffs of my warm breath on the cold air clouded my vision. I let go of the wall as I stumbled towards the end of the street.

A sleek, black car pulled to a sudden halt right in front of me. A smile of relief spread over my face and I reached out with one limp arm as I staggered onto the uneven cobbles. The pool of light from the street lamp was inches from my outstretched fingers.

The car door opened and a be-suited, male foot stepped out of the back seat of the car. Antonio to my rescue.

Relief washed over me and I collapsed sideways, still cloaked in shadow. I didn't hit the floor. Cool arms caught me as I fell. A gloved hand closed over my mouth and I was pulled back into the shadows, towards the trees. I tried to scream but lacked the strength to fight against whoever held me. No sound escaped. I kicked my feet against the cobbles hopelessly.

My eyes tried to focus on the car and the man stepping out of it. I hoped that Antonio would hear my struggle. I thrashed wildly in the tight grip of my captor.

But it wasn't Antonio by the car. Adrenaline kicked in and cleared my vision enough to see Roberto Esposito in his grey suit and long, black coat standing by the car. He looked up and down the street, then gave a small gesture of beckoning with his gloved hand.

I was lifted, still kicking madly, and carried swiftly to the car.

'Excellent,' Esposito said with a smirk. He stood aside and I was tossed into the back of the car. I spun around to see Dante's dark face looking back at me. 'Good catch,' Esposito said to him. They exchanged nods and Dante climbed into the front passenger seat, while Esposito slid smoothly into the back seat next to me.

'What are you doing? Let me go!'

'Not a chance,' he said, still smirking at me. 'I'm taking you straight to Lucia.'

'You think she'll reward you? She doesn't care about me. She just saw me and left me alone.'

The car set off, silently speeding away from the flashing blue lights outside the front of Peter's house.

'I think she had a change of heart and sent Dante to collect you.'

I peered over the back of the seat in front of him and saw Dante glance over his shoulder at me. His dark eyes were dangerous and hungry. The unfamiliar driver next to him ignored everything. There was no point appealing to him. I pressed myself against the door and felt for the handle. Maybe I could throw myself out if we stopped at a red light? In this state that might kill me, but it was worth the risk. Antonio had to be close by. If I could scream then maybe he would hear me.

We sped past the end of my street, the empty roads giving the driver no cause to brake.

'Why does she want me?'

'Maybe she thinks you'll taste good.' Esposito didn't take his eyes off me and I suddenly felt more apprehensive of his intentions than any of the vampires.

'Well there's not much blood in me right now,' I snapped at him.

'Weak little girl got into trouble playing with shit she didn't understand.'

'I understand more than you think.'

'I don't think so,' Esposito replied.

There was a red light ahead, now was my moment. I gripped the handle and waited. The car slowed as it approached the red light and I yanked on the handle. But the door was locked and didn't budge. Esposito laughed cruelly. 'This isn't my first rodeo.'

I hit the button to open the window and it rolled slowly down as Esposito's face fell.

'Antonio!' I hollered at the top of my lungs. I reached up and grabbed the roof of the car, heaving myself up out of the window.

Esposito lunged across the back seat and grabbed my legs, yanking me roughly back into the car. I screamed again with all my might. Even if Antonio didn't hear, somebody should see or hear something.

The car set off again, wheels spinning noisily on the tarmac. I thrashed and screamed against Esposito as he wrestled me down onto the seat and out of sight of the window. He clamped a hand over my mouth and lay over me, pressing his weight down on me and I fell still.

'Struggle again,' he hissed. 'I like it like that.'

My head spun, my eyes rolled back and everything went black.

CHAPTER THIRTY-THREE

I saw a hundred bloody corpses, including some shifter faces I recognised. I heard a chorus of triumphant shouts and jeers. I saw Roberto Esposito sporting new fangs; Lucia was smearing bright red blood across his forehead with her thumb. He'd finally got what he'd always wanted and the glee in his face was unmistakably cruel and twisted. There was fire everywhere and demons clawing their way across the veil between worlds, with Lucia and Esposito leading the way to the city.

'What is wrong with her? Why are her eyes doing that?' Lucia's cold voice cut into the vision and pulled me back into the real world. Before I opened my eyes I knew I was no longer in the car. I was tied to a chair, a gag in my mouth. I whimpered and tugged against the bonds around my wrists and ankles. How long had I been unconscious?

'She's coming to.' I didn't recognise that voice. My eyes flickered open and strained to focus; everything swam in a blur. Firelight licked up the walls of a cave, casting eerie shadows that danced. Figures moved around me. I swayed, my head turned and tried to orient itself upright on my neck.

'There's something wrong with her.' Esposito's cold voice jarred in my mind and my head settled. My eyes finally focused and I found him standing just behind Lucia, his arms crossed over his chest and a scowl on his face.

'That's just sour grapes because Dante stopped you raping her,' Lucia said sharply. 'Unspoiled, I said. Didn't I?'

'I wasn't going to leave any marks.'

'That is entirely beside the point.'

'I thought it would irk your brother more.'

'Stop trying to defend yourself,' Lucia said, venom in her voice.

He looked as if he wanted to protest, but thought better of it and fell silent. My eyes searched for Dante. I wanted to thank him, even though it was him who'd grabbed me from the street in the first place. But he wasn't there.

The other vampire who'd been in the Wilkes's kitchen was straddling a chair next to me, his arms resting on the back of it. He looked at me quizzically. He had alarmingly blue eyes and fair hair. His face looked like it could have been carved out of marble, perfectly chiselled. A suit jacket hung over the back of the chair, under his arms, and his shirt sleeves were rolled up. The way he looked at me sent a shiver up my spine.

'She's been fed on recently. Too much, by the looks of it.' His was the voice I hadn't been able to place as I came around. He poked my shoulder and my whole body swayed. The only thing keeping me from slipping off the chair was the rope tying me to it. 'If we take any more we might kill her.'

'I know that, Celino,' Lucia said in a bored voice. 'She's only here as leverage. While the shifters are busy dealing with the mess I left in their kitchen we will sort out my brother.'

My eyes focused on my surroundings. The flickering light came from three tall candles in an old, elaborate brass candleholder on a stone plinth just behind Celino. We were in a cave very like the one beneath my basement, if a little larger. The walls and floor were the same, light sandy colour. I couldn't see any way in or out, but I could feel a cool draught on my back.

'She's perking up,' Esposito said, a vicious snap in his words.

'Eve, darling,' Lucia said, bending over me and grinning. 'Welcome to the party.'

I glared at her with the most withering look I could summon in the state I was in. She must have got the gist, as she chuckled at me and stood up straight to tower over me. She was immaculate in skinny jeans and a cream, roll-neck sweater. Her thick, dark hair was tied in a neat bun and her lips were coated in matte, dark red lipstick. She pulled her phone from her back pocket and held it up in front of me. 'Say cheese.'

I scowled and growled at her through my cloth gag as she took my picture, the flash dazzling me for a moment. 'Go to the surface and send that to my brother, then go and check on how Laguardia is getting on in the other cave.' She passed her phone to Esposito, who rolled his eyes and strolled past me. I craned my neck to watch him go and sure enough, there was a narrow passage right behind me.

'Now, girl talk time, Eve.' She waved a hand at Celino. He leapt from his chair and passed it to her. She turned it to face me, placed it right in front of me and sat down, crossing one impossibly long leg over the other. She folded her hands neatly in her lap and pursed her lips. 'Are you following in Mummy and Daddy's footsteps?'

I narrowed my eyes and clenched my teeth on the gag.

Lucia tilted her head to one side and smiled sweetly. 'Now, we can do this one of two ways. I promise you, this is the easy way. You don't want to experience the hard way.'

I felt Celino move behind me, partially blocking the draught and standing much too close for comfort. 'It's best if you agree to answer my questions. You saw what happened to Marianne Wilkes.'

Anger flared up inside me. How dare she mention my friend's mother right now. I rocked my chair and pulled forward on the ropes tying my wrists, feeling the burn as they scraped over my skin.

'That's more like it,' Lucia said, still smiling. 'Now, are you trying to influence my brother in order to overthrow our grip on the shifters?'

I rocked the chair again, snarling at her as I tried desperately to inch myself close enough to her to inflict some sort of injury. I knew it was pointless, but I had to fight, resist.

She twitched her head in Celino's direction and his hands grabbed my shoulders, holding me firmly back in the chair. I tried to pull away from his grip but I didn't budge.

'Nod if the answer is yes. Are you trying to loosen our grip on the shifters?'

I growled and struggled against Celino's grasp. His fingers dug painfully into me. Lucia sighed. 'You understand that I will hurt you if you refuse to cooperate. Don't you?'

I nodded, reluctantly.

'Good. So, are you trying to use my brother?'

I narrowed my eyes even further and refused to respond. She closed her eyes for a moment. When she opened them she looked up at Celino and gave the tiniest nod. He let go of my shoulders and grabbed my right hand, roughly pulling my thumb back. My eyes popped wide open and I tried to scream and struggle. He did nothing more, simply held my thumb ready to snap it back at Lucia's signal. I whimpered and tried to pull free, but he held me firmly in place.

'Answer my question,' Lucia said. She was no longer smiling. 'Are you trying to manipulate my brother?'

I glared at her but held fast. I couldn't break. I couldn't give her what she wanted, no matter what the cost. Kirk had refused to break and it had cost him his wife. I knew the price would be high, but what the shifters were doing was too important. It was just a thumb.

There was a snap and pain seared up my wrist. I screamed and tears streamed down my face. The gag muffled my scream and I bit down hard on it. The pain was like nothing I had ever felt before. I'd never broken a bone.

Celino moved my fingers again, targeting my index finger next. I closed my eyes.

'Are you manipulating my brother?'

I groaned and shook the chair.

Celino broke my finger.

I cried out again, the gag swallowing the bulk of the noise.

'Are you manipulating my brother?'

I could hardly see through my tears and my blood pounded in my temples. I whimpered as Celino lined up my next finger. I couldn't do it, I couldn't cope with the pain. It was awful. I struggled again and roared against the gag.

Snap.

I screamed and rocked hard in the chair, hard enough to shuffle it a few inches towards Lucia. She leaned away from me, a slightly alarmed expression flickering across her face.

'Well?' Lucia shouted at me, finally losing some of her cool.

'NO!' I roared into my gag. As muffled as my voice was, the simple word's meaning got through. She narrowed her eyes at me and leaned closer.

'Are you in love with him?'

I stopped struggling and went limp. I closed my eyes and nodded once. Celino released my broken hand and stepped back. My hand hung limply from where it was tied to the back of the chair. My broken fingers throbbed and I couldn't move my hand at all. I whimpered. The pain was unbearable.

'That's an interesting development,' Esposito said softly from behind me. I heard his footsteps on the stone floor and managed to peel my eyes open to look up at him as he handed Lucia's phone back to her. 'Message received. You realise that if he loves her back you've just invited his ire?'

'If that's the case then there may be no redemption for him anyway.' Lucia stood up and moved around her chair. She leaned against the back of it to peer closely at my face. 'Are you working with the shifters, Eve?'

I shook my head. It was all I could do.

'She's obviously lying,' Esposito said with an indignant huff. Lucia glared at him.

'She is broken, you idiot. Look at her.'

I lowered my gaze.

'Break another finger and check,' Esposito suggested, smirking.

I was aware of Celino twitching behind me, but he waited for Lucia to confirm the order. She stood, arms crossed, glaring down at me. She turned her head towards Esposito and smiled that dangerous smile of hers. She moved at lightning speed, grabbing him by the throat and slamming him against the wall. A little shower of dust fell over him and he blinked furiously as it fell into his eyes.

'Tell me what to do again.' She snarled at him, showing her fangs as they slowly grew out of her gums.

'I'm sorry,' he said, struggling against her grip.

'How is Laguardia doing?'

'He's ready for you,' Esposito croaked.

The light from the candles flickered more vigorously, throwing dark shadows across the rocky walls. I peered up through my bleary eyelashes to see a shadow peel away from the wall and take the form of a man in a top hat with a sallow face. My eyes widened and I strained slightly against my restraints. The demon cleared its throat.

Lucia dropped Esposito and he slumped sideways, clutching his bruised throat. Lucia turned to the demon and straightened her clothes before addressing him.

'Yes?'

'Trouble,' the shadow man whispered. The candles flickered again and one of them blew out. 'In the tunnels. Company.'

'My brother?'

The shadow man nodded and rippled back into the wall.

I craned my neck as Dante flew into the cave, his bulk taking up almost the whole passage. His face was as unreadable as ever, but Lucia's nostrils were flaring angrily. 'Grab her and get her into the catacombs.' She jerked her head in my direction. Dante nodded and stooped to untie me.

My hand seared in agony and a ripple of pain shot up my arm the moment the rope was loosened. Dante worked quickly to remove the rope around my ankles and my other hand. He met my eyes and there was something in the way he looked at me, barely perceptible, but there nonetheless. Sympathy. And something more. Regret?

He scooped me gently from the chair and hoisted me up over his shoulder, sending blood rushing to my head. I groaned against my gag, which was soaked through and digging painfully into the corners of my mouth.

Dante ran up the passage with me over his shoulder. It was pitch black, but I heard the hurried footsteps of the others behind us as we ascended from the cave. The passage was relatively short, and light met my pained eyes again as we emerged into a larger cave. We took a hard left and Dante jogged quickly and smoothly down a narrow set of neatly carved steps. I lifted my head enough to see the others go a different way and I heard a shout.

We reached the bottom of the steps, turned a corner into a wider passage, and Dante broke into a run, jostling me painfully. My head was spinning dangerously and I feared that I was about to pass out again.

He skidded to a halt and carefully lowered me to the ground, sitting me on the smooth cobbles that lined this passage and leaning me against the wall. It was so dark I could hardly see him. He gently removed my gag and carefully ran his hands down my arm to my broken hand. I winced and recoiled from his touch, but he took my hand with such tenderness I was caught off guard.

'Dante?' My voice was hoarse and it hurt to speak. 'What are you doing?'

He didn't reply. I'd never heard him speak, I realised. He held my broken hand gently between the palms of his ham-sized hands. I reached out with my mind, trying desperately to see into his. He held still, his head slightly bowed, just holding my hand. His palms were cool and dry, unlike my sweaty hands. I had the very strong feeling that my broken hand was also covered in blood, though I hadn't dared look at it, or had much light to do so.

A thought that didn't belong to me fluttered through my mind and I reached out for it, trying to grasp it. It was

Dante, I was sure of it.

'Here to help,' he thought, very deliberately. He knew about my gift. That was why he was touching me like that.

My uninjured hand was rising before I knew what I was doing. I felt for his face in the dark and found his full lips. My fingers traced them.

'You can't talk.'

He shook his head.

'She took out your tongue, didn't she?'

He nodded.

'You're loyal to Antonio?'

He nodded again.

'Is he coming?'

One last nod, and relief flooded my body.

CHAPTER THIRTY-FOUR

THE RELIEF WAS FLEETING. Antonio wasn't here yet. Dante had risked blowing his cover to make sure I was all right.

'She thinks you're hers. She'll kill you if she finds out you betrayed her.'

He pulled away from me and gently released my hand. It felt a little better. It definitely hurt less. He put my hand down to rest on my lap and stood up, looking both ways along the passage.

My eyes were adjusting to the dark slightly and I could make out the shape of him. His whole body tensed and he turned to look away from the direction we'd come.

A moment later I heard footsteps pounding on the cobbles and saw the light from a flame bobbing in the distance, throwing jagged shadows on the walls.

'Eve?!' Peter's voice called.

'Peter!' I called back, my throat tearing painfully. There were multiple figures running behind the light. I could make them out as they drew nearer: Peter, Kirk, Weaver, Crystal and Strikes Twice were sprinting towards us, Weaver wielding a flame in her hand. Dante stood over me, his fists clenched at his sides, his face set in a determined expression in the light from Weaver's outstretched hand.

Strikes Twice barrelled into Dante and pinned him against the wall with his axe across Dante's chest. 'Stop! No! He got me out,' I shouted, my voice cracking in the middle. Strikes Twice grudgingly released the vampire, but kept his narrowed eyes fixed on Dante.

Peter stooped down to examine me, his brow furrowed and his jaw tight.

'What happened?'

'She interrogated me.' I inclined my head down to my broken hand. I could see it now in the flickering light. The thumb and two fingers lay at odd angles and dried blood was crusted all over them. A wave of nausea rolled up from my stomach.

'Oh god. I should never have let you leave the house alone. I'm so sorry.' Peter hung his head.

'Walker, we need to go,' Weaver hissed, looking anxiously up and down the passage. It took me a second to realise she was addressing Peter. 'Eve, I'm sorry, but we need to move. Now.' She set off at a brisk walk away up the passage.

Peter hoisted me up and wrapped my left arm across his shoulders.

'Can you walk?'

'I don't know. Maybe.' We moved a few steps, but my whole body collapsed against Peter.

'Stop!' Peter shouted at Weaver's retreating back.

Dante stepped in and lifted me as easily as if I were a rag doll, draping me across his chest. I wrapped my good arm behind his neck and smiled at him. Peter scowled and set off after Weaver.

Dante ran behind the shifters, smoothly and quietly compared to their pounding feet. We were heading back the way the shifters had come, away from the steps that Dante had carried me down. I didn't know what Lucia's plan had been, where he was supposed to take me, or if she was going to meet us there. But whatever her plan had been, she would soon be realising that it had gone awry.

I held a little tighter to his broad shoulders and closed my eyes. Where was Antonio? I needed him more than anything else.

We turned a corner into a narrower passage with a lower ceiling and Dante had to stoop a little, hunching over me as he ran. The light ahead bobbed wildly and the shadows danced eerily on the walls.

The shifters ahead of us lurched to a halt and Dante almost bumped into Strikes Twice. He glanced down at me apologetically.

'There you are,' Peter said with an irritated tone.

'Where is she?' Antonio's voice was ragged and desperate. The shifters parted, throwing light down the passage to us at the back. Antonio sped between the others and took me from Dante. He pulled me into his arms and cradled my head. My feet found the floor, but couldn't take my weight and I leaned heavily against him. 'Dante, thank you for getting her to me. I can't ever repay you.'

Antonio held me away from him so he could look into my face. I tried to smile, but my mouth wouldn't form the right shape. My eyes fluttered closed and I dropped to the floor. Antonio dropped with me, guiding me gently into a sitting position. 'There now, it's going to be all right.'

My eyelids flickered open and fixed on his dark eyes. He raised his hand and I saw his thumb nail morph into a pointed claw. He pierced his index finger with it and a little drop of blood appeared. 'You need this. Trust me, please.' He gently rubbed his bloody finger against the inside of my bottom lip and my tongue darted out reflexively to lick the blood. My eyes met his and asked the silent question:

Will this change me?

He shook his head with a small smile.

'No, you have to die first. You haven't lost nearly enough blood for this to make you a vampire.' He eased his fingertip into my mouth. I sucked on it, drawing more of his blood. It tasted sweet and salty at the same time and lacked that metallic note of normal blood.

'You healed me with your blood yesterday, now it is my turn to heal you.'

Warmth spread from my lips into my cheeks and brow. The ache I'd felt in my throat and behind my tired eyes eased away. The sensation spread quickly over my scalp and down my neck into my chest. My shoulders relaxed just as I realised how tense they'd been. It was like a ripple running right through my body.

My injured hand felt hot, and there was a series of little pops as the bones clicked back into place. Each one sent a shot of pain up my wrist, but by the time I'd winced the pain was already gone. Energy trickled back into my body and I no longer had to strain in the dark passage to see clearly.

'Can you stand?'

'Yes.' I went to move and Antonio was on his feet in an instant, pulling me up by my hands. There was no pain left in the one that Celino had broken and I stared at it in wonder.

The flickering light seemed brighter and more alive, the shadows fainter. I stared at the shifters behind Antonio, every eye was on me and more than one face looked wary. 'I'm okay. I'm good. Where do we need to be?'

'Lucia is summoning her demons.' Antonio's voice was grave.

'I know, I saw. I had a vision.' I nodded earnestly.

'She tried to bait me into coming to rescue you.'

'It worked, didn't it? You're here.'

'Well, yes. She hasn't seen me yet.' A darkness crossed

his face that I didn't like one bit.

'Are you going to kill her?'

'If I have to.'

'Let's go,' Weaver urged from the far end of the passage. She set off, taking the light with her. The other shifters fell into step behind her, Peter casting me a serious look before turning away. Antonio took my healed hand and led me after them, with Dante bringing up the rear.

I could hear more voices ahead and the roar of a large fire. The passage opened up wider and we turned a corner, stepping out into the familiar cavern. Many other shapeshifters were gathered and every one of them turned our way as we entered. Snarls and shouts ripped through the air over the roar of the huge fire that burned at one end of the cave.

Antonio's grip on my hand tightened and Dante slipped fluidly past us to position himself between the baying beasts and Antonio.

'They're with us!' Weaver called, her hands raised and the fire in her palm dancing dangerously.

'There are a lot more of them than I realised,' Antonio whispered, a light smile playing on his lips. 'You could have warned me.'

'Sorry,' I said, grinning sheepishly. 'I was never quite sure if I could trust you or not.'

Weaver didn't seem to have persuaded anyone. Several shifters erupted into their Agrius forms and

Antonio just hesitated for a moment, his smile faltering. I squeezed his hand.

'We don't have time!' Weaver shouted. 'Lucia is summoning a horde of demons right now. She knows that her brother has betrayed her and she killed one of our own, Moon Caller's wife. Lucia abducted Eve and tortured her. She killed Eve's parents, she acted alone. It is Lucia that we must focus on. Antonio is on our side. I swear it.'

Peter threw a glance our way and flinched when he saw us huddled so close, hands entwined. I wanted to apologise to him, but now wasn't the moment.

Weaver seemed to have settled the initial outburst at the entrance of the vampires into their midst, but the looks issuing from almost every face, human and Agrius alike, were unmistakably hostile. I held Antonio's hand firmly in mine and stepped out from behind Dante, drawing level with Weaver.

'It's true. And Dante here risked his own life to get me out of Lucia's grasp. We have this one opportunity to defeat Lucia and we have the numbers. We can do this and be free of her evil for good.'

'What about him?' someone shouted from the crowd. 'We want justice for what he's done.'

'There is no justice in violence,' I called back. 'Once we've dealt with the immediate threat then we can discuss the rest. Right now, Antonio is not a threat to you. He can even help you as you negotiate the deals you need to make to take on your role as guardians of the veil. But all of that can wait. Right now we have to track down Lucia and stop her. We don't have time to argue.'

I turned to Antonio. 'Do you know where she is?'

He nodded silently and squeezed my hand. He set off at a brisk walk, right past the war party of bristling shifters, not sparing them a glance. He led me past the raging fire and I glanced over my shoulder to see Peter's pack following us. Some of the others were falling into step beside him and others were still looking angrily towards Antonio.

He walked quickly into a wide passage at the head of the cavern and into the dark. Weaver was just behind me, her fire still glowing in her hand. Soon it was the only light, but I wasn't struggling to see. My eyesight was sharper than ever and I could hear every footfall from the thirty shifters behind us.

We were an army and Antonio and I were leading the charge.

CHAPTER THIRTY-FIVE

A RUMBLE AHEAD IN THE DARK BROUGHT OUR PARTY TO A HALT. The whole floor of the passage trembled and dust fell from the ceiling.

'How does she know how to summon demons?' I asked Antonio out of the corner of my mouth.

'When we arrived in the city and began to set down roots here, we made deals with some demons to give us power and influence. We learned about the veil together. It was a few decades later, when we discovered the shapeshifters, that I took on guarding the veil. Lucia knew. She understood the value in doing it but had little interest in helping me. But she knew about the demons and how to bargain with them.'

'What do you think she's summoned to help her now?'

'Something formidable.' He glanced down at me; light flickered on his skin from Weaver's burning hand. 'Let's go.' We set off walking again, the shifters in our wake.

Another rumble shook the passage and a low groan of anguish followed it. Something large objected to being ripped across the veil.

An unpleasant squirm took place in the deepest part of my gut and I glanced at Weaver and Peter walking along on one side of me, then over to Antonio on my other side. I lacked their strength, speed and agility. What could I possibly do here?

A warm draught swept down the wide passage towards us. It lifted my hair and warmed my face. But what followed was a ground-shaking roar. Something knew we were there.

The shifters were growing agitated behind me. I heard snarling and was swept along with them as they picked up the pace. Peter shifted form as he ran; his human feet in trainers that pounded lightly on the stone became huge, hair-covered feet that thundered towards whatever lay in wait for us.

Everyone around me seemed to be erupting into their bestial forms. Weapons were being drawn and teeth bared. Antonio kept tight hold of my hand as we ran amidst the beasts. Dante jogged silently just behind Antonio, though I noticed his fangs had protracted and his mouth hung open in an angry but silent snarl.

There was a warm glow in the tunnel ahead and the shadows of the shifters around me bobbed erratically up the curved walls. Dust showered down on us now as the army of shifters thundered towards the oncoming battle.

My heart was pounding and I was growing a little

breathless as we raced ahead. I could hear the large something stumbling around in the catacombs, bumping into the walls and thudding hard against the floor.

I knew I should be afraid, but my body was pumped full of adrenaline and all I really felt was a dark sort of thrill that all of this madness was coming to a head.

The passage opened up into a vast cavern that resembled an old underground railway station. The high walls curved up to form the ceiling and everything was lined with neat, black tiles. Torches burned in brackets along the walls, the tiles reflecting the flickering light.

Somewhere above us, I knew, was the centre of the city. Humans were going about their night oblivious to what was happening beneath them. Would they hear the fight? Or feel the vibrations? Would the news be reporting some sort of earthquake?

I couldn't worry about that now, though. I returned my attention to what lay ahead.

In the centre of the cavern was a crack in the ground that ran right from one side to the other. Weaver growled and bared her teeth. I understood why, a little. Like the door that Antonio had opened in my kitchen, I could see across the veil where the crack in the ground was. On the other side was a place of fire, smoke and shadows. Roars, snarls and the spitting of fire could be heard drifting up through the crack.

Although my mind struggled to wrap itself around

what I was seeing, and it made my temples throb, I could perceive the veil itself wafting on either side of the crack, as if a great tear had been made in it. Damage like that to the veil must be a terrible crime to shifters, I thought.

The flame in Weaver's hand was extinguished as she leapt into the air towards the crack. My eyes had to strain to see past the tear and settle on what lay beyond it. On the other side of the very physical crack in the ground, was a vast demon. It filled the cavern with its dark body of writhing tentacles.

The demon was covered in scales that glittered in the flickering torchlight. It didn't have a distinct neck. But it had a head set into its vast, reptilian body. Many eyes like a huge insect blinked and glinted in the firelight and a vast mouth glowed with fire deep inside and spat sparks each time it roared. Heat blasted us from the huge maw and the whip-like tentacles flailed out across the crack in the ground.

Crystal and two other shifters made their way quickly to one side of where we had entered and began getting out stones, salt, candles and whatever else they needed for their ritual. I didn't understand half of what there was to know about the veil, but I knew that a tear like this was bad news and would need to be mended with magic.

Antonio pulled me gently towards them as most of the shifters bounded past us to leap into combat with the giant demon. The air was filled with their roars and the clang of metal blades on the hard, glistening scales of the demon.

I searched the shadows for a sign of Lucia. She had to be here somewhere. But all I could see was the demon, the crack, and the thirty or so shifters that were leaping over the crack and into the fray.

I'd lost sight of Dante, Peter and Weaver. Antonio tugged on my arm and brought my attention back to him. I must have looked terrified because he turned to face me, took gentle hold of my face in both of his hands and looked deep into my eyes.

'Eve. Are you here with me?'

'Yes.' I nodded, my face still cupped in his palms.

'I need to help them handle Lucia. You need to stay out of harm's way. Do you understand?'

I nodded again. He kissed me swiftly then released me and sprinted towards the crack. He leapt over it in a single bound, seeming almost to float across it and land lightly on the other side.

'I can't just stand here while everyone fights,' I said to no one in particular.

'Eve!' Crystal called from nearby. I turned towards her. 'Come and help us!'

I ran over and she thrust a red candle into my hands. One of the others, an older lady with wispy grey hair and a crossbow on her back, was scraping strange shapes into the dusty ground. The other shifter, a young man wearing cut-off jeans and sporting a shaved head, was squatting down and grinding something with a mortar and pestle.

'What can I do?' I asked, looking around at the ritualists and then over at the fight.

'Light these,' Crystal replied, thrusting another candle into my hand. 'We have to mend the veil. Hurry!'

I took the lighter she offered me and, with shaking fingers, lit both candles. Crystal took one of them from me. 'Great, now stand there.' She pointed to one of the strange markings on the ground. I went and stood on it and looked down at it. It was two vertical lines with a wavy one drawn across the top of them and two small dots on the right side. It looked a bit like a rune, but not one I recognised. The other markings on the floor formed a square and the three shifters each took up position on one of them.

The young man in the cut-offs walked around the outside of the circle we formed, sprinkling the herbs he'd been grinding to form a circle around us. I watched in awe as blue light shone from the ground where the herbs lay and a dome of light formed around us.

Crystal raised the candle over her head and nodded across at me. I copied her, holding the candle up. The little flame seemed to touch the blue dome over my head and small, white sparks showered down on me. They were cool and disappeared the moment they touched my hands and arms.

I glanced over my shoulder towards the raging battle. It was like looking through blue-tinted glass. Ripping, roaring and clanging sounds rent the air and the demon was writhing around, swatting the shifters away with its great tentacles.

Something unsettling coiled around my insides. I turned my attention back to the ritual. Crystal was chanting something in words I didn't understand. I yearned to break from the circle and go in search of my loved ones.

I needed Antonio and to know where Peter was. But more than anything, I wanted Lucia. I wanted to fight her. Rage surged in my veins for the way she'd tortured me and for her killing Peter's mother.

I looked towards the tear in the veil and watched in wonder as I saw the blue light from the dome reaching out like a tendril towards the start of the tear near to where we stood. It seemed to be drawing the torn pieces of the veil back together, neatly sewing them back in place. Whatever we were doing, it was working and I couldn't move.

The blue tendril worked its way slowly across the crack, gently tugging the veil back together and gradually fixing it.

A pair of shifters were swatted away from the demon and skidded across the ground, right towards the crack. One of them tumbled through it with a scream, disappearing into the fiery pit below. The other grabbed hold of the edge and pulled himself back up, with a furious roar over his shoulder at his lost comrade.

'Crystal!' I shouted. 'Wait. Someone's on the other side!'

'We can't stop, Eve,' she called back. Her face looked strained and sweat ran down either side of her forehead. 'I'm sorry. We've lost a few people, but we can't get them back.'

'They'll die over there!'

'I know. I'm sorry.'

'Do you still need me?'

'Yes!'

'I can help them!'

The three shifters looked at me sceptically. There wasn't time to explain. The tear was still mending, slowly closing the gap. I was certain that once it was fully mended I wouldn't be able to do anything.

I stepped off my mark and passed the candle to the young shifter. 'I'm sorry. I have to do something.'

'Eve!' Crystal called as I stepped out of the ritual circle. It was like stepping into an icy waterfall. The blue light was shockingly cold against my skin as I passed through the dome. But once I was through it the air was hot. I ran to the crack in the ground and stooped to peer through the tear in the veil.

It was the strangest sensation. I was on the edge of a precipice, with a very real, physical crack in the ground that disappeared into a dark abyss. But layered over that crack in the human world, was this gateway into what looked like hell.

Fires raged, demons with bat-like wings flew below me and others the size of the biggest dinosaurs stomped about below on dark, rocky slopes between fires and flowing lava. There was a steady stream of demons heading up towards us.

At the same time, I could see a starry sky and the smooth crystals of Hepethia. I saw trees of diamonds and a smooth, clear lake. It was as if all of the different realms imaginable all coexisted in this one place. All you had to do was pick one layer to focus on and that was what you could see.

I felt sick and dizzy as I gazed into the tear. Blue light was working its way slowly towards me, the tear coming together and making the hole between worlds smaller and smaller.

I searched the fiery hell for signs of shifters. Just below me, on a ridge right above a stream of lava, was the shifter I'd seen tumble into the hole. He looked up at me and his mouth formed a scream, but I couldn't hear him over the roars in the cavern around me.

I reached out a hand and focused with all of the mental energy I could muster. I'd made Peter fly sideways when I needed to get him away from Antonio. I could pull this stranded shifter towards me. I knew it.

My eyes rolled back in my head and everything went black as I strained to move him. There was a great rush of wind and something touched my outstretched fingers. A hand was grasping mine, and my eyes popped open.

The shifter, back in his human form, was gazing up at me with wide eyes. I heaved him up out of the crack and the blue light knitted its way quickly towards us. It sealed up the gap a split second after his feet were clear.

'How did you do that?' he asked, staring at me. He was covered in ash, his blazing eyes bored into mine.

'Don't overthink it,' I said, trying to smile.

'Thank you, you saved my life.'

'Well, you can swear a blood oath of allegiance later. Right now we have a demon to vanquish.' He laughed and jumped to his feet. He shifted into his Agrius form and rejoined the fight.

There was one small gap still in the veil and I watched as the blue light halted its course. I looked back at Crystal and the others and saw them watching me with wonder. I ran back over to them and stood outside the dome, looking in.

'We need to send it back before we close the tear fully,' Crystal said, her voice muffled through the shimmering blue light.

I turned back to the fight. The shifters had driven the demon over to the precipice. Many of its tentacles had been dismembered and lay discarded around the cavern floor. Black shadow seemed to ooze from dozens of wounds and the demon writhed and roared in apparent agony.

I caught sight of Antonio and Dante, in there among the shifters. Antonio had hold of a tentacle and Dante had grasped it in his huge hands. He was ripping it, tendon by tendon, from the demon's body.

Strikes Twice strode over it, his axe raised over his head, and sliced the blade through the partially severed tentacle. It dropped to the ground, out of the hands of the two vampires, and that strange, liquid shadow seeped out of the open wound on the demon's body. Strikes Twice nodded at Dante, then turned and leapt high up on the demon, driving his axe into its head.

The demon crashed to the ground and writhed hopelessly, roaring and groaning in pain. The shifters pounced on it, stabbing it with their blades and claws. I began to feel pity for the creature. It didn't know where it was, it was only defending itself. I looked from it to the nearby hole in the veil. Demons still swarmed towards us. I'd never moved anything anywhere near as big as the demon before. I locked my gaze onto one of the remaining tentacles and saw myself reaching out and grasping it in my hands. The tentacle went rigid, jutting right out towards me. I pulled and it lurched towards me.

I ran to the remaining gap in the veil and watched in awe as the tentacle followed me. The shifters fighting it began to fall back, watching as they picked up on what was happening.

The demon flailed wildly as I pulled the whole thing closer towards the gap. I was reaching out with both hands, straining the muscles as if pulling on a great rope, but it was my mind doing all of the real work.

The fight died down, although the demon continued to roar and wail in fear and shock. It tried to grasp hold of something to hold it in place, but its tentacles couldn't grip anything.

Shifters scattered out of the way and I saw Peter and Kirk among them, staring in awe at me. Weaver joined them and resumed her human form. One side of her mouth cocked up in a smile and she nodded in encouragement.

I heaved the demon closer and fed the tentacle I had mental hold of into the gap. The hole was much too small for the entire demon, only a few feet wide. But I was getting the hang of this stuff. It was all energy and perception. I saw the demon being squeezed and shrinking as I threaded the tentacle through the hole. I fed the whole entity swiftly back into hell and the blue light immediately went back to sewing the tear. Moments later, it was sealed and a huge cheer swelled up, filling the cavern with thunderous jubilation.

I was swamped by the shifters as they bounded over to me and piled on top of me, each trying to embrace me and thump me on the back. Crushed by the weight of them, I pushed bodies away from me with surprising strength.

'Let her go!' Peter shouted above the din. 'You'll crush her.'

Bodies flew away from me, some releasing me of their own accord, but Peter appeared, dragging one of the shifters off me and tossing her aside. He grabbed me and pulled me into a tight embrace.

I found myself laughing, but it became a hysterical cry and tears streamed down my face.

'Impressive,' said Weaver softly behind me. Peter released me and I turned to face her. She pulled me into a hug too and patted me on the back. 'You have surprising gifts, Eve.'

'Tell me about it.'

Antonio appeared by my side out of nowhere and scooped me up into his arms, spinning me around.

'You were incredible,' he said softly so that only I could hear. He placed me gently on the ground and captured my lips in a passionate kiss. My head was still spinning from being twirled about and the kiss didn't help matters.

'You fought with honour,' a deep voice behind me said. I looked around at Strikes Twice as he sheathed his axe across his back. He was looking at Antonio. 'You helped us.'

'I did what I could. Dante too,' Antonio said, indicating Dante, who was hoisting a pair of giant tentacles across his broad shoulders. He carried them a few feet and dropped them on top of a pile of the slimy things, silently tidying up.

'Where's Lucia?' I asked, searching the cavern for a sign of her.

'I don't know. I haven't seen Lucia at all.' There was a dark tone to Weaver's voice and her eyes were slightly narrowed.

'We have to find her,' I said, looking from Weaver to Antonio. 'We have to finish this.'

CHAPTER THIRTY-SIX

'No!' The shriek came from the dark recesses of the vast cavern and was unmistakably Lucia. It seemed we wouldn't need to find her after all. 'What have you done?' The vampire swept into the cave with Celino and a man who had to be Laguardia flanking her. Esposito lurked behind her, his face ghostly pale and covered in sweat and grime.

Lucia looked wild. Her hair had fallen loose and was a tangled mess around her face. Her eyes were wide and dangerous. Her pristine, cream sweater was stained with blood and dirt.

Antonio tensed at my side and gripped my hand. I glanced up into his face and saw contempt etched on his handsome features.

'We sent your pet back to hell, where it belongs,' Kirk shouted, his voice carrying clearly across the cavern and echoing off the high walls.

'You have my brother. I want him back.' Lucia brushed off Kirk's remark about the demon. Her initial outrage flickered off her beautiful face and she turned her attention to more pressing concerns. She looked right at Antonio and her eyes narrowed when they saw our clasped hands. She tilted her head to one side and crossed her arms. 'Your hand seems to have healed remarkably quickly, my dear,' she said, looking pointedly at me. Her accent thickened as she spoke.

'Maybe there's more to me than meets the eye,' I called back. My voice was strong and certain, no trace of a flicker, even though my stomach was doing somersaults.

'I think that must be true. Antonio, come here to me. She has bewitched you, I think.'

Antonio's hand tightened on mine.

'You're wrong, Lucia. I've known that what you're doing is wrong since before I even met Eve. I was working with her parents to undo some of your dark work. I saw you kill them. You will find that you have precious little support left in the business. I've been at this for some time.' There was a snide smirk on her lips but it faded as he spoke. Her upper lip twitched towards a snarl a few times, but she kept it at bay.

'Dante?' Lucia turned her attention to the silent vampire behind Antonio. 'My love. Why are you siding with them?'

Dante raised an eyebrow and Lucia withered. It seemed to be finally dawning on her that torturing and punishing her supposed allies probably wasn't the wisest course of action.

'It's time to turn yourself over to the shifters for whatever justice they deem fit,' I said, my voice still surprisingly strong. Antonio twitched beside me and I gave his hand a firm squeeze of reassurance without looking at him. 'You've lost. You have nothing. No power, no influence and precious few friends left at your side.' Lucia glanced at the three men standing with her. The two vampires were eyeing up her and Antonio, as well as the army of shifters. They were clearly weighing their own options. Esposito was still hiding at the back, one eye on the exit, I noticed.

Just behind me, Crystal and one of her fellow ritualists were discreetly passing each other things and muttering under their breath. I tuned in to their thoughts and saw them preparing to open a door to the hell dimension we'd sent the demon to. I tugged free of Antonio's grip and stepped forward. Lucia locked her narrow eyes on me and took a few steps forward herself.

'You had to meddle, didn't you? Just like your parents. They were thorns in my side for years.'

'You should have known that killing them wouldn't end your problems. Humans tend to value family quite a lot.'

'They weren't human,' she said. She looked me up and down. 'And I don't quite know what you are. You don't need to lecture me on family. We Camorra know what truly matters. In the end you will never be able to hold his heart.

He is my brother and he knows where his true loyalty lies.'

'Lucia,' I said, shaking my head. 'I never intended to come between you. I still don't want to do that. You both made your own choices and now you stand on opposite sides. I don't know if reconciliation is possible, but you took my parents from me and you have to pay for that.'

There was a shimmer in the veil just behind her. I kept my eyes focused on her as the shimmer intensified. Celino, Laguardia and Esposito all began backing away from Lucia. She was glaring at me, with apparently no idea of the disturbance out of sight.

'He'll get bored of you. He is over two hundred years old. Do you think you're the first pretty girl to turn his head? With or without my influence, he'll either see you die or lose interest. As for your parents, they defied their masters. It's as simple as that. They failed to know their place.'

'You still think you control them, don't you? You think you'll get your power back and everything will go back to the way it was. That's never going to happen.'

The shimmer became a hole through which I could see the fire and shadows of that awful place. Lucia's head began to turn towards the doorway. Now was my only chance.

I gave a great mental shove, thrusting my hands out in front of me as if to push Lucia, even though she was out of my reach. My mind whipped out and thrust her backwards. Her face caught in an expression of surprise, her mouth wide and eyes unblinking as she went flying backwards into the hole in reality.

'Lucia!' Esposito yelled and lunged forward to grab her, but he was too late. She fell through the hole in the veil and was tumbling down into a pit of fire. Esposito leapt after her, loyal to the last.

The shifters behind me swept the door closed in the blink of an eye, cutting the hell realm off from us and trapping Lucia and Esposito there. Celino and Laguardia had staggered backwards, away from the hole, and now stood looking awkwardly from each other to the rest of us on the other side of the cavern.

Before anyone could react to what had happened, the vampires disappeared down the dark passage behind them, running so fast they were mere blurs in the flickering torchlight.

A great roar erupted behind me, making me jump. The shifters burst into celebration, many of them shifting form and scooping each other up in embraces of passionate camaraderie. I turned to watch, a light laugh of disbelief escaping my lips.

A few wary eyes were being cast towards Antonio, who stood frozen amid the shifters, his eyes locked on where his sister had disappeared from view.

Peter appeared at his side and hurried him away from the celebrations towards me. He pushed Antonio into my arms and turned away, returning to his father and pack mates. I wrapped my arms around Antonio's neck and pulled his face close to mine.

'Are you all right?'

'Yes, I think so.' He held me close and kissed me. When our lips parted he stroked my hair and looked into my eyes. 'You didn't let me deal with her.'

'No, I'm sorry about that.'

'It's probably for the best. I don't think I could have done what you did. She's my sister.'

'Well, she has food, so maybe she'll find a way to survive down there.' I gave him a wry smile. He chuckled and shook his head in disbelief.

'You will never stop surprising me.'

'I don't know, maybe one day. Maybe she was right about you getting bored of me.'

'Never.' He pressed his mouth to mine, capturing me in a deep and passionate kiss. I believed him, for better or worse.

In the days that followed I hardly had a moment to myself. The shifters had divided up the city between them before the final battle, but now began the hard task of taking over the job of guarding the veil. None of them wanted to talk to Antonio, or get his advice.

He stayed in his house, away from trouble. He had his own problems to resolve now that Lucia was gone. He had sent his people out to track down Celino and Laguardia, but so far no sign of them had been found.

I didn't have time to go to him. I was being paraded about like a hero, given tours of every piece of territory and introduced to every pack. It all passed in a blur and when I was allowed to sleep I dreamed of the hell realm and of Lucia's face as she fell into it.

I'd expected to feel a sense of vindication when I avenged my parents' deaths, but I was restless and alone, even when I was surrounded by people.

It was on the fourth day that I had a moment alone with Weaver. She came to my house and I made her a cup of tea. We sat in silence for minutes that dragged.

'You're leaving,' I said at last.

'I have to get back to Caerton,' she replied.

'Of course.'

'You have my number.'

'Yes. I assume Kirk does, too.'

'He does. I'll be available if you need any help. If you need to get out of Oris you'd be welcome to visit.'

'I'm still toying with the idea of going back to university.'

'Oh?' She raised her eyebrows and kept her gaze fixed on me as she sipped her tea.

'You don't approve.'

'Well, it's just that your world has changed so much. Is it even possible to go back?'

'No, not really. But I like to finish the things I start. It might be a good idea to get away from here for a while. There's too much awkwardness.'

'Because of Antonio?'

'Yes, and Peter and everything. I'm no hero. I hate the attention. I hate everyone knowing me and wanting a piece of me.'

'That'll die down, in time.'

'I guess.'

'Well, if you do come back to Caerton, let me know.'

'I will.'

Weaver finished her tea and stood up. I walked her to the door.

'If you need any more help with that gift of yours, you call me.'

'Sure.' I smiled and allowed Weaver to pull me into a tight embrace. She released me and opened the door. Antonio stood there with one hand raised to knock.

'Well, goodnight,' Weaver said, looking from his surprised face to mine.

'Safe journey,' I said as she stepped past Antonio. She glanced back at the pair of us and gave me a parting smile of caution. She approved of us about as much as Peter did. But she was leaving. I watched her walk away into the night, her long skirt and coat blowing slightly in the cold,

December wind. Antonio's Maserati was parked by my gate, his driver and Dante next to it, both watching us intently. 'Come in,' I said to Antonio, stepping aside to admit him. He stepped over the threshold and closed the door.

'How are you?'

'Busy. You?'

'The same.'

I set off back towards the kitchen and he followed.

The heightened senses I'd experienced after taking his blood had worn off and left me a little tired and feeling as though I was lacking something.

'Why is Dante with you?'

'I don't go anywhere without him these days. We have to look out for each other.'

'I don't think the shifters are going to hurt you.' I poured myself more tea and turned to face him. He stood in the kitchen doorway, one hand in his trouser pocket, the other hanging loosely by his side.

'Hmm. We can't quite take the chance that one or more of them won't revolt against the group.'

'They're not baseless animals.'

'I know. They're people. But they're passionate and have been badly hurt by me and my kind. Vengeance would be natural.'

'I suppose.'

'How have you been feeling?'

'Tired.'

'You've been through a lot.'

'Yeah, well, your sister tortured me and then I sent her to hell, so...' I let out a mirthless chuckle. He didn't smile.

'Eve, I can never express how much I regret what happened.'

'I know. It's okay.'

'It's really not.' He moved closer to me and took my cup from my hands, placing it on the kitchen worktop behind me. He pressed close to me and I felt that familiar swooping sensation of getting lost in my desire for him. He took hold of my face in both of his hands and looked deep into my eyes. 'I love you so much. I never want any harm to come to you again.'

'But I'm a fragile human.'

'Yes, you are.' He kissed me softly. 'But for now, you are whole and more or less well. Let's try and keep it that way, shall we?' He smiled.

'Sure.' I smiled back and pressed myself against him.

'Your friends will never approve of us.'

'No, they won't. Peter especially.'

'Well, no one will ever be good enough for you in his eyes.' Antonio allowed a small smile to grace his lips.

'You have no idea how true that is.'

'I think I do.'

'You know how he feels about me?' I looked up at him, not really surprised.

'Of course. I knew before you did.' He grinned down at me.

'Does it bother you?'

'Not really. I'm not the jealous type. Besides, I know your heart lies with me.'

His self-confidence was soothing to my permanent sense of confusion and self-doubt. I leaned against him and rested my head on his chest.

'How are you getting along with dismantling your criminal empire?' I asked, not looking up at him.

'Fine. I am waiting on a few things to conclude, but no new crime, I promise.' There was a smile in his voice. That would have to do, for now. I looked up into his dark eyes. It might not make sense to the outside world, but it felt right to me.

'I might be going back to Caerton, to finish my degree.'

'I thought that might be the case.' He nodded solemnly.

'Would you come with me?'

'Now there's a thought.'

'Have you ever been there?'

'Yes. I have a good friend there.'

'Oh?'

'A very old friend. I could always look him up. But, Eve, if you want to focus on your studies, it might be best if I weren't there to distract you.'

'True. I don't have to decide now. In the new year I

will though.'

'Well, let's enjoy our time together until then, shall we?' He grinned and scooped me up into his arms. I giggled and caressed his cool face. Yes, for now I could lose myself in the moment with him and revel in our freedom.

PLEASE LEAVE A REVIEW

I hope you enjoyed *In The Blood*. I would really appreciate it if you could take a few minutes now to review the book on your favourite retailer.

Independent authors rely heavily on reader reviews, they really are like oxygen. Reviews help other readers decide whether a book is a good fit for them or not. Much as I want everyone to love my books, I also know that it's important to find the right readers, so just a few words from you could help me to do that and reach other readers who will enjoy my dark and twisted tales!

Thank you!

Join My Tribe

If you enjoyed this book and would like to check out more of my world, you can get short story collection *Little Lies the Dead Tell* for free when you subscribe to my reader Tribe. I'll also email you regularly with news and offers.

Get your copy here: https://BookHip.com/NCMACX

ABOUT THE AUTHOR

H.B. Lyne is an urban fantasy author, podcaster and bullet journal enthusiast with a knack for organisation and getting stuff done.

She lives in Yorkshire with her husbeast, two children and midwife cat. When not juggling family commitments, she writes dark urban fantasy novels, purging her imagination of its demons. Inspired by the King of Horror himself, Holly aspires to be at least half as prolific and successful and promises to limit herself to only one tome of The Stand-like proportions in her career.

For More Information

hblyne.com

Follow me on Instagram: @hblyne

And on Facebook: facebook.com/authorhblyne

ALSO BY H.B. LYNE

In the Shifters of Caerton series:

Fate of the Blue Moon

Ghosts of Winter

Demons of the Past

Rise of the Furies

Dark Echoes: Tales from the Shadows

From Ashes to Echoes

In the Jones & Maxwell Casefiles series:

The Hidden City

In the Lies the Dead Tell series:

In the Blood

The Power of Blood